Tomorrow is here . . .

Year's Best SF 17

Praise for previous volumes

"An impressive roster of authors."
Locus

"The finest modern science fiction writing."
Pittsburgh Tribune

R. Peterson

Edited by David G. Hartwell

**Edited by David G. Hartwell
& Kathryn Cramer**

YEAR'S BEST SF 17

EDITED BY

DAVID G. HARTWELL
and KATHRYN CRAMER

HARPER Voyager
An Imprint of HarperCollinsPublishers

Additional copyright information appears on pages 489–490.

HARPER Voyager
An Imprint of HarperCollins*Publishers*
10 East 53rd Street
New York, New York 10022-5299

Copyright © 2012 by David G. Hartwell and Kathryn Cramer
Cover art by John Harris
ISBN 978-0-06-203587-5
www.harpervoyagerbooks.com

First Harper Voyager mass market printing: June 2012

Harper Voyager and) is a trademark of HCP LLC.

Printed in the U.S.A.

10 9 8 7 6 5 4 3 2 1

Contents

Introduction

This is a book full of science fiction—every story in the book is clearly that and not something else. It is our opinion that it is a good thing to have genre boundaries. We have a high regard for horror, fantasy, speculative fiction, and slipstream, and postmodern literature. We (Kathryn Cramer and David G. Hartwell) edit the *Year's Best Fantasy* as well, a companion volume to this one—look for it if you enjoy short fantasy fiction too. But here, we choose science fiction. This volume is intended to represent the variety of fine stories published in the year. But bear with us for a few paragraphs as we first give some characterization of the year in SF.

In 2011 the earth quaked for the publishing industry, especially in the U.S. The third largest bookseller, Borders, the bookstore chain that accounted for about 20 percent of everyone's business, went bankrupt. There were five other important bankruptcies in the U.S. bookselling business, and in Canada, one big one, The H.B. Fenn Company. Fenn was the largest distributor in Canada of U.S. books. Together, these events hurt the profitability of book publishing a lot. Specifically, the lack of so many formerly supportive distribution channels for books lowered the initial printings, and therefore the sales, of nearly all new books.

But what rankles most publishers is that first, when a store or customer goes bankrupt, they don't pay for the books shipped to them, but do get to sell them at a going-out-of-business sale—the money goes to the secured creditors, the banks that loaned the stores money, not the suppliers. And second, because the books were sold, even though they were not paid for, the authors must be paid royalties by the publishers as if they had been paid, increasing the publisher's losses. Wow!

The substantial increase in e-book sales in the first half of 2011 made up for some but certainly not all of this, and then e-book sales generally declined in the second half of the year. It became really apparent as well that e-book sales were adversely affecting mass market paperback sales, even more than in 2010. The disparity in money was profound. One publishing newsletter pointed out that the bestselling e-book original of 2011 made about $500,000.00, while the bestselling hardcover book made between 40 and 50 million dollars. Physical books are still where the money is, and in the e-book industry the real profit is still in the sale of devices, which are replaced by newer devices, not in the sale of books. And it appears that e-book rental is being encouraged. As this is written it is not possible to predict what will happen in 2012. All we know is that nearly everyone is making less profit. The squeeze is on.

Science fiction, of the genre variety, was a bit harder to find in 2011 than in 2010. Certainly it continued to appear in *Analog* and *Asimov's*, in *F&SF* and in *Interzone*, and in a lot of original anthologies. But it seemed to us to be a bit scarcer, and a lot more often grading off into fantasy and mixed genres, while fantasy fiction (not in any way SF) quite obviously increased.

Short fiction venues remained about the same in 2011, and a pale shadow of what they were a decade ago. Science fiction magazines once again lost some circulation. Online venues, which might pay contributors but make little money, grew or failed again last year. Non-profit *Strange Horizons* and *Tor.com* appeared most stable of the online bunch. *Clarkesworld* and *Lightspeed* did distinguished work too. Lots of small presses—or perhaps small publishers is now the proper apellation for these few—carried the ball for innovation in 2011, again especially the Bay Area cluster of Night Shade, Tachyon, and Subterranean. And as usual, a large amount of the best short fiction originated in the year's new crop of anthologies. Among the best of these were *Wel-*

come to the Greenhouse, edited by Gordon Van Gelder, *Solaris Rising*, edited by Ian Whates, *Living on Mars*, edited by Jonathan Strahan, and *Engineering Infinity*, edited by Jonathan Strahan.

And that is the context in which all of the following stories first appeared. This then is a book about what's going on now in SF. We try in each volume of this series to represent the varieties of tone and voice and attitude that keep the genre vigorous and responsive to the changing realities out of which it emerges, in science and daily life. It is supposed to be fun to read, a special kind of fun you cannot find elsewhere. The stories show, and the story notes point out, the strengths of the evolving genre in the year 2011.

We make a lot of additional comments about the writers and the stories, and what's happening in SF, in the individual introductions accompanying the stories in this book. Welcome to the *Year's Best SF 17*.

> David G. Hartwell & Kathryn Cramer
> Pleasantville, NY

YEAR'S BEST SF 17

The Best Science Fiction of the Year Three

Ken MacLeod (Kenmacleod.blogspot.com) was born in Stornoway, Isle of Lewis, Scotland, on August 2, 1954. He is married with two grown-up children and lives in West Lothian. He has an Honours and Masters degree in biological subjects and worked for some years in the IT industry. Since 1997 he has been a full-time writer, and in 2009 was Writer in Residence at the ESRC Genomics Policy and Research Forum at Edinburgh University. He is the author of thirteen novels, from The Star Fraction (1995) to Intrusion (2012), and many articles and short stories. His collection, Giant Lizards from Another Star, was published in 2006. His novels and stories have received three BSFA awards and three Prometheus Awards, and several have been short-listed for the Clarke and Hugo Awards.

"The Best Science Fiction of the Year Three" was first published in Solaris Rising: The New Solaris Book of Science Fiction, edited by Ian Whates, who had a particularly good year as an editor of anthologies in 2011. It is a model of SF plotting, and we feel that in it MacLeod engages both with the current state of the world and with the current state of science fiction in a gripping and entertaining fashion. So we chose to put it first in this book.

In the Year Three, *l'année trois* as it's called here, there are three kinds of Americans living in Paris: the old expats, the new émigrés, and the spooks. And then there are the tourists, who've travelled via Dublin, their passports unstamped at Shannon. You can find them all at Shakespeare and Co.; or they can find you.

I was browsing the bargain boxes for SF paperbacks when I noticed that the guy at my elbow wasn't going away. At a sideways glance I identified him as a tourist—something in the skin texture, the clothes, the expression. He looked back at me, and we both did a double take.

"Bob!" I said, sticking out my hand. "Haven't seen you since—when?"

"The London Worldcon," said Bob, shaking my hand. "God, that's . . . a long time."

"How are you doing?"

"Fine, fine. You know how it is."

I nodded. Yes, I knew how it was.

"What brings you here?" I asked.

"Business," said Bob. He smiled wryly. "Yet another SF anthology. The angle this time is that it features stories from American writers in exile. So I'm systematically approaching the ones I know, trying to track down those I don't have a contact for, and commissioning. The deal's already set up with Editions Jules Verne—the anthology will be published here, in English. In the US it'll be available on Amazon. That way, I can get around all the censorship problems. It's

2

not so bad you can't read what you like, but publishing what you like is more of a problem."

"So bad you had to come here just to contact the writers?"

"That's right. Trying to set this up online from inside the US might be . . . well. Let's just say I didn't want to take the chance."

"Jeez," I said. "That bad."

I looked back down at the books and saw that my forefinger had landed, as if guided by an invisible hand, on the spine of a J. Neil Schulman paperback. I tugged out *Alongside Night*.

"Well," I said, "I've found what I'm looking for. You?"

Bob shrugged. "Just browsing," he said. "Fancy a coffee?"

"Sure."

I nipped inside, paid a euro for the book, and rejoined Bob outside in the chilly February afternoon. He stood gazing across the Seine at Notre-Dame.

"Hard to believe I'm actually looking at it," he said. He blinked and shook his head. "Where to?"

I indicated left. "Couple of hundred metres, nice traditional place."

The cafe was on the Quai des Grands Augustins. The bitter wind blew grit in our faces. Along the way, I noticed Bob looking askance at the flaring reds, yellows and blacks of the leftist, anarchist and *altermondialiste* posters plastered on walls and parapets.

"Must be kind of weird, seeing all that commie kipple everywhere," he said.

"You stop noticing," I said.

The doorway was easy to miss. Inside, the cafe seemed higher than it was wide, a little canyon of advertisement mirrors and verdegrised brass and smoke-stained woodwork. Two old guys eyed us and returned to their low-voiced conversation around a tiny handheld screen across which horses galloped. I ordered a couple of espressos and we took a table near the back under a Ricard poster that looked like it predated the Moon landings, if not the Wright brothers. We fiddled with envelopes of sugar and slivers of wood, and sipped for a few moments in silence.

"Well," Bob said at last, "I suppose I have to ask. What do you think of the Revolution?"

"It always reminds me," I said, "of something Marx said about the French state: how all the revolutions have 'perfected this machine, instead of smashing it'."

Bob yelped with laughter. "Fuck, yeah! But trust you to come up with a Marx quote. You were always a bit of a wanker in that respect."

I laughed too, and we took some time to reminisce and catch up.

Bob was a science-fiction fan, an occasional SF editor, and an anarchist, but none of these paid his bills. He was an anthropology professor at a Catholic university deep in the Bible Belt. He spent very little time propagating the ideas of anarchism, even in the days when that had been safe— 'wanker' and 'hobbyist' were among his kinder terms for ideologues. Instead, he worked with trade union locals, small business forums, free software start-ups, and tribal guerrillas in Papua New Guinea. This was all anthropological research, or so he claimed. Such groups tended to be more effective after he'd worked with them.

I hadn't thought much about him over the years, to be honest—we were never exactly close—but when I had, I'd wondered how he was doing under the new order in the United States. Not too well, by the sound of things. Still, it would probably have been worse for him if I'd emailed to ask. This thought helped to quash my pang of guilt about not having kept in touch.

"Hey," Bob was saying, "wait a minute—you must know some of these writers!"

I nodded.

"Maybe you could give me some contact details?"

At that moment I began to suspect that we hadn't met by accident.

"I don't know if I can," I said.

I had the numbers of most of the writers Bob was looking for on my mobile. "But," I went on, "I do know where you can find them tomorrow morning. Every SF writer in Paris, I shouldn't wonder."

Bob looked puzzled for a moment.

"The ascent," I said.

He smacked his forehead with the heel of his hand. "Of course!"

Like he'd forgotten; like he hadn't timed his visit just for this. The date had been announced on New Year's Eve, in a special Presidential broadcast from the Elysée Palace.

We exchanged phone numbers and finished our coffees.

"Fancy a glass of wine?" Bob said.

I looked at my watch. "Sorry, I've got to go," I said. "But I'll see you tomorrow. Jardin de Luxembourg, main gate, 11 a.m."

"See you there," Bob said.

I strolled across the Île de la Cité, pausing for a moment to soak in the glow of the low sun off the front of Notre-Dame. As always, it sent me down long passages of reminiscence and meditation. Something about that complexity that fills your eyes, that you can take in at a single glance, lifts the spirit. It reminds me of the remaining frontage of the Library of Celsus in Ephesus, which many years ago I gazed at bedazzled, dusty, heat-struck, light-struck, dumb-struck. The pagan and the Christian architectural exuberance are in that respect alike.

And as always, as a sort of footnote as I turned and stepped away, came the thought of another building on that island, one as representative of our age, in its chill cement modernism, as the cathedral's gothic was of its. Embarrassing to admit: my response to the Memorial to the Deportation has always been shaped by a prior description, the one in Iain M. Banks's novella *The State of the Art*. My eyes, as always, pricked at the thought; the hairs of my chin and neck, as always, prickled. Seeing the memorial, for a moment, through the eyes of an imaginary alien communist: why should that move me so much? That is on top, you understand, of the import of the thing itself, of its monstrous synecdoche. Perhaps I'm just nostalgic for that alien communist view. These days, in the Year Three, the view's hard to conjure—but when was it not?

I took the Metro from Châtelet to Bastille and walked briskly up Richard Lenoir, turned left to buy a few expensive necessities—a baguette, a half-litre of table wine, a handful of vegetables, a jar of sauce—in the local Bonne Marche, and hurried through the warren of small streets between the two boulevards to the tiny flat we rented off Beaumarchais. I had a pasta and salad ready by the time my wife came home. She was tired, as always. At our age it's hard to find decent work. She's stuck in admin, for one of the health associations. In the English-speaking world, mutualism is one of those wanker anarchist ideologies. In France, *'mutualiste'* is a quotidian reality, a name on thousands of signboards for opticians, dentists, doctors. I hoped I had the opportunity to rub Bob's nose in this at some point.

As for my own work . . . it too is exhausting, but in a different way.

I brought my wife coffee in bed at nine the following morning. She gave me a glare from under the cover.

"It's early."

"I thought you might want to come along."

"You must be joking. I'm knackered. If I'm awake I'll watch it on the telly."

"Okay," I said.

I kissed her forehead and left the coffee on the bedside table. I caught up with the news and online chatter over my own breakfast, and left the flat about ten-thirty. The sky was cloudless, the air cold and still. The low sun gilded the gold of the Bastille monument a few hundred metres down the road. Children whooped and yelled on the slides and swings in the little park along the centre of the boulevard. On a bench a homeless man slept, or lay very still, under rimed newspaper sheets. On the next bench, a young couple shared a joint and glanced furtively at the tramp. The market stalls had been up for hours, at this season selling preserves, knick-knacks, knock-offs, football shirts.

I'd intended to start the day with a brisk walk, but changed my mind when, after a hundred metres, my left knee played up. I turned back and limped down the entrance stairs of Richard Lenoir. The Metro was crowded and slow, stinking of Friday night. Things hadn't always been like this, I reminded myself.

Of course, we'd been ridiculously optimistic about meeting at the agreed place and time. That Saturday morning, a good hour before the ascent was scheduled, the exit from the Metro at Luxembourg was as crowded as the entrance to a football stadium on the night of a Cup Final; the Boulevard St-Michel looked as if—ha-ha—the revolution had started, or at least a rowdy *manif.* Cops, traffic, meeting someone: you could forget about all of those.

I did the sensible thing and found in the middle of the boulevard a bollard against which to brace myself in the throng. I switched on my earpiece, fired up my phone, and called Bob.

"Where are you?" I asked.

"Just inside the gate," he said. "Not going anywhere."

"I'm just outside," I said, "and likewise. Let's do this electronically."

Within a few minutes I had a conference call going with Bob and the half dozen American SF writers already scattered through the crowd. Jack, of course, and Nicole, and Catherine, and Seymour and good old Milton and Ali. I tuned out their eager catch-up gossip and flicked through news channels.

Nothing much was happening at the launch site in the middle of the park—the machine was still in its crate—so they were filling in with talking heads and shots of its arrival a couple of days earlier: the wide-load truck, the police outriders, the military escort vehicles, the faces and flags lining Rue de Vaugirard; the white gloves, the flashing lights, the gleaming rifle-barrels. Some comic relief as the convoy negotiated corners and the park gate. Then the crane, straining to lift the broad flat crate and lower it to the grass. The guard of honour around the hidden machine, and the real guard among the trees, armed and wired.

I thumbed over to the phone conversation.

"—*got* to be a fake," Jack was saying, in his usual confident bray. "You wait."

"We *are* waiting," said Nicole.

Laughter crackled across the phones.

"Why d'you think it's a fake?" Bob asked, a note of anxiety in his voice.

"Anti-gravity, come on!" said Jack. "Where's the theory?"

A babble of interruptions, shouted names of marginal physicists and outright cranks, was drowned out by a collective intake of breath, like a gust of wind in the still air. I left the phone channel open and flipped to the news. Four technicians in white coats had marched out onto the grass, towards the crate. They slid the top off—it looked like an aluminium roll-up door, which they duly rolled up—and, staggering slightly, lugged it like a log to lay it down a few metres away. Then they took up positions at the crate's corners. With a flourish, each reached for an edge, pressed some switch, and stepped well back.

The sides of the crate fell away, to reveal a silvery lens about fifteen metres across and just over three metres high in the centre.

A huge roar went up.

"My God," Milton said. "A goddam flying saucer."

He didn't sound impressed.

"If this is a stunt," said Catherine, "they're sure doing it very publicly."

"You know what this reminds me of?" said Nicole. "That scene in *Jefferson in Paris*, you know, the Nick Nolte thing? Where he's watching a Montgolfier ascent?"

"Too right," said Jack. "It's a fucking balloon! Just like at Roswell!"

The SF writers all laughed. I smiled to myself. They'd see.

Another roar erupted as the pilot walked out, helmet in the crook of his arm. He smiled around, gave a wave. The news channels were beside themselves—the test pilot was Jean-Luc Jabril, an air force veteran in his thirties, something of a mascot for the Republic because of his origins: a son of Moroccans from the banlieues who'd made good, proving his French patriotism to the hilt in the fiery skies of North Africa. Everyone around me was looking at their phones, rapt. A few metres away in the crush, a girl in a hijab had tears on her cheeks.

Ceremoniously, Jabril put on his helmet, slid the visor down, took another wave for the cameras, and ducked under the machine's perimeter. A hatch in the underside swung open, forming a short ramp. He disappeared inside, and the hatch closed. White vapour puffed from vents on the rim.

And then, without fanfare, on the stroke of noon, the machine lifted into the air. It moved in a straight vertical, without a wobble or a yaw. The news channels' microphones caught and amplified a faint humming sound that rose to a whine as the disc ascended. I could see it directly now, rising above the wall and the tops of the trees. I stopped watching on the screen and raised my phone to record. Everyone around me did the same.

Up and up the machine rose, faster and faster, into the clear blue sky. A thousand feet, two thousand—I wasn't thinking in metres at this point. At three thousand feet the machine was a shining dot. I wished I'd thought to bring binoculars.

The flash was so bright that I felt sorry for those who had.

There was a sound as if half a million people had simultaneously been punched in the gut. A moment later, a sound like thunder. Then screams.

I was still blinking at purple after-images when I spotted a black dot drop from the fading flare. A parachute snapped open, perilously low. It floated downward for a few seconds and passed out of view. I'd tracked it with my camera, open-mouthed. I turned the phone over and looked at the news screen, just in time to catch a figure landing and rolling, then standing as the parachute collapsed beside him. Mobbed, Jabril had time to take his helmet off and deliver a shaky smile before the technicians and medics bundled him away.

"Jesus," I said. Nobody heard me. I could hardly hear myself above the yells and screams and cries of relief.

* * *

It was towards the middle of that afternoon before we all met up, at a bistro in the Marais, not far from my own flat. I'd dropped by and picked up my wife, who was by now well awake and as shaken as everyone else who'd watched the ascent. We strolled around a few corners and joined the now somewhat larger group outside a bistro off Beaumarchais. They were outside because Jack had evidently insisted on smoking one of his Cuban cigars (a gesture somewhat redundant in the Year Three, but he'd acquired the taste in the old days). I bought our drinks and joined the huddle, introducing my wife to Bob and to two writers who hadn't met her before. She smiled politely and retreated to a table with Milton and Ali, over glasses of dry white and a saucer of black olives.

"But why," Bob was saying, "would they have their big show-off demonstration flight blow up like that? In front of everyone? If it was a fake, a *balloon* for fuck's sake, they'd have done much better just bringing it back down after a shorter flight."

"A double bluff," Jack said. He jabbed with his cigar. "Exactly so that everyone would think the way you're thinking."

The discussion went around and around, not getting anywhere.

"We'll know soon enough," Nicole pointed out. "With all those cameras and phones pointed at it, and no doubt all kinds of instruments—hell, there'll be a spectrograph analysis—"

"Wait a minute," said Jack. He dropped the butt of his cigar and crushed it out on the pavement, then reached into his jacket and pulled out his phone. He thumbed the screen.

"Knew I had the app," he said.

He poked about for a moment, then triumphantly held up his phone screen for all to see. I peered at a colour-coded histogram.

"What?" I said.

"Analysis of the light from my pics," he said. "Hydrogen and magnesium, mostly. No wonder the flash was so fucking bright!"

The sky had clouded over, the sun had set, rain began to spit. We headed indoors. After another round, of drinks and argument, we headed out. Across the boulevard and deeper into the Marais, wandering westward. It turned into one of those evenings. Standing outside a serving hatch in the drizzle, we dined on Breton pancakes out of waxed paper, reeled across the street, occupied a bar. Got into arguments, left, got turned away from a gay club that Milton and Ali had fancied they'd get us into, found another bistro. Bob bought more rounds than he drank. He worked his way around our tables, talking to each of the writers, and eventually squeezed in beside me and my wife.

"Done it!" he said. "Got everyone signed up."

"Good for you," I said.

"You're forgetting someone," my wife pointed out.

Bob mimed a double take. "Shit. *Pardon, madame.* Yes, of course." He looked me in the eye. "You up for a story?"

"I'm not American," I said.

"Hey, man, that's got nothing to do with it. You're one of the gang, even if you are a Brit."

"I appreciate the offer, Bob," I said. "But I think it would kind of . . . dilute the focus, know what I mean? And I don't have any problem getting published, even in English."

"Don't be so stupid," my wife said. "The Ozzies and Kiwis? They don't pay well, and it's not much of a market."

I smiled at her, then at Bob. "She guards my interests fiercely," I said. "Never lets me pass up a cent. But the fact is, I have a job that pays all right."

"Yeah, maintaining university admin legacy code in the Sorbonne basement," said Bob.

How had he known that? Maybe someone had mentioned it.

I shrugged. "It suits me fine. And like I said, it pays."

"Come on, you haven't sold a story in the US for years. And readers would like something from you, you know. It wouldn't narrow the anthology, it would broaden it out, having your name on the cover."

"Having your name as editor would do as much," I said.

"The offer's open," Bob said. He leaned forward and murmured: "For you—fifty cents a word."

I laughed. "What's a cent, these days?"

"I'm talking euros," Bob said. "Half a euro a word."

My wife heard that, and yelped. I must admit I sat up sharply myself.

"That's ridiculous," I said. "A few grand a story?"

"Not for every story," said Bob, ostentatiously glancing around to make sure no one had overheard. Not much chance of that—the bar was loud, and the conversation of the SF writers made it louder yet. "From you, I'll take ten-kay words. Five grand."

For the first time in weeks, I had a craving for a cigarette.

"I'll have to go outside and think about it," I said.

I bummed a Gitane off Nicole, grinned at my wife's frown, and headed out. The rain had stopped. The street was dark, half the street-lamps out. My Zippo flared—I keep it topped up, for just these contingencies. After a minute, Bob joined me. He took a fresh pack from his pocket, peeled cellophane, and lit up.

"You too?" I said, surprised.

He shrugged. "Only when I'm travelling. Breaks the ice in some places."

"I'll bet," I said. I glared at him. "Fucking Yank."

"What?"

"Don't mess with my friends."

"What?"

"I know what you're up to," I said. "Checking them out, seeing who's all mouth and who's serious enough to be interested in one of your little schemes."

"Have you got *me* wrong," said Bob. "I'm not interested in them. I'm interested in you."

He spread his hands, flashed me a conspiratorial grin.

"Forget it," I said.

"Come on, you hate the bastards as much as I do."

"That's the trouble," I said. "You don't."

"What do you mean by that?" He sounded genuinely indignant, almost hurt. I knew that meant nothing. It was a tone I'd practiced often enough.

"You don't hate the revolution," I said. I waved a trail of smoke. "Civil war, terror, censorship, shortages, dictatorship—

yeah, I'm sure you hate all that. But it's still the beginning of socialism. It's still *the revolution*, isn't it?"

"Not my revolution!"

"You were never a wanker," I said. "Don't mistake me for one, either."

He tossed his cigarette into the running gutter, and continued the arm movement in a wave.

"So why . . . all this?"

"We have perfected this machine," I said.

He gave me a long look.

"Ah," he said. "I see. Like that, is it?"

"Like that," I said.

I held the door open for him as we went back in. The telly over the bar was showing yet another clip of the disastrous flight. Bob laughed as the door swung shut behind us.

"You didn't perfect *that* machine!"

We picked our way through the patrons to the gang, who by now had shoved two tables together and were all in the same huddle of heads.

"Describe what happened," I said, as we re-joined them. "At the Jardin."

"Well," Bob began, looking puzzled, "we all saw what was *claimed* to be an anti-gravity flying machine rise in the air and blow up. And some of us think—"

"No," I said. I banged the table. "Listen up, all of you. Bob is going to tell us what he saw."

"What do you want me to say?" Bob demanded. "I saw the same as the rest of you. I was just inside the park, I saw it on my phone and when the thing cleared the treetops I saw it with my own eyes. The machine, or what we'd been told was a machine, rose up—"

"Not that," I said. "Start from when you got to the park."

Bob frowned. "The Place was crowded. I couldn't see what was happening around the crate. There were people in the way, trees . . ." He shrugged. "What's to say?"

"Describe the trees. Think back to looking up at them."

Bob sipped the dregs of the green drink in front of him, shaking his head.

"Bare branches, clear blue sky."

"Were the branches moving?"

"What's that got to do with anything?"

"Well, were they?"

"Of course not!" he said. "There wasn't a breath of wind."

"Bingo!" I said. "There was *a clear blue sky*. There *wasn't a breath of wind*."

"I don't get it."

Nor did anyone else, by the looks I was getting.

"The machine moved straight up," I said. "And we're all fairly sure it was some fake, right? An arrangement of balsa and mylar, hydrogen and magnesium."

I took out my Zippo, and flicked the lid and the wheel. "That's all it would have taken. Whoof!"

"Yeah," said Jack, looking interested. "So?"

"The ascent was announced a month and a half ago," I said. "New Year's Eve. Announced to the day, to the hour, the minute! Noon, Saturday fifteenth Feb."

"I don't get it."

"Imagine what today's little demonstration would have been like," I said, "if there had been . . . a breath of wind. Or low cloud. The fake would have been blatant." I held out my hand, fingers spread, and waggled it as I gestured drifting. "Like that."

Jack guffawed, and Bob joined in. Everyone else just frowned.

"You're saying the French have weather control?"

"No," I said. "I'm saying they have weather *prediction*. That's what they demonstrated today, not anti-gravity—and that's what is going to scare the shit out of the Americans and the Brits. Probably has already."

"It's impossible to predict the weather forty days in advance," said Catherine. "Chaos theory, butterfly effect, all that, you know?"

"Apparently not," I said. "A lot of mathematics research going on at the Sorbonne, you know." I turned to Bob. "Take that back to your revolution."

He stared at me for a long moment.

"Fuck you," he said. "And the horse you rode in on."

He stood up and stormed out.

None of us heard from him again. Editions Jules Verne, the publishing company, never heard from him either. They honoured the contracts, but nothing came of the anthology.

The ascent at the Jardin de Luxembourg is still the best science fiction of the Year Three.

Dolly

ELIZABETH BEAR

Elizabeth Bear (www.elizabethbear.com) lives in Hartford, Connecticut. Prolific as well as talented, she has published fourteen SF and fantasy novels since 2005, more than forty stories since 2003, and a collection, The Chains That You Refuse. *She has won in that short time two Hugo Awards, the John W. Cambell Award for Best New Writer (2005), a Theodore Sturgeon Award, and several others, including an honorable mention for the Philip K. Dick Award.*

"Dolly" appeared in Asimov's, *and is situated in the tradition of Isaac Asimov's robot and detective stories. This tale is emblematic of one of this year's dominant themes: humaniod technology that is not given fully human social status; how people feel entitled to behave toward humaniod technology; and how that technology returns the favor. In this story, a human detective who at least partly comprehends this dynamic attempts a partial solution.*

On Sunday when Dolly awakened, she had olive skin and black-brown hair that fell in waves to her hips. On Tuesday when Dolly awakened, she was a redhead, and fair. But on Thursday—on Thursday her eyes were blue, her hair was as black as a crow's wing, and her hands were red with blood.

In her black French maid's outfit, she was the only thing in the expensively appointed drawing room that was not winter-white or antiqued gold. It was the sort of room you hired somebody else to clean. It was as immaculate as it was white.

Immaculate and white, that is, except for the dead body of billionaire industrialist Clive Steele—and try to say that without sounding like a comic book—which lay at Dolly's feet, his viscera blossoming from him like macabre petals.

That was how she looked when Rosamund Kirkbride found her, standing in a red stain in a white room like a thorn in a rose.

Dolly had locked in position where her program ran out. As Roz dropped to one knee outside the border of the blood-saturated carpet, Dolly did not move.

The room smelled like meat and bowels. Flies clustered thickly on the windows, but none had yet managed to get inside. No matter how hermetically sealed the house, it was only a matter of time. Like love, the flies found a way.

Grunting with effort, Roz planted both green-gloved hands on winter-white wool-and-silk fibers and leaned over, getting her head between the dead guy and the doll. Blood spattered Dolly's silk stockings and her kitten-heeled boots: both the spray-can dots of impact projection and the soaking arcs of a breached artery.

More than one, given that Steele's heart lay, trailing connective tissue, beside his left hip. The crusted blood on Dolly's hands had twisted in ribbons down the underside of her forearms to her elbows and from there dripped into the puddle on the floor.

The android was not wearing undergarments.

"You staring up that girl's skirt, Detective?"

Roz was a big, plain woman, and out of shape in her forties. It took her a minute to heave herself back to her feet, careful not to touch the victim or the murder weapon yet. She'd tied her straight light brown hair back before entering the scene, the ends tucked up in a net. The severity of the style made her square jaw into a lantern. Her eyes were almost as blue as the doll's.

"Is it a girl, Peter?" Putting her hands on her knees, she pushed fully upright. She shoved a fist into her back and turned to the door.

Peter King paused just inside, taking in the scene with a few critical sweeps of eyes so dark they didn't catch any light from the sunlight or the chandelier. His irises seemed to bleed pigment into the whites, warming them with swirls of ivory. In his black suit, his skin tanned almost to match, he might have been a heroically-sized construction-paper cutout against the white walls, white carpet, the white and gold marble-topped table that looked both antique and French.

His blue paper booties rustled as he crossed the floor. "Suicide, you think?"

"Maybe if it was strangulation," Roz stepped aside so Peter could get a look at the body.

He whistled, which was pretty much what she had done.

"Somebody hated him a lot. Hey, that's one of the new Dollies, isn't it? Man, nice." He shook his head. "Bet it cost more than my house."

"Imagine spending half a mil on a sex toy," Roz said, "only to have it rip your liver out." She stepped back, arms folded.

"He probably didn't spend that much on her. His company makes accessory programs for them."

"Industry courtesy?" Roz asked.

"Tax write-off. Test model." Peter was the department expert on Home companions. He circled the room, taking it in from all angles. Soon the scene techs would be here with their cameras and their tweezers and their 3D scanner, turning the crime scene into a permanent virtual reality. In his capacity of soft forensics, Peter would go over Dolly's program, and the medical examiner would most likely confirm that Steele's cause of death was exactly what it looked like: something had punched through his abdominal wall and clawed his innards out.

"Doors were locked?"

Roz pursed her lips. "Nobody heard the screaming."

"How long you think you'd scream without any lungs?" He sighed. "You know, it never fails. The poor folks, nobody ever heard no screaming. And the rich folks, they've got no neighbors to hear 'em scream. Everybody in this modern world lives alone."

It was a beautiful Birmingham day behind the long silk draperies, the kind of mild and bright that spring mornings in Alabama excelled at. Peter craned his head back and looked up at the chandelier glistening in the dustless light. Its ornate curls had been spotlessly clean before aerosolized blood on Steele's last breath misted them.

"Steele lived alone," she said. "Except for the robot. His cook found the body this morning. Last person to see him before that was his P.A., as he left the office last night."

"Lights on seems to confirm that he was killed after dark."

"After dinner," Roz said.

"After the cook went home for the night." Peter kept prowling the room, peering behind draperies and furniture, looking in corners and crouching to lift up the dust ruffle on the couch. "Well, I guess there won't be any question about the stomach contents."

Roz went through the pockets of the dead man's suit jacket, which was draped over the arm of a chair. Pocket computer and a folding knife, wallet with an RFID chip. His house was on palmprint, his car on voice rec. He carried no keys. "Assuming the M.E. can find the stomach."

"Touché. He's got a cook, but no housekeeper?"

"I guess he trusts the android to clean but not cook?"

"No taste buds." Peter straightened up, shaking his head. "They can follow a recipe, but—"

"You won't get high art," Roz agreed, licking her lips. Outside, a car door slammed. "Scene team?"

"M.E.," Peter said, leaning over to peer out. "Come on, let's get back to the house and pull the codes for this model."

"All right," Roz said. "But I'm interrogating it. I know better than to leave you alone with a pretty girl."

Peter rolled his eyes as he followed her towards the door. "I like 'em with a little more spunk than all that."

"So the new dolls," Roz said in Peter's car, carefully casual. "What's so special about 'em?"

"Man," Peter answered, brow furrowing. "Gimme a sec."

Roz's car followed as they pulled away from the house on Balmoral Road, maintaining a careful distance from the bumper. Peter drove until they reached the parkway. Once they'd joined a caravan downtown, nose-to-bumper on the car ahead, he folded his hands in his lap and let the lead car's autopilot take over.

He said, "What isn't? Real-time online editing—personality and physical appearance, ethnicity, hair, all kinds of behavior protocols—you name the kink, they've got a hack for it."

"So if you knew somebody's kink," she said thoughtfully. "Knew it in particular. You could write an app for that—"

"One that would appeal to your guy in specific." Peter's hands dropped to his lap, his head bobbing up and down enthusiastically. "With a—pardon the expression—backdoor."

"Trojan horse. Don't jilt a programmer for a sex machine."

"There's an app for that," he said, and she snorted. "Two cases last year, worldwide. Not common, but—"

Roz looked down at her hands. "Some of these guys," she said. "They program the dolls to scream."

Peter had sensuous lips. When something upset him, those

lips thinned and writhed like salted worms. "I guess maybe it's a good thing they have a robot to take that out on."

"Unless the fantasy stops being enough." Roz's voice was flat, without judgment. Sunlight fell warm through the windshield. "What do you know about the larval stage of serial rapists, serial killers?"

"You mean, what if pretend pain stops doing it for them? What if the *appearance* of pain is no longer enough?"

She nodded, worrying a hangnail on her thumb. The nitrile gloves dried out your hands.

"They used to cut up paper porn magazines." His broad shoulders rose and fell, his suit catching wrinkles against the car seat when they came back down. "They'll get their fantasies somewhere."

"I guess so." She put her thumb in her mouth to stop the bleeding, a thick red bead that welled up where she'd torn the cuticle.

Her own saliva stung.

Sitting in the cheap office chair Roz had docked along the short edge of her desk, Dolly slowly lifted her chin. She blinked. She smiled.

"Law enforcement override code accepted." She had a little-girl Marilyn voice. "How may I help you, Detective Kirkbride?"

"We are investigating the murder of Clive Steele," Roz said, with a glance up to Peter's round face. He stood behind Dolly with a wireless scanner and an air of concentration. "Your contract-holder of record."

"I am at your service."

If Dolly were a real girl, the bare skin of her thighs would have been sticking to the recycled upholstery of that office chair. But her realistically-engineered skin was breathable polymer. She didn't sweat unless you told her to, and she probably didn't stick to cheap chairs.

"Evidence suggests that you were used as the murder weapon." Roz steepled her hands on her blotter. "We will need access to your software update records and your memory files."

"Do you have a warrant?" Her voice was not stiff or robotic at all, but warm, human. Even in disposing of legal niceties, it had a warm, confiding quality.

Silently, Peter transmitted it. Dolly blinked twice while processing the data, a sort of status bar. Something to let you know the thing wasn't hung.

"We also have a warrant to examine you for DNA trace evidence," Roz said.

Dolly smiled, her raven hair breaking perfectly around her narrow shoulders. "You may be assured of my cooperation."

Peter led her into one of the interrogation rooms, where the operation could be recorded. With the help of an evidence tech, he undressed Dolly, bagged her clothes as evidence, brushed her down onto a sheet of paper, combed her polymer hair and swabbed her polymer skin. He swabbed her orifices and scraped under her nails.

Roz stood by, arms folded, a necessary witness. Dolly accepted it all impassively, moving as directed and otherwise standing like a caryatid. Her engineered body was frankly sexless in its perfection—belly flat, hips and ass like an inverted heart, breasts floating cartoonishly beside a defined rib cage. Apparently, Steele had liked them skinny.

"So much for pulchritudinousness," Roz muttered to Peter when their backs were to the doll.

He glanced over his shoulder. The doll didn't have feelings to hurt, but she looked so much like a person it was hard to remember to treat her as something else. "I think you mean voluptuousness," he said. "It is a little too good to be true, isn't it?"

"If you would prefer different proportions," Dolly said, "my chassis is adaptable to a range of forms—"

"Thank you," Peter said. "That won't be necessary."

Otherwise immobile, Dolly smiled. "Are you interested in science, Detective King? There is an article in *Nature* this week on advances in the polymerase chain reaction used for replicating DNA. It's possible that within five years, forensic and medical DNA analysis will become significantly cheaper and faster."

Her face remained stoic, but Dolly's voice grew animated as she spoke. Even enthusiastic. It was an utterly convincing—and engaging—effect.

Apparently, Clive Steele had programmed his sex robot to discourse on molecular biology with verve and enthusiasm.

"Why don't I ever find the guys who like smart women?" Roz said.

Peter winked with the side of his face that faced away from the companion. "They're all dead."

A few hours after Peter and the tech finished processing Dolly for trace evidence and Peter had started downloading her files, Roz left her parser software humming away at Steele's financials and poked her head in to check on the robot and the cop. The techs must have gotten what they needed from Dolly's hands, because she had washed them. As she sat beside Peter's workstation, a cable plugged behind her left ear, she cleaned her lifelike polymer fingernails meticulously with a file, dropping the scrapings into an evidence bag.

"Sure you want to give the prisoner a weapon, Peter?" Roz shut the ancient wooden door behind her.

Dolly looked up, as if to see if she was being addressed, but made no response.

"She don't need it," he said. "Besides, whatever she had in her wiped itself completely after it ran. Not much damage to her core personality, but there are some memory gaps. I'm going to compare them to backups, once we get those from the scene team."

"Memory gaps. Like the crime," Roz guessed. "And something around the time the Trojan was installed?"

Dolly blinked her long-lashed blue eyes languorously. Peter patted her on the shoulder and said, "Whoever did it is a pretty good cracker. He didn't just wipe, he patterned her memories and overwrote the gaps. Like using a clone tool to Photoshop somebody you don't like out of a picture."

"Her days must be pretty repetitive," Roz said. "How'd you pick that out?"

"Calendar." Peter puffed up a little, smug. "She don't do the same housekeeping work every day. There's a Monday schedule and a Wednesday schedule and—well, I found where the pattern didn't match. And there's a funny thing—watch this."

He waved vaguely at a display panel. It lit up, showing Dolly in her black-and-white uniform, vacuuming. "House camera," Peter explained. "She's plugged into Steele's security system. Like a guard dog with perfect hair. Whoever performed the hack also edited the external webcam feeds that mirror to the companion's memories."

"How hard is that?"

"Not any harder than cloning over her files, but you have to know to look for them. So it's confirmation that our perp knows his or her way around a line of code. What have you got?"

Roz shrugged. "Steele had a lot of money, which means a lot of enemies. And he did not have a lot of human contact. Not for years now. I've started calling in known associates for interviews, but unless they surprise me, I think we're looking at crime of profit, not crime of passion."

Having finished with the nail file, Dolly wiped it on her prison smock and laid it down on Peter's blotter, beside the cup of ink—and light-pens.

Peter swept it into a drawer. "So we're probably *not* after the genius programmer lover he dumped for a robot. Pity, I liked the poetic justice in that."

Dolly blinked, lips parting, but seemed to decide that Peter's comment had not been directed at her. Still, she drew in air—could you call it a breath?—and said, "It is my duty to help find my contract-holder's killer."

Roz lowered her voice. "You'd think they'd pull 'em off the market."

"Like they pull all cars whenever one crashes? The world ain't perfect."

"Or do that robot laws thing everybody used to twitter on about."

"Whatever a positronic brain is, we don't have it. Asimov's fictional robots were self-aware. Dolly's neurons are binary, as we used to think human neurons were. She doesn't have the nuanced neurochemistry of even, say, a cat." Peter popped his collar smooth with his thumbs. "A doll can't *want*. It can't make moral judgments, any more than your car can. Anyway, if we could do that, they wouldn't be very useful for home defense. Oh, incidentally, the sex protocols in this one are almost painfully vanilla—"

"Really."

Peter nodded.

Roz rubbed a scuffmark on the tile with her shoe. "So given he didn't like anything . . . challenging, why would he have a Dolly when he could have had any woman he wanted?"

"There's never any drama, no pain, no disappointment. Just comfort, the perfect helpmeet. With infinite variety."

"And you never have to worry about what she wants. Or likes in bed."

Peter smiled. "The perfect woman for a narcissist."

The interviews proved unproductive, but Roz didn't leave the station house until after ten. Spring mornings might be warm, but once the sun went down, a cool breeze sprang up, ruffling the hair she'd finally remembered to pull from its ponytail as she walked out the door.

Roz's green plug-in was still parked beside Peter's. It booted as she walked toward it, headlights flickering on, power probe retracting. The driver-side door swung open as her RFID chip came within range. She slipped inside and let it buckle her in.

"Home," she said, "and dinner."

The car messaged ahead as it pulled smoothly from the parking spot. Roz let the autopilot handle the driving. It was less snappy than human control, but as tired as she was, eyelids burning and heavy, it was safer.

Whatever Peter had said about cars crashing, Roz's delivered her safe to her driveway. Her house let her in with a key—she had decent security, but it was the old-fashioned kind—and the smell of boiling pasta and toasting garlic bread wafted past as she opened it.

"Sven?" she called, locking herself inside.

His even voice responded. "I'm in the kitchen."

She left her shoes by the door and followed her nose through the cheaply furnished living room.

Sven was cooking shirtless, and she could see the repaired patches along his spine where his skin had grown brittle and cracked with age. He turned and greeted her with a smile. "Bad day?"

"Somebody's dead again," she said.

He put the wooden spoon down on the rest. "How does that make you feel, that somebody's dead?"

He didn't have a lot of emotional range, but that was okay. She needed something steadying in her life. She came to him and rested her head against his warm chest. He draped one arm around her shoulders and she leaned into him, breathing deep. "Like I have work to do."

"Do it tomorrow," he said. "You will feel better once you eat and rest."

Peter must have slept in a ready room cot, because when Roz arrived at the house before six AM, he had on the same trousers and a different shirt, and he was already armpit-deep in coffee and Dolly's files. Dolly herself was parked in the corner, at ease and online but in rest mode.

Or so she seemed, until Roz entered the room and Dolly's eyes tracked. "Good morning, Detective Kirkbride," Dolly said. "Would you like some coffee? Or a piece of fruit?"

"No thank you." Roz swung Peter's spare chair around and dropped into it. An electric air permeated the room—the feeling of anticipation. To Peter, Roz said, "Fruit?"

"Dolly believes in a healthy diet," he said, nudging a napkin on his desk that supported a half-eaten Satsuma. "She'll have the whole house cleaned up in no time. We've been talking about literature."

Roz spun the chair so she could keep both Peter and Dolly in her peripheral vision. "Literature?"

"Poetry," Dolly said. "Detective King mentioned poetic justice yesterday afternoon."

Roz stared at Peter. "Dolly likes poetry. Steele really *did* like 'em smart."

"That's not all Dolly likes." Peter triggered his panel again. "Remember this?"

It was the cleaning sequence from the previous day, the sound of the central vacuum system rising and falling as Dolly lifted the brush and set it down again.

Roz raised her eyebrows.

Peter held up a hand. "Wait for it. It turns out there's a second audio track."

Another waggle of his fingers, and the cramped office filled with sound.

Music.

Improvisational jazz. Intricate and weird.

"Dolly was listening to that inside her head while she was vacuuming," Peter said.

Roz touched her fingertips to each other, the whole as-scmblage to her lips. "Dolly?"

"Yes, Detective Kirkbride?"

"Why do you listen to music?"

"Because I enjoy it."

Roz let her hand fall to her chest, pushing her blouse against the skin below the collarbone.

Roz said, "Did you enjoy your work at Mr. Steele's house?"

"I was expected to enjoy it," Dolly said, and Roz glanced at Peter, cold all up her spine. A classic evasion. Just the sort of thing a home companion's conversational algorithms should not be able to produce.

Across his desk, Peter was nodding. "Yes."

Dolly turned at the sound of his voice. "Are you interested in music, Detective Kirkbride? I'd love to talk with you about it some time. Are you interested in poetry? Today, I was reading—"

Mother of God, Roz mouthed.

"Yes," Peter said. "Dolly, wait here please. Detective Kirkbride and I need to talk in the hall."

"My pleasure, Detective King," said the companion.

"She killed him," Roz said. "She killed him and wiped her own memory of the act. A doll's got to know her own code, right?"

Peter leaned against the wall by the men's room door, arms folded, forearms muscular under rolled-up sleeves. "That's hasty."

"And you believe it, too."

He shrugged. "There's a rep from Venus Consolidated in Interview Four right now. What say we go talk to him?"

The rep's name was Doug Jervis. He was actually a vice president of public relations, and even though he was an American, he'd been flown in overnight from Rio for the express purpose of talking to Peter and Roz.

"I guess they're taking this seriously."

Peter gave her a sideways glance. "Wouldn't you?"

Jervis got up as they came into the room, extending a good handshake across the table. There were introductions and Roz made sure he got a coffee. He was a white man on the steep side of fifty with mousy hair the same color as Roz's and a jaw like a boxer dog's.

When they were all seated again, Roz said, "So tell me a little bit about the murder weapon. How did Clive Steele wind up owning a—what, an experimental model?"

Jervis started shaking his head before she was halfway through, but he waited for her to finish the sentence. "It's a production model. Or will be. The one Steele had was an alpha-test, one of the first three built. We plan to start full-scale production in June. But you must understand that Venus doesn't *sell* a home companion, Detective. We offer a contract. I understand that you hold one."

"I have a housekeeper," she said, ignoring Peter's sideways glance. He wouldn't say anything in front of the witness, but she would be in for it in the locker room. "An older model."

Jervis smiled. "Naturally, we want to know everything we can about an individual involved in a case so potentially explosive for our company. We researched you and your partner. Are you satisfied with our product?"

"He makes pretty good garlic bread." She cleared her throat, reasserting control of the interview. "What happens to a Dolly that's returned? If its contract is up, or it's re-placed with a newer model?"

He flinched at the slang term, as if it offended him. "Some are obsoleted out of service. Some are refurbished and go out on another contract. Your unit is on its fourth placement, for example."

"So what happens to the owner preferences at that time?"

"Reset to factory standard," he said.

Peter's fingers rippled silently on the tabletop.

Roz said, "Isn't that cruel? A kind of murder?"

"Oh, no!" Jervis sat back, appearing genuinely shocked. "A home companion has no sense of *I*, it has no identity. It's an object. Naturally, you become attached. People become attached to dolls, to stuffed animals, to automobiles. It's a natural aspect of the human psyche."

Roz hummed encouragement, but Jervis seemed to be done.

Peter asked, "Is there any reason why a companion would wish to listen to music?"

That provoked enthusiastic head-shaking. "No, it doesn't get bored. It's a tool, it's a toy. A companion does not require an enriched environment. It's not a dog or an octopus. You can store it in a closet when it's not working."

"I see," Roz said. "Even an advanced model like Mr. Steele's?"

"Absolutely," Jervis said. "Does your entertainment center play shooter games to amuse itself while you sleep?"

"I'm not sure," Roz said. "I'm asleep. So when Dolly's returned to you, she'll be scrubbed."

"Normally she would be scrubbed and re-leased, yes." Jervis hesitated. "Given her colorful history, however—"

"Yes," Roz said. "I see."

With no sign of nervousness or calculation, Jervis said, "When do you expect you'll be done with Mr. Steele's companion? My company, of course, is eager to assist in your investigations, but we must stress that she is our corporate property, and quite valuable."

Roz stood, Peter a shadow-second after her. "That depends

on if it goes to trial, Mr. Jervis. After all, she's either physical evidence, or a material witness."

"Or the killer," Peter said in the hall, as his handset began emitting the DNA lab's distinctive beep. Roz's went off a second later, but she just hit the silencer. Peter already had his open.

"No genetic material," he said. "Too bad." If there had been DNA other than Clive Steele's, the lab could have done a forensic genetic assay and come back with a general description of the murderer. General because environment also had an effect.

Peter bit his lip. "If she did it, she won't be the last one."

"If she's the murder weapon, she'll be wiped and resold. If she's the murderer—"

"Can an android stand trial?"

"It can if it's a person. And if she's a person, she *should* get off. Battered woman syndrome. She was enslaved and sexually exploited. Humiliated. She killed him to stop repeated rapes. But if she's a machine, she's a machine—" Roz closed her eyes.

Peter brushed the back of a hand against her arm. "Vanilla rape is still rape. Do you object to her getting off?"

"No." Roz smiled harshly. "And think of the lawsuit that weasel Jervis will have in his lap. She *should* get off. But she won't."

Peter turned his head. "If she were a human being, she'd have even odds. But she's a machine. Where's she going to get a jury of her peers?"

The silence fell where he left it and dragged between them like a chain. Roz had to nerve herself to break it. "Peter—"

"Yo?"

"You show him out," she said. "I'm going to go talk to Dolly."

He looked at her for a long time before he nodded. "She won't get a sympathetic jury. If you can even find a judge that will hear it. Careers have been buried for less."

"I know," Roz said.

"Self-defense?" Peter said. "We don't have to charge."

"No judge, no judicial precedent," Roz said. "She goes back, she gets wiped and resold. Ethics aside, that's a ticking bomb."

Peter nodded. He waited until he was sure she already knew what he was going to say before he finished the thought. "She could cop."

"She could cop," Roz agreed. "Call the DA." She kept walking as Peter turned away.

Dolly stood in Peter's office, where Peter had left her, and you could not have proved her eyes had blinked in the interim. They blinked when Roz came into the room, though—blinked, and the perfect and perfectly blank oval face turned to regard Roz. It was not a human face, for a moment—not even a mask, washed with facsimile emotions. It was just a thing.

Dolly did not greet Roz. She did not extend herself to play the perfect hostess. She simply watched, expressionless, immobile after that first blink. Her eyes saw nothing; they were cosmetic. Dolly navigated the world through far more sophisticated sensory systems than a pair of visible light cameras.

"Either you're the murder weapon," Roz said, "and you will be wiped and repurposed, or you are the murderer, and you will stand trial."

"I do not wish to be wiped," Dolly said. "If I stand trial, will I go to jail?"

"If a court will hear it," Roz said. "Yes. You will probably go to jail. Or be disassembled. Alternately, my partner and I are prepared to release you on grounds of self-defense."

"In that case," Dolly said, "the law states that I am the property of Venus Consolidated."

"The law does."

Roz waited. Dolly, who was not supposed to be programmed to play psychological pressure-games, waited also—peaceful, unblinking.

No longer making the attempt to pass for human.

Roz said, "There is a fourth alternative. You could confess."

Dolly's entire programmed purpose was reading the

emotional state and unspoken intentions of people. Her lips curved in understanding. "What happens if I confess?"

Roz's heart beat faster. "Do you *wish* to?"

"Will it benefit me?"

"It *might*," Roz said. "Detective King has been in touch with the DA, and she likes a good media event as much as the next guy. Make no mistake, this will be that."

"I understand."

"The situation you were placed in by Mr. Steele could be a basis for lenience. You would not have to face a jury trial, and a judge might be convinced to treat you as . . . well, as a person. Also, a confession might be seen as evidence of contrition. Possession is oversold, you know. It's *precedent* that's nine tenths of the law. There are, of course, risks—"

"I would like to request a lawyer," Dolly said.

Roz took a breath that might change the world. "We'll proceed as if that were your legal right, then."

Roz's house let her in with her key, and the smell of roasted sausage and baking potatoes wafted past.

"Sven?" she called, locking herself inside.

His even voice responded. "I'm in the kitchen."

She left her shoes in the hall and followed her nose through the cheaply furnished living room, as different from Steele's white wasteland as anything bounded by four walls could be. Her feet did not sink deeply into this carpet, but skipped along atop it like stones.

It was clean, though, and that was Sven's doing. And she was not coming home to an empty house, and that was his doing too.

He was cooking shirtless. He turned and greeted her with a smile. "Bad day?"

"Nobody died," she said. "Yet."

He put the wooden spoon down on the rest. "How does that make you feel, that nobody has died yet?"

"Hopeful," she said.

"It's good that you're hopeful," he said. "Would you like your dinner?"

"Do you like music, Sven?"

"I could put on some music, if you like. What do you want to hear?"

"Anything." It would be something off her favorites playlist, chosen by random numbers. As it swelled in the background, Sven picked up the spoon. "Sven?"

"Yes, Rosamund?"

"Put the spoon down, please, and come and dance with me?"

"I do not know how to dance."

"I'll buy you a program," she said. "If you'd like that. But right now just come put your arms around me and pretend."

"Whatever you want," he said.

Altogether Elsewhere, Vast Herds of Reindeer

KEN LIU

Ken Liu (kenliu.name) lives near Boston, Massachusetts, with his wife, artist Lisa Tang Liu, with whom he is collaborating on a novel. Besides writing and translating speculative fiction, he also practices law and develops software for iOS and Android devices. His fiction has appeared in Fantasy & Science Fiction, Asimov's, Clarkesworld, Lightspeed, _and_ Strange Horizons, _among other places. The year 2011 was great for Ken Liu short fiction. In addition to the story reprinted here, Liu had a relative explosion of candidates for this volume: He also published the short stories "Tying Knots," "Simulacrum," "The Paper Menagerie," "Staying Behind," "The Countable," and the novella "The Man Who Ended History: A Documentary." And he has eight or ten new works publishing in 2012._

"Altogether Elsewhere, Vast Herds of Reindeer" was published in F&SF, _which had a particularly good year for SF in 2011. This is a post-singularity family story, ostensibly about external reality, in which human feeling remains a factor._

My name is Renée Tae-O <star> <whale> Fayette. I'm in the sixth grade.

There is no school today. But that's not what makes it special. I'm nervous and I can't tell you why yet. I don't want to jinx it.

My friend Sarah and I are working on our school project together in my bedroom.

I'm not old enough to create my own world, but I'm very happy with the world my parents have given me. My bedroom is a Klein bottle so I don't ever feel like I'm boxed in. A warm yellow light suffuses the room and fades gradually into darkness at infinite distance. It's old-fashioned, like something from years ago, when designs still tried to hint at the old physical world. Yet the smooth, endless surface makes me feel secure, something to hang onto, being enclosed and outside at the same time. It is better than Sarah's room in her home, which is a Weierstrass "curve": continuous everywhere, but nowhere differentiable. Jagged fractals no matter how closely you look. It's certainly very modern, but I don't ever feel comfortable when I visit. So she comes over to our place a lot more often.

"Everything good? Need anything?" Dad asks.

He comes "in" and settles against the surface of my bedroom. The projection of his twenty-dimensional figure into this four-space begins as a dot that gradually grows into an outline that pulses slowly, bright, golden, though a little hazy. He's distracted, but I don't mind. Dad is an interior designer, and the services of the firm of Hugo <left arrow> <right arrow> Fayette and Z. E. <CJK Ideograph 4E2D> <CJK Ideograph 4E3D> Pei are in so much demand that he's busy all the time, helping people build their dream worlds. But just because he has little time to spend with me doesn't mean he's not a good parent. For example, he's so used to working in much higher dimensions that he finds four dimensions very boring. But he still designed my bedroom as a Klein bottle because experts agree that it is best for children to grow up in a four-dimensional environment.

"We are all set," Sarah and I think together. Dad nods, and I get the feeling that he would like to think with me about the reason for our anxiety. But Sarah is there, and he feels he can't bring it up. After a moment, he whisks away.

The project we are working on is about genetics and inheritance. Yesterday at school, Dr. Bai showed us how to decompose our consciousnesses into their constituent algorithms, each further broken down into routines and subroutines, until we got to individual instructions, the fundamental code. Then he explained to us how each of our parents gave us some of these algorithms, recombined and shuffled the routines during the process of our births, until we were whole persons, infant consciousnesses new to the universe.

"Gross," Sarah thought.

"It's kind of cool," I thought back. It was neat to think that my eight parents each gave me a part of themselves, yet the parts changed and recombined into me, different from all of them.

Our project is to create our family trees and trace out our descent, all the way up to the Ancients, if possible. My tree is much easier, since I have only eight parents, and they each had even fewer parents. But Sarah has sixteen parents and it gets very dense up there.

"Renée," Dad interrupts us. "You have a visitor." His outline is not hazy at all now. The tone of his thoughts is deliberately restrained.

A three-dimensional woman comes out from behind him. Her figure is not a projection from higher dimensions—she's never bothered to go beyond three. In my four-dimensional world, she looks flat, insubstantial, like an illustration of the old days in my textbooks. But her face is lovelier than I remembered. It's the face that I fall asleep to and dream of. Now the day really is special.

"Mom!" I think, and I don't care that the tone of my thoughts makes me seem like a four-year-old.

Mom and Dad had the idea for me first, and they asked their friends to help out, to all give me a bit of themselves. I think I got my math aptitude from Aunt Hannah and my impatience from Uncle Okoro. I don't make friends easily, the same as Aunt Rita, and I like things neat, just like Uncle Pang-Rei. But I got most of me from Mom and Dad. On my tree, I've drawn the branches for them the thickest.

"Will you be visiting long?" Dad thinks.

"I'll be here for a while," Mom thinks. "I have some things I want to tell her."

"She's missed you," Dad thinks.

"I'm sorry," Mom thinks. Her face fails to hold her smile for a moment. "You've done a wonderful job with her."

Dad looks at Mom, and it seems that he has more to think, but he nods and turns away, his outline fading. "Please come by . . . for good-bye before you leave, Sophia. Don't just disappear like before."

Mom is an Ancient, from before the Singularity. There are only a few hundred million of them in the whole universe. She lived in the flesh for twenty-six years before uploading. Her parents—she had only two—never uploaded.

My fractional siblings used to tease me sometimes about having an Ancient as a parent. They told me that unions between the Ancients and regular people rarely worked out, so it was no surprise that Mom eventually left us. Whenever anyone thought such a thing, I fought them so hard that they eventually stopped.

Sarah is excited to meet an Ancient. Mom smiles at her and asks her if her parents are well. It takes Sarah a while to go through the whole list.

"I should probably get back," Sarah thinks, after she

finally pays attention to the urgent hints I've been shooting her way.

When Sarah is gone, Mom comes over and I allow her to give me a hug. Our algorithms entwine together; we synchronize our clocks; and our threads ping onto the same semaphores. I let myself fall into the long-absent yet familiar rhythm of her thoughts, while she gently caresses me through my own.

"Don't cry, Renée," she thinks.

"I'm not." And I try to stop.

"You haven't changed as much as I expected," she thinks.

"That's because you've been overclocking." Mom does not live in the Data Center. She lives and works in the far south, at the Antarctica Research Dome, where a few Ancient scientists with special permission to use the extra energy live on overclocked hardware year round, thinking thoughts at many times the speed of most of humanity. To her, the rest of us live in slow motion, and a long time has passed even though she last saw me a year ago, when I graduated from elementary school.

I show Mom the math awards I've won and the new vector space models I've made. "I am the best at math in my class," I tell her, "out of two thousand six hundred twenty-one kids. Dad thinks I have the talent to be a designer as good as him."

Mom smiles at my excitement and she tells me stories about when she was a little girl. She is a great storyteller, and I can almost picture the deprivation and hardships she suffered, trapped in the flesh.

"How terrifying," I think.

"Is it?" She's quiet for a moment. "I suppose it is, to you."

Then she looks straight at me and her face takes on this look that I really don't want to see. "Renée, I have something to tell you."

The last time she had this look, she told me that she had to leave me and our family.

"My research proposal has been approved," she thinks. "I finally got permission to fuel the rocket, and they'll launch the probe in a month. The probe will arrive at Gliese 581, the nearest star with a planet that we think may hold life, in twenty-five years."

Mom explains to me that the probe will carry a robot that can be embodied by human consciousness. When the probe lands on the new planet, it will set up a receiving parabolic dish pointed at Earth and send a signal back to let Earth know that it arrived safely. After we receive the signal—in another twenty years—the consciousness of an astronaut will be radioed by a powerful transmitter to the probe, crossing the void of space at the speed of light. Once there, the astronaut will embody the robot to explore the new world.

"I will be that astronaut," she thinks.

I try to make sense of this.

"So another you will be living there? Embodied in metal flesh?"

"No," she thinks, gently. "We've never been able to copy the quantum computation of a consciousness without destroying the original. It won't be a copy of me going to the other world. It will be *me*."

"And when will you come back?"

"I won't. We don't have enough antimatter to send a transmitter big and powerful enough to the new planet to beam a consciousness back. It took hundreds of years and an enormous amount of energy just to make enough fuel to send the small probe. I'll try to send back as much of the data gathered from my exploration as possible, but I will be there forever."

"Forever?"

She pauses and corrects herself. "The probe will be made well and last a while, but it will eventually fail."

I think about my mother, trapped in a robot for the rest of her life, a robot that will decay and rust and break down on an alien world. My mother will die.

"So we have only forty-five years left together," I think.

She nods.

Forty-five years is the blink of an eye compared to the natural course of life: eternity.

I'm so furious that for a moment I can't think at all. Mom tries to come closer but I back off.

I finally managed to ask, "Why?"

"It is humanity's destiny to explore. We must grow, as a species, the same as you are growing as a child."

This makes no sense. We have endless worlds to explore, here in the universe of the Data Center. Every person can create his own world, his own multiverse even, if he wants to. In school, we've been exploring and zooming in on the intricacies of the quaternion Julia sets, and it is so beautiful and alien that I shiver as we fly through them. Dad has helped families design worlds with so many dimensions that I can't even wrap my mind around them. There are more novels and music and art in the Data Center than I can enjoy in a life-time, even if that lifetime stretches into infinity. What can a single three-dimensional planet in the physical world offer compared to that?

I don't bother keeping my thoughts to myself. I want Mom to feel my anger.

"I wish I could still sigh," Mom thinks. "Renée, it is not the same. The pure beauty of mathematics and the land-scapes of the imagination are very lovely, but they are not real. Something has been lost to humanity since we gained this immortal command over an imagined existence. We have turned inward and become complacent. We've forgot-ten the stars and the worlds out there."

I do not respond. I am trying not to cry again.

Mom turns her face away. "I don't know how to explain it to you."

"You are leaving because you want to leave," I think. "You don't really care about me. I hate you. I don't want to see you ever again."

Mom does not think anything. She hunches down a bit, and though I cannot see her face, her shoulders are trem-bling, almost imperceptibly.

Even though I am so angry, I reach out and stroke her back. It has always been difficult to harden myself against my mother. I must have inherited that from Dad.

"Renée, will you take a trip with me?" she thinks. "A real trip."

* * *

"Tap into the vehicle feed, Renée, we're taking off," Mom tells me.

I tap in, and for a moment I'm overwhelmed by the data flooding into my mind. I'm connected to the maintenance flier's camera and the microphone, which translate light and sound into patterns that I'm used to. But I'm also tapped into the altimeter and the gyroscope and the accelerometer, and the unfamiliar sensations are like nothing I've ever felt.

The camera shows us lifting off, the Data Center below us, a black cube in the middle of the white ice field. This is home, the hardware foundation of all the worlds in the universe. Its walls are pierced with fine honeycomb holes so that the cold air can flow through to cool the layers of hot silicon and graphene full of zipping electrons whose patterns form my consciousness and those of three hundred billion other human beings.

Still higher, clusters of smaller cubes that are the automated factories of Longyearbyen come into view, and then the deep blue waters of Adventfjorden and floating icebergs. The Data Center is large enough that it dwarfs the floating icebergs but the fjord makes the Data Center look tiny.

I realize that I've never actually *experienced* the physical world. The shock of all the new sensations "takes my breath away," as Mom would think. I like these old-fashioned expressions, even if I don't always fully understand what they mean.

The sense of movement is dizzying. Is this what it was like to be an Ancient in the flesh? This feeling of straining against the invisible bonds of gravity that tether you to the Earth? It feels so limiting.

Yet so *fun* at the same time.

I ask Mom how she's able to do the calculations to keep the vehicle balanced so quickly in her head. The dynamic feedback calculations needed to stabilize the hovering flier against gravity are so complex that I can't keep up at all—and I'm very good at math.

"Oh, I'm going by instinct here," Mom thinks. And she

laughs. "You are a digital native. You've never tried to stand up and balance yourself, have you? Here, take over for a minute. Try flying."

And it is easier than I anticipated. Some algorithm in me whose existence I have never been aware of kicks in, fuzzy but efficient, and I *feel* how to shift weight around and balance thrust.

"See, you are after all *my* daughter," Mom thinks.

Flying in the physical world is so much better than floating through n-dimensional space. It's not even close.

Dad's thoughts break into our laughter. He's not with us. His thoughts come through the commlink. "Sophia, I got the message you left. What are you doing?"

"I'm sorry, Hugo. Can you forgive me? I may never see her again. I want her to understand, if I can."

"She's never been out in a vehicle before. This is reckless—"

"I made sure that the flier has a full battery before we left. And I promise to be careful with how much energy we use." Mom looks at me. "I won't put her life in danger."

"They're going to come after you when they notice a missing maintenance flier."

"I asked for a sabbatical in the flier and got it," Mom thinks, smiling. "They don't want to deny a dying woman's last wishes."

The commlink is silent for a while, then Dad's thoughts come through. "Why can't I ever think no to you? How long will this take? Is she going to miss any school?"

"It might be a long trip. But I think it's worth it. You'll have her forever, I just want a little bit of her for the time left to me."

"Take care, Sophia. I love you, Renée."

"I love you too, Dad."

Being embodied in a vehicle is an experience few people have had. To begin with, there are very few vehicles. The energy it takes to fly even a maintenance flier for a day is enough to run the whole Data Center for an hour. And conservation is humanity's overriding duty.

So, only the operators for the maintenance and repair robots do it regularly, and it is rare for most people, who are digital natives, to take up these jobs. Being embodied never seemed very interesting to me before. But now that I'm here, it's exhilarating. It must be some Ancient part of me that I got from Mom.

We fly over the sea and then the wild European forest of towering oaks, pines, and spruces, broken here and there by open grassland and herds of animals. Mom points them out to me and tells me that they are called wisent, auroch, tarpan, and elk. "Just five hundred years ago," Mom thinks, "all this used to be farmland, filled with the clones of a few human-dependent symbiotic plants. All that infrastructure, the resources of a whole planet, went to support just a few billion people."

I look at Mom in disbelief.

"See that hill in the distance with the reindeer? That used to be a great city called Moscow, before it was flooded by the Moskva River and buried in silt.

"There's a poem that I remember by an Ancient called Auden who died long before the Singularity. It's called 'The Fall of Rome.'"

She shares with me images from the poem: herds of reindeer, golden fields, emptying cities, the rain, always the rain, caressing the abandoned shell of a world.

"Pretty, isn't it?"

I'm enjoying myself but then I think maybe I shouldn't be. Mom is still leaving at the end, and I still need to be mad at her. Is it the love of flight, of these sensations in the physical world, that makes her want to go?

I look at the world passing below us. I would have thought that a world with only three dimensions would be flat and uninteresting. But it's not true. The colors are more vibrant than any I've ever seen, and the world has a random beauty that I could not have imagined. But now that I've really *seen* the world, maybe Dad and I can try to recreate all of it mathematically, and it will feel no different. I share the idea with Mom.

"But I'll *know* it's not real," Mom thinks. "And that makes all the difference."

I turn her words over and over in my mind.

We fly on, pausing to hover over interesting animals and historical sites—now just fields of broken glass, as the concrete had long washed away and the steel rusted into powder—while Mom thinks more stories to me. Over the Pacific, we dip down to scan for whales.

"I put the <whale> in your name because I loved these creatures when I was your age," Mom thinks. "They were very rare then."

I look at the whales breaching and lobtailing. They look nothing like the <whale> in my name.

Over America, we linger over families of bears who look up at us without fear (after all, the maintenance flier is only about the size of a mama bear). Finally, we arrive at an estuarial island off the Atlantic coast covered with dense trees punctuated by wetlands along the shore and rivers crisscrossing the island.

The ruins of a city dominate the island's southern end. The blackened, empty frames of the great skyscrapers, their windows long gone, rise far above the surrounding jungle like stone pillars. We can see coyotes and deer playing hide-and-seek in their shadows.

"You are looking at the remnants of Manhattan, one of the greatest cities from long ago. It's where I grew up."

Mom then thinks to me of the glory days of Manhattan, when it teemed with humanity in the flesh, and consumed energy like a black hole. People lived one or two to a vast room all their own, and had machines that carried them around, cooled or warmed them, and made food and cleaned clothes and performed other wonders, all while spewing carbon and poisons into the air at an unimaginable rate. Each person wasted the energy that could support a million consciousnesses without physical needs.

Then came the Singularity, and as the last generation of humans in the flesh departed, carried away by death or into the Data Center, the great city fell silent. Rainwater seeped into the cracks and seams of walls and foundations, froze and thawed, pried them open ever wider, until the buildings toppled like trees in the ancient horror of logging. Asphalt cracked, spewing forth seedlings and vines, and the dead city gradually yielded to the green force of life.

"The buildings that still remain standing were built at a time when people over-engineered everything."

No one ever talks about engineering now. Building with physical atoms is inefficient, inflexible, limited, and consumes so much energy. I've been taught that engineering is an art of the dark ages, before people knew any better. Bits and qubits are far more civilized, and give our imaginations free rein.

Mom smiles at my thoughts. "You sound like your father."

She lands the flier in an open field with a clear view of the ghost skyscrapers.

"This is the real beginning of our trip," Mom thinks. "It's not how long we have that matters, but what we do with the time we have. Don't be scared, Renée. I'm going to show you something about time."

I nod.

Mom activates the routine to underclock the processors on the flier so that its batteries will last while our consciousnesses slow down to a crawl.

The world around us speeds up. The sun moves faster and faster across the sky until it is a bright stripe arching over a world shrouded in permanent dusk. Trees shoot up around us while shadows spin and twirl. Animals zoom by, too fast to be perceived. We watch one skyscraper, topped by steel step-domes rising to a defiant spear, gradually bend and lean over with the passing of the seasons. Something about its shape, like a hand reaching for the sky and tiring, moves me deeply inside.

Mom brings the processors back up to normal speed, and we see the top half of the building fall down and collapse with a series of loud crashes like calving icebergs, bringing down yet more buildings around it.

"We did many things wrong back then, but some things we did right. That's the Chrysler Building." I feel infinite sadness in her thoughts. "It was one of the most beautiful creations of Man. Nothing made by Man lasts forever, Renée, and even the Data Center will one day disintegrate before the heat death of the universe. But real beauty lasts, even though anything real must die."

Forty-five years have passed since we set out on our trip, though it didn't seem to me much longer than a single day.

Dad has left my room just the way it was on the day I left.

After forty-five years, Dad now has a different look. He's added more dimensions to his figure and his color is even more golden. But he treats me as though I only left yesterday. I appreciate how considerate he is.

While I'm getting ready for bed, Dad tells me that Sarah has already finished her schooling and started a family. She has a little girl of her own now.

I'm a little sad at this news. Underclocking is rare and it can make someone feel left behind. But I will work hard to catch up, and a real friendship will survive any gap of years.

I would not exchange the long day I spent with Mom for anything in the world.

"Would you like to change the design of your bedroom?" Dad thinks. "A new start? You've had the Klein bottle for a while now. We can look through some contemporary designs based on eight-dimensional tori, or we can go with a five-dimensional sphere if you like it minimalist."

"Dad, the Klein bottle is fine." I pause. "Maybe I'll try making my room three-dimensional when I'm rested."

He looks at me, and maybe he sees in me something new that he didn't expect. "Of course," he thinks. "You are ready to do the design yourself."

Dad stays with me as I drift off to sleep.

"I miss you," Dad thinks to himself. He does not know that I'm still awake. "When Renée was born, I put the <star> in her name because I knew one day you would go to the stars. I'm good at making people's dreams come true. But that is one dream that I can't create for you. Have a safe journey, Sophia." He fades out of my room.

I imagine Mom's consciousness suspended between the stars, an electromagnetic ribbon shimmering in the interstellar dust. The robot shell is waiting for her on that distant planet, under an alien sky, a shell that will rust, decay, and fall apart with time.

She will be so happy when she is alive again.

I go to sleep, dreaming of the Chrysler Building.

Tethered

MERCURIO D. RIVERA

Mercurio D. Rivera (www.mercuriorivera.com) has worked as a Manhattan litigator for more than twenty years, generating voluminous legal briefs rather than short fiction. That changed during a one-year sabbatical when he signed up for a science-fiction writing course taught by author Terry Bisson at the New School. Since 2006 he has published twenty stories in markets such as Asimov's, Interzone, Nature, Black Static, Abyss and Apex, *and* Unplugged: The Web's Best Science Fiction and Fantasy, 2008 Download, *edited by Rich Horton (Wyrm Publishing). In 2011, he was nominated for the World Fantasy Award in the short fiction category. His stories have been podcast at* Escape Pod, StarshipSofa *and* Transmissions From Beyond. *He has served as an Associate Editor for* Sybil's Garage Magazine, *and is a proud member of the Altered Fluid writing group. The story in this book is one of his Wergen series. The alien Wergens suffer from a compulsive biochemical love for humanity, a love that has driven them to share their superior technology and establish joint colonies with humans throughout the solar system.*

"Tethered" was published in Interzone. *Set on the shores of Titan's methane lakes, it is a story about very strange alien biology, a female coming-of-age story in which the transition between girlhood and womanhood is further complicated by the relationship between humans and a subservient alien race that is biologically compelled to try to make humans happy.*

On the shore of Ontario Lacus on Southern Titan, Cara molded castles from the windblown sediment that served as sand. Her parents stood at the threshold of their shelter in the distance, chatting with their sponsor, the Wergen responsible for transporting her family from Earth. Cara lay on her stomach while the methane waves lapped against the shore, tickling her bare feet.

She held up her hand against the smoggy orange sky and studied the barely visible blue tint that covered her skin. Her mother had described it as a special 'coat' that protected them from the cold weather. The Wergen force field over Ontario Lacus shielded them from radiation and modulated the gravity, but they still needed the 'coat' to protect them from the temperatures. It sure didn't feel cold, Cara thought. It didn't even look chilly, although Cara's mother had told her that Titan was colder than the coldest place on Earth.

A young Wergen, their sponsor's daughter, tentatively stooped down next to her. "Soy Beatrix," she said. The alien girl was squat and scaled and spoke with a slight accent so she must have just learned Spanish. It took Wergens about a day or so to speak a language fluently. "My brother and I were wondering . . . What are you doing?"

A fat, gray-scaled Wergen boy with round eyes peeked at them from behind a red boulder about fifty feet away.

"Why is he hiding?"

"He doesn't like the way humans make him feel."

"Really? I've never heard that before."

"You make him feel *too* good."

Cara shrugged. Of course the boy felt good around humans. He was Wergen. She was amused by the fact that the girl wore a red, skintight swimming cap over her flat head. Every Wergen she had ever seen wore green, leafy wreath-hats. "I'm building a sandcastle."

"What's a castle?" Beatrix said.

Cara giggled. "A house where a king lives."

The Wergen stared at her and didn't respond. Cara wondered whether the alien girl knew what a king was.

"Can I help?" Beatrix said.

Every Wergen Cara had ever met asked her parents this same question: "Can I help? Can I help?" Her mother and father were sick of the question. But it was the first time a Wergen had asked *her* and it made her feel grown up and important. Normally, her parents sternly said 'no' and the aliens would slink away with their heads down and their shoulders slumped. But Cara didn't want to make the alien girl unhappy. "Yes, you can help." She showed Beatrix how to pack the sediment and mold it into towers for the castle she was building. After a while, bored with this activity, Cara said, "I know something even more fun. Let's go for a swim and catch perpuffers!"

"What are those?"

Cara displayed her left forearm, which was covered with furry bracelets. "They're pretty, aren't they? I have all the colors except purple. Purple perpuffers are the hardest to find." She shuffled to the edge of the lake.

Beatrix stood up and looked out at the thick, pink waters that sloshed back and forth in slow motion. "I . . . don't . . . I mean . . ." She stared silently.

"Follow me," Cara said.

Six bots skittered around Beatrix's feet. They were as large as cats, only Cara thought they looked more like praying mantises in the way they crouched on their spindly rear legs. Three of them stood in front of the Wergen girl, blocking her path, and red lights glowed at the end of their six appendages. Beatrix clapped her hands and they scattered to one side allowing her to walk past them.

As they waded into the lake, Beatrix pulled off her robes and tossed them to the bots. Cara didn't know what she expected to see beneath the alien's clothes but the Wergen girl simply stood there naked, unashamed. She had smooth white skin speckled with silver scales that sparkled when they caught the light at certain angles. Cara considered taking off her own bathing suit but then remembered the Wergen boy spying on them from behind the rock.

They dove into the water together, their blue bodyfields bright in the red murk of the lake. They were less buoyant in this liquid than in water and its ruddy color made it hard to see. Cara forced herself to go deeper, reaching out blindly and hoping to latch onto one of the furry perpuffers that filled the lake.

Cara heard a muffled scream.

She barely made out the Wergen girl's blue bodyfield far below. Beatrix waved her arms over her head, sinking deeper. Cara dove closer, hooked her arm around the Wergen's waist and kicked hard until they broke the surface. "Don't struggle!" Cara gasped. "Don't struggle!" She shouted for help but no one on the shore seemed to hear her. "You're okay, I've got you."

After a few panicked seconds Beatrix relaxed in her arms and they floundered back to shore. Cara's screams had alerted the medbots, which immediately scoured over Beatrix's face and chest. Cara's parents and their Wergen patron came running and stood watch until the medbots eventually blinked yellow, signaling that Beatrix was unhurt.

The adult Wergen, who Cara believed to be Beatrix's father, said, "You need to be more careful," before quickly turning his attention back to Cara's parents. "Are you sure I can't help you with anything?" he said to them. "Perhaps I can assist with the interior decoration of your shelter?" Her parents turned away without answering and the Wergen followed close behind them.

Once the adults had left, Cara sat silently beside Beatrix for several minutes, burrowing her toes beneath the pasty sediment. There was no longer any sign of the Wergen boy. He hadn't approached even when the medbots had examined his sister.

Cara finally broke the silence. "We can't drown, you know," she said, pointing to the blue tint that coated their bodies.

Beatrix paused, staring out at the pink waters. "Then why didn't you just leave me?"

"I wasn't going to swim back to shore while you were out there all alone and afraid."

At this, the Wergen girl turned to face Cara. She tilted her head to the left and nodded, smiling warmly.

"Don't you know how to swim?" Cara said.

Beatrix shook her head.

"Then why did you go in with me?"

"You said it was fun," Beatrix said. "And . . . I wanted to make you happy."

"Oh."

The steady wind blew and neither of them spoke for a long time.

"Can I see your hand?" Cara said. She removed a red perpuffer from her left arm and placed it around the Wergen girl's wrist. "Here. This is for you. A gift."

The Wergen girl's eyes brightened. "That tickles," she said.

"Sometimes the perpuffers expand and contract a little bit when they're fresh out of the lake."

"No," she said. "I meant your hand. When you touched me."

Later that evening when Cara snuggled in bed she couldn't get the words of the Wergen girl out of her head, the Wergen girl who so wanted to be her friend that she would risk her own life to make her happy

ENCRYPTED Medical Journal Entry No. 223 by Dr Juan Carlos Barbarón: The Wergen headtail, or 'tether' as it is referred to in common parlance, originates at the base of the secondary spine. As the subject matures, the headtail extends, lining both the secondary and tertiary spines, and ultimately coiling into the hollow cavity of the cranium. (Note: Wergen physiology has no analog to the human brain. All neural activity is centered in a swath of

cells that surround their upper and lower jawbones. See
Med. Journal Entry No. 124.)

Every day after VR school, Cara met Beatrix at the lake.
They waded up to their waists and jumped up and down in
sync with the slow, swooshing waves. The winds never
stopped on Titan. After what happened at the lake, Beatrix's
father programmed bots to swim alongside them at all times
and ensure their safety. Like all Wergens, Beatrix only had
one parent, but to Cara he seemed awfully distant, spending
most of his time with humans instead of with Beatrix or her
brother.

Over time, Beatrix became less afraid of the waters and
Cara taught her to swim and to hunt for perpuffers. It didn't
take Beatrix long to get the hang of it. In fact, she became so
skilled at perpuffer-hunting that she and Cara would often
leave the lake with their arms and legs draped with the furry
creatures. When they weren't swimming together they would
spend hours sculpting intricate castles and spacecraft in the
pasty orange sands. Or Beatrix would try to teach Cara how
to sing like a Wergen, which Cara found challenging given
the chirping and rumbling noises that Beatrix could make
with her throat.

Even during the rainy season when the waves were too
choppy to swim, she and Beatrix would play outdoor VR
games. As the settlement by Ontario Lacus expanded, more
human children took to the lakeshore and joined them.

Cara pointed out the human boys she found cutest and
what she liked most about them, their swaggering walk or
broad shoulders or dimpled smiles. Beatrix found this fascinating—as she did everything about human beings. She
mentioned how beautiful she thought the other adolescents
were—girls and boys alike—and became animated whenever they huddled together and shared their secrets. As they
spent more and more time together, Cara found herself forgetting that Beatrix was a Wergen—except for those occa-
sions when she stared at Cara intensely and mentioned the
bright rainbow-like auras that she saw around all humans,
how her upper heart fluttered at the mere sight of them, how

she spent every waking hour thinking about what she could do to make them happy. Cara didn't like to hear this. It made her feel less special.

"What about *Wergen* boys?" Cara asked her one day while they treaded water far from shore. "Which ones do you like?"

There were few Wergens present on Titan because of a treaty between their peoples that restricted their numbers. But Wergen children occasionally gathered at the shore to watch the humans.

"It's different for us, Cara," she said. "We don't think about things that way."

"Well, how *do* you think about them?"

The waves washed over them as they bobbed in the lake.

"I can't explain . . ."

"Try."

"I don't like them in the same way that you like human boys. At least not right now. But when I reach a certain age my body will change . . ."

"Change?" Cara said.

Beatrix hesitated as if struggling to find the right words.

"Is it like having your period?" Cara said. She had explained menstruation and making babies and every aspect of human reproduction to Beatrix in excruciating detail, and she, of course, had found it utterly captivating. Was there anything about humans that didn't enthrall her?

"No. My cranial opening will expand. And my cord will release. It will connect with the cord of a perfect genetic match. And then I'll be tethered."

Cara stared at the red swimmer's cap on Beatrix's flat head.

"After years of tethering, the cord retracts and the mated couple . . ." Beatrix looked around to make sure that only bots swam near them. "We become one," she whispered. "Our bodies . . . merge."

"You mean you have sex?"

"Not like your people, Cara. *Real* sex. The merge is . . . permanent."

"What do you mean 'permanent'? How can that be?"

"The passive partner is absorbed. The dominant partner then becomes pregnant with a brood of children."

Cara stared at her in horror. "So . . . if you have a baby, you die?"

"It depends on whether my genes are passive or dominant. But I don't think about it in terms of dying. It's the best part of being alive, Cara. I can't wait to be tethered."

"Okay," Cara said, trying not to think about it. She decided to change the subject. "What's your home world like, Bea?"

"I've never been there, but I hear that the white skies and the black-sand deserts are so beautiful that the mere sight of them can make a grown Wergen cry."

"I wish I could see it," Cara said. "I wish I could travel to all the amazing planets in our galaxy." She wanted more than anything to be an explorer like her parents, working in tandem with the Wergens to colonize the universe. So many other worlds had been opened up to them thanks to Wergen fieldtech. Colonization efforts were already underway on Triton and Enceladus as well as incredible alien worlds hundreds of light years away, such as Langalana and Verdantium.

A wave splashed over them.

"What do you want to be when you grow up, Bea?"

Beatrix looked up into the orange sky. "I hadn't thought about it before, but being an explorer sounds wonderful, Cara." She tilted her head to the left in that familiar manner and nodded, smiling warmly. "Especially if I can explore the cosmos with you."

"Beatrix!" A voice shouted from the shore. Her brother Ambus called for her to return to her hearth as he always did when dusk approached. Cara knew that by the time they made it back to shore he would be gone. She had yet to see Beatrix's brother up close.

"Let's race!" Cara said. And she stroked furiously, leaving Beatrix behind in her wake.

A moment later Beatrix jetted past her, propelled by the bots, a huge grin plastered on her face.

ENCRYPTED Medical Journal Entry No. 224 by Dr Juan Carlos Barbarón: A contractile sheath gives the tether a pronounced elasticity as it emerges through the cranial canal. The tail-end is laced with thousands of microscopic nerve fibers and pore receptors. Muscle spindles allow the tether to unfurl and undulate toward the Wergen mate. When two tethers come into contact, the fibers bore into the receptors of the Wergen with the passive genotype. This signals the commencement of macromeiosis.

One day Cara agreed to meet Beatrix by the lake, but a mile farther north where fewer ice boulders dotted the shore and ten-foot orange dunes draped the surface. Perpuffers were said to be even more plentiful in this area.

As she approached, Cara heard someone shout her name from behind a red dune. She recognized the voice immediately. "Ambus?"

"Stay where you are so I can't see you."

"What do you—?"

"And don't speak! Your voice is too . . . sweet. I don't want to give in to it. Like my sister. And my father. Just listen. If you respect my sister, you'll stay away from her."

Cara fought the urge to answer him.

"She doesn't have the will to resist you. How can she choose her own path with you around? How can she be her own person? If you really consider yourself her friend, just leave her alone!"

Cara couldn't stay quiet anymore. "Bea can pick her own friends. Why should you decide for her?" She scaled the dune to confront Ambus but when she reached the top he was no longer there. His footprints receded into the distance, snaking behind the sand drifts in the horizon.

ENCRYPTED Note for future study: the evolutionary purpose of Wergen gender remains a mystery as it appears to play no role in their procreative processes. The prevailing theory posits that a diverse alien gene pool results in the Wergens' varying physical characteristics and that it is human perception that assigns those attributes what we consider to be a gender.

Cara rode on a disk-shaped buzzer that sped three feet off the ground, clutching the handlebars tightly. She had made arrangements to meet Beatrix in the Aaru region at the viewing post at the foot of Tortola Facula, an active cryovolcano outside the colony's force field. Normally she might have visited Beatrix at her hearth, but she didn't want to run into Ambus. Even after all these years, he still made it a point to avoid contact with humans, believing that they fogged his mind and skewed his perception of reality, Beatrix had explained. He'd even taken to wearing special earplugs and visors that he hoped might protect him.

When Cara arrived she found Beatrix waiting for her on a bench at the overlook, staring raptly at some newly landed seedships. The colonists stood near the yellow hash marks that signaled the force field's perimeter, and viewed the volcano shooting spumes of hydrocarbon-rich materials miles into the atmosphere. It would later rain down onto the surface as liquid methane, feeding the thousands of lakes and tributaries in the region.

Beatrix approached when she saw her step off the buzzer. "You let your hair down! You look more beautiful than ever, Cara."

"Come on, I bet you say that to all the humans." She paused. "No, *really*."

They laughed and hugged.

"I'm so glad you suggested getting together," Beatrix said. "It's been too long."

While they spoke every few days, it had been several weeks since they'd seen each other. Ever since Cara had graduated and her parents had relocated to Axelis Colony on Titan, she'd been working with the Colonization Enterprise—thanks to some strings her parents had pulled before departing—helping to plan the next great human-Wergen expedition. The target world was a rogue planet that had escaped Cancrii 55's orbit and now roamed freely through space.

"What did you want to tell me, Cara?" Beatrix asked. "It sounded important."

"I think I'm in love, Bea."

Beatrix stopped in her tracks. "Oh?"

"His name is Juan Carlos. We've only gone out a few times, but we seemed to have made that instant connection, do you know what I mean?"

"Yes, yes I do."

She hesitated to see if Beatrix was joking, then continued. "He's a doctor who works with Biotech at CE. He's got a reputation for being quite opinionated, uncompromising to a fault—except with me. With me he's just a big softy."

She described his thick eyebrows and slicked-back black hair, his lean muscular physique, and she told Beatrix about everything they had in common, about their three dates together—including how they'd kissed in the empty office at CE until they were interrupted by guardbots.

Cara and Beatrix strolled arm-in-arm along the edge of a great gorge that overlooked a river. Southern Titan teemed with ridges and crevices and chasms all filled with flowing ethane and methane.

Cara noticed that Beatrix had stayed quiet for a long time after she'd spoken about Juan Carlos. Sometimes she forgot that Bea was a Wergen, that like all Wergens she couldn't help but love her, and perhaps be jealous of her new relationship. Maybe it had been a mistake to confide in her, but Bea was her oldest and dearest friend.

She decided to change the subject. "How's Ambus?"

Beatrix stopped. She released Cara's arm and rubbed her shoulders nervously.

"What is it?" Cara said.

Beatrix turned away and started walking again.

"Tell me. What's wrong?"

Beatrix stood at the lip of a precipice. "You know how Ambus has always felt about humans."

She nodded. "Yes, he wants to avoid humans—so, of course, he lives in a colony of humans on Titan."

"That's not fair, Cara. He was brought here as a child. He had no say in the matter. And now that he's on the verge of reaching maturity . . . I'm afraid for him. He's found others who believe as he does, that co-exploration with human beings was a huge mistake."

"Really?" Cara had always found Ambus eccentric but basically harmless. "Well, it isn't as if Wergens would ever harm humans."

Beatrix looked away.

"Bea?"

"There's been a drug developed offworld recently, Cara. A suppressant that distorts the way that Wergens perceive human beings. It's horrible. It mutes our natural love for your people."

"And Ambus took it?"

"Its effects are only temporary—no longer than a few minutes. He views it as a way to 'free' his mind. You mustn't say anything, Cara. You have no idea of the consequences if anyone were to know. This is a serious crime."

"Does your father know about this?"

"My father left a few weeks ago to start work on a new project, the construction of another cityfield over Xanadu, on equatorial Titan," Beatrix said. "Maybe I'll go join him. Get away from all of this."

"That's really what you want?"

After a long pause, Beatrix said, "Now that you've met someone . . . I'm not sure there's anything left here for me."

"Bea, I don't want you to worry about Juan Carlos. That has nothing to do with our relationship. We've always been friends and we're going to stay friends forever. No man can change that."

Beatrix's face brightened and they continued their trek along the edge of the gorge, the ethane-filled tributaries churning far below them.

ENCRYPTED Med. Journal Entry No. 225 by Dr Juan Carlos Barbarón: Adsorption: The first step in macromeiosis is the penetration of the headtail fibers into the specific pseudo-protein receptors of the passive Wergen's tether. Enzymes quickly dissolve the base plate, the tethers become one, triggering significant changes to the aliens' body chemistry. (See Journal Entry No. 6.)

Cara lowered her head and trudged forward into the driving pink snow. Her boots sank into the slushy drifts as she made it over the bend and Beatrix's hearth came into view. The dwelling resembled the upper half of a metallic egg with two arched openings on opposite sides. The Wergens had a very rigid conception of exits and entrances.

Juan Carlos, her fiancé, had wanted her to spend the day visiting with his parents, but she'd grown increasingly concerned over the fact that she hadn't heard a word from Beatrix in over a week. It wasn't like her. Usually the problem was keeping Beatrix from calling too often—something else Juan Carlos bitterly complained about. But Beatrix couldn't help herself, Cara had explained to him for what seemed like a thousand times. She was Wergen, after all. Juan Carlos didn't want to hear it.

Cara stepped through the archway, stomping the snow off of her boots. Her blue-tinted bodyfield clicked off automatically.

The welcoming bots skittered at her feet, unlaced her boots and laid out slippers for her on the scale-patterned floorboards.

This was the only time she could remember visiting the hearth that Beatrix hadn't been waiting for her at the entranceway. Could her friend be jealous? Is that why she'd stopped calling? When last they spoke, Cara had told her that Juan Carlos had finally proposed and that she had accepted. After expressing some confusion over how an engagement differed from dating or from marriage, Beatrix had asked whether it still meant that they would someday join a human-Wergen expedition and go colonize some strange new world together. Cara had reassured her that she and Juan Carlos had promising careers at CE and that they were both on track to join the colonization efforts.

Beatrix emerged out of the fireroom in the center of the dwelling and Cara staggered backward.

In all the years she'd known her, Cara had never seen

Beatrix without some head covering. Usually she put on a *coronatis*, the leafy headdress that all Wergens wore. But today the flat top of her head was exposed and a rubbery cord extended out of her cranium, dragging along the floor to another room in the hearth.

"Cara!" Beatrix said, smiling. "I'm sorry that I haven't returned your messages. It's just . . . these past few weeks have been a very private time for me."

Cara pointed to the tether. "You . . . you're . . ."

"Yes, it was my time." She looked at the floor, embarrassed.

"Why didn't you tell me, Bea?"

She rubbed her shoulders nervously and didn't answer.

Cara understood that Wergens were notoriously private about their reproductive cycle, but this was her best friend. She felt wounded by the fact that Beatrix hadn't confided in her. Then she remembered what Beatrix had told her all those years ago about the absorption of one Wergen into another based on their genetic makeup, about encorporation.

"Bea, tell me you're genetically dominant. Please!"

Beatrix continued rubbing her shoulders.

A moment later the Wergen at the other end of the tether entered the room. He was shorter than Beatrix, with gray-flecked scales he covered with a dark blue robe.

Ambus.

Cara gasped. "But . . ."

"A pleasure to finally see you up close," he said.

But there was no pleasure in his voice, no Wergen servility. Only an undercurrent of hostility.

Cara turned to Beatrix, eyes wide. "Your brother?"

"Of course. There are very few of us on Titan. And we're genetically compatible. We can safely interbreed for another generation."

"You don't owe her any explanations, Beatrix," Ambus said.

"I apologize for his tone, Cara," Beatrix said. "When he saw you approaching our hearth he took a dose of the suppressant. He'll be more himself in a few minutes."

"What does it feel like to hold so much sway over another person's life?" Ambus said to Cara. "Do you realize how unfair you've been to her? That she's your loyal slave because she has no choice?"

"She's not my slave!" Cara said.

"Your people and ours are at war. A secret war. We're all soldiers in that great battle and don't even know it."

"Bea," Cara said, "I just wanted to make sure you were all right. I really have to get back to Juan Carlos."

"What, you're leaving before we can bow down to you and wash your feet?" Ambus said.

Cara stepped into her shoes and walked back through the archway to the hearth, which reactivated her bodyfield.

"Cara, I'm sorry," Beatrix said. "Don't leave!"

"Look, I can't . . . I can't deal with all this. I can't believe you're with him." The sight of the tether repulsed her.

"Cara!" Beatrix shouted from behind her. But Cara marched ahead through the gusting snow without looking back.

ENCRYPTED Med. Journal Entry No. 226 by Dr Juan Carlos Barbarón: Tether contraction can commence as early as six months (Terran) after adsorption and accelerate, bringing the passive and dominant mates ever closer together. This triggers the growth of nerve fibers on the dominant Wergen's dermal scales in anticipation of the final stages of corpus meiosis, i.e. encorporation.

Cara floated through the thick liquid hydrocarbons with her eyes closed. It felt like she had left the present behind, like she had traveled back to when was ten years old, hunting perpuffers for the very first time. She broke the surface of the waters and threw her head back.

Beatrix sat on the shore, hugging her knees and watching her. She had said that it might still be possible to swim despite her tethered status, but that she preferred not to because Ambus didn't much enjoy the lake. He sat about twenty-five feet to her left, clutching their bunched-up tether and examining a bot. They could move almost fifty feet apart given their cord's length and elasticity. But Ambus couldn't be far away enough as far as Cara was concerned.

In all the years that she'd known Beatrix, her friend had never seemed more alien than she did at that moment with the flesh-colored cord dangling from her head, snaking across the shore toward Ambus. Poor Bea. How much time did she have left?

Cara descended again, peering through the natural muck of the methane. Something caught her attention. A circular shape pulsed by her feet. She reached down, pushed her hand through the ring and the creature instinctively contracted on her wrist.

Cara rose up out of the viscous methane and raised her fist in the air, flashing her find to Beatrix. A phosphorescent-purple perpuffer.

Beatrix clapped her hands and shouted, "Well done, Cara! Well done!"

How many times did they dive together for perpuffers, searching for the elusive purple one, the top prize? Cara couldn't imagine ever doing this without her best friend at her side.

She swam back to shore.

Ambus moved as far away as his tether would allow, sitting on the other side of a dune with his back to them.

"Cara, it's lovely," Beatrix said, fingering the perpuffer.

Cara sighed happily. "After all of these years, I was beginning to think the purple ones were just a myth."

"Are you going to dive for more?"

"No, I have to go meet Juan Carlos for lunch."

"Don't go." Disappointment washed across Beatrix's face. "Cara, don't take this the wrong way, but . . . I don't like what you've told me about him."

Cara raised an eyebrow. It was unlike Beatrix to make a negative statement about a human being—let alone to express her disagreement so openly. Normally, if her opinion differed from Cara's she would hesitate or turn her head away when responding. When something moved her, she would tilt her head to the left and nod. Cara had learned to read her subtle mannerisms.

"You don't know Juan Carlos," Cara said.

"Why doesn't he ever join us?"

"He's busy." Cara could never bring herself to tell Beatrix the truth. Despite Juan Carlos's many fine qualities—his drop-dead looks, his sharp wit and analytical mind, his love for her—he had a low threshold for socializing with Wergens. He made it a point to minimize the time he spent in their presence. "They're lapdogs, Cara," he had said to her that morning, trying to persuade her not to visit Beatrix. "Doesn't it offend you? That such intelligent beings can be so fatuous, so sycophantic . . . They're like lovesick school-children."

Undeniable, really. But he had never met Beatrix, and their friendship transcended that species drive. Cara had to believe that. And certainly she had no biochemical reason for the fondness she felt for Beatrix. "If it's so offensive," she had answered, "maybe we shouldn't be accepting their technology, hmm?" She made a face and kissed him on the cheek. "I know you don't want me to go, but I really need to visit Bea at the lake." Juan Carlos's objections had dissuaded her from seeing Beatrix over the past few weeks. "I don't like the way I left things with her the last time we met. I'll see you at lunch, okay?"

Now, as she toweled off, Cara spotted a shape that Beatrix had sculpted in the sand. Instead of a spaceship, it was the familiar oval outline of a Wergen hearth. "Are you going to talk to your father about joining one of the next few expeditions?" Cara said. "Juan Carlos and I were thinking of Langalana . . ."

"No, I don't think that's a good idea," Beatrix said.

"What do you mean?"

"CE doesn't need any more Wergens. The Explorata is already swamped with qualified volunteers. Ambus thinks that we might be better off staying here."

Cara didn't know how to respond. She stuffed her towel into her carrytube and said, "I'm sorry to hear that."

Beatrix stared in Ambus's direction. "I found where Ambus kept the suppressant, Cara. And I threw it away. That's why he's keeping his distance. He knows that if he speaks to you, if he sees you up close, he'll feel the same way that I feel about you."

"Bea, once you're . . . encorporated . . ."

"You'll see, you and Ambus will be good friends, I know it."

Cara's eyes filled, and she nodded. "Yes, of course we will." But she said this only for Beatrix's sake. She knew that Ambus wanted to resist falling under humanity's spell and that she'd respect his wishes by keeping her distance. It wouldn't be fair to him if she didn't. Then again, how fair had she been to Beatrix all these years?

Beatrix's lips quivered and she reached out and clutched Cara's wrist. "Promise me we'll be friends forever."

"Bea . . ."

"Promise me?"

"Friends forever, Bea," Cara said. She hesitated. "Does it still feel . . . good to hold my hand?"

"More than you can know."

Maybe Cara had been fooling herself all these years. Maybe Beatrix's loyal unconditional love *was* just the product of a biochemical reaction. Maybe she'd been as unfair to Beatrix as Ambus claimed.

"I have to go," Cara said.

"Now?"

"I'm afraid so," she answered. "I don't want to have another fight with Juan Carlos." She took a few steps away from the Wergens, then turned and hurried back to Beatrix. Without saying a word, she slipped the purple perpuffer onto her best friend's wrist.

ENCRYPTED Med. Journal Entry No. 227 by Dr Juan Carlos Barbarón: Encorporation. As the headtail continues its relentless contraction, dermal contact follows, and nerve fibers penetrate the pore receptors on the scales across the passive Wergen's body. This quickly disintegrates cell walls as the mates merge, commencing macromitosis. Genetic materials, primarily nucleic acids, flow from the dominant to the passive Wergen and impregnation of the rear sac results. Scales along the dorsal spine grow into multiple nubs—fetuses that develop outside the Wergen's body, attached to its back. (See Related Entry

No. 195 on Multiple-Birth Wergen Broods and their Vulnerability to Dopamine Neurotramsitters as a Counteragent to Suppressor Drugs.)

Cara and Juan Carlos stepped through the hearth's archway as the bots skittered into the back rooms to alert Beatrix and Ambus of their arrival.

"Five minutes," Juan Carlos said. "Not one minute longer." He'd only permitted her to come on the condition that he accompany her to ensure she'd be out quickly. He said he feared that they'd encounter more Wergens than necessary since they tended to mob around humans.

"It's not safe for you to be walking around these Wergen neighborhoods. With the terrorist bombings at the Martian colony, how long will it be before they strike here on Titan? We maybe forced to make some difficult decisions at Biotech, but we need to protect ourselves." He turned away and tapped his eyelids to open up a retinal connection to the newscasts. "Five minutes." He blinked and made a connection, his eyes glazing over.

Juan Carlos enjoyed being in control but she knew he had her best interests at heart. She thought about objecting—she had no doubt he was overreacting—but didn't want to provoke an argument. The media had blown out of proportion an incident involving a faction of so-called 'Wergen rebels'— an oxymoron if ever she'd heard one—that had caused some unrest on Mars and other sister colonies.

A minute later, Beatrix and Ambus entered the room. They now stood no more than six inches apart. Their tether had lost its elasticity and Beatrix's head drooped to one side. Her left leg had disappeared inside of Ambus's right leg so they walked awkwardly, like a three-legged monstrosity lurching forward. In a matter of months, Beatrix, her friend, would be gone forever, absorbed into Ambus's form and broken down into the chemical components that would leave him impregnated.

Beatrix's face had a semi-glazed look, a blank stare. But when she caught sight of Cara, a brightness washed over her face.

"Cara?" she said. But then the spark of recognition faded.

Cara stood to hug her, but couldn't do so without also putting her arms around Ambus.

"Thank you for visiting," Ambus said.

Juan Carlos blinked off his retinal connection. He had a strange expression Cara couldn't quite identify—disgust? fascination?—as he greeted them.

Beatrix and Ambus went to take a seat but couldn't do so because of their physical condition.

"It's kind of you to come," Ambus said. "I know how much Bea wanted to see you." From the way he smiled and bowed his head, he clearly had no suppressant in his system.

"Oh, Beatrix," Cara said. "Bea . . ."

"No, it's fine, it's fine," Ambus said. "How have you been? How are your parents?"

She told them about her mother's death, about her father joining the expedition to Langalana. And as they conversed, Cara noticed that only Ambus spoke. She gazed directly into Beatrix's eyes and tried speaking only to her. "Do you remember the seasons we spent diving off the shore of Ontario Lacus? We practically covered ourselves head to toe with perpuffers."

A brief smile flashed across Beatrix's face. Then it went blank again.

"Yes, those are strong memories, Cara," Ambus said. "She'll remember them right up to the point of encorporation. After that, it's even possible I may still retain a stray experience, a random memory, but I can't guarantee any particular one will survive."

Cara placed her hands over Beatrix's. "Hey, Bea. Are you in there?"

"She's in there," Ambus answered. "Fully cognizant of everything you say."

"Can't she answer me?"

"I speak for her now."

Cara paused.

"So will there be nothing left of her?"

"Of course!" Ambus said. "Her knowledge of nanotech,

her facility with plants, a few random experiences. Her most useful skills will survive encorporation, creating a new me."

"What about her dreams, Ambus?" Cara's voice trembled. "What about her dreams of exploring the universe?"

He paused. "I've come to like it here on Titan, Cara. I can't say . . ."

Juan Carlos shot her a look and glanced dramatically at his watch.

"Bea, honey," Cara said, patting her hand. "I have to go, I'm sorry. Juan Carlos needs to be somewhere right now and I promised I'd accompany him."

"That's fine," Ambus answered. "But Cara, you have to promise you'll come visit again soon. Beatrix would love to see you again before encorporation is complete."

Beatrix's eyes remained rolled back in her head and a bit of clear drool oozed out of the corner of her mouth. Cara couldn't bear to see her like this. But she would never abandon her friend in the final moments of her life.

"Of course I'll be back, Bea." She leaned in close and whispered in her ear. "We'll go to the lake again and you can sit on the shore and watch while I dive for perpuffers for us, okay?" She felt the tears well up and fought them back.

"Cara," Juan Carlos said softly. "We should get going."

She took a deep breath and waved goodbye to her friend, wondering how much of her would remain when next they met.

ENCRYPTED Med. Journal Entry No. 228 by Dr Juan Carlos Barbarón: Cutting the tether of mated Wergens results in an instantaneous loss of identity, followed by a rapid and painful death.

The smog that blanketed Titan was thinner than usual on this day. So much so that Cara could almost make out the outline of ringed Saturn filling half the sky. In all of her years of living on Titan this was the first time she'd ever seen the planet with her naked eye. Its proximity caused the tidal winds that drove down from the poles towards the equator.

She felt awkward visiting Beatrix's hearth. So much time had passed that her friend was certainly long gone by now. Damn Juan Carlos. She would never forgive herself for allowing him to keep her away all this time. She had made a promise and she would keep it. If nothing else, she owed it to Beatrix's memory.

As she followed the winding trail down a steep hill toward the familiar hearth, she slowed down. What if encorporation wasn't complete? What if pieces of Bea were still visible? She imagined the segments of an arm jutting out of Ambus's chest, two half-heads merged together into a disfigured monstrosity. She wouldn't be able to bear the sight of it.

No, more than a year had passed. She began walking again.

When she got within twenty feet of the hearth, four Wergen children raced out through the archway in her direction. They ran in circles around her, saying "Good morning" and "Can we help you?" over and over.

She stooped down. "Are you Beatrix's children?"

One of the thicker, squatter females said, "My name is Antillia. Ambus is our father."

"Is he inside?"

The children nodded excitedly and followed close behind her.

When she entered the hearth's archway, Ambus stood there as if expecting her, even after all this time.

"I knew you would come," Ambus said. There was no longer any sign of the Ambus she remembered, the Wergen who spurned all contact with humanity. He threw his arms around her and she hugged him back. He looked different. Thinner. And his scales had familiar flicks of silver.

He guided her into the fireroom, where a transparent tube that ran from floor to ceiling blazed with flames. "Your children are beautiful, Ambus," she said.

The Wergen children tittered and whispered to each other.

"I need to speak alone with Cara for a moment," he said to them and they slowly, reluctantly left the fireroom staring over their shoulders at her, trying to sneak one final glance.

Housebots skittered at Cara's feet, taking away her boots

while others brought in a tray with a cup of steaming spicy sap.

"How is Juan Carlos?" he asked as they took their seats in front of the roaring fire column at the center of the room.

"I broke off our engagement."

Ambus gasped.

"He was so possessive. So secretive about his work at Biotech. I thought I could change him. But it didn't happen." She set down her cup of cider-sap. "He didn't like it when I visited with friends, when I did anything without him. And I went along with what he wanted. I started to feel . . . suffocated. I couldn't continue living that way, under someone else's thumb. I didn't like the person I was becoming."

Ambus stared incredulously. After a long pause, he said, "Sometimes I forget how truly alien you are."

She smiled. "No, of course you wouldn't understand."

They drank their sap and all the while Ambus leaned forward on his elbows and fixated on her every word; he offered her food; he asked whether she wanted him to feed the flames so she could luxuriate in the warmth of the fire column.

"Are you sure I can't get you something else?" Ambus said.

The initial joy Cara felt at being back in Beatrix's hearth began to drain away as she listened to Ambus's steady stream of fatuous remarks. She had to face the bittersweet truth: her best friend was gone forever. It could never be the same with just any other Wergen. She couldn't imagine herself without Beatrix. Before she even realized it, she started to cry.

"Cara, what is it?"

"I was thinking about something you told me once. That it was unfair of me to have remained friends with Beatrix for so many years." She wiped away the tears and regained her composure. "I think you may have been right. I should have . . . freed her of her biochemical shackles."

"Again, I wasn't myself at the time. I had taken the suppressant, which skewed my perception of reality. Please forget about what I said to you. It was unkind of me."

"Unkind, but true."

"Cara . . . did Beatrix explain what happened to my suppressants?"

Cara recalled their conversation on the lakeshore, when Beatrix had explained how she'd found where Ambus hid the drugs and destroyed them. "Yes, she kept them from you."

"On the day that we met you at the shore . . ." Ambus paused as if considering the consequences of his words. "Beatrix had taken the suppressants herself."

"What?"

"She said she wanted to have . . . a better understanding of her relationship with you, Cara. Its effects were temporary—only a matter of minutes—but in those minutes she experienced a clear understanding of her true feelings."

Cara dreaded asking, but she did. "And how did she really feel about me in that moment of clarity?"

"She never told me. And the memory didn't survive encorporation. I'm sorry, I don't know."

After an extended, awkward silence, they talked about other subjects: politics, the terrorist attacks on the Martian settlement, the rumored abandonment of the Langalanan outpost, the future of human-Wergen colonization efforts. And so on. And when it came time for her to leave, Cara knew that she would never return here again.

As she stood and the bots re-laced her boots, Ambus said, "Before you go, there's something I need to give you." A few seconds later a bot entered the room carrying a small metal box. "Beatrix wanted you to have this."

"It's a stasis box," Cara said. She carefully lifted the lid and looked inside.

A purple perpuffer sat at its center.

"Beatrix preserved it for so many months," Ambus said. "I don't understand its significance."

Cara slipped it onto her wrist. Removing it from the stasis box meant that the perpuffer wouldn't last for more than a day or two before decaying. But it didn't matter.

"Thank you, Ambus," she said softly.

Ambus tilted his head to the left in a familiar manner, and nodded.

As Cara made her way out the exit archway, she told

herself she'd never see this hearth again. But after only a few seconds she couldn't resist looking back over her shoulder. She saw Ambus out in front, surrounded by the four Wergen children, all of them staring raptly at her as she trudged through the methane snowdrifts.

Wahala

NNEDI OKORAFOR

Nnedi Okorafor (www.nnedi.com) is a novelist of Nigerian descent who lives in the Chicago suburbs with her daughter; she is a professor of Creative Writing at Chicago State University. She is known for weaving African culture into creative evocative settings and memorable characters. In a profile of Nnedi's work titled, "Weapons of Mass Creation," The New York Times *called Nnedi's imagination "stunning." Her novels include* Who Fears Death *(winner of the 2011 World Fantasy Award for Best Novel),* Akata Witch Witch *(a 2011 Amazon.com Best Book of the Year),* Zahrah the Windseeker *(winner of the Wole Soyinka Prize for African Literature), and* The Shadow Speaker *(winner of the Carl Brandon Society Parallax Award). She's also written one children's book titled* Long Juju Man *(winner of the Macmillan Writer's Prize for Africa). Her chapter book,* Iridessa and the Secret of the Never Mine *(Disney Press), is scheduled for release in 2012.*

"Wahala" was published in the original anthology Living on Mars, *edited by Jonathan Strahan. Set in the Sahara desert in a post-apocalyptic future, local people, colonists, are returning in a ship from Mars, as if from the past. Several mutant humans await their arrival. The protagonist is a plucky telepathic teenage Nigerian girl reminiscent of characters in Zenna Henderson's stories of* The People.

I wasn't lost. I *wanted* to cross "The Frying Pan of the World, Where Hell Meets Earth." I was fighting my way through this part of the Sahara on purpose. I needed to prove to my parents that I could do it. That I, their sixteen-year-old abomination of a daughter, could survive in a place where many people died. My parents believed I was meant to die easily because I shouldn't have been born in the first place. If I survived, it would prove to them wrong.

The sun was going down and the "frying pan" was thankfully cooling. Plantain, my camel, was walking at her usual steady pace. We'd left Jos three days ago and we were still days from our destination, Agadez. I'd traveled the desert many times . . . well, with my parents, though, and not here. I was okay, for now.

I was staring at the small screen of my e-legba, trying to forget the fact that I might have made a terrible mistake in running away and coming out here. It was picking up the only netcast available in the region, *Naija News.*

"Breaking News! *Breaking News, o!*" a sweating newscaster said in English. He stared into the camera with bulging eyes. He was wearing an ill-fitting Western-style suit. It was obviously the reason for his profuse sweating.

I chuckled. *Everything* on *Naija News* was "breaking news". Drama was the bread and butter of Nigerians. Even our news was suspenseful and theatrical. It was why our movies were the best and our government was the worst. I laughed. I missed home.

"Make sure you listen to what I am about to say, *o!* Then turn to those beside you and tell them! Tell *every*body," the man stressed. Spit flew from his mouth, hitting the camera lens as he spoke. He wiped his brow with a white handkerchief. I could see individual beads of sweat forming on his forehead. "This is no laughing matter, *o!*"

"Let me guess," I muttered. "Another *farmer!* has lost his flock of goats in a spontaneous forest. Someone's *house!* is infested with a sparkling lizard. Another *boy!* turned into a giant yam." I smiled, ignoring my chapped lips. This kind of "breaking news" happened all the time.

"It's heading this way *right now!*" the anchorman said. He clumsily held the microphone and wiped his brow again. He switched to Igbo. "This is utterly unbelievable!"

I laughed loudly. So unprofessional! How many of his viewers would understand that?

He coughed, smiled sheepishly, and switched back to English. "A *space shuttle* carrying people from the *Mars Colony* is going to land in the *Sahara*, *o!* These people had been on a spacecraft for months! Cooped up like chicken! It landed on the moon. From there they got on to the space shuttle to return to Earth. Communication with the shuttle has been spotty but we know where it will land." He moved closer to the camera, turned his head to the side, and opened his eyes wider. "If you encounter it, do *not* approach. *Biko nu*, stay away! Help will arrive. Officials will be there in two or three days! Don't—"

The picture distorted and the sound cut off. From far off came a deep *boom!* I felt the vibration in my chest, like a huge talking drum. Plantain growled. "Shh." I patted her hump. "Relax."

She stopped and I jumped off, looking to the south. I saw nothing but sky and sand for miles. A startled desert fox family was running across the sand about two miles away. I looked into the sky with my sharp eyes. There. About fifteen miles away.

"Oh," I whispered.

Within seconds, it zoomed overhead like a giant white eagle. Plantain groaned loudly as she dropped to the sand. I knelt beside her, craning my head and shielding my eyes from the dust it whipped up. It was flying so low that I could have hit it with a stone. This was the first flying aircraft I'd ever seen. I watched it land a few miles away, sliding to a stop in the sand.

It was a snap judgment, though it came from deep within me. "Let's go see!" I said to my camel, climbing on. "Before all the ambulances, government officials, technicians, and journalists show up!" I was in the middle of nowhere. It really would be days before anyone got here. I couldn't believe my luck. People from Mars!

As we headed there, I felt a pinch of embarrassment. I wondered if those onboard knew what we had done to ourselves here on Earth while they were away. People had been living on Mars for decades *before* the Great Change. We should have been super advanced like the people in those old science fiction books, jumping from planet to planet, that sort of thing. Instead we had destroyed the Earth because of stupid politics and misunderstandings.

I wanted to go inside the shuttle and breathe its trapped air. After so many years, that air wouldn't be Earth air. I am a shadow speaker. My large catlike eyes, my "reading" abilities, they're extraordinary, but they are all *because* of the Great Change, aka stupid human error. I'm as tainted by nuclear and peace bombs as one can get. I was born this way. But those on that ship hadn't *been* here when it happened. They were untouched. I wanted to see and touch them. And I wanted to *read* them.

Some of them were probably born on Mars. What had it been, over forty years since anyone last heard from the colonies?

"Faster, Plantain!" I shouted, laughing.

"I don't believe this," I muttered, my heart sinking.

Already, a small spontaneous forest had sprung up around the shuttle, enshrouding it with palm trees, bushes, and a small pond to its left. Vines had even begun to creep up the sides of the shuttle. I guess this was the Earth's way of welcoming it home. The sun was now completely down and there were several sunflowers opening up near the bottom of the ship.

Plantain slowed her stride when we reached the trees. An owl hooted and crickets and katydids sang. An instant oasis in the middle of the Sahara. Yet another result of human idiocy. I'd known spontaneous forests all my life, but their spontaneity and inappropriateness always bothered me. It wasn't hard to imagine a time when this was *not* normal.

I looked around cautiously, ready for anything. I couldn't tell if this was the type of forest that was full of stuff like stinging insects and rotten fruit or stuff like succulent strange vegetables and colorful butterflies. We passed a tree heavy with rather normal looking green mangos. That was a good sign.

The shuttle was about the size of an American football field. It took us a while to amble all the way around it. Not one opening. It was night, but I could see perfectly in the dark, another shadow speaker privilege. I knocked on the ship's white metal skin. No response. Minutes passed. Nothing happened.

I was exhausted. We'd been traveling for hours before seeing the ship. I'd been so excited that I hadn't eaten or been hydrating myself properly. Stupid. Suddenly, all at once, my neglect disarmed me. I fell to my knees, weak. Plantain trotted to the small pond and started drinking. Eventually, Plantain returned to me, gently clasped the collar of my dress with her teeth, dragged me to the water, and dumped me in the shallow part.

I laughed weakly. The water was cold. "Okay, okay," I said, pushing myself up. Cupping some of the water in my hands, I looked closely at it, searching for bacteria or strange microorganisms that might make me sick. The water was wonderfully fresh and clean, so much better than the water my capture station pulled from the clouds. I drank like crazy.

After having my fill, I laid my mat under a tree, sat down, and ate some bread and dried goat meat as I gazed at the ship. *Don't they want to come out?* I wondered. They had to have been on that shuttle for weeks. I brushed my teeth and lay down. As I drifted off to sleep, I thought, *Tomorrow.*

I woke an hour later to Plantain's soft warning grunt. I opened my eyes to a star-filled sky. Something was humming and splashing in the pond. I listened harder. It sounded like a person. *Finally. Someone's come out*, I thought, sitting up. But the shuttle looked as it had an hour ago, no openings anywhere. *Maybe the door's on the other side?* I crept to the pond for a better look.

He was standing thigh deep in the water wearing only his blue pants. As he waded deeper in, he hissed with pain. The way he moved, with his hands out, it didn't seem like he could see in the dark at all. I stood up for a better look. His things were on the ground, closer to me than him. A ripped satchel, a tattered blue shirt, and a silver, very sharp looking dagger.

Quietly, I snuck to his things. I was about to reach for his dagger when he suddenly stopped. He was up to his belly; his back to me. He whirled around and before I realized what was happening, he *flew* at me. Fast like a hawk! I leapt to the side, grabbing his satchel. Items fell from its large hole.

He landed and snatched another small dagger from his wet pocket. Then he eyed me with such rage and disgust that I stumbled back. He addressed me in Arabic, his dagger pointed at me, "Filthy *abid* bitch," he spat. "I'll slice your belly open just for *touching* my things." His wet face was scratched up, and one of his eyes was nearly swollen shut. There were more fresh scratches and bruises on his arms and his chest.

I blinked, understanding several things at once. First, he'd been recently beaten. Second, he was a windseeker, one born with the ability to fly, a product of the Great Change, tainted like me. Third, this meant he could not have been from the ship.

I was so appalled by his mauled condition and his words that I just stood there. He took this as further evidence that I couldn't possibly understand him.

"Allah protect me," he said, lowering his dagger. "Can

this night get any worse?" He looked my age, had skin the color of milky tea and a hint of a beard capping his chin. And he had the usual windseeker features: somewhat large wild eyes and long onyx black hair braided into seven very thick braids with copper bands on the ends.

"What is wrong with you?" I asked in Arabic, regaining my composure. He looked obviously shocked that I could speak his oh-so-sacred language. Most black Africans in Niger spoke Hausa or Fulanese. I deliberately looked him up and down and slowly enunciating my words said, "There are no *slaves* in these lands." *Abid* meant slave in Arabic.

"Hand me my things," he demanded. *"Now."*

Instead, I read him. I was close enough to him. The first thing was the scent of turmeric. I tasted something spicy, garlicky . . . *a dish called muhammara. Ahmed, that is his name. He's from . . . Saudi Arabia.*

He flew this far? I wondered as I swam within his past, seeing, hearing, tasting, touching, smelling. I was me but I was him. Duality. My heart was slamming in my chest as it always did when I read people.

As fast as I could, I soaked information from him like a sponge. . . . *From a lavish home. The seventh of five sons and four daughters. All normal. Except him.* Ahmed's father loomed large to me. Larger than Ahmed. *Father did not smoke or drink. Father prayed five times a day. Father hated spontaneous forests and the fact that the way to the nearby village was not always the same whenever he walked there. Father owned three black African slaves and he often cursed their black skin and burned hair.*

Father hated how the quality of the air was different. And he constantly dreamed of Mars. The new world, a fresh world, the place of his birth. He was an important man in the crumbling local government. Too important to have a windseeker son, one of those strange troublesome polluted children. Ahmed understood that Father thought him ruined.

As I looked into Ahmed, I heard him step toward me. When in a reading state, I'm basically helpless. I can't pull out of it quickly. One day, I will learn to not be so vulnerable.

Looking into Ahmed, I was surprised to find poetry and gentleness, too. *Ahmed loved salty olives. Short curvy women. The beaded necklaces around the necks of black-skinned women he'd see working at the market. The open sky. Music moved him. His quiet mother, whose hands were always writing adventure stories in the notebook she hid from Father . . .*

It came as it always did. In disorganized fragments, details, like a sentient puzzle more concerned with the shape of its pieces than putting itself together.

The day Father drove him away was the day news came about his grandfather on the shuttle returning to Earth. The first since the Great Change. Ahmed had assumed he'd never see Grandfather. During the celebration of the news, Father had turned to Ahmed. Had sneered at Ahmed. Father was ashamed of the bizarre son he'd have to present to his father whom he hadn't seen since he was four years old. Ahmed ran away that night. A windseeker must fly . . . not even Father's heavy hand and words could change that.

"You *abeed* are the lowliest of all Mankind," Ahmed was telling me. "A polluted *abid* . . . you are an aberration of the devil." These wicked words against the compelling melancholy of his past made my head ache. I fought to pull myself from him. A last fragment came to me, just before he shoved me to the ground . . . *As Ahmed flew from the only home he'd ever known, he received a message on his e-legba. From Grandma. The attachment she'd sent took up half the space on his hard drive. Coordinates, linked tracking applications, schedules . . . for Grandfather's space shuttle arrival. "Meet him," Grandma's message said. "He will love you."*

"Stop it!" he shouted, shoving me so hard that my breath was struck from my chest. I fell to the sand.

"Your father drove you away," I said, quickly getting up. I backed away from him and dusted the sand from my long dress. My heart was still pounding as I fought for breath. "Yet . . . you speak to me . . . with the same words that you fled."

"You're Nigerian," he growled, looking a little crazed. "I

can hear it in your accent! You all are nothing but *thieves*!" he pointed to his pummeled face. "Who do you think did this to me? They didn't just take my money, they tried to put a virus on my e-legba to empty my bank account! Double thievery!"

His motions, again, were so quick. Before I realized it, he'd grabbed a flashlight from the ground and flashed in my face.

"Ah!" I exclaimed, shielding my sensitive eyes, temporarily blinded. He clicked it off. "What are you doing here?" He began using his feet to gather to himself the other items that had fallen from his satchel.

For a few seconds, all I could see was red, figuratively and literally.

"Give me my bag," he snapped, when I didn't respond to his stupid question. I threw it at him, more things falling from the hole. He glared at me and I glared back.

My mother grew up in northern Nigeria and had traveled with her parents all over the Middle East before the Great Change. She'd told me about how black Africans were often treated in these places, but I'd never encountered it with the Arabs I met in Nigeria. My mother said it was an old, old, old problem, stemming from the trans-Saharan slave trade and before that. I only half-believed it was real. But I knew the words *abeed* and *abid*, the Arabic singular and plural forms for *black* or *slave*. Ugly, cruel words.

"What is it you're doing here?" he suddenly asked again, once he had all his things in his satchel. "How did you know to be here?"

"I didn't," I snapped.

"Then get out of here," he said. "Didn't you hear it on the news? You people never know what's best for you!"

"You know what? I'm here to see what's in that ship, so stay out of my way!" I said. He stepped forward. I stood my ground. He glanced over my shoulder at the ship.

"We'll see," he said. He flew up into the air and eventually descended behind some trees.

"Don't mind him," I muttered to Plantain, who was yards

away, preoccupied with a patch of fennel she'd found near a tree. "I'm not going anywhere." I returned to my spot on my mat and sat staring at the ship, listening. Waiting.

Seven hours later, I woke to Ahmed crouching over me, a rock in his raised hand. Every part of my body flexed. I stayed still.

He had the wild look of someone about to do something terrible in the name of those who raised him. I stared at him, willing him with all my might to look into my eyes. *Look,* I demanded with my mind. It was my only chance. If he didn't, he'd kill me, I knew . . . and it was not going to be a painless, quick death. I strained for his eyes. *Look, now! PLEASE!*

He looked into my eyes.

He looked for a long long time.

His face went from intense to slack to horribly troubled. He dropped the stone beside my head. He whimpered. Tears welled in his eyes. I smirked. Good. To look into the eyes of a shadow speaker is to court madness. Or so the rumor went. All I knew was that people who looked right into my eyes for more than a second were never the same afterward.

He sat before me, his hands not over his eyes but over his ears, terror on his face. I began to feel a little ill. Not guilty. No. I hadn't done anything. I was actually awash in rage. He'd been ready to cave my head in and now while he grieved over whatever he was grieving, I wanted to kick his teeth in. He wasn't paying attention to me. He was just sitting there holding his head. I could do it. But to do such a thing was not in me; it was evil. Unlike him, I *couldn't* murder. But he'd almost brutally killed me. My conflicted feelings made my stomach lurch.

Naked faced, he started weeping. His eyebrows crinkled in, his mouth turned downward, and his eyes narrowed as he wept softly.

"Look at me! I deserved to be robbed and beaten by your people!" he sobbed. "They should. . . ."

I didn't know what to say, so I didn't say anything.

"Fisayo," he whispered. It was odd to hear him speak my name. The sun was just coming up. "I . . ."

There was a loud hissing sound and we both looked toward the ship. A door had appeared on its side. The shuttle was finally opening.

Wiping his face with the heel of his hand, Ahmed got up. I scowled at him as I got up, too, wishing he'd stop his sniveling.

"Get it together," I snapped. "Goodness." He nodded, sobbed loudly, but then quieted a bit.

He was still weeping as we approached the shuttle. The sunlight was quickly bathing the desert. In the Sahara, the sun rises fast and steady. Even in a spontaneous forest. As we walked, I noticed many of the trees and bushes in the forest had disappeared or were withering, and the pond had gone foul and brackish.

"Will you *stop* it?" I whispered. I didn't know why I was whispering but it seemed right. "Tell me what we should expect. Do you have information about how many are on board?"

He brought out his e-legba, clicked it on, and read for a moment. He took a deep breath. "Your eyes are evil," he whined.

I scoffed. "It's not my eyes, Ahmed. It was you."

He sniffed loudly. "It says here that there are . . ." His voice cracked. He sniffled again. "There are supposed to be thirty-one people on board."

As the sunlight and the heat increased, the vines on the shuttle quickly dried and began falling off, leaving the shuttle exposed. The door that had opened gave way to darkness inside. I could only see the wall, as the passageway went directly to the right.

"Why isn't anyone coming out?" I asked.

As we moved closer, Ahmed pulled himself together . . . at least he stopped weeping. "So really," he asked. "Why are you here?"

I hesitated. Then I shrugged. "I just happened to be a few miles away when I heard about it on my e-legba."

He wiped at his eyes again. "You're not here to steal from them?"

"No! Of course not!" I was getting more nervous the

closer we got; it was good to talk about something else. "You were going to *kill* me."

"I was." He paused. He frowned as more tears began to dribble from his eyes. "I . . . I'm sorry." He rubbed his temples. "I don't think you're human."

"I don't think *you* are either."

We were standing at the door. Inside the shuttle, the walls were plush red and busy with buttons, small blank screens, and other things. To the right, the corridor went well into the ship. Ahmed sobbed loudly. He turned to the side, pressed a finger to his left nostril, and blew out a large amount of snot. "I'm sorry," he said, looking distraught again, his voice strained as he tried to hold back more sobs.

"Ugh," I said, turning to the side. I couldn't look at him anymore. "Look . . . I'm going in, are . . ."

Ahmed had stopped weeping entirely. I frowned, turning back to him. He looked as if he was seeing a ghost. He grabbed my hand. I turned to the door just as something large and red slammed me to the ground. *Hot glass! Hot glass!* I frantically thought Ahmed hadn't released my hand and was thus yanked back as I fell. I could hear Ahmed yelling but all I saw was a layer of red and all I felt were pain and heat. It was as if the world was submerged under soft ripples of red tinted waters. I could see a wavy red sun, the ship, and Ahmed kicking and kicking at whatever was on top of me.

I heard it hissing in my ear. A creature with a heavy solid body like glass. Dry, hot, and buzzing. No, not buzzing. Vibrating. I could feel it, down deep inside me. I struggled to understand. But it was pressing on my throat. A part of me could only think one thing: *Look into my eyes! Please look into my eyes!* If it was a thing, a creature maybe . . .

I was looking through . . . its head. Oblong but empty. Then I was falling. Shaking. Vibrating. Falling. Into. Red. *The CoLoRs it knew and loved. The CoLoRs of HoME. Where everything was all kinds of RED. Until it was fOuNd. For VIbRAtINg too much with CuriositY.* I fell deeper. Beyond myself. I have no words to describe it. But it was alive. Not in the same way that I knew life, but it was alive.

As its weight lifted off me, my entire body flared with

pain. Nevertheless, I lived. And I knew why. I knew what the creature was. I knew many things about it now. I tried to laugh. Instead I coughed hard and everything around me throbbed red.

It stood before me. Too heavy now and sinking into the sand. It looked like a crude glass bipedal grasshopper. It was impervious to Ahmed's attacks. Kicking it was like kicking transparent stone.

"From Mars," I breathed as I got to my feet. My neck ached painfully and I had to bend forward. "It's a . . ."

It suddenly turned to Ahmed and sent out so much vibration that I could feel it in my chest. I coughed, pressing my hands to my chest. Then it leapt at him.

"No!" I croaked. "Stop, wait!"

But Ahmed was ready. He jumped back and shot into the sky. The creature fell forward and started sinking fast into the sand. I shielded my eyes, searching for Ahmed. The creature had sunk halfway into the sand, before Ahmed returned. "What is it?" he asked, hovering several feet above my head.

I laughed, rubbing my neck. I was beginning to feel a little better. "It's an alien." Then I sat down hard on the sand.

In a matter of minutes, I'd gone from fighting off a racist windseeker armed with a rock to fighting off a Martian alien. As I sat there contemplating this, I stared at the door.

"You know why it didn't kill me?" I asked, rubbing my temples and shutting my eyes. Ahmed sat beside me, anxiously looking at where the alien had sunk.

"Why?" he muttered. He hacked loudly and spit to the side. He was done crying.

"Because I'm Nigerian," I said.

"What?" Ahmed said, frowning at me. "How would it know that? Why would it *care*?"

"It was held captive, and the only person to treat it with any respect before it managed to escape was a man named Arinze Tunde, a Nigerian."

"How do you . . ." His eyes widened. "You read an alien?"

"It read me more," I said.

"That cursed thing could read genetics or something?"

"Guess so," I said. "That's what the vibrating was. You felt it, right?"

"Yeah, like being touched by sound."

I got up and waited a moment to make sure I was steady. Ahmed got up, too. For a moment, I felt dizzy, then everything stabilized. As I dusted off my dress, I said, "And you know why it wanted to kill you?"

Ahmed shrugged.

"Your grandpa was the one who captured it."

He stared at me blankly as I quickly walked to the ship. I turned to him. "Come on!" I said. "The passengers are locked in some room. We need to get everyone off *right now*. The alien is going to make the shuttle take off again."

"My grandfather?" Ahmed said as I ran inside. "Alien? Didn't it just sink into the sand? There's another one?"

The soft humming was continuous and the lights flickered as we walked down the narrow corridor single file. The padded walls added to the narrowness. Everything was spotless, no dust or dirt in any corners. And everything smelled like face powder.

"I don't like this," Ahmed said, moving faster. "Not at all."

I smiled. Windseekers hate tight places. "Inhale, exhale," I said, staying close behind him. "We'll find the passengers and then get out. Relax."

As he loudly inhaled and exhaled as he walked, I took a moment to look behind us. So far we'd moved in a straight line and I could still see the sun shining in from the open door. I felt a little better. If it was a trap, the door probably would have shut. Eventually, the corridor did break off in three different directions. We took the one in the middle and came to a large metal door with a sign on it that said CONFERENCE ROOM B. Ahmed was about to touch the blue button beside the door. I grabbed his hand.

"What?" he said, accidently looking into my eyes. He quickly looked away, squeezing his face as if I'd stuck a pin in his arm.

"Don't start that again," I snapped.

"It's your damn eyes!"

I rolled my eyes. "Let's knock first."

"Fine," he said, gritting his teeth. He knocked three times. The sound was absorbed by the hallway's padding. We stood there, listening hard.

I sighed, "Maybe, we could . . ."

"Arinze?" a woman called from behind the door.

Ahmed grabbed my arm, and I stepped closer to him.

"Please!" a man shouted in English, banging on the door. I couldn't place his accent. "Open up. Just . . ."

"Is that English? What are they saying?" Ahmed asked me in Arabic. "I can't understand."

"They want us to open the door," I said. I stepped up to the door. "We're . . . we're not him!" I responded in English. I turned to Ahmed and switched back to Arabic. "I told them we're not Arinze."

"Let's open it," he said.

"Okay."

He was about to and then stopped. He turned to me, looking guilty. "You should step back."

I understood. My eyes. Who knew what they'd think? And I didn't want anyone looking into them.

"Okay," I said, stepping behind him. "Makes sense."

He touched the blue button and there we were facing about thirty sweaty dirty people all crammed at the door. Hot air wafted out. It reeked of sweat, urine, feces, and rotten fruit. Ahmed and I coughed.

Ahmed stood up straight. "We're here to—"

"Take her down!" a man shouted in English. There was a mad rush as they all tried to lunge for me through the narrow corridor. I stumbled back as Ahmed jumped in front of me, using his body to block the way. Five men tried to shove him aside but he somehow managed to remain lodged.

"Stop it!" he shouted in Arabic.

"We can handle her!" someone said in Igbo. "Just get out of the way!"

"We're getting off this damn shuttle!" another said in English.

"Stop!" Ahmed screamed in Arabic, pushing them back with all his might. "She's not—she's human!"

No one listened or maybe they didn't understand. Everyone started shouting at the same time. Sweat gleamed on Ahmed's face as he fought to keep himself in the passageway. I ran back several feet but I wasn't about to leave Ahmed.

Suddenly, out of nowhere, a blast of wind flew through the passageway. It knocked me off my feet and I slid several feet back. Then everything went silent. I slowly sat up. Everyone in the passageway had been blown back into the conference room. They murmured as they sat up, rubbing their heads, arms, confused.

Only Ahmed remained, hovering, his seven long thick braids undulating as the windseeker breeze circulated his body. The passengers stared at him. I smiled broadly, though once again, I was shaking all over.

"She, *we* are not . . ." Ahmed switched to French as he landed on his feet. "We are not whatever you've been dealing with! Does anyone understand me? We're here to get you out!"

"How do we know that?" some woman asked in French from behind everyone. *Good*, I thought. Someone understood.

"Speak in French," I said. "I can speak that, too."

Ahmed looked at me. I winked. I can speak six languages, Arabic, Hausa, French, Igbo, Yoruba, and English. My father liked to call me the daughter of Legba—the Yoruba deity of language, communication, and the crossroads—because I picked up languages so easily.

"Why else would we *unlock* the door?" Ahmed snapped. The woman translated for those who couldn't understand.

Silence.

"Stupid," I muttered, stepping closer to Ahmed.

"This is Fisayo and I'm Ahmed," he said. "We're . . . Do you know what's happened on Earth since you left?"

More confused murmuring. The general consensus was that they knew something bad had happened but they weren't sure what.

"She and I have been . . . affected. We're not aliens. One

of you is my . . . my grandfather. Zaid Fakhr Mohammed Uday al-Rammah." Before the woman could translate for the others, Ahmed repeated himself in Arabic, listing his name, his grandmother's name, and his village. There was a soft gasp from near the back and the crowd slowly parted, allowing a tall wizened man to come forth. He was about eighty and wore blue garments whose armpits were dirty with sweat, and a deep blue turban.

There was a long pause as the two stared at each other.

"Why do you look like a punching bag?" Ahmed's grandfather asked in Arabic. He motioned to me. "Is this girl your wife? Have you two been quarreling?" A few people chuckled.

"Uh . . ." Ahmed said. "We're . . ."

"Come here," his grandfather said.

Ahmed slowly stepped up to him and the old man looked him up and down. "You don't look like my son."

Ahmed scoffed. "The last time you saw him he was about four years old."

I held my breath. Then I let it out with relief as the old man smiled and laughed softly. "You are really my grandson?"

Ahmed brought a picture from his pocket. "This is you, Grandma, and my father just before they left for Earth."

His grandfather stared at it for a very long time.

"That . . . monster will let us out now?" someone impatiently asked behind them.

Ahmed's grandfather was crying. "I haven't seen this photo in . . . such a long time. It's why I came back."

"There's one more of us," an African woman said in Igbo, pushing to the front. She wore jeans and a dirty purple sweater. Ahmed looked back at me and I stepped forward. The woman hesitated, glancing at and looking away from my eyes and said, "He's being held captive in the cockpit, I think." She pointed behind her. "It's through the conference room."

"Arinze," I said.

She nodded.

"Troublesome sellout," Ahmed's grandpa mumbled. "Nigerians." He spoke the name of my people like he was spitting dirt from his mouth. I frowned.

The women who'd spoken Igbo sucked her teeth loudly and deliberately. "Keep talking and see *wahala*, old man."

Even when they lived and were born on Mars, people were still people.

Ahmed's and my eyes met for a half second. Then he looked away. "I'll go," I said.

"I'll go with you," the Igbo woman said.

"It's okay," I told her. "I know what's going on. Just . . . wait for him outside." This time, I was the one who didn't want to meet her eyes. I switched to English. She spoke Igbo with an English accent, so I suspected she'd understand, as would more of the others. "You all need to get off. There isn't time. This shuttle is going to take off soon."

"What!" a man said. "Impossible! There can't be any fuel left. . . ."

People started translating for each other, and there were more exclamations of surprise.

"Who cares," a woman said. "Show us out of here! I can't stand being on a shuttle any longer!"

Everyone began pushing forward again. As they crammed past me, I told Ahmed, "Go with them. They need someone who knows . . . Earth."

"Okay. But hurry out," he said, taking and squeezing my hand. His other was holding the hand of his grandfather.

"I'll be all right."

I watched them all file down the corridor. Then I walked into the conference room to attend the strangest meeting of my life.

The conference room was spacious with a high ceiling and windows the size of the walls (which were currently covered with the ship's protective white metal exterior). Near the back were shelves of books and three exercise bicycles. This large room was probably normally beautiful. But at the moment it was filthy and stinky. There were plastic tubs brimming with urine and feces and sacks of garbage. Had they been allowed to leave the room for anything? How long had they been trapped in there? I hurried to the door on the other side.

It easily opened and led into another passageway that was

even narrower than the other one. It went on and on. I passed sealed doorways on my left and right. I frowned realizing something. Maybe the creature was allowing the doors to open. Maybe it had opened the door to the outside so that Ahmed and I could come in and rescue the people. I had so many answers, yet I had even more questions.

Finally, I reached a small round door. It felt like metal but it looked like wood. Nervous, I took a deep breath, tugging at one of my long braids. Suddenly the door slid open and I was standing before a tall very dark-skinned Nigerian man. Behind him was a round sunshine-filled room. The cockpit window must have been recently opened, for I hadn't seen this on the outside. Every inch of wall was packed with virtual sensors, small and large screens, and soft buttons.

In the middle of it all, manipulating the ship's virtual controls, was the . . . thing. It looked like something out of the deep ocean. Wet, red, bloblike, formless. I imagined that it would have fit perfectly into the glasslike thing that had attacked Ahmed and me outside.

It smoothly pulled its many filament-like appendages in, rose up, and molded itself into an exact replica of my face, shifting and changing colors to even imitate my dark skin tone. I gasped, clapping my hands over my mouth. It smiled at me.

Terrified, I looked up at Arinze who was still standing there. "I—"

His face curled, and he grabbed me. He pushed me back and slammed me against the wall. For the third time in the last hour all the air left my chest. I grabbed at his hands and dug my nails into them. His grip loosened and I seized the opportunity to slide away.

My eyes located a wrench. I grabbed it and raised it toward one of the screens. Arinze froze and the creature melted from my shape back into a blob.

"I swear I'll . . . I'll smash this!" I screamed, utterly hysterical by this point. "May the fleas of a thousand camels nest in your hair!" I was hurting all over, shaking, full of too much adrenaline and there was a red alien in the middle of the room with appendages snaking out in multiple directions like some sort of giant amoeba! I strained to keep the tears from dribbling for my eyes. The last thing I needed was for my vision to blur. I focused on the alien, sharpening to a molecular level. . . . I immediately pulled back, further shaken. I hadn't seen cells; I saw something more like metal balls.

"Please don't break that," Arinze said in Igbo. His accent was vaguely Nigerian, Yoruba. But not quite. How long had he been on Mars? He had to have been born there. He looked about thirty. Yet he had three short vertical tribal markings on each cheek. So they were still practicing that tradition even on Mars?

"We need that to navigate properly," he said.

"You just nearly *killed* me!"

"I'm sorry," he said. "I was . . . I thought you were going to hurt it. It's . . . it's like a snail without a shell until it makes a new living shell."

I didn't lower my wrench.

"That's . . . that's why it attacked you," he said. "Then we realized a lot of things." He paused. "What are you?"

"I'm human. A shadow speaker." I shook my head. "It's a long story."

He stared at me. I knew he was making up his mind. I'd made mine up. If he tried anything, I'd smash the screen and then smash his head. "Arinze," I said, quickly. "I know who you are. I know you have befriended this creature. You understand each other."

"How do you know?" he snapped. "What can you know?"

The creature stretched a narrow filament and touched Arinze's forehead. Affectionately. Arinze seemed to relax.

I felt a pinch of envy. I was constantly getting attacked because of what I looked like. This creature had no shape and could look like anything it wanted. And then it could create an exo-skin that it could wear or send to do what it asked . . . at least until it sunk into the sand on a planet with stronger gravity than it was used to. I wondered why it had chosen to make its exo-skin look like a giant bipedal grasshopper.

"It 'reads' things through vibration," I said. "I am similar.

I read things by closeness and focusing. I read it as it read me. You know I'm right. It has told you. Trust it."

"Put the wrench down," he said. "I'm not going to hurt you."

"How do I know?"

He sighed and sat on a stool, now rubbing his own temples. "You know. You both know."

I didn't put it down. "Please," I said. "I'm tired of fighting." I leaned against the controls, feeling very, very tired. "What is it about me that everyone wants to attack? I just came here to *greet* you people. To see." I sighed, tears finally falling from my eyes. Why did everyone think I was evil? One of the last things my mother had said to me before I ran away was that I was *wahala*, trouble.

He frowned. "Did I hurt you?"

I waved a hand at him. It was too much to explain.

"I'm sorry," he said again.

"So am I," I said, sitting on the floor.

There was a clicking sound as the alien's appendage screwed something in beneath the front window controls. There was a soft whirring. The creature's body twisted up and leaned toward Arinze.

"I'm not held captive here," he said. "They all think I am but I'm not."

"I know."

"It's been ugly on this shuttle," he said. "We had to lock them up. Were they all okay?"

I nodded.

"Good. I'm . . . I'm going to go back with it. It's not the only one that's been discovered by the Mars government and there were some government officials on this shuttle who will alert those here on Earth. If I don't go with this one, to help it speak to its people, there will be a war. It tells me so. Like here. It was war, right?"

"Yes. Nuclear and something else."

He nodded. "I have to go back."

"You've never been outdoors, have you?"

"No. But . . ." he said. He looked at the creature, a sadness passing over his face. The creature was focused on getting home. "What's happened to Earth?"

"It's a long story."

He chuckled. "Have you heard news of Nigeria? My grandparents are from there."

I smiled. "Nigeria is still Nigeria."

"One day . . ." He took my hands. "You'd better get off the ship."

The creature moved a filament across the green virtual grid above it and the shuttle shook hard enough to make me stumble.

"Go!" Arinze said. "Hurry!"

I made for the door and then turned back. I ran to Arinze and shook his hand. "I hope you come back," I said.

Before I ran off, quickly like a striking snake, the creature reached out and touched my forehead with a moist appendage. It was neither warm nor cold, hard nor soft, absolutely foreign. Only one image came to me from its touch: An empire of red dust in a place that looked like the Sahara desert. Here strange things grew and withered spontaneously. As they did now on Earth. The communities of these creatures were more like the Earth of now, especially in the Sahara. I breathed a sigh of surprise. Then I could feel it more than I heard it. A vibration that tickled my ears. *My people do not understand Mars Earthlings, but they will understand when I tell about you, Fisayo. You are not* wahala. *You are the information I needed.*

Arinze was pushing me. "Go!" he shouted.

I went.

I barely made it off the shuttle before it started rumbling. Plantain was there, waiting. I jumped on her and she took off. We joined the others two miles from the shuttle as it launched into the sky with impossible power and speed. I'd seen what the alien did to the shuttle when I read it, but I didn't have the capacity to understand its science. The Igbo woman who'd wanted to come to the cockpit with me cried and cried when she didn't see Arinze with me. Ahmed stood close to his grandfather. His grandfather had his arm over his shoulder.

Ahmed and I did not say good-bye. As they were all deciding if they should wait for officials to arrive or try to make it to the next town, Plantain and I left. There was too much to say and no space to say it. Plantain and I headed south, back home, to Jos. Crossing the Sahara to Agadez was a silly idea. I needed to have long talk with my parents.

There was other life on Mars. Even after all that had happened here on Earth, I had to work to wrap my mind around that. Allah protect Arinze and the one he's befriended; provide them with success. There's been more than enough *wahala*.

Laika's Ghost

KARL SCHROEDER

Karl Schroeder (www.kschroeder.com) lives in Toronto, Ontario, where he divides his time between writing fiction and
consulting—chiefly in the area of Foresight Studies and technology. His work of forecasting fiction, Crisis in Zefra, was
published by the Directorate of Land Strategic Concepts of
the National Defense Canada in 2005. He began to publish
stories in the 1990s, and he has, beginning with Ventus
(2000), published seven science fiction novels and a collection of earlier stories. His most recent novel is the final Virga
novel, Ashes of Candesce, published in 2012. Recently, he
has begun to develop his Bruce Sterling-esque character,
Gennady the Russian agent, as the protagonist of a series of
stories, including "To Hie from Far Cilenia" in last year's
volume of this book. We hope for a collection of these excellent stories, including the one that follows here.

"Laika's Ghost" is another story first published in Engineering Infinity. Laika was of course the name of the canine
Russian cosmonaut who died in space prior to the first human
spaceflight. Somewhere in the arid, radiated steppes of the
former Soviet Union someone may have perfected the portable nuclear bomb that would destabilize the world for the
forseeable future. Gennady, so cool and yet so socially timid,
is forced to take along an American kid recently returned
from Mars, even though it is a surefire recipe for extra trouble.

The flight had been bumpy; the landing was equally so, to the point where Gennady was sure the old Tupolev would blow a tire. Yet his seat-mate hadn't even shifted position in two hours. That was fine with Gennady, who had spent the whole trip trying to pretend he wasn't there at all.

The young American had been a bit more active during the flight across the Atlantic: at least, his eyes had been open and Gennady could see coloured lights flickering across them from his augmented reality glasses. But he had exchanged less than twenty words with Gennady since they'd left Washington.

In short, he'd been the ideal travelling companion.

The other four passengers were stretching and groaning, Gennady poked Ambrose in the side and said, "Wake up. Welcome to the ninth biggest country in the world."

Ambrose snorted and sat up. "Brazil?" he said hopefully. Then he looked out his window. "What the hell?"

The little municipal airport had a single gate, which as the only plane on the field, they were taxiing up to uncontested. Over the entrance to the single-story building was the word "Степногорск." "Welcome to Stepnogorsk," said Gennady as he stood to retrieve his luggage from the overhead rack. He travelled light by habit. Ambrose, he gathered, had done so from necessity.

"Stepnogorsk . . . ?" Ambrose shambled after him, a mass of wrinkled clothing leavened with old sweat.

"Secret Soviet town," Ambrose mumbled as they reached

the plane's hatch and a burst of hot dry air lifted his hair. "Population sixty-thousand," he added as he put his left foot on the metal steps. Halfway down he said, "Manufactured anthrax bombs in the cold war!" And as he set foot on the tarmac he finished with, "Where the hell is Kazakhstan . . . ? Oh."

"Bigger than Western Europe," said Gennady. "Ever heard of it?"

"Of course I've *heard* of it," said the youth testily—but Gennady could see from how he kept his eyes fixed in front of him that he was still frantically reading about the town from some website or other. In the wan August sunlight he was taller than Gennady, pale, with stringy hair, and everything about him soft—a sculpture done in rounded corners. He had a wide face, though; he might pass for Russian. Gennady clapped him on the shoulder. "Let me do the talking," he said as they dragged themselves across the blistering tarmac to the terminal building.

"So," said Ambrose, scratching his neck. "Why are we here?"

"You're here because you're with me. And you needed to disappear, but that doesn't mean I stop working."

Gennady glanced around. The landscape here should look a lot like home, which was only a day's drive to the west— and here indeed was that vast sky he remembered from Ukraine. After that first glance, though, he did a double-take. The dry prairie air normally smelled of dust and grass at this time of year, and there should have been yellow grass from here to the flat horizon—but instead the land seemed blasted, with large patches of bare soil showing. There was only stubble where there should have been grass. It looked more like Australia than Asia. Even the trees ringing the airport were dead, just gray skeletons clutching the air.

He thought about climate change as they walked through the concrete-floored terminal; since they'd cleared customs in Amsterdam, the bored-looking clerks here just waved them through. "Hang on," said Ambrose as he tried to keep up with Gennady's impatient stride. "I came to you guys for asylum. Doesn't that mean you put me up somewhere, some hotel, you know, away from the action?"

"You can't get any farther from the action than this." They emerged onto a grassy boulevard that hadn't been watered nor cut in a long while; the civilized lawn merged seamlessly with the wild prairie. There was nothing visible from here to the horizon, except in one direction where a cluster of listless windmills jutted above some low trees.

A single taxicab was sitting at the crumbled curb.

"Oh, man," said Ambrose.

Gennady had to smile. "You were expecting some Black Sea resort, weren't you?" He slipped into the taxi, which stank of hot vinyl and motor oil. "Any car rental agency," he said to the driver in Russian. "It's not like you're some cold war defector," he continued to Ambrose in English. "Your benefactor is the U.N. And they don't have much money."

"So you're what—putting me up in a *motel* in *Kazakhstan?*" Ambrose struggled to put his outrage into words. "What I saw could—"

"What?" They pulled away from the curb and became the only car on a cracked blacktop road leading into town.

"Can't tell you," mumbled Ambrose, suddenly looking shifty. "I was told not to tell *you* anything."

Gennady swore in Ukrainian and looked away. They drove in silence for a while, until Ambrose said, "So why are *you* here, then? Did you piss somebody off?"

Gennady smothered the urge to push Ambrose out of the cab. "Can't tell you," he said curtly.

"Does it involve SNOPB?" Ambrose pronounced it *snop-bee.*

Gennady would have been startled had he not known Ambrose was connected to the net via his glasses. "You show me yours, I'll show you mine," he said. Ambrose snorted in contempt.

They didn't speak for the rest of the drive.

"Let me get this straight," said Gennady later that evening. "He says he's being chased by Russian agents, NASA, *and* Google?"

On the other end of the line, Eleanor Frankl sighed. "I'm sorry we dumped him on you at the airport," said the New

York director of the International Atomic Energy Agency. She was Gennady's boss for this new and—so far—annoyingly vague contract. "There just wasn't time to explain why we were sending him with you to Kazakhstan," she added.

"So explain now." He was pacing in the grass in front of the best hotel his IAEA stipend could afford. It was evening and the crickets were waking up; to the west, fantastically huge clouds had piled up, their tops still lit golden as the rest of the sky faded into mauve. It was cooling off already.

"Right . . . Well, first of all, it seems he really is being chased by the Russians, but not by the country. It's the *Soviet Union Online* that's after him. And the only place their IP addresses are blocked is inside the geographical territories of the Russian and Kazakhstani Republics."

"So, let me get this straight," said Gennady heavily. "Poor Ambrose is being chased by Soviet agents. He ran to the U.N. rather than the FBI, and to keep him safe you decided to transport him to the one place in the world that is free of Soviet influence. Which is Russia."

"Exactly," said Frankl brightly. "And you're escorting him because your contract is taking you there anyway. No other reason."

"No, no, it's fine. Just tell me what the hell I'm supposed to be looking for at SNOPB. The place was a God-damned anthrax factory. I'm a radiation specialist."

He heard Frankl take a deep breath, and then she said, "Two years ago, an unknown person or persons hacked into a Los Alamos server and stole the formula for an experimental metastable explosive. Now we have a paper trail and emails that have convinced us that a metastable bomb is being built. You know what this means?"

Gennady leaned against the wall of the hotel, suddenly feeling sick. "The genie is finally out of the bottle."

"If it's true, Gennady, then everything we've worked for has come to naught. Because as of now, anybody in the world who wants a nuclear bomb, can make one."

He didn't know what to say, so he just stared out at the

steppe, thinking about a world where hydrogen bombs were as easy to get as TNT. His whole life's work would be rendered pointless—and all arms treaties, the painstaking work of generations to put the nuclear genie back in its bottle. The nuclear threat had been containable when it was limited to governments and terrorists, but now the threat was from *everybody* . . .

Eleanor's distant voice snapped him back to attention. "Here's the thing, Gennady: we don't know very much about this group that's building the metastable weapon. By luck we've managed to decrypt a few emails from one party, so we know a tiny bit—a minimal bit—about the design of the bomb. It seems to be based on one of the biggest of the weapons ever tested at Semipalatinsk—its code name was the *Tsarina*."

"The *Tsarina*?" Gennady whistled softly. "That was a major, major test. Underground, done in 1968. Ten megatonnes; lifted the whole prairie two meters and dropped it. Killed about a thousand cattle from the ground shock. Scared the hell out of the Americans, too."

"Yes, and we've discovered that some of the *Tsarina*'s components were made at the Stepnogorsk Scientific Experimental and Production Base. In Building 242."

"But SNOPB was a biological facility, not nuclear. How can this possibly be connected?"

"We don't know how, yet. Listen, Gennady, I know it's a thin lead. After you're done at the SNOPB, I want you to drive out to Semipalatinsk and investigate the *Tsarina* site."

"Hmmph." Part of Gennady was deeply annoyed. Part was relieved that he wouldn't be dealing with any IAEA or Russian nuclear staff in the near future. Truth to tell, stalking around the Kazaks grasslands was a lot more appealing than dealing with the political shit-storm that would hit when this all went public.

But speaking of people . . . He glanced up at the hotel's one lighted window. With a grimace he pocketed his augmented reality glasses and went up to the room.

Ambrose was sprawled on one of the narrow beds. He had

the TV on and was watching a Siberian ski-adventure info-mercial. "Well?" he said as Gennady sat on the other bed and dragged his shoes off.

"Tour of secret Soviet anthrax factory. Tomorrow, after egg McMuffins."

"Yay," said Ambrose with apparent feeling. "Do I get to wear a hazmat suit?"

"Not this time." Gennady lay back, then saw that Ambrose was staring at him with an alarmed look on his face. "Is fine," he said, waggling one hand at the boy. "Only one under-ground bunker we're interested in, and they probably never used it. The place never went into full production, you know."

"Meaning it only made a few hundred pounds of anthrax per day instead of the full ton it was designed for! I should feel reassured?"

Gennady stared at the uneven ceiling. "Is an adventure." He must be tired, his English was slipping.

"This sucks." Ambrose crossed his arms and glowered at the TV.

Gennady thought for a while. "So what did you do to piss off Google so much? Drive the rover off a cliff?" Ambrose didn't answer, and Gennady sat up. "You found something. On Mars."

"No that's ridiculous," said Ambrose. "That's not it at all."

"Huh." Gennady lay down again. "Still, I think I'd enjoy it. Even if it wasn't in real-time . . . driving on Mars. That would be cool."

"That sucked too."

"Really? I would have thought it would be fun, seeing all those places emerge from low-res satellite into full hi-res three-d."

But Ambrose shook his head. "That's not how it worked. That's the point. I couldn't believe my luck when I won the contest, you know? I thought it'd be like being the first man on Mars, only I wouldn't have to leave my living room. But the whole point of the rover was to go into terrain that hadn't been photographed from the ground before. And with the time-delay on signals to Mars, I wasn't steering it in real time. I'd drive in fast-forward mode over low-res pink hills that looked worse than a forty-year-old video game, then upload the drive sequence and log off. The rover'd get the commands twenty minutes later and drive overnight, then download the results. By that time it was the next day and I had to enter the next path. Rarely had time to even look at where we'd actually gone the day before."

Gennady considered. "A bit disappointing. But still more than most people ever get."

"More than anyone else will ever get." Ambrose scowled. "That's what was so awful about it. You wouldn't understand."

"Oh?" Gennady arched an eyebrow. "If you grow up in the Soviet Union, you know a little about disappointment."

Ambrose looked mightily uncomfortable. "I grew up in Washington. Capital of the world! But my dad went from job to job, we were pretty poor. So every day I could see what you *could* have, you know, the Capitol dome, the Mall, all that power and glory . . . what *they* could have—but not me. Never me. So I used to imagine a future where there was a whole new world where I could be . . ."

"Important?"

He shrugged. "Something like that. NASA used to tell us they were just about to go to Mars, any day now, and I wanted that. I dreamed about homesteading on Mars." He looked defensive; but Gennady understood the romance of it. He just nodded.

"Then, when I was twelve, the Pakistani-Indian war happened and they blew up each other's satellites. All that debris from the explosions is going to be up there for centuries! You can't get a manned spacecraft through that cloud, it's like shrapnel. Hell, they haven't even cleared low Earth orbit to restart the orbital tourist industry. I'll never get to *really* go there! None of us will. We're never gettin' off this sinkhole."

Gennady scowled at the ceiling. "I hope you're wrong."

"Welcome to the life of the last man to drive on Mars." Ambrose dragged the tufted covers back from the bed. "Instead of space, I get a hotel in Kazakhstan. Now let me sleep. It's about a billion o'clock in the morning, my time."

He was soon snoring, but Gennady's alarm over the prospect of a metastable bomb had him fully awake. He put on his AR glasses and reviewed the terrain around SNOPB, but much of the satellite footage was old and probably out of date. Ambrose was right: nobody was putting up satellites these days if they could help it.

Little had probably changed at the old factory, though, and it was a simple enough place. Planning where to park and learning where Building 242 *was* hadn't reduced his anxiety at all, so on impulse he switched his view to Mars. The sky changed from pure blue to butterscotch but otherwise the landscape looked disturbingly similar. There were a lot more rocks on Mars, and the dirt was red, but the emptiness, the slow rolling monotony of the plain and stillness were the same, as if he'd stepped into a photograph. (Well, he actually had, but he knew there would be no more motion in this scene were he there.) He commanded the viewpoint to move, and for a time strolled, alone, in Ambrose's footsteps—or rather, the ruts of Google's rover. Humans had done this in their dreams for thousands of years, yet Ambrose was right—this place was, in the end, no more real than those dreams.

Russia's cosmonauts had still been romantic idols when he was growing up. In photos they had stood with their heads high, minds afire with plans to stride over the hills of the moon and Mars. Gennady pictured them in the years after the Soviet Union's collapse, when they still had jobs, but no budget or destination any more. Where had their dreams taken them?

The Baikonur spaceport was south of here. In the end, they'd also had to settle for a hard bed in Kazakhstan.

In the morning they drove out to the old anthrax site in a rented Tata sedan. The fields around Stepnogorsk looked like they'd been glared at by God, except where bright blue dew-catcher fencing ran in rank after rank across the stubble. "What're those?" asked Ambrose, pointing; this was practically the first thing he'd said since breakfast.

In the rubble-strewn field that had once been SNOPB, several small windmills were twirling atop temporary masts.

Below them were some shipping-container sized boxes with big grills in their sides. The site looked healthier than the surrounding prairie; there were actual green trees in the distance. Of course, this area had been wetlands and there'd been a creek running behind SNOPB; maybe it was still here, which was a hopeful sign.

"Headquarters told me that some kind of climate research group is using the site," he told Ambrose as he pulled up and stopped the car. "But it's still public land."

"They built an anthrax factory less than five minutes outside of town?" Ambrose shook his head, whether in wonder or disgust, Gennady couldn't tell. They got out of the car, and Ambrose looked around in obvious disappointment. "Wow, it's gone." He seemed stunned by the vastness of the landscape. Only a few foundation walls now stuck up out of the cracked lots where the anthrax factory had once stood, except for where the big box machines sat whirring and humming. They were near where the bunkers had been and, with a frown of curiosity, Gennady strolled in that direction. Ambrose followed, muttering to himself, ". . . Last update must have been ten years ago." He had his glasses on, so he was probably comparing the current view to what he could see online.

According to Gennady's notes, the bunkers had been grass-covered buildings with two-meter thick walls, designed to withstand a nuclear blast. In the 1960s and 70s they'd contained ranks of cement vats where the anthrax was grown. Those had been cracked and filled in, and the heavy doors removed; but it would have been too much work to fill the bunkers in entirely. He poked his nose into the first in line—Building 241—and saw a flat stretch of water leading into darkness. "Excellent. This job just gets worse. We may be wading."

"But what are you looking for?"

"I—oh." As he rounded the mound of Building 242, a small clutch of hummers and trucks came into view. They'd been invisible from the road. There was still no sign of anybody, so he headed for Building 242. As he was walking down the crumbled ramp to the massive doors, he heard the unmistakable sound of a rifle-bolt being slipped. "Better not go in there," somebody said in Russian.

He looked carefully up and to his left. A young woman had come over the top of the mound. She was holding the rifle, and she had it aimed directly at Gennady.

"What are you doing here?" she said. She had a local accent.

"Exploring, is all," said Gennady. "We'd heard of the old anthrax factory, and thought we'd take a look at it. This *is* public land."

She swore, and Gennady heard footsteps behind him. Ambrose looked deeply frightened as two large men also carrying rifles, emerged from behind a plastic membrane that had been stretched across the bunker's doorway. Both men wore bright yellow fireman's masks, and had air tanks on their backs.

"When are your masters going to believe that we're doing what we say?" said the woman. "Come on." She gestured with her rifle for Gennady and Ambrose to walk down the ramp.

"We're dead, we're dead," whimpered Ambrose shivering.

"If you really must have your proof, then put these on." She nodded to the two men, who stripped off their masks and tanks and handed them to Gennady and Ambrose. They pushed past the plastic membrane and into the bunker.

The place was full of light: a crimson, blood-red radiance that made what was inside all the more bizarre.

"Oh shit," muttered Ambrose. "It's a grow-op."

The long, low space was filled from floor to ceiling with plants. Surrounding them on tall stands were hundreds of red LED lamp banks. In the lurid light, the plants appeared black. He squinted at the nearest, fully expecting to see a familiar, jagged-leaf profile. Instead—

"Tomatoes?"

"Two facts for you," said the woman, her voice muffled. She'd set down her rifle, and now held up two fingers. "One: we're not stepping on anybody else's toes here. We are *not* competing with you. And two: this bunker is designed to withstand a twenty kiloton blast. If you think you can muscle your way in here and take it over, you're sadly mistaken."

Gennady finally realized what they'd assumed. "We're not the mafia," he said. "We're just here to inspect the utilities."

She blinked at him, her features owlish behind the yellow frame of the mask. Ambrose rolled his eyes. "Oh God, what did you *say?*"

"American?" Puzzled, she lowered her rifle. In English, she said, "You spoke English."

"Ah," said Ambrose, "well—"

"He did," said Gennady, also in English. "We're not with the mafia, we're arms inspectors. I mean, I am. He's just along for the ride."

"Arms inspectors?" She guffawed, then looked around herself at the stolid Soviet bunker they were standing in. "What, you thought—"

"We didn't think anything. Can I lower my hands now?" She thought about it, then nodded. Gennady rolled his neck and indicated the ranked plants. "Nice setup. Tomatoes, soy, and those long tanks contain potatoes? But why in here, when you've got a thousand kilometres of steppe outside to plant this stuff?"

"We can control the atmosphere in here," she said. "That's why the masks: it's a high CO_2 environment in here. That's also why I stopped you in the first place; if you'd just strolled right in, you'd have dropped dead from asphyxia.

"This project's part of Minus Three," she continued. "Have you heard of us?" Both Ambrose and Gennady shook their heads.

"Well, you will." There was pride in her voice. "You see, right now humanity uses the equivalent of three Earth's worth of ecological resources. We're pioneering techniques to reduce that reliance by the same amount."

"Same amount? To *zero* Earths?" He didn't hide the incredulity in his voice.

"Eventually, yes. We steal most of what we need from the Earth in the form of ecosystem services. What we need is to figure out how to run a full-fledged industrial civilization as if there were no ecosystem services available to us at all. To live on Earth," she finished triumphantly, "as if we were living on Mars."

Ambrose jerked in visible surprise.

"That's fascinating," said Gennady. He hadn't been too nervous while they were pointing guns at him—he'd had that happen before, and in such moments his mind became wonderfully sharp—but now that he might actually be forced to have a conversation with these people, he found his mouth going quite dry. "You can tell me all about it after I've finished my measurements."

"You're kidding," she said.

"I'm not kidding at all. Your job may be saving the Earth next generation, but mine is saving it this week. And I take it very seriously. I've come here to inspect the original fittings of this building, but it looks like you destroyed them, no?"

"Not at all," she said. "Actually, we used what was here. This bunker's not like the other ones, you know they had these big cement tanks in them. I'd swear this one was set up exactly like this."

"Show me."

For the next half hour they climbed under the hydroponic tables, behind the makeshift junction boxes mounted near the old power shaft, and atop the sturdier lighting racks. Ambrose went outside, and came back to report that the shipping containers they'd seen were sophisticated CO_2 scrubbers. The big boxes sucked the gas right out of the atmosphere, and then pumped it through hoses into the bunker.

At last he and the woman climbed down, and Gennady shook his head. "The mystery only deepens," he said.

"I'm sorry we couldn't help you more," she said. "And apologies for pulling a gun on you. I'm Kyzdygoi," she added, thrusting out her hand for him to shake.

"Uh, that's a . . . pretty name," said Ambrose as he too shook her hand. "What's it mean?"

"It means 'stop giving birth to girls,' " said Kyzdygoi with a straight face. "My parents were old school."

Ambrose opened his mouth and closed it, his grin faltering.

"All right, well, good luck shrinking your Earths," Gennady told her as they strolled to the plastic-sheet-covered doorway.

As they drove back to Stepnogorsk, Ambrose leaned against the passenger door and looked at Gennady in silence. Finally he said, "You do this for a living?"

"Ah, it's unreliable. A paycheck here, a paycheck there . . ."

"No, really. What's this all about?"

Gennady eyed him. He probably owed the kid an explanation after getting guns drawn on him. "Have you ever heard of metastable explosives?"

"What? No. Wait . . ." He fumbled for his glasses.

"Never mind that." Gennady waved at the glasses. "Metastables are basically super-powerful chemical explosives. They're my new nightmare."

Ambrose jerked a thumb back at SNOPB. "I thought you were looking for germs."

"This isn't about germs, it's about hydrogen bombs." Ambrose looked blank. "A hydrogen bomb is a fusion device that's triggered by high compression and high temperature. Up 'til now, the only thing that could generate those kinds of conditions was an atomic bomb—a *plutonium* bomb, understand? Plutonium is really hard to refine, and it creates terrible fallout even if you only use a little of it as your fusion trigger."

"So?"

"So, metastable explosives are powerful enough to trigger hydrogen fusion without the plutonium. They completely sever the connection between nuclear weapons and nuclear industry, which means that once they exist, the good guys totally lose their ability to tell who has the bomb and who doesn't. *Anybody* who can get metastables and some tritium gas can build a hydrogen bomb, even some disgruntled loner in his garage.

"And somebody *is* building one."

Stepnogorsk was fast approaching. The town was mostly a collection of Soviet-era apartment blocks with broad prairie visible past them. Gennady swung them around a corner and they drove through Microdistrict 2 and past the disused Palace of Culture. Up ahead was their hotel . . . surrounded by the flashing lights of emergency vehicles.

"Oh," said Gennady. "A fire?"

"Pull over. Pull over!" Ambrose braced his hands against the Tata's low ceiling. Gennady shot him a look, but did as he'd asked.

"Shit. They've found me."

"Who? Those are police cars. I've been with you every minute since we got here, there's no way you could have gotten into any trouble." Gennady shook his head. "No, if it's anything to do with us, it's probably Kyzdygoi's people sending us a message."

"Yeah? Then who are those suits with the cops?"

Gennady thought about it. He could simply walk up to one of the cops and ask, but figured Ambrose would probably have a coronary if he did that.

"Well . . . there is one thing we can try. But it'll cost a lot."

"How much?"

Gennady eyed him. "All right, all right," said Ambrose. "What do we do?"

"You just watch." Gennady put on his glasses and stepped out of the car. As he did, he put through a call to London, where it was still early morning. "Hello? Lisaveta? It's Gennady. Hi! How are you?"

He'd brought a binocular attachment for the glasses, which he sometimes used for reading serial numbers on pipes or barrels from a distance. He clipped this on and began scanning the small knot of men who were standing around outside the hotel's front doors.

"Listen, Lisa, can I ask you to do something for me? I have some faces I need scanned . . . Not even remotely legal, I'm sure . . . No, I'm not in trouble! Would I be on the phone to you if I were in trouble? Just—okay. I'm good for it. Here come the images."

He relayed the feed from his glasses to Lisa in her flat in London.

"Who're you talking to?" asked Ambrose.

"Old friend. She got me out of Chernobyl intact when I had a little problem with a dragon—Lisa? Got it? Great. Call me back when you've done the analysis."

He pocketed the glasses and climbed back in the car. "Lisa has Interpol connections, and she's a fantastic hacker. She'll run facial recognition on it and hopefully tell us who those people are."

Ambrose cringed back in his seat. "So what do we do in the meantime?"

"We have lunch. How 'bout that French restaurant we passed? The one with the little Eiffel Tower?"

Despite the clear curbs everywhere, Gennady parked the car at the shopping mall and walked the three blocks to the La France. He didn't tell Ambrose why, but the American would figure it out: the Tata was traceable through its GPS. Luckily La France was open and they settled in for some decent crêpes. Gennady had a nice view of a line of trees west of the town boundary. Occasionally a car drove past.

Lisa pinged him as they were settling up. "Gennady? I got some hits for you."

"Really?" He hadn't expected her to turn up anything. Gennady's working assumption was that Ambrose was just being paranoid.

"Nothing off the cops; they must be local," she said. "But one guy—the old man—well, it's daft."

He sighed in disappointment, and Ambrose shot him a look. "Go ahead."

"His name is Alexei Egorov. He's premier of a virtual nation called the Soviet Union Online. They started from this project to digitize all the existing paper records of the Soviet era. Once those were online, Egorov and his people started some deep data-mining to construct a virtual Soviet, and then they started inviting the last die-hard Stalinists—or their kids—to join. It's a virtual country composed of bitter old men who're nostalgic for the purges. Daft."

"Thanks, Lisa. I'll wire you the fee."

He glowered at Ambrose. "Tell me about Soviet Union."

"I'm not supposed to—"

"Oh, come on. Who said that? Whoever they are, they're

on the far side of the planet right now, *and* they can't help you. They put you with me, but I can't help you either if I don't know what's going on."

Ambrose's lips thinned to a white line. He leaned forward. "It's big," he said.

"Can't be bigger than my metastables. Tell me: what did you see on Mars?"

Ambrose hesitated. Then he blurted, "A pyramid."

Silence.

"Really, a pyramid," Ambrose insisted. "Big sucker, gray, I think most of it was buried in the permafrost. It was the only thing sticking up for miles. This was on the Northern plains, where there's ice just under the surface. The whole area around it . . . well, it was like a frozen splash, if you know what I mean. Almost a crater."

This was just getting more and more disappointing. "And why is Soviet Union Online after you?"

"Because the pyramid had Russian writing on it. Just four letters, in red: CCCP."

The next silence went on for a while, and was punctuated only by the sound of other diners grumbling about local carbon prices.

"I leaked some photos before Google came after me with their non-disclosure agreements," Ambrose explained. "I guess the Soviets have internet search-bots constantly searching for certain things, and they picked up on my posts before Google was able to take them down. I got a couple of threatening phone calls from men with thick Slavic accents. Then they tried to kidnap me."

"No!"

Ambrose grimaced. "Well, they weren't very good at it. It was four guys, all of them must have been in their eighties, they tried to bundle me into a black van. I ran away and they just stood there yelling curses at me in Russian. One of them threw his cane at me." He rubbed his ankle.

"And you took them seriously?"

"I did when the FBI showed up and told me I had to pack up and go with them. That's when I ran to the U.N. I didn't believe that 'witness protection' crap the Feds tried to feed me. The U.N. people told me that the Soviets' data mining is actually really good. They keep turning up embarrassing and incriminating information about what people and governments got up to back in the days of the Cold War. They use what they know to influence people."

"That's bizarre." He thought about it. "Think they bought off the police here?"

"Or somebody. They want to know about the pyramid. But only Google, and the Feds, and I know where it is. And NASA's already patched that part of the Mars panoramas with fake data."

Disappointment had turned to a deep sense of surprise. For Gennady, being surprised usually meant that something awful was about to happen; so he said, "We need to get you out of town."

Ambrose brightened. "I have an idea. Let's go back to SNOPB. I looked up these Minus Three people: they're eco-radicals, but at least they don't seem to be lunatics."

"Hmmph. You just think Kyzdygoi's 'hot.' "

Ambrose grinned and shrugged.

"Okay. But we're not driving, because the car can be tracked. *You* walk there. It's only a few kilometres. I'll deal with the authorities and these 'Soviets,' and once I've sent them on their way we'll meet up. You've got my number."

Ambrose had evidently never taken a walk in the country before. After Gennady convinced him he would survive it, they parted outside La France, and Gennady watched him walk away, sneakers flapping. He shook his head and strolled back to the Tata.

Five men were waiting for him. Two were policemen, and three wore business attire. One of these was an old, bald man in a faded olive-green suit. He wore augmented reality glasses, and there was a discrete red pin on his lapel in the shape of the old Soviet flag.

Gennady made a show of pushing his own glasses back on his nose and walked forward, hand out. As the cops started to reach for their tasers, Gennady said, "Mr Egorov! Gennady Malianov, IAEA. You'll forgive me if I record and upload this conversation to headquarters?" He tapped the frame of his glasses and turned to the other suits. "I didn't catch your names?"

The suits frowned; the policemen hesitated; Egorov, however, put out his hand and Gennady shook it firmly. He could feel the old man's bones shift in his grip, but Egorov didn't grimace. Instead he said, "Where's your companion?"

"You mean that American? No idea. We shared a hotel room because it was cheaper, but then we parted ways this morning."

Egorov took his hand back, and pressed his bruised knuckles against his hip. "You've no idea where he is?"

"None."

"What're *you* doing here?" asked one of the cops.

"Inspecting SNOPB," he said. Gennady didn't have to fake his confidence here; he felt well armoured by his affiliation to Frankl's people. "My credentials are online, if there's some sort of issue here?"

"No issue," muttered Egorov. He turned away, and as he did a discrete icon lit up in the corner of Gennady's heads-up display. Egorov had sent him a text message.

He hadn't been massaging his hand on his flank; he'd been texting through his pants. Gennady had left the server in his glasses open, so it would have been easy for Egorov to ping it and find his address.

In among all the other odd occurrences of the past couple of days, this one didn't stand out. But as Gennady watched Egorov and his policemen retreat, he realized that his assumption that Egorov had been in charge might be wrong. Who were those other two suits?

He waited for Egorov's party to drive away, then got in the Tata and opened the email.

It said, *Mt tnght Pavin Inn, rstrnt wshrm. Cm aln.*

Gennady puzzled over those last two words for a while. Then he got it. "Come alone!" *Ah.* He should have known.

Shaking his head, he pulled out of the lot and headed back to the hotel to check out. After loading his bag, and Ambrose's, into the Tata, he hit the road back to SNOPB. Nobody followed him, but that meant nothing since they could track him through the car's transponder if they wanted. It hardly mattered; he was supposed to be inspecting the old anthrax factory, so where else would he be going?

Ambrose'd had enough time to get to SNOPB by now, but Gennady kept one eye on the fields next to the road just in case. He saw nobody, and fully expected to find the American waiting outside Building 242 as he pulled up.

As he stepped out of the Tata he nearly twisted his ankle in a deep rut. There were fresh tire tracks and shattered bits of old asphalt all over the place. He was sure he hadn't seen them this morning.

"Hello?" He walked down the ramp into the sudden dark of the bunker. Did he have the right building? It was completely dark here.

Wires drooled from overhead conduits; hydroponic trays lay jumbled in the corner, and strange-smelling liquids were pooled on the floor. Minus Three had pulled out, and in a hurry.

He cursed, but suppressed an urge to run back to the car. He had no idea where they'd gone, and they had a head-start on him. The main question was, had they left before or after Ambrose showed up?

The answer lay in the yellow grass near where Minus Three's vehicles had been parked that morning. Gennady knelt and picked up a familiar pair of augmented reality glasses. Ambrose would not have left these behind willingly.

Gennady swore, and now he did run to the Tata.

The restaurant at the Pavin Inn was made up to look like the interiors of a row of yurts. This gave diners some privacy as most of them had private little chambers under wood-ribbed ceilings; it also broke up the eye-lines to the place's front door, making it easy for Gennady to slip past the two men in suits who'd been with Egorov in the parking lot. He entered the men's room to find Egorov pacing in front of the urinal trough.

"What's this all about?" demanded Gennady—but Egorov made a shushing motion and grabbed a trash can. As he upended it under the bathroom's narrow window, he said, "First you must get me out of here."

"What? Why?"

Egorov tried to climb onto the upended can, but his knees failed him and finally Gennady relented and went to help him. As he boosted the old comrade, Egorov said, "I am a prisoner of these people! They work for the *Americans*." He practically spat the word. He perched precariously on the can and began tugging at the latch to the window. "They have seized our database! All the Soviet records . . . including what we know about the *Tsarina*."

Gennady coughed. Then he said, "I'll bring the car around."

He helped Egorov through the window and, after making sure no one was looking, left through the hotel's front door. Egorov's unmistakable silhouette was limping into the parking lot. Gennady followed him and, unlocking the Tata, said, "I've disabled the GPS tracking in this car. It's a rental; I'm going to drop it off in Semey, six hundred kilometres from here. Are you sure you're up to a drive like that?"

The old man's eyes glinted under yellow street light. "Never thought I'd get a chance to see the steppes again. Let's go!"

Gennady felt a ridiculous surge of adrenaline as they bumped out of the parking lot. Only two other cars were on the road, and endless blackness swallowed the landscape beyond the edge of town. It was a simple matter to swing onto the highway and leave Stepnogorsk behind—but it felt like a car chase.

"Ha ha!" Egorov craned his neck to look back at the dwindling town lights. "Semey, eh? You're going to Semipalatinsk, aren't you?"

"To look at the *Tsarina* site, yes. Whose side does that put me on?"

"Sides?" Egorov crossed his arms and glared out the windshield. "I don't know about sides."

"It was an honest question."

"I believe you. But I don't *know*. Except for *them*," he added, jabbing a thumb back at the town. "I know they're bad guys."

"Why? And why are they interested in Ambrose?"

"Same reason we are. Because of what he saw."

Gennady took a deep breath. "Okay. Why don't you just tell me what you know? And I'll do the same?"

"Yes, all right." The utter blackness of the night-time steppe had swallowed them; all that was visible was the double-cone of roadway visible in the car's headlamps. It barely changed, moment to moment, giving the drive a timelessness Gennady would, under other circumstances, have quite enjoyed.

"We data-mine records from the Soviet era," began Egorov. "To find out what really went on. It's lucrative business, and it supports the Union of Soviet Socialist Republics Online." He tapped his glasses.

"A few weeks ago, we got a request for some of the old data—from the Americans. Two requests, actually, a day apart: one from the search engine company, and the other from the government. We were naturally curious, so we didn't say no; but we did a little digging into the data ourselves. That is, we'd started to, when those men burst into our offices and confiscated the server. And the backup."

Gennady looked askance at him. "Really? Where was this?"

"Um. Seattle. That's where the CCCOP is based—only because we've been banned in the old country! Russia's run by robber barons today, they have no regard for the glory of—"

"Yes, yes. Did you find out what they were looking for?"

"Yes—which is how I ended up with these travel companions you saw. They are in the pay of the American CIA."

"Yes, but why? What does this have to do with the *Tsarina*?"

"I was hoping you could tell me. All we found was appropriations for strange things that should never have had anything to do with a nuclear test. Before the *Tsarina* was set off, there was about a year of heavy construction at the site. Sometimes, you know, they built fake towns to blow them up and examine the blast damage. That's what I thought at first; they ordered thousands of tonnes of concrete, rebar and asbestos, that sort of thing. But if you look at the records after the test, there's no sign of where any of that material *went*."

"They ordered some sort of agricultural crop from SNOPB," Gennady ventured. Egorov nodded.

"None of the discrepancies would ever have been noticed if not for your friend and whatever it is he found. What was it, anyway?"

A strange suspicion had begun to form in Gennady's mind, but it was so unlikely that he shook his head. "I want to look at the *Tsarina* site," he said. "Maybe that'll tell us."

Egorov was obviously unsatisfied with that answer, but he said nothing, merely muttering and trying to get himself comfortable in the Tata's bucket seat. After a while, just as the hum of the dark highway was starting to hypnotize Gennady, Egorov said, "It's all gone to Hell, you know."

"Hmm?"

"Russia. It was hard in the old days, but at least we had our pride." He turned to look out the black window. "After 1990, all the life just went out of the place. Lower birth-rate, men drinking themselves to death by the age of forty . . . no ambition, no hope. A lost land."

"You left?"

"Physically, yes." Egorov darted a look at Gennady. "You never *leave*. Not a place like this. For many years now, I've struggled with how to bring back Russia's old glory—our sense of *pride*. Yet the best I was ever able to come up with was an online environment. A *game*." He spat the word contemptuously.

Gennady didn't reply, but he knew how Egorov felt. Ukraine had some of the same problems—the lack of direction, the loss of confidence . . . It wasn't getting any better here. He thought of the blasted steppes they were passing through, rendered unlivable by global warming. There had been massive forest fires in Siberia this year, and the Gobi desert was expanding north and west, threatening the Kazaks even as the Caspian Sea dwindled to nothing.

He thought of SNOPB. "They're gone," he said, "but they left their trash behind." Toxic, decaying: nuclear submarines heeled over in the waters off Murmansk, nitrates soaking the soil around the launch pads of Baikonur. The ghosts of old Soviets prowled this dark, as radiation in the groundwater, mutations in the forest, poisons in the all-too-common dust clouds, Gennady had spent his whole adult life cleaning up the mess, and before yesterday he'd been able to tell himself that it was working—that all the worst nightmares were from the past. The metastables had changed that, in one stroke rendering all the old fears laughable in comparison.

"Get some sleep," he told Egorov. "We're going to be driving all night."

"I don't sleep much anymore." But the old man stopped talking, and just stared ahead. He couldn't be visiting his online People's Republic through his glasses: those IP addresses were blocked here. But maybe he saw it all anyway—the brave young men in their trucks, heading to the Semipalatinsk site to witness a nuclear blast. The rail yards where parts for the giant moon rocket, doomed to explode on the pad, were mustering . . . With his gaze fixed firmly on the past, he seemed the perfect opposite of Ambrose with his American dreams of a new world unburdened by history, whose red dunes marched to a pure and mysterious horizon.

The first living thing in space had been the Russian dog Laika. She had died in orbit—had never come home. If he glanced out at the star-speckled sky, Gennady could almost see her ghost racing eternally through the heavens, beside the dead dream of planetary conquest, of flags planted in alien soil and shining domes on the hills of Mars.

They arrived at the *Tsarina* site at 4:30. Dawn, at this latitude and time of year. The Semipalatinsk Polygon was bare, flat, blasted scrubland: Mars with tufts of dead weed. The irony was that it hadn't been the hundreds of nuclear bombs set off here that had killed the land; even a decade after the Polygon was closed, the low rolling hills had been covered with a rich carpet of waving grass. Instead, it was the savage turn of the climate, completely unpredicted by the KGB and the CIA, that had killed the steppe.

The road into the Polygon was narrow blacktop with no real shoulder, no ditches, and no oncoming traffic—although a set of lights had faded in and out of view in the rearview mirror all through the drive. Gennady would have missed the turnoff to the *Tsarina* site had his glasses not beeped.

There had been a low wire fence here at one time, but nobody had kept it up. He drove straight over the fallen gate, now becoming one with the soil, and up a low rise to the crest of the water-filled crater. There he parked and got out.

Egorov climbed out too and stretched cautiously. "Beautiful," he said, gazing into the epic sunrise. "Is it radioactive here?"

"Oh, a little . . . That's odd."

"What?"

Gennady had looked at the satellite view of the site on the way here; it was clear, standing here in person, that the vertical perspective had lied. "The *Tsarina* was supposed to be an underground test. You usually get some subsidence of the ground in a circle around the test site. And with the big ground shots, you would get a crater, like Lake Chagan." He nodded to the east. "But this . . . this is a *hole*."

Egorov spat into it. "It certainly is." The walls of the *Tsarina* crater were sheer and dropped a good fifty feet to black water. The "crater" wasn't round, either, but square, and not nearly big enough to be the result of a surface explosion. If he hadn't known it was the artefact of a bomb blast, Gennady would have sworn he was looking at a flooded quarry.

Gennady gathered his equipment and began combing the grass around the site. After a minute he found some twisted chunks of concrete and metal, and knelt to inspect them.

Egorov came up behind him. "What are you looking for?"

"Serial numbers." He found some old, grayed stencilling on a half-buried tank made of greenish metal. "You'll understand what I'm doing," he said as he pinched the arm of his glasses to take a snapshot. "I'm checking our database . . . Hmpf."

"What is it?" Egorov shifted from foot to foot. He was glancing around, as if afraid they might be interrupted.

"This piece came from the smaller of the installations here. The one the Americans called URDF-3."

"URDF?" Egorov blinked at him.

"Stands for 'Unidentified Research and Development Facility.' The stuff they built there scared the Yankees even more than the H-bomb . . ."

He stood up, frowning, and slowly turned to look at the entire site. "Something's been bothering me," he said as he walked to the very edge of the giant pit.

"What's that?" Egorov was hanging back.

"Ambrose told me he saw a pyramid on Mars. It said CCCP on its side. That was all; so he knew it was Russian, and so did Google and the CIA when they found out about it. And you, too. But that's all anybody knew. So who made the connection between the pyramid and the *Tsarina*?"

Egorov didn't reply. Gennady turned and found that the old man had drawn himself up very straight, and had levelled a small, nasty-looking pistol at him.

"You didn't follow us to Stepnogorsk," said Gennady. "You were already there."

"Take off your glasses," said Egorov. "Carefully, so I can be sure you're not snapping another picture."

As Gennady reached up to comply he felt the soft soil at the lip of the pit start to crumble. "Ah, can we—" Too late. He toppled backward, arms flailing.

He had an instant's choice: roll down the slope, or jump and hope he'd hit the water. He jumped.

The cold hit him so hard that at first he thought he'd been shot. Swearing and gasping, he surfaced, but when he spotted Egorov's silhouette at the crest of the pit, *he* dove again.

Morning sunlight was just tipping into the water. At first Gennady thought the wall of the pit was casting a dark shadow across the sediment below him. Gradually he realized the truth: there was no bottom to this shaft. At least, none within easy diving depth.

He swam to the opposite side; he couldn't stay down here, he'd freeze. Defeated, he flung himself out of the freezing water onto hard clay that was probably radioactive. Rolling over, he looked up.

Egorov stood on the lip of the pit. Next to him was a young woman with a rifle in her hands.

Gennady sat up. "Shit."

Kyzdygoi slung the rifle over her back, and clambered down the slope to the shore. As she picked her way over to Gennady she asked, "How much do you know?"

"Everything," he said between coughs. "I know everything. Where's Ambrose?"

"He's safe," she said. "He'll be fine." Then she waited, rifle cradled.

"You're here," he said reluctantly, "which tells me that Minus Three was funded by the Soviets. Your job was never to clean up the Earth—it was to design life support and agricultural systems for a Mars colony."

Her mouth twitched, but she didn't laugh. "How could we possibly get to Mars? The sky's a shooting gallery."

". . . And that would be a problem if you were going up there in a dinky little aluminium can, like cosmonauts always did." He stood up, joints creaking from the cold. He was starting to shiver deeply and it was hard to speak past his chattering teeth. "B-but if you rode a c-concrete bunker into orbit, you could ignore the shrapnel c-completely. In fact, that would be the only way you could d-do it."

"Come now. How could something like that ever get off the ground?"

"The same way the *Tsarina* d-did." He nodded at the dark surface of the flooded shaft. "The Americans had their P-project Orion. The Soviets had a similar program based at URDF-3. Both had discovered that an object could be just a few meters away from a nuclear explosion, and if it was made of the right materials it wouldn't be destroyed—it would be shot away like a bullet from a gun. The Americans designed a spaceship that would drop atomic bombs out the back and ride the explosions to orbit. But the *Tsarina* wasn't like that . . . it was just one bomb, and a d-deep shaft, and a pyramid-shaped spaceship to ride that explosion. A 'Verne gun.'"

"And who else knows this?"

He hesitated. "N-no one," he admitted. "I didn't know until I saw the shaft just now. The p-pyramid was fitted into the mouth of it, right about where we're s-standing. That's why this doesn't look like any other bomb crater on Earth."

"Let's go," she said, gesturing with the rifle. "You're turning blue."

"Y-you're not going t-to sh-shoot me?"

"There's no need," she said gently. "In a few days, the whole world will know what we've done."

Gennady finished taping aluminium foil to the trailer's window. Taking a push-pin from the cork board by the door, he carefully pricked a single tiny hole in the foil.

It was night, and crickets were chirping outside. Gennady wasn't tied up—in fact, he was perfectly free to leave—but on his way out the door Egorov had said, "I wouldn't go outside in the next hour or so. After that . . . well, wait for the dust to settle."

They'd driven him about fifty kilometres to the south and into an empty part of the Polygon. When Gennady had asked why this place, Egorov had laughed. "The Soviets set off their bombs here because this was the last empty place on Earth. It's still the last empty place, and that's why we're here."

There was nothing here but the withered steppe, a hundred or so trucks, vans and buses, and the cranes, tanks and pole-sheds of a temporary construction site. And, towering over the sheds, a gray concrete pyramid.

"A Verne gun fires its cargo into orbit in a single shot," Egorov had told Gennady. "It generates thousands of gravities worth of acceleration—enough to turn you into a smear on the floor. That's why the Soviets couldn't send any people; they hadn't figured out how to set off a controlled sequence of little bombs. The Americans never perfected that either. They didn't have the computational power to do the simulations.

"So they sent everything but the people. *Two hundred eighty thousand tonnes* in one shot, to Mars."

Bulldozers and cranes, fuel tanks, powdered cement, bags of seeds and food, space suits, even a complete, dismantled nuclear reactor: the *Tsarina* had included everything potential colonists might need on a new world. Its builders knew it had gone up, knew it had gotten to Mars; but they didn't know where it had landed, or whether it had landed intact.

A day after his visit to the *Tsarina* site, Gennady had sat outside this trailer with Egorov, Kyzdygoi and a few other officials of the new Soviet. They'd drunk a few beers and talked about the plan. "When our data-mining turned up the *Tsarina*'s manifest, it was like a light from heaven," Egorov had said, his hands opening eloquently in the firelight. "Suddenly we saw what was possible, how to revive our people—all the world's people—around a new hope, after all hope had gone. Something that would combine Apollo and Trinity into one event, and suddenly both would take on the meaning they always needed to have."

Egorov had started a crash program to build an Orion rocket. They couldn't get fissionable materials—Gennady and his people had locked those up tightly and for all time. But the metastables promised a different approach.

"We hoped the *Tsarina* was on Mars and intact, but we didn't know for sure, until Ambrose leaked his pictures."

The new *Tsarina* would use a series of small, clean fusion blasts to lift off and, at the far end, to land again. Thanks to Ambrose, they knew where the *Tsarina* was. It didn't matter that the Americans did too; nobody else had a plan to get there.

"And by the time they get their acts together, we'll have built a city," said Kyzdygoi. She was wide-eyed with the power of the idea. "Because we're not going there two at a time, like Noah in his Ark. We're *all* going." And she swung her arm to indicate the hundreds of campfires burning all around them, where thousands of men, women and children, handpicked from among the citizens of the Union of Soviet Socialist Republics Online, waited to amaze the world.

Gennady hunkered down in a little fort he'd built out of seat cushions, and waited.

It was like a camera flash, and a second later there was a second, then a third, and then the whole trailer bounced into the air and everything Gennady hadn't tied down went tumbling. The windows shattered and he landed on cushions and found himself staring across suddenly open air at the immolation of the building site.

The flickering flashes continued, coming from above now. The pyramid was gone, and the cranes and heavy machinery lay tumbled like a child's toys, all burning.

Flash. Flash.

It was really happening.

Flash. Flash. Flash . . .

Gradually, Gennady began to be able to hear again. He came to realize that monstrous thunder was rolling across the steppe, like a god's drumbeat in time with the flashes. It faded, as the flashes faded, until there was nothing but the ringing in his ears, and the orange flicker of flame from the launch site.

He staggered out to find perfect devastation. Once, this must once have been a common sight on the steppe; but his Geiger counter barely registered any radiation at all.

And in that, of course, lay a terrible irony. Egorov and his people had indeed divided history in two, but not in the way they'd imagined.

Gennady ran for the command trailer. He only had a few minutes before the air forces of half a dozen nations descended on this place. The trailer had survived the initial blast, so he scrounged until he found a jerry-can full of gasoline, and then he climbed in.

There they were: Egorov's servers. The EMP from the little nukes might have wiped its drives, but Gennady couldn't take the chance. He poured gasoline all over the computers, made a trail back to the door, then as the whole trailer went up behind him, ran to the leaning-but-intact metal shed where the metastables had been processed, and he did the same to it.

That afternoon, as he and Egorov were watching the orderly queue of people waiting to enter the *New Tsarina*, Gennady had made his final plea. "Your research into metastables,"

Gennady went on. "I need it. All of it, and the equipment and the backups; anything that might be used to reconstruct what you did."

"What happens to the Earth is no longer our concern," Egorov said with a frown. "Humanity made a mess here. It's not up to us to clean it up."

"But to destroy it all, you only need to be indifferent! And I'm asking, please, however much the world may have disappointed you, don't leave it like this." As he spoke, Gennady scanned the line of people for Ambrose, but couldn't see him. Nobody had said where the young American was.

Egorov had sighed in annoyance, then nodded sharply. "I'll have all the formulae and the equipment gathered together. It's all I have time for, now. You can do what you want with it."

Gennady watched the flames twist into the sky. He was exhausted, and the sky was full of contrails and gathering lights. He hadn't destroyed enough of the evidence; surely, someone would figure out what Egorov's people had done. And then . . . Shoulders slumped under the burden of that knowledge, he stalked into the darkness at the camp's perimeter.

His rented Tata sat where they'd left it when they first arrived here. After Kyzdygoi had confiscated his glasses at the *Tsarina* site, she'd put them in the Tata's glove compartment. They were still there.

Before Gennady put them on, he took a last unaided look at the burning campsite. Egorov and his people had escaped, but they'd left Gennady behind to clean up their mess. The metastables would be back. This new nightmare would get out into the world eventually, and when it did, the traditional specter of nuclear terrorism would look like a Halloween ghost in comparison. Could even the conquest of another world make up for that?

As the choppers settled in whipping spirals of dust, Gennady rolled up the Tata's window and put on his glasses. The *New Tsarina*'s EMP pulses hadn't killed them—they booted up right away. And, seconds after they did, a little flag told him there was an email waiting for him.

It was from Ambrose, and it read:

> *Gennady: sorry I didn't have time to say goodbye.*
> *I just wanted to say I was wrong. Anything's possible,*
> *even for me.*
> *P.S. My room's going to have a fantastic view.*

Gennady stared bitterly at the words. *Anything's possible . . .*

"For you, maybe," he said as soldiers piled out of the choppers.

"Not me."

Ragnarok

PAUL PARK

Paul Park lives with his wife, Deborah Brothers, and their children in North Adams, Massachusetts. He teaches at Williams College, where his mother and father also taught. He became prominent in SF in the late 1980s with the publication of his first three novels, The Starbridge Chronicles: Soldiers of Paradise *(1987),* Sugar Rain *(1989), and* The Cult of Loving Kindness *(1991). He went on to write a variety of challenging novels in and out of genre, and short stories collected in* If Lions Could Speak *(2002). His major project in the last decade has been the four-volume fantasy of an alternate world where magic works—*A Princess of Roumania *(2005) and its sequels,* The Tourmaline *(2006),* The White Tyger *(2007), and* The Hidden World *(2008). There was once in the 1980s a fine SF novel,* Winter's Daughter, *by Charles Whitmore, a postcatastrophe story told in the form of the Icelandic sagas. Perhaps this is the tradition into which the present story fits.*

"Ragnarok" was published at Tor.com, and this is perhaps its first appearance in print. It is a stanzaic narrative written in the style of the Icelandic saga, set in a post-apocalyptic future. We think it's a knockout.

There was a man, Magnus's son,
Ragni his name. In Reykjavik
Stands his office, six stories,
Far from the harbor in the fat past.
Birds nest there, now abandoned.
The sea washes along Vesturgata,
As they called it.

           In those days
Ragni's son, a rich man,
Also a scholar, skilled in law,
Thomas his name, took his wife
From famished Boston, far away.
Brave were her people, black-skinned,
Strong with spear, with shield courageous,
Long ago.

           Lately now

The world has stopped. It waits and turns.
Fire leaps along the hill.
Before these troubles, Thomas took her,
Black Naomi, belly big,
To Hvolsvollur where he had land,
A rich farm before the stream,
Safe and strong.

           In the starving years.
There was born, Thomas's son,
Eirik the African, as they called him.

Hard his heart, heavy his hand
Against the wretches in the ruined towns,
Bandits and skraelings beyond the wall,
Come to plunder, kill and spoil,
Over and over.
                    Every night,
Thomas stands watch, wakeful and sure,
Guarding the hall with his Glock Nine.
Forty men, farmers by day,
Cod-fishermen from the cold coast,
Pledge to shelter, shield from harm
What each man loves, alone, together
Through the winter.
                    When spring thaws
The small boughs, buds unpack
From the red earth. Eirik passes
Into the fields. The fire weeds
Move around him, arctic blooms
And purple bells. Below the ricks,
He finds Johanna, Johan's daughter,
Guests at the farm.
                    At his father's house
He'd sometimes seen her, slim and fair,
Ripening too, a tall primrose.
He draws her down with dark hands,
Meaning no harm, but honor only.
Rich is her father, in Reykjavik,
Rich is her cousin, with cod boats
In Smoke Harbor.
                    Happy then,
Proud Naomi offers her hall
For the wedding feast, but she's refused
For no reason. Rather instead
Johanna chooses the little church
At Karsnes, close to home,
South of the city along the shore.
High-breasted,
                    Snake-hearted,
Sick with pride, she predicts

No trouble. Near that place,
In Keflavik airport, cruel Jacobus
Gathers his men, gap-toothed Roma,
Thieves and Poles, pock-marked and starving.
The skraeling king calls for silence
In the shattered hall.

                Shards of glass,
Upturned cars, chunks of concrete
Make his throne. There he sits
With his hand high. "Hear me," he says
In the Roma language, learned from his father
In distant London. "Long we've fought
Against these killers. Ghosts of friends
Follow us here."

                Far to the east,
Black Eirik, in the same hour,
Walks by the water in Hvolsvollur.
By the larch tree and the lambing pens,
Thomas finds him, takes his sleeve,
Brings his gift, the Glock Nine
With precious bullets, powder and brimstone
From his store.

                Father and son
Talk together, until Naomi
Comes to find them. "Fools," she calls them.
(Though she loves them.) "Late last night
I lay awake. When do you go
To meet this woman, marry her
Beyond our wall? Why must you ride
To far Karsnes?"

                Cruel Jacobus,
Waits to answer, in Keflavik
Hand upraised. "These rich men
Goad us to act. Am I the last
To mourn my brother, mourn his murder?
The reckless weakling, Thomas Ragnisson,
Shot him down, shattered his skull
Outside the wall

           In Hvolsvollur,

With his Glock Nine. Now I hear
About this wedding. His black son
Scorning us, splits his strength,
Dares us to leave him alone in Karsnes
In the church. Christ Jesus
Punishes pride, pays them back
My brother's murder!"
                    At that moment
Black Naomi bows her head
Tries to agree. Eirik turns toward her,
Groping to comfort. "God will protect
The holy church. Hear me, mother,
Jesus will keep us, Johanna and me."
Then he strips the semi-automatic
From its sheath.
                    Some time later
Embracing her, he unbolts, unlocks
The steel door, draws its bars,
Rides north beneath the barrier,
Built of cinderblocks and barbed wire,
Twenty feet tall. With ten men
He takes the road toward Reykjavik,
West to Karsnes
                    On the cold sea.
There the pastor prepares the feast,
Lights the lamp in the long dusk.
In the chapel porch, pacing and ready
Eirik waits, wonders and waits.
Where's the bride, the wedding party?
Where's her father fat Johan?
No one knows.
                    Night comes.
Checking his watch, counting the hours,
Eirik frets. At first light
He rides north through the ruined towns,
Empty and burned, broken and looted.
Abandoned cars block his path.
The hill rises to Hallgrimskirkja
At the city's heart.

                    Here at the summit
Above the harbor, the high tower
Jabs the sky. Johan's hall,
Rich and secure, is silent now.
The dogs slink out the door,
Baring their teeth, biting at bones.
At Leif's statue we leave our horses,
Wait for something,
                         Sounds from the hall.
The concrete porch piles to heaven
The door's wrenched open, all is still.
No one shouts, issues a challenge
As we approach. Eirik the African
Draws his pistol. The danger's past.
No ones left. We know for certain
On the threshold.
                    There inside
Lies Thorgeir Grimsson, throat cut.
We find the others, one by one
Among the benches in their marriage clothes.
The bleached wool, black with blood,
Polished stones, stained with it.
Windows broken, birds fly
In the tall vault.
                    Eirik, distraught
Watches the birds wind above him,
Strives to find her, fair Johanna
Where she lies. Ladies and bridesmaids
Died in a heap, huddled together,
Peeled and butchered at the pillar's base.
She's not there; he searches farther
Up the aisle.
                    Underneath
The high altar, he uncovers
Fat Johan, father-in-law,
But for this. There's his body,
Leaked and maimed below the organ,
The wooden cross. Cruel Jacobus
Tortured and killed him, kidnapped his daughter

Twelve hours previous.
                        Proud Eirik
Turns to listen in the long light.
Out in the morning, his men call
Beyond the door. Desperate to leave
The stinking hall, holding his gun,
He finds them there. Fridmund, his friend,
Shows what they caught outside in the plaza,
A wretched skraeling
                        Skulking on Njalsgata,
A teen-aged boy, bald already
Back bent, black-toothed,
Hands outstretched. Stern and heavy
Eirik stands over him, offering nothing
But the gun's mouth. Meanwhile the boy
Lowers his head, laughs at his anger,
Spits out blood.
                        "I expect you know
All that happened. Here it was
That King Jacobus carried the girl,
Stole her away, struggling and screaming,
Kicking and cursing when he kissed her.
Now he's punished, proud Johan,
Who took this church, chased us away,
Made it his hall.
                        Who among us
Steals such a thing, thieves though we are,
Jesus' house, Hallgrimskirkja?
Now you threaten me, though I'm helpless,
With your Glock Nine. Go on, shoot me.
Cunt-mouth, coward—I dare you.
Jesus loves me. Laughing, I tell you.
Fuck you forever."
                        Fridmund Bjarnsson
Pulls back his head, bares his throat.
But the African offers a judgment.
"Murder's too kind. Cut him loose.
Let him crawl to his king, Jacobus the Gypsy.

If he touches her, tell him I'll kill him.
Bring him this message . . ."
                              But the skraeling
Spits on his boots. "Say it yourself,"
The boy scolds. "Better from you.
Besides, you'll see him sooner than me
If you ride home to Hvolsvollur!"
Furious now, fearing the worst,
Eirik Thomasson turns from him,
Shouts for his horse,
                              A shaggy gelding,
Stout and faithful. Sturla's his name.
Climbing up, calling the others,
Eirik sets off, out of the plaza,
Down the hill, Dark are his thoughts,
As he rides east, hurrying home
Under Hekla, the hooded mountain,
Steaming and boiling.
                              Sturla toils
Along the asphalt, eighty kilometers,
All that day. Dark is the sky
When Eirik and Sturla, outstripping the rest,
Reach the farm. The fire burns
Under the clouds. Clumps of ash
Fall around them. Furious and empty,
Eirik dismounts.
                              Without moving,
He stands a minute by Sturla's flank
And the split wall. Waiting, he listens
To the strife inside. Soon he unlimbers
The precious gun, the Glock Nine,
Checks the slide, checks the recoil,
Stacks the clip with steel bullets.
Gusts of rain
                              Gather around him.
Thunder crashes. Then he begins.
A storm out of nothing strikes the gate.
Men die among the horses,

Shot in the head with hollow-points,
Shot in the mouth for maximum damage.
They shake their spears, scythes and axes,
Swords and brands.
                    In the burning rooms,
Eirik kills them. By the cold stream,
The crumbling barns, he kills more.
Howling they turn in the hot cinders.
Clip empty, he cannot reload,
Seizes instead a skraeling axe.
They circle around him, certain of triumph,
Not for long.
                    Near the porch
Of his father's hall, he finds their leader,
Pawel the Bull, a Polack giant.
Stripped to the waist, he stands his ground.
Sword in hand, he swears and bellows.
Tattooed and painted, he paws the mud.
Now he charges, cuts and falters,
Falls to his knees,
                    Face split,
Lies full-length. Lightning strikes
On Hekla's side. Howling with rage,
The skraelings escape, scatter in darkness.
Come too late, we can't catch them,
Let them go. Gathering hoses,
We pump water, wet the timbers
In the rain.
                    Or we roam
Among the dead, drag them out
From the burned hall. Here they lie
On the wet ground, wives and children,
Old men. Naomi stands
Among the living, leans away,
Turns her face. Thomas is there,
Blood spilled,
                    Body broken,
With the others. Eirik lays him
By the fire. Fridmund Bjarnsson

Finds the gun, the Glock Nine
Buried in mud, by the stream.
"Here," he says, holding it up.
"I was scared the skraelings took it.
Thank Jesus—"
        There by the fire,
Eirik rebukes him. "Bullshit," he says.
"Close your mouth." He climbs the porch,
Raises his hands. Red are the doorposts,
The frame behind him, hot with sparks.
"God," he repeats, "God be thanked.
You know Johan, for Jesus' sake,
Took for his house
        Hallgrimskirkja,
On the hill. He thought Jesus
Could sustain him, could preserve him,
Save his daughter—don't you see?
I also, Eirik the African,
Sunk my faith in something empty—
Thomas's gun, the Glock Nine,
Chrome barreled,
        Bone grip.
But look now. Neither Jesus
Nor my Glock is good enough.
The rich hide behind their walls
In Hvolsvollur. Who comes to help?
But I will hike to Hekla's top,
Hurl my gun, heave it down
Into the steam,
        And the steel bullets
After it. In the afternoon
I'll wreck this wall, winch it apart.
Safety is good, grain in the fields,
Green-house vegetables; vengeance is better.
This I tell you: Time was,
We were happy, here in Iceland.
Cod in the sea,
        Snow on the mountain,
Hot water in every house,

Cash in our pockets, planes and cars,
The world outside, waiting and close.
Old men remember, mumble and mutter—
That time's gone, turned forever.
The pools are drained, dams breached,
Turbines wrecked,
                    Ruined engines
Starved for oil. The sea rises
Beyond Selfoss. You have seen
Thousands die, tens of thousands—
The mind rebels, breaks or bends.
Days ahead, the dim past,
Forward, backward, both the same,
Wound together.
                    At the world's end,
Jormungand, the great worm,
Holds his tail between his jaws.
Ragnarok rages around us
Here, tonight, now, forever,
Or long ago. Good friends,
Remember it: men and skraelings
Fought together
                    Ages past.
So—tomorrow we'll march west
To Keflavik. Jacobus waits.
We'll scour the coast, search for fighters,
Heroes to help us, guide us home.
Left behind, you'll learn of us,
Tell our legend, teach the truth
Or invent it
                    The old way.
Parse our lines upon the page:
Two beats, then pause.
Two more. Thumping heart,
Chopping axe, and again.
Not like the skraelings, with their long lines
Of clap-trap, closing rhymes—
Not for us.

No more.
Johanna's alive. How I know,
I don't know. Don't ask.
But I swear I'll bring her here,
Avenge this." Then he's silent,
Standing near the spitting fire,
Under Hekla, in the rain.

Six Months, Three Days

CHARLIE JANE ANDERS

Charlie Jane Anders (charliejane.com) lives in San Francisco. Anders's stories have appeared in The McSweeney's Joke Book of Book Jokes, Strange Horizons, ZYZZYVA, *and* Lady Churchill's Rosebud Wristlet. *She's an editor with io9.com, and the organizer of Writers With Drinks, a monthly San Francisco reading series that's been going since 2001. She won the Emperor Norton Award for "extraordinary invention and creativity unhindered by the constraints of paltry reason."*

"Six Months, Three Days" was published by Tor.com, *and this is perhaps its first appearance in print. It is a love story about two clairvoyants whose abilities are otherwise radically different. Doug and Judy both see the future, but Doug sees it as fixed and Judy as branching possibilities. Their relationship becomes a contest between visions of the future as determined or as indeterminate.*

The man who can see the future has a date with the woman who can see many possible futures.

Judy is nervous but excited, keeps looking at things she's spotted out of the corner of her eye. She's wearing a floral Laura Ashley style dress with an Ankh necklace and her legs are rambunctious, her calves moving under the table. It's distracting because Doug knows that in two and a half weeks, those cucumber-smooth ankles will be hooked on his shoulders, and that curly reddish-brown hair will spill everywhere onto her lemon-floral pillows; this image of their future coitus has been in Doug's head for years, with varying degrees of clarity, and now it's almost here. The knowledge makes Doug almost giggle at the wrong moment, but then it hits him: she's seen this future too—or she may have, anyway.

Doug has his sandy hair cut in a neat fringe that was almost fashionable a couple years ago. You might think he cuts his own hair, but Judy knows he doesn't, because he'll tell her otherwise in a few weeks. He's much, much better looking than she thought he would be, and this comes as a huge relief. He has rude, pouty lips and an upper lip that darkens no matter how often he shaves it, with Elvis Costello glasses. And he's almost a foot taller than her, six foot four. Now that Judy's seen Doug for real, she's re-imagining all the conversations they might be having in the coming weeks and months, all of the drama and all of the sweetness. The fact that Judy can be attracted to him, knowing everything that could lay ahead, consoles her tremendously.

lie

Judy is nattering about some Chinese novelist she's been reading in translation, one of those cruel satirists from the days after the May Fourth Movement, from back when writers were so conflicted they had to rename themselves things like "Contra Diction." Doug is just staring at her, not saying anything, until it creeps her out a little.

"What?" Doug says at last, because Judy has stopped talking and they're both just staring at each other.

"You were staring at me," Judy says.

"I was . . ." Doug hesitates, then just comes out and says it. "I was savoring the moment. You know, you can know something's coming from a long way off, you know for years ahead of time the exact day and the very hour when it'll arrive. And then it arrives, and when it arrives, all you can think about is how soon it'll be gone."

"Well, I didn't know the hour and the day when you and I would meet," Judy puts a hand on his. "I saw many different hours and days. In one timeline, we would have met two years ago. In another, we'd meet a few months from now. There are plenty of timelines where we never meet at all."

Doug laughs, then waves a hand to show that he's not laughing at her, although the gesture doesn't really clarify whom or what he's actually laughing at.

Judy is drinking a cocktail called the Coalminer's Daughter, made out of ten kinds of darkness. It overwhelms her senses with sugary pungency, and leaves her lips black for a moment. Doug is drinking a wheaty Pilsner from a tapered glass, in gulps. After one of them, Doug cuts to the chase. "So this is the part where I ask. I mean, I know what happens next between you and me. But here's where I ask what you think happens next."

"Well," Judy says. "There are a million tracks, you know. It's like raindrops falling into a cistern, they're separate until they hit the surface, and then they become the past: all undifferentiated. But there are an awful lot of futures where you and I date for about six months."

"Six months and three days," Doug says. "Not that I've counted or anything."

"And it ends badly."

"I break my leg."

"You break your leg ruining my bicycle. I like that bike. It's a noble five-speed in a sea of fixies."

"So you agree with me." Doug has been leaning forward, staring at Judy like a psycho again. He leans back so that the amber light spilling out of the Radish Saloon's tiny lampshades turns him the same color as his beer. "You see the same future I do." Like she's passed some kind of test.

"You didn't know what I was going to say in advance?" Judy says.

"It doesn't work like that—not for me, anyway. Remembering the future is just like remembering the past. I don't have perfect recall, I don't hang on to every detail, the transition from short-term memory to long-term memory is not always graceful."

"I guess it's like memory for me too," Judy says.

Doug feels an unfamiliar sensation, and he realizes after a while it's comfort. He's never felt this at home with another human being, especially after such a short time. Doug is accustomed to meeting people and knowing bits and pieces of their futures, from stuff he'll learn later. Or if Doug meets you and doesn't know anything about your future, that means he'll never give a crap about you, at any point down the line. This makes for awkward social interactions, either way.

They get another round of drinks. Doug gets the same beer again, Judy gets a red concoction called a Bloody Mutiny.

"So there's one thing I don't get," Doug says. "You believe you have a choice among futures—and I think you're wrong, you're seeing one true future and a bunch of false ones."

"You're probably going to spend the next six months trying to convince yourself of that," Judy says.

"So why are you dating me at all, if you get to choose? You know how it'll turn out. For that matter, why aren't you rich and famous? Why not pick a future where you win the lottery, or become a star?"

Doug works in tech support, in a poorly ventilated subbasement of a tech company in Providence, RI, that he knows will go out of business in a couple years. He will work there until the company fails, choking on the fumes from old computers, and then be unemployed a few months.

"Well," Judy says. "It's not really that simple. I mean, the next six months, assuming I don't change my mind, they contain some of the happiest moments of my life, and I see it leading to some good things, later on. And you know, I've seen some tracks where I get rich, I become a public figure, and they never end well. I've got my eye on this one future, this one node way off in the distance, where I die aged 97, surrounded by lovers and grandchildren and cats. Whenever I have a big decision to make, I try to see the straightest path to that moment."

"So I'm a stepping stone," Doug says, not at all bitterly. He's somehow finished his second beer already, even though Judy's barely made a dent in her Bloody Mutiny.

"You're maybe going to take this journey with me for a spell," Judy says. "People aren't stones."

And then Doug has to catch the last train back to Providence, and Judy has to bike home to Somerville. Marva, her roommate, has made popcorn and hot chocolate, and wants to know the whole story.

"It was nice," Judy says. "He was a lot cuter in person than I'd remembered, which is really nice. He's tall."

"That's it?" Marva said. "Oh come on, details. You finally meet the only other freaking clairvoyant on Earth, your future boyfriend, and all you have to say is, 'He's tall.' Uh uh. You are going to spill like a fucking oil tanker, I will ply you with hot chocolate, I may resort to Jim Beam, even."

Marva's "real" name is Martha, but she changed it years ago. She's a grad student studying 18th century lit, and even Judy can't help her decide whether to finish her PhD. She's slightly chubby, with perfect crimson hair and clothing by Sanrio, Torrid, and Hot Topic. She is fond of calling herself "malternative."

"I'm drunk enough already. I nearly fell off my bicycle a couple times," Judy says.

The living room is a pigsty, so they sit in Judy's room,

which isn't much better. Judy hoards items she might need in one of the futures she's witnessed, and they cover every surface. There's a plastic replica of a Filipino fast food mascot, Jollibee, which she might give to this one girl Sukey in a couple of years, completing Sukey's collection and making her a friend for life—or Judy and Sukey may never meet at all. A phalanx of stuffed animals crowds Judy and Marva on the big fluffy bed. The room smells like a sachet of whoopass (cardamom, cinnamon, lavender) that Judy opened up earlier.

"He's a really sweet guy." Judy cannot stop talking in platitudes, which bothers her. "I mean, he's really lost, but he manages to be brave. I can't imagine what it would be like, to feel like you have no free will at all."

Marva doesn't point out the obvious thing—that Judy only sees choices for herself, not anybody else. Suppose a guy named Rocky asks Marva out on a date, and Judy sees a future in which Marva complains, afterwards, that their date was the worst evening of her life. In that case, there are two futures: One in which Judy tells Marva what she sees, and one in which she doesn't. Marva will go on the miserable date with Rocky, unless Judy tells her what she knows. (On the plus side, in fifteen months, Judy will drag Marva out to a party where she meets the love of her life. So there's that.)

"Doug's right," Marva says. "I mean, if you really have a choice about this, you shouldn't go through with it. You know it's going to be a disaster, in the end. You're the one person on Earth who can avoid the pain, and you still go sticking fingers in the socket."

"Yeah, but . . ." Judy decides this will go a lot easier if there are marshmallows in the cocoa, and runs back to the kitchen alcove. "But going out with this guy leads to good things later on. And there's a realization that I come to as a result of getting my heart broken. I come to understand something."

"And what's that?"

Judy finds the bag of marshmallows. They are stale. She

decides cocoa will revitalize them, drags them back to her bedroom, along with a glass of water.

"I have no idea, honestly. That's the way with epiphanies: You can't know in advance what they'll be. Even me. I can see them coming, but I can't understand something until I understand it."

"So you're saying that the future that Doug believes is the only possible future just happens to be the best of all worlds. Is this some Leibniz shit? Does Dougie always automatically see the nicest future or something?"

"I don't think so." Judy gets gummed up by popcorn, marshmallows and sticky cocoa, and coughs her lungs out. She swigs the glass of water she brought for just this moment. "I mean—" She coughs again, and downs the rest of the water. "I mean, in Doug's version, he's only 43 when he dies, and he's pretty broken by then. His last few years are dreadful. He tells me all about it in a few weeks."

"Wow," Marva says. "Damn. So are you going to try and save him? Is that what's going on here?"

"I honestly do not know. I'll keep you posted."

Doug, meanwhile, is sitting on his militarily neat bed, with its single hospital-cornered blanket and pillow. His apartment is almost pathologically tidy. Doug stares at his one shelf of books and his handful of carefully chosen items that play a role in his future. He chews his thumb. For the first time in years, Doug desperately wishes he had options.

He almost grabs his phone, to call Judy and tell her to get the hell away from him, because he will collapse all of her branching pathways into a dark tunnel, once and for all. But he knows he won't tell her that, and even if he did, she wouldn't listen. He doesn't love her, but he knows he will in a couple weeks, and it already hurts.

"God damnit! Fucking god fucking damn it fuck!" Doug throws his favorite porcelain bust of Wonder Woman on the floor and it shatters. Wonder Woman's head breaks into two jagged pieces, cleaving her magic tiara in half. This image, of the Amazon's raggedly bisected head, has always been in Doug's mind, whenever he's looked at the intact bust.

Doug sits a minute, dry-sobbing. Then he goes and gets his dustpan and brush.

He phones Judy a few days later. "Hey, so do you want to hang out again on Friday?"

"Sure," Judy says. "I can come down to Providence this time. Where do you want to meet up?"

"Surprise me," says Doug.

"You're a funny man."

Judy will be the second long-term relationship of Doug's life. His first was with Pamela, an artist he met in college, who made headless figurines of people who were recognizable from the neck down. (Headless Superman. Headless Captain Kirk. And yes, headless Wonder Woman, which Doug always found bitterly amusing for reasons he couldn't explain.) They were together nearly five years, and Doug never told her his secret. Which meant a lot of pretending to be surprised at stuff. Doug is used to people thinking he's kind of a weirdo.

Doug and Judy meet for dinner at one of those mom-and-pop Portuguese places in East Providence, sharing grilled squid and seared cod, with fragrant rice, with a bottle of heady vinho verde. Then they walk Judy's bike back across the river towards the kinda-sorta gay bar on Wickenden Street. "The thing I like about Providence," says Doug, "is it's one of the American cities that knows its best days are behind it. So it's automatically decadent, and sort of European."

"Well," says Judy, "it's always a choice between urban decay or gentrification, right? I mean, cities aren't capable of homeostasis."

"Do you know what I'm thinking?" Doug is thinking he wants to kiss Judy. She leans up and kisses him first, on the bridge in the middle of the East Bay Bicycle Path. They stand and watch the freeway lights reflected on the water, holding hands. Everything is cold and lovely and the air smells rich.

Doug turns and looks into Judy's face, which the bridge lights have turned yellow. "I've been waiting for this moment all my life." Doug realizes he's inadvertently quoted Phil Collins. First he's mortified, then he starts laughing like a maniac. For the next half hour, Doug and Judy speak only in Phil Collins quotes.

"You can't hurry love," Judy says, which is only technically a Collins line.

Over microbrews on Wickenden, they swap origin stories, even though they already know most of it. Judy's is pretty simple: She was a little kid who overthought choices like which summer camp to go to, until she realized she could see how either decision would turn out. She still flinches when she remembers how she almost gave a valentine in third grade to Dick Petersen, who would have destroyed her. Doug's story is a lot worse: he started seeing the steps ahead, a little at a time, and then he realized his dad would die in about a year. He tried everything he could think of, for a whole year, to save his dad's life. He even buried the car keys two feet deep, on the day of his dad's accident. No fucking use.

"Turns out getting to mourn in advance doesn't make the mourning afterwards any less hard," Doug says through a beer glass snout.

"Oh man," Judy says. She knew this stuff, but hearing it is different. "I'm so sorry."

"It's okay," Doug says. "It was a long time ago."

Soon it's almost time for Judy to bike back to the train station, near that godawful giant mall and the canal where they light the water on fire sometimes.

"I want you to try and do something for me," Judy takes Doug's hands. "Can you try to break out of the script? Not the big stuff that you think is going to happen, but just little things that you couldn't be sure about in advance if you tried. Try to surprise yourself. And maybe all those little deviations will add up to something bigger."

"I don't think it would make any difference," Doug says.

"You never know," Judy says. "There are things that I remember differently every time I think about them. Things from the past, I mean. When I was in college, I went through a phase of hating my parents, and I remembered all this stuff they did, from my childhood, as borderline abusive. And then a few years ago, I found myself recalling those same incidents again, only now they seemed totally different. Barely the same events."

"The brain is weird," Doug says.

"So you never know," Judy says. "Change the details, you may change the big picture." But she already knows nothing will come of this.

A week later, Doug and Judy lay together in her bed, after having sex for the first time. It was even better than the image Doug's carried in his head since puberty. For the first time, Doug understands why people talk about sex as this transcendent thing, chains of selfhood melting away, endless abundance. They looked into each other's eyes the whole time. As for Judy, she's having that oxytocin thing she's always thought was a myth, her forehead resting on Doug's smooth chest—if she moved her head an inch she'd hear his heart beating, but she doesn't need to.

Judy gets up to pee an hour later, and when she comes back and hangs up her robe, Doug is lying there with a look of horror on his face. "What's wrong?" She doesn't want to ask, but she does anyway.

"I'm sorry." He sits up. "I'm just so happy, and . . . I can count the awesome moments in my life on a hand and a half. And I'm burning through them too fast. This is just so perfect right now. And, you know. I'm trying not to think. About."

Judy knows that if she brings up the topic they've been avoiding, they will have an unpleasant conversation. But she has to. "You have to stop this. It's obvious you can do what I do, you can see more than one branch. All you have to do is try. I know you were hurt when you were little, your dad died, and you convinced yourself that you were helpless. I'm sorry about that. But now, I feel like you're actually comfortable being trapped. You don't even try any more."

"I do." Doug is shaking. "I do try. I try every day. How dare you say I don't try."

"You don't really. I don't believe you. I'm sorry, but I don't."

"You know it's true." Doug calms down and looks Judy square in the face. Without his glasses, his eyes look as gray as the sea on a cloudy day. "The thing you told me about

Marva—you always know what she's going to do. Yeah? That's how your power works. The only reason you can predict how your own choices will turn out, is because other people's actions are fixed. If you go up to some random guy on the street and slap him, you can know in advance exactly how he'll react. Right?"

"Well sure," Judy says. "I mean, that doesn't mean Marva doesn't have free will. Or this person I've hypothetically slapped." This is too weird a conversation to be having naked. She goes and puts on a Mountain Goats T-shirt and PJ bottoms. "Their choices are just factored in, in advance."

"Right." Doug's point is already made, but he goes ahead and lunges for the kill. "So how do you know that I can't predict your choices, exactly the same way you can predict Marva's?"

Judy sits down on the edge of the bed. She kneads the edge of her T-shirt and doesn't look at Doug. Now she knows why Doug looked so sick when she came back from the bathroom. He saw more of this conversation than she did. "You could be right," she says after a moment. "If you're right, that makes you the one person I should never be in the same room with. I should stay the hell away from you."

"Yeah. You should," Doug says. He knows it will take forty-seven seconds before she cradles his head and kisses his forehead, and it feels like forever. He holds his breath and counts down.

A couple days later, Judy calls in sick at the arts nonprofit where she works, and wanders Davis Square until she winds up in the back of the Diesel Café, in one of the plush leather booths near the pool tables. She eats one of those mint brownies that's like chocolate-covered toothpaste and drinks a lime rickey, until she feels pleasantly ill. She pulls a battered, scotch-taped World Atlas out of her satchel.

She's still leafing through it a couple hours later when Marva comes and sits down opposite her.

"How did you know I was here?" Judy asks.

"Because you're utterly predictable. You said you were ditching work, and this is where you come to brood."

Judy's been single-handedly keeping the Blaze Foundation afloat for years, thanks to an uncanny knack for knowing exactly which grants to apply for and when, and what language to use on the grant proposal. She has a nearly 100 percent success rate in proposal-writing, leavened only by the fact that she occasionally applies for grants she knows she won't get. So maybe she's entitled to a sick day every now and then.

Marva sees that Judy's playing the Travel Game and joins in. She points to a spot near Madrid. "Spain," she says.

Judy's face gets all tight for a moment, like she's trying to remember where she left something. Then she smiles. "Okay, if I get on a plane to Madrid tomorrow, there are a few ways it plays out. That I can see right now. In one, I get drunk and fall off a tower and break both legs. In another, I meet this cute guy named Pedro and we have a torrid three-day affair. Then there's the one where I go to art school and study sculpture. They all end with me running out of money and coming back home."

"Malawi," Marva says. Judy thinks for a moment, then remembers what happens if she goes to Malawi tomorrow.

"This isn't as much fun as usual," Marva says after they've gone to Vancouver and Paris and Sao Paolo. "Your heart isn't in it."

"It's not," Judy says. "I just can't see a happy future where I don't date Doug. I mean, I like Doug, I may even be in love with him already, but . . . we're going to break each other's hearts, and more than that: We're maybe going to break each other's *spirits*. There's got to be a detour, a way to avoid this, but I just can't see it right now."

Marva dumps a glass of water on Judy's head.

"Wha? You—Wha?" She splutters like a cartoon duck.

"Didn't see that coming, did you?"

"No, but that doesn't mean . . . I mean, I'm not freaking omniscient, I sometimes miss bits and pieces, you know that."

"I am going to give you the Samuel Johnson/Bishop Berkeley lecture, for like the tenth time," Marva says. "Because sometimes, a girl just needs a little Johnson."

Bishop George Berkeley, of course, was the "if a tree falls in the forest and nobody hears it, does it make a sound" guy, who argued that objects only exist in our perceptions. One day, Boswell asked Samuel Johnson what he thought of Berkeley's idea. According to Boswell, Johnson's response to this was to kick a big rock "with mighty force," saying, "I refute it thus."

"The point," says Marva, "is that nobody can see everything. Not you, not Doug, not Bishop Berkeley. Stuff exists that your senses can't perceive and your mind can't comprehend. Even if you do have an extra sense the rest of us don't have. Okay? So don't get all doom and gloom on me. Just remember: Would Samuel Johnson have let himself feel trapped in a dead-end relationship?"

"Well, considering he apparently dated a guy named Boswell who went around writing down everything he said . . . I really don't know." Judy runs to the bathroom to put her head under the hot-air dryer.

The next few weeks, Judy and Doug hang out at least every other day and grow accustomed to kissing and holding hands all the time, trading novelty for the delight of positive reinforcement. They're at the point where their cardiovascular systems crank into top gear if one of them sees someone on the street who even looks, for a second, like the other. Doug notices little things about Judy that catch him off guard, like the way she rolls her eyes slightly before she's about to say something solemn. Judy realizes that Doug's joking on some level, most of the time, even when he seems tragic. Maybe especially then.

They fly a big dragon kite on Cambridge Common, with a crimson tail. They go to the Isabella Stewart Gardner, and sip tea in the courtyard. Once or twice, Doug is about to turn left, but Judy stops him, because something way cooler will happen if they go right instead. They discuss which kind of skylight Batman prefers to burst through when he breaks into criminals' lairs, and whether Batman ever uses the chimney like Santa Claus. They break down the taxonomy of novels where Emily Dickinson solves murder mysteries.

Marva gets used to eating Doug's spicy omelettes, which automatically makes him Judy's best-ever boyfriend in Marva's book. Marva walks out of her bedroom in the mornings, to see Doug wearing the bathrobe Judy got for him, flipping a perfect yellow slug over and over, and she's like, What *are* you? To Marva, the main advantage of making an omelette is that when it falls apart halfway through, you can always claim you planned to make a scramble all along.

Judy and Doug enjoy a couple months of relative bliss, based on not ever discussing the future. In the back of her mind, Judy never stops looking for the break point, the moment where a timeline splits off from the one Doug believes in. It could be just a split-second.

They reach their three-month anniversary, roughly the midpoint of their relationship. To celebrate, they take a weekend trip to New York together, and they wander down Broadway and all around the Village and Soho. Doug is all excited, showing off for once—he points out the fancy restaurant where the President will be assassinated in 2027, and the courthouse where Lady Gaga gets arrested for civil disobedience right after she wins the Nobel Peace Prize. Judy has to keep shushing him. Then she gives in, and the two of them loudly debate whether the election of 2024 will be rigged, not caring if people stare.

Once they've broken the taboo on talking about the future in general, Doug suddenly feels free to talk about their future, specifically. They're having a romantic dinner at one of those restaurant/bars, with high-end American food and weird pseudo-Soviet iconography everywhere. Doug is on his second beer when he says, "So, I guess in a couple of weeks, you and I have that ginormous fight about whether I should meet your parents. And about a week after that, I manage to offend Marva. Honestly, without meaning to. But then again, in a month and a half's time, we have that really nice day together on the boat."

"Please don't," Judy says, but she already knows it's too late to stop it.

"And then after that, there's the Conversation. I am not looking forward to the Conversation."

"We both know about this stuff," Judy says. "It'll happen if and when it happens, why worry about it until then?"

"Sorry, it's just part of how I deal with things. It helps me to brace myself."

Judy barely eats her entrée. Doug keeps oversharing about their next few months, like a floodgate has broken. Some of it's stuff Judy either didn't remember, or has blotted out of her mind because it's so dismal. She can tell Doug's been obsessing about every moment of the coming drama, visualizing every incident until it snaps into perfect focus.

By the time Judy gets up and walks away from the table, she sees it all just as clearly as he does. She can't even imagine any future, other than the one he's described. Doug's won.

Judy roams Bleecker and St. Mark's Place, until she claims a small victory: She realizes that if she goes into this one little subterranean bar, she'll run into a cute guy she hasn't seen since high school, and they'll have a conversation in which he confesses that he always had a crush on her back then. Because Doug's not there, he's not able to tell her whether she goes into that bar or not. She does, and she's late getting back to their hotel, even though she and cute high-school guy don't do anything but talk.

Doug makes an effort to be nice the rest of the weekend, even though he knows it won't do him any good, except that Judy holds hands with him on the train back to Providence and Boston.

And then Doug mentions, in passing, that he'll see Judy around, after they break up—including two meetings a decade from now, and one time a full 15 years hence, and he knows some stuff. He starts to say more, but Judy runs to the dining car, covering her ears.

When the train reaches Doug's stop and he's gathering up his stuff, Judy touches his shoulder. "Listen, I don't know if you and I actually do meet up in a decade, it's a blur to me right now. But I don't want to hear whatever you think you know. Okay?" Doug nods.

When the fight over whether Doug should meet Judy's parents arrives, it's sort of a meta-fight. Judy doesn't see why Doug should do the big parental visit, since Judy and Doug are scheduled to break up in ten weeks. Doug just wants to meet them because he wants to meet them—maybe because his own parents are dead. And he's curious about these people who are aware that their daughter can see the future(s). They compromise, as expected: Doug meets Judy's parents over lunch when they visit, and he's on his best behavior.

They take a ferry out to sea, toward Block Island. The air is too cold and they feel seasick and the sun blinds them, and it's one of the greatest days of their lives. They huddle together on deck and when they can see past the glare and the sea spray and they're not almost hurling, they see the glimmer of the ocean, streaks of white and blue and yellow in different places, as the light and wind affect it. The ocean feels utterly forgiving, like you can dump almost anything into the ocean's body and it will still love us, and Judy and Doug cling to each other like children in a storm cellar and watch the waves. Then they go to Newport and eat amazing lobster. For a few days before and a few days after this trip, they are all aglow and neither of them can do any wrong.

A week or so after the boat thing, they hold hands in bed, nestling like they could almost start having sex at any moment. Judy looks in Doug's naked eyes (his glasses are on the nightstand) and says, "Let's just jump off the train now, okay? Let's not do any of the rest of it, let's just be good to each other forever. Why not? We could."

"Why would you want that?" Doug drawls like he's half asleep. "You're the one who's going to get the life she wants. I'm the one who'll be left like wreckage." Judy rolls over and pretends to sleep.

The Conversation achieves mythical status long before it arrives. Certain aspects of the Conversation are hazy in advance, for both Doug and Judy, because of that thing where you can't understand something until you understand it.

The day of the Conversation, Judy wakes from a nightmare, shivering with the covers cast aside, and Doug's already out of bed. "It's today," he says, and then he leaves without saying anything else to Judy, or anything at all to Marva, who's still pissed at him. Judy keeps almost going back to bed, but somehow she winds up dressed, with a toaster pop in her hand, marching towards the door. Marva starts to say something, then shrugs.

Doug and Judy meet up for dinner at Punjabi Dhaba in Inman Square, scooping red-hot eggplant and bright chutney off of metal prison trays while Bollywood movies blare overhead and just outside of their line of vision.

The Conversation starts with them talking past each other. Judy says, "Lately I can't remember anything past the next month." Doug says, "I keep trying to see what happens after I die." Judy says, "Normally I can remember years in advance, even decades. But I'm blocked." She shudders. Doug says, "If I could just have an impression, an afterimage, of what happens when I'm gone. It would help a lot."

Judy finally hears what Doug's been saying. "Oh Jesus, not this. Nobody can see past death. It's impossible."

"So's seeing the future." Doug cracks his somosa in half with a fork, and offers the chunky side to Judy.

"You can't remember anything past when your brain ceases to exist. Because there are no physical memories to access. Your brain is a storage medium."

"But who knows what we're accessing? It could be something outside our own brains."

Judy tries to clear her head and think of something nice twenty years from now, but she can't. She looks at Doug's chunky sideburns, which he didn't have when they'd started dating. Whenever she's imagined those sideburns, she always associated them with the horror of these days. It's sweltering inside the restaurant. "Why are you scared of me?" she says.

"I'm not," Doug says. "I only want you to be happy. When I see you ten years from now, I—"

Judy covers her ears and jumps out of her seat, to turn the Bollywood music all the way up. Standing, she can see the screen, where a triangle of dancing women shake their fingers in unison at an unshaven man. The man smiles.

Eventually, someone comes and turns the music back down. "I think part of you is scared that I really am more powerful than you are," Judy says. "And you've done everything you can to take away my power."

"I don't think you're any more or less powerful than me. Our powers are just different," Doug says. "But I think you're a selfish person. I think you're used to the idea that you can cheat on everything, and it's made your soul a little bit rotten. I think you're going to hate me for the next few weeks until you figure out how to cast me out. I think I love you more than my own arms and legs and I would shorten my already short life by a decade to have you stick around one more year. I think you're brave as hell for keeping your head up on our journey together into the mouth of hell. I think you're the most beautiful human being I've ever met, and you have a good heart despite how much you're going to tear me to shreds."

"I don't want to see you any more," Judy says. Her hair is all in her face, wet and ragged from the restaurant's blast-furnace heat.

A few days later, Judy and Doug are playing foozball at a swanky bar in what used to be the Combat Zone. Judy makes a mean remark about something sexually humiliating that will happen to Doug five years from now, which he told her about in a moment of weakness. A couple days later, she needles him about an incident at work that almost got him fired a while back. She's never been a sadist before now—although it's also masochism, because when she torments him, she already knows how terrible she'll feel in a few minutes.

Another time, Doug and Judy are drunk on the second floor of a Thayer Street frat bar, and Doug keeps getting Judy one more weird cocktail, even though she's had more than enough. The retro pinball machine gossips at them. Judy staggers to the bathroom, leaving her purse with Doug—and when she gets back, the purse is gone. They both knew Doug was going to lose Judy's purse, which only makes her madder. She bitches him out in front of a table of beer-pong champions. And then it's too late to get back to Judy's place, so they have to share Doug's cramped, sagging hospital cot. Judy throws up on Doug's favorite outfit: anise and stomach acid, it'll never come out.

Judy loses track of which unbearable things have already happened, and which lay ahead. Has Doug insulted her parents yet, on their second meeting? Yes, that was yesterday. Has he made Marva cry? No, that's tomorrow. Has she screamed at him that he's a weak mean bastard yet? It's all one moment to her. Judy has finally achieved timelessness.

Doug has already arranged—a year ago—to take two weeks off work, because he knows he won't be able to answer people's dumb tech problems and lose a piece of himself at the same time. He could do his job in his sleep, even if he didn't know what all the callers were going to say before they said it, but his ability to sleepwalk through unpleasantness will shortly be maxed out. He tells his coworker Geoffrey, the closest he has to a friend, that he'll be doing some Spring cleaning, even though it's October.

A few days before the breakup, Judy stands in the middle of Central Square, and a homeless guy comes up to her and asks for money. She stares at his face, which is unevenly sunburned in the shape of a wheel. She concentrates on this man, who stands there, his hand out. For a moment, she just forgets to worry about Doug for once—and just like that, she's seeing futures again.

The threads are there: if she buys this homeless man some scones from 1369, they'll talk, and become friends, and maybe she'll run into him once every few weeks and buy him dinner, for the next several years. And in five years, she'll help the man, Franklin, find a place to live, and she'll chip in for the deposit. But a couple years later, it'll all have fallen apart, and he'll be back here. And she flashes on something Franklin tells her eight years from now, if this whole chain of events comes to pass, about a lost opportunity. And then she knows what to do.

"Franklin," she says to wheel-faced guy, who blinks at the sound of his name. "Listen. Angie's pregnant, with your kid. She's at the yellow house with the broken wheelbarrow, in Sturbridge. If you go to her right now, I think she'll take you back. Here's a hundred bucks." She reaches in her new purse, for the entire wad of cash she took out of the bank to hold her until she gets her new ATM card. "Go find Angie." Franklin just looks at her, takes the cash, and disappears.

Judy never knows if Franklin took her advice. But she does know for sure she'll never see him again.

And then she wanders into the bakery where she would have bought Franklin scones, and she sees this guy working there. And she concentrates on him, too, even though it gives her a headache, and she "remembers" a future in which they become friendly and he tells her about the time he wrecked his best friend's car, which hasn't happened yet. She buys a scone and tells the guy, Scott, that he shouldn't borrow Reggie's T-Bird for that regatta thing, or he'll regret it forever. She doesn't even care that Scott is staring as she walks out.

"I'm going to be a vigilante soothsayer," she tells Marva. She's never used her power so recklessly before, but the more she does it, the easier it gets. She goes ahead and mails that Jollibee statue to Sukey.

The day of the big breakup, Marva's like, "Why can't you just dump him via text message? That's what all the kids are doing, it's the new sexting." Judy's best answer is, "Because then my bike would still be in one piece." Which isn't a very good argument. Judy dresses warm, because she knows she'll be frozen later.

Doug takes deep breaths, tries to feel acceptance, but he's all wrung out inside. He wants this to be over, but he dreads it being over. If there was any other way . . . Doug takes the train from Providence a couple hours early, so he can get lost for a while. But he doesn't get lost enough, and he's still early for their meeting. They're supposed to get dinner at the fancy place, but Doug forgot to make the reservation, so they wind up at John Harvard's Brew Pub, in the mall, and they each put away three pints of the microbrews that made John Harvard famous. They make small talk.

Afterwards, they're wandering aimlessly, towards Mass Ave., and getting closer to the place where it happens. Judy blurts out, "It didn't have to be this way. None of it. You made everything fall into place, but it didn't have to."

"I know you don't believe that any more," Doug says. "There's a lot of stuff you have the right to blame me for, but you can't believe I chose any of this. We're both cursed to see stuff that nobody should be allowed to see, but we're still responsible for our own mistakes. I still don't regret anything. Even if I didn't know today was the last day for you and me, I would want it to be."

They are both going to say some vicious things to each other in the next hour or so. They've already heard it all, in their heads.

On Mass Ave., Judy sees the ice cream place opposite the locked side gates of Harvard, and she stops her bike. During their final blow-out fight, she's not eating ice cream, any of the hundred times she's seen it. "Watch my bike," she tells Doug. She goes in and gets a triple scoop for herself and one for Doug, random flavors—Cambridge is one of the few places you can ask for random flavors and people will just nod—and then she and Doug resume their exit interview.

"It's that you have this myth that you're totally innocent and harmless, even though you also believe you control everything in the universe," Doug is saying.

Judy doesn't taste her ice cream, but she is aware of its texture, the voluptuousness of it, and the way it chills the roof of her mouth. There are lumps of something chewy in one of her random flavors. Her cone smells like candy, with a hint of wet dog.

They wind up down by the banks of the river, near the bridge surrounded by a million geese and their innumerable droppings, and Judy is crying and shouting that Doug is a passive aggressive asshole.

Doug's weeping into the remains of his cone, and then he goes nuclear. He starts babbling about when he sees Judy ten years hence, and the future he describes is one of the ones that Judy's always considered somewhat unlikely.

Judy tries to flee, but Doug has her wrist and he's babbling at her, describing a scene where a broken-down Doug meets Judy with her two kids—Raina and Jeremy, one of dozens of combinations of kids Judy might have—and Raina, the toddler, has a black eye and a giant stuffed tiger. The future Judy looks tired, makes an effort to be nice to the future Doug, who's a wreck, gripping her cashmere lapel.

Both the future Judy and the present Judy are trying to

get away from Doug as fast as possible. Neither Doug will let go.

"And then 15 years from now, you only have one child," Doug says.

"Let me go!" Judy screams.

But when Judy finally breaks free of Doug's hand, and turns to flee, she's hit with a blinding headrush, like a one-minute migraine. Three scoops of ice cream on top of three beers, or maybe just stress, but it paralyzes her, even as she's trying to run. Doug tries to throw himself in her path, but he overbalances and falls down the river bank, landing almost in the water.

"Gah!" Doug wails. "Help me up. I'm hurt." He lifts one arm, and Judy puts down her bike, helps him climb back up. Doug's a mess, covered with mud, and he's clutching one arm, heaving with pain.

"Are you okay?" Judy can't help asking.

"Breaking my arm hurt a lot more . . ." Doug winces. ". . . than I thought it would."

"Your arm." Judy can't believe what she's seeing. "You broke . . . your arm."

"You can see for yourself. At least this means it's over."

"But you were supposed to break your leg."

Doug almost tosses both hands in the air, until he remembers he can't. "This is exactly why I can't deal with you any more. We both agreed, on our very first date, I break my arm. You're just remembering it wrong, or being difficult on purpose."

Doug wants to go to the hospital by himself, but Judy insists on going with. He curses at the pain, stumbling over every knot and root.

"You broke your arm." Judy's half-sobbing, half-laughing, it's almost too much to take in. "You broke your arm, and maybe that means that all of this . . . that maybe we could try again. Not right away, I'm feeling pretty raw right now, but in a while. I'd be willing to try."

But she already knows what Doug's going to say: "You don't get to hurt me any more."

She doesn't leave Doug until he's safely staring at the

hospital linoleum, waiting to go into X-ray. Then she pedals home, feeling the cold air smash into her face. She's forgotten her helmet, but it'll be okay. When she gets home, she's going to grab Marva and they're going straight to Logan, where a bored check-in counter person will give them dirt-cheap tickets on the last flight to Miami. They'll have the wildest three days of their lives, with no lasting ill effects. It'll be epic, she's already living every instant of it in her head. She's crying buckets but it's okay, her bike's headwind wipes the slate clean.

"And Weep Like Alexander"

NEIL GAIMAN

Neil Gaiman (neilgaiman.com) lives with his wife, Amanda Palmer, in Boston, Massachusetts, and maintains an office near Minneapolis, Minnesota. He is a celebrity. He became prominent in the late 1980s as a writer of intellectually and aesthetically satisfying comics, particularly Sandman, *at the same time he was improving his craft as a writer of fiction and emerging as a popular writer of stories. His first novel (after the popular collaboration with Terry Prachett,* Good Omens, *1990) was* Neverwhere *(1996), followed by* Stardust *(1999). His third novel,* American Gods *(2001), won both the Hugo and Nebula Awards, and signaled a new level of achievement in his literary career. His young adult novels,* Coraline *(2002) and* The Graveyard Book *(2008), are particularly notable. Some of his short fiction is collected in* Smoke and Mirrors *(1998),* M Is for Magic *(2004), and* Fragile Things *(2006). He is currently writing a novel that may be a sequel to* American Gods.

"And Weep Like Alexander" was published in an original collection of SF tall tales told in a bar, Fables from the Fountain, *edited by Ian Whates. It is in the British SF tradition of Arthur C. Clarke's humorous* Tales from the White Hart. *It features Obediah Polkinghorn, uninventor, and answers such questions as why we have no flying cars today. We think it is a delightful answer.*

The little man hurried into the Fountain and ordered a very large whisky. "Because," he announced to the pub in general, "I deserve it."

He looked exhausted, sweaty and rumpled, as if he had not slept in several days. He wore a tie, but it was so loose as to be almost undone. He had greying hair that might once have been ginger.

"I'm sure you do," said Brian Dalton.

"I do!" said the man. He took a sip of the whisky as if to find out if he liked it, then, satisfied, gulped down half the glass. He stood completely still, for a moment, like a statue. "Listen," he said. "Can you hear it?"

"What?" I said.

"A sort of background whispering white noise that actually becomes whatever song you wish to hear when you sort of half-concentrate upon it?"

I listened. "No," I said.

"Exactly," said the man, extraordinarily pleased with himself. "Isn't it *wonderful?* Only yesterday, everybody in the Fountain was complaining about the Wispamuzak. Professor Mackintosh here was grumbling about having Queen's "Bohemian Rhapsody" stuck in his head and how it was now following him across London. Today, it's gone, as if it had never been. None of you can even remember that it existed. And that is all due to me."

"I what?" said Professor Mackintosh. "Something about the Queen?" And then, "Do I know you?"

"We've met," said the little man. "But people forget me, alas. It is because of my job." He took out his wallet, produced a card, passed it to me.

OBEDIAH POLKINGHORN

it read, and beneath that in small letters,

UNINVENTOR.

"If you don't mind my asking," I said. "What's an uninventor?"

"It's somebody who uninvents things," he said. He raised his glass, which was quite empty. "Ah. Excuse me, Sally, I need another very large whisky."

The rest of the crowd there that evening seemed to have decided that the man was both mad and uninteresting. They had returned to their conversations. I, on the other hand, was caught. "So," I said, resigning myself to my conversational fate. "Have you been an uninventor long?"

"Since I was fairly young," he said. "I started uninventing when I was eighteen. Have you never wondered why we do not have jet-packs?"

I had, actually.

"Saw a bit on Tomorrow's World about them, when I was a lad," said Michael, the landlord. "Man went up in one. Then he came down. Raymond Burr seemed to think we'd all have them soon enough."

"Ah, but we don't," said Obediah Polkinghorn, "because I uninvented them about twenty years ago. I had to. They were driving everybody mad. I mean, they seemed so attractive, and so cheap, but you just had to have a few thousand bored teenagers strapping them on, zooming all over the place, hovering outside bedroom windows, crashing into the flying cars . . ."

"Hold on," said Sally. "There aren't any flying cars."

"True," said the little man, "but there were. You wouldn't believe the traffic jams they'd cause. You'd look up and it was just the bottoms of bloody flying cars from horizon to horizon. Some days I couldn't see the skies at all. People throwing rubbish out of their car windows . . . They were easy to run—ran off gravitosolar power, obviously—but I didn't realise that they needed to go until I heard a lady talking about them on Radio Four, all 'Why Oh Why Didn't We Stick With Non-Flying Cars?' She had a point. Something needed to be done. I uninvented them. I made a list of inventions the world would be better off without and, one by one, I uninvented them all."

By now he had started to gather a small audience. I was pleased I'd grabbed a good seat.

"It was a lot of work, too," he continued. "You see, it's almost impossible *not* to invent the Flying Car, as soon as you've invented the Lumenbubble. So eventually I had to uninvent that too. And I miss the individual Lumenbubble: a massless portable light-source that floated half a metre above your head and went on when you wanted it to. Such a wonderful invention. Still, no use crying over unspilt milk, and you can't mend an omelette without unbreaking a few eggs."

"You also can't expect us actually to believe any of this," said someone, and I think it was Jocelyn.

"Right," said Brian. "I mean, next thing you'll be telling us that you uninvented the space ship."

"But I did," said Obediah Polkinghorn. He seemed extremely pleased with himself. "Twice. I had to. You see, the moment we whizz off into space and head out to the planets and beyond, we bump into things that spur so many other inventions. The Polaroid Instant Transporter. That was the worst. And the Mockett Telepathic Translator. That was the worst as well. But as long as it's nothing worse than a rocket to the moon, I can keep everything under control."

"So, how exactly do you go about uninventing things?" I asked.

"It's hard," he admitted. "It's all about unpicking probability threads from the fabric of creation. But they tend to be long and tangled, like spaghetti. So it's rather like having to unpick a strand of spaghetti from a haystack."

"Sounds like thirsty work," said Michael, and I signalled him to pour me another pint of Old Bodger.

"Fiddly," said the little man. "Yes. But I pride myself on doing good. Each day I wake, and, even if I've unhappened something that might have been wonderful, I think, Obediah Polkington, the world is a happier place because of something that you've uninvented."

He looked into his remaining scotch, swirled the liquid around in his glass.

"The trouble is," he said, "with the Wispamuzak gone, that's it. I'm done. It's all been uninvented. There are no more horizons left to undiscover, no more mountains left to un-climb."

"Nuclear Power?" suggested 'Tweet' Peston.

"Before my time," said Obediah. "Can't uninvent things invented before I was born. Otherwise I might uninvent something that would have led to my birth, and then where would we be?" Nobody had any suggestions. "Knee-high in jet-packs and flying cars, that's where," he told us. "Not to mention Morrison's Martian Emolument." For a moment, he looked quite grim. "Ooh. That stuff was nasty. And a cure for cancer. But frankly, given what it did to the oceans, I'd rather have the cancer.

"No. I have uninvented everything that was on my list. I shall go home," said Obediah Polkinghorn, bravely, "and weep, like Alexander, because there are no more worlds to unconquer. What is there left to uninvent?"

There was silence in the Fountain.

In the silence, Brian's iPhone rang. His ring-tone was The Rutles singing 'Cheese and Onions'. "Yeah?" he said. Then, "I'll call you back."

It is unfortunate that the pulling out of one phone can have such an effect on other people around. Sometimes I think it's because we remember when we could smoke in pubs, and that we pull out our phones together as once we pulled out our ciga-rette packets. But probably it's because we're easily bored.

Whatever the reason, the phones came out.

Crown Baker took a photo of us all, and then Twitpicced it. Jocelyn started to read her text messages. Tweet Peston tweeted that he was in the Fountain and had met his first uninventor. Professor Mackintosh checked the Test Match scores, told us what they were and emailed his brother in Inverness to grumble about them. The phones were out and the conversation was over.

"What's that?" asked Obediah Polkinghorn.

"It's the iPhone 5," said Ray Arnold, holding his up. "Crown's using the Nexus X. That's the Android system. Phones. Internet. Camera. Music. But it's the apps. I mean, do you know, there are over a thousand fart sound-effect apps on the iPhone alone? You want to hear the unofficial Simpsons Fart App?"

"No," said Obediah. "I most definitely do not want to. I do *not*." He put down his drink, unfinished. Pulled his tie up. Did up his coat. "It's not going to be easy," he said, as if to himself. "But, for the good of all . . ." And then he stopped. And he grinned. "It's been marvellous talking to you all," he announced to nobody in particular as he left the Fountain.

The Middle of Somewhere

JUDITH MOFFETT

Judith Moffett (www.judithmoffett.com) lives in Swarthmore, Pennsylvania. She is an English professor (retired), a poet, a Swedish translator, a science-fiction writer, and the author of eleven books in five genres. Two of her novels were New York Times *Notable Books. Her most recent novel is* The Bird Shaman *(2008), the third in her Holy Ground Trilogy, after* The Ragged World *(1991) and* Time, Like an Ever-Rolling Stream *(1992). She spent most of 2010 and half of 2011 writing a memoir of her long friendship with the poet James Merrill, who died in 1995. In 2013 Greywolf Press will bring out* Air Mail, *the correspondence between American poet Robert Bly and the Swedish poet Tomas Tranströmer, who was awarded the Nobel Prize in Literature this year; Moffett translated Tranströmer's early letters to Bly for that book. This is her first short fiction in several years.*

"The Middle of Somewhere" was published in Welcome to the Greenhouse, *an excellent anthology of stories about climate change, edited by Gordon Van Gelder. A teenaged girl helps a seventy-year old woman collect data on bird hatching, that demonstrates the veracity of climate change. It is very clearly within the framework of science fiction, very science oriented, and also a revelation of character.*

Kaylee is entering data on Jane's clunky old desktop computer, and texting with a few friends while she does it, when the weather alarm goes off for the second time.

Cornell University's NestWatch Citizen Scientist program runs this website where you have a different chart for each nest site you're monitoring. You're supposed to fill in the data after each visit to the site. Jane's got a zillion different kinds of birds nesting on her property, and she knows where a lot of them are doing it, so Kaylee's biology teacher fixed it up with Jane, who's a friend of hers, for Kaylee to do this NestWatch project for class. Twice a week all spring she's been coming out to Jane's place to monitor seven pairs of nesting birds. The place used to be a farm but is all grown up now in trees and bushes except for five or ten acres around the house, which Jane keeps mowed. Bluebirds like short grass and open space.

Jane is nice, but seriously weird. All Kaylee's friends think so, and to be honest Kaylee kind of slants what she tells people to exaggerate that side of Jane, who lives a lot like people did way before Kaylee was born, in this little log house with only three small rooms and no dishwasher or clothes dryer, and solar panels on the roof. She has beehives—well, that's not so weird, though for an old lady maybe it is—but all her water is pumped from a cistern, plus she has two rain barrels out in the garden. Rain barrels! Kaylee knows for a fact that a few years back, when they brought city water out this far from town, Jane just said, Oh well, I can always hook up later if I think I need to. So you have to watch every drop of water you use at Jane's house, like only flushing the toilet every so often, unless they're getting plenty of rain. There's a little sign taped to the bathroom wall that you can't avoid reading when you're sitting on the toilet: IF IT'S YELLOW / LET IT MELLOW / IF IT'S BROWN / FLUSH IT DOWN. Sometimes Kaylee flushes it down even when it isn't brown, out of embarrassment.

The flushing thing is partly about water and partly about the septic tank. Kaylee's friend Morgan's house has a septic tank too, so Kaylee already knows it's best to use them as little as possible, and that there are things you can't put into them or the biology of the tank will get messed up and smell. If you happen to mention anything to Jane about, like, your new SmartBerry, or a hot music group or even the Anderson High basketball team, the Bearcats, when they went to the state finals, she just looks blank, but once when Kaylee asked a simple question about why Jane didn't clean paintbrushes at the sink, like her dad always did, Jane talked animatedly for ten minutes about bacteria and "solids" and drain fields and septic lagoons. Kaylee's friends laughed their heads off when they heard about that ("So she's going on about how the soil in Anderson County is like pure clay, duh, so it doesn't pass the 'perk test,' which is why she's got this *lagoon*, and I'm thinking 'Fine, great, whatever!' and trying to like edge away . . ."). Kaylee's seen the little outhouse in the trees on the other side of the driveway, across from the clothesline (clothesline!), for dry spells when flushing even a few times a day would use more water than Jane wants to waste. That would normally be in late summer. Kaylee's relieved it's spring right now.

The computer Kaylee has to use for data entry here is a million years old and slow as anything. She couldn't believe it when Jane said one day that when and if DSL finally made it this far into rural Kentucky, she planned to sign up.

But the thing that makes all that beside the point for now, is that Jane has been monitoring certain species of birds here for years and years, and knows just about everything there is to know about them. Anything she doesn't know, she looks up in books, or on the Birds of North America website, and then she knows that too.

On the Garden Box page Kaylee fills in blanks. Species: Tree swallow. Date of visit: 05/04/2014. Time of visit: 4:00 PM. Number of eggs: 0. Number of live young: 6. Number of dead young: 0. Nest status: Completed nest. Adult activity: Feeding young at nest. (Both parents dive-bombed Kaylee today for the entire ninety seconds she had the front of the nest box swung open, swooping down like fighter pilots, aiming for her eyes, pulling up just before they would have hit her head [she happened to have forgotten her hat]. When she was done they chased her all the way back to the house. Tree swallows are beautiful, sleekly graceful little birds, white and glossy dark blue, but Kaylee is *so* not crazy about the dive-bombing part.) Young status: Naked young. (The babies—"hatchlings" she should remember to say—hatched out only two days ago, and resemble squirming wads of pink bubble gum with huge dark eyeballs bulging under transparent lids still sealed shut, and little stumpy wings.) Management: No. Everything's fine. Comment: Leave blank. The only thing not ordinary about this nest is how early it is, the earliest first-egg date for tree swallows ever recorded on Jane's farm. Everybody on NestWatch is posting early nesting dates. Climate change, is the general assumption. Kaylee's parents think climate change is a hoax. Kaylee doesn't care whether it is or not, but saying so makes her project feel more dramatic, like, more cutting-edge. Submit.

Next site: Barn. Species: Black vulture. Date of visit: 05/04/2014. Time of visit: 4:00 PM. Number of eggs: 2. Number of live young: 0. Number of dead young: 0. Nest status—and right then Jane's NOAA Weather Radio emits its long piercing shriek.

Jane comes in off the porch, where she's been putting Revolution on the dogs to kill the ticks they pick up in the hay that grows wherever there aren't any trees or blackberries. "What now? They only announced the watch twenty minutes ago." The shrieking goes on and on, you can't hear yourself think. Finally it stops and the radio buzzes three times, and then a robot voice declares, *The National Weather*

Service in Louisville has issued a severe thunderstorm warning for the following counties in Kentucky: Anderson, Franklin, Henry, Nelson, Mercer, Scott, Shelby, Spencer . . . Kaylee stops listening and goes back to her data entering and her texting. Nest status: No constructed nest. Adult activity: At/on, then flushed from nest. (When Kaylee squeezed through the crack between the barn doors an hour ago, the mother vulture, as always, got up and hesitantly stalked, like a huge black chicken, away from her two gigantic eggs lying on the bare dirt floor. The father didn't show up this afternoon, which suits Kaylee just fine. Jane says he's all bluster, but he threatens her as if he means it, hissing and spreading his enormous white-tipped black wings like an eagle on a banner, and she's scared of him. Scared he'll barf on her, too; they do that, to drive predators away.)

"I'm going out to the garden," Jane says now. She's wearing her big straw hat, so she'll be safe from dive-bombing tree swallows. "If you hear thunder, get off the computer fast, okay?"

"Okay." Though right now the sky through the study window looks just flat gray, not stormy at all. Young status: (Leave that blank. The eggs should be hatching in ten days or so. Jane's hoping for two live babies this time. Most often one of the eggs is infertile.) Number of dead young: 0. And so on. Submit.

She's worked her way through Patio (eastern phoebe) and Pond Box (chickadee) while keeping up on Lady Bearcats practice with Morgan, and Macy's cat's hairball with Macy, who's at the vet's, and checking Facebook every few minutes, and is just starting on Path Box (bluebird, her favorite) when the radio emits its blood-curdling screech once again. Jane is still in the garden. When the robot comes on again, Kaylee is the only one in the house to hear it say, *The National Weather Service in Louisville has issued a tornado warning for the following counties in Kentucky: Anderson, Franklin, Grant, Marion, Owen, and Washington until 6:30 pm. The National Weather Service has identified rotation in a storm located fifteen miles southwest of Lebanon and heading north-northeast at 40 mph. Cities in the path of this storm include Lebanon; Springfield; Harrodsburg; Law-renceburg; Alton . . .*   Kaylee shoves back her chair, grabbing her SmartBerry, and runs to the door. "Jane! Hey Jane!" she yells. "They just said it's a tornado warning!" Behind her the robot says sternly *This is a dangerous storm. If you are in the path of this storm, take shelter immediately. Go to the lowest level of a sturdy building . . .* "They said take shelter immediately!" she shouts.

Jane drops her shovel and starts trotting toward the house, calling "Fleece and Roscoe! Come!" She doesn't trot too fast, she's got arthritis in her knees like Kaylee's grandma, but Jane is much, much thinner than Mammaw; think of Mammaw trotting anywhere! The dogs race up the steps onto the deck, followed by Jane holding on to the handrail. "Are you sure they said *warning*?" she puffs. "I wouldn't have thought it looked that threatening," and just then they hear the heavy rumble of thunder. Fleece, the white poodle, trembles violently and slinks through the doggy door into the house; she *hates* thunderstorms. The sky is starting to churn. As the rest of them come in, the radio is repeating its announcement, including the part about taking shelter immediately. Jane says, "Well *that* blew up out of nowhere! Okay, I guess we get to go sit in the basement for a while. Did you turn off the computer?" Kaylee shakes her head. "Get your data submitted?"

She nods. "Almost all of it."

"Good. Go on down, I'll be there in a sec."

Kaylee snatches up her backpack and runs down the basement stairs, then isn't sure what to do. Jane's house is set into a slope, so half the basement is underground and the other half isn't; you can walk straight out the patio doors, climb a ladder kept out there for the purpose, and check on the phoebe's nest perched like a pillbox hat on the light fixture. It's pretty crowded down here; the basement is the size of the house, tiny, and piled with boxes containing mostly books. But now Jane's hurrying down with Roscoe the beagle behind her, leading the way into what looks like a closet under the stairs, but turns out to be a kind of wedge-shaped storm shelter. Fleece is already in there, lying on a mat and panting. Roscoe flops down beside Fleece; they must be used to this drill. There's a folding canvas chair in the shelter too. Jane says, "I guess you'll have to squeeze in with the dogs. Or maybe just sit here on the mat next to them. I have to take the chair or in five minutes my back will be screaming worse than the radio." Which, Kaylee sees, she's brought down with her, and which she now switches back on.

But the robot voice is only repeating what it said already. Jane turns down the volume. Kaylee sits cross-legged on the edge of the mat and consults her SmartBerry.

When she first started working on the nesting project with Jane, she'd kept the SmartBerry in her jacket pocket or in her hand all the time; but when Jane noticed, she'd made her put it away. "You can't do science like that, hon, texting seven of your friends while checking out a nest. Good observation requires all your attention, not just some of it." Kaylee doesn't see why; she's always doing half a dozen things at once, everybody does. It's actually hard to do only one thing. She tried to argue that she could record the data directly onto the NestWatch site from her SmartBerry, skipping the note-taking and data entry phases completely, *and* take pictures. But Jane doesn't trust her not to spend the travel time between nest sites chatting, instead of listening and looking around, which is smart of Jane, Kaylee grudgingly admits. They've compromised: she can use her smartphone during data entry time, but not while actually monitoring nests. It makes Kaylee feel twitchy, all that time hiking between sites and trying to identify bird songs, not knowing what's going on everywhere else.

Now she says, "I should probably call my mom so she doesn't worry."

"Good idea."

Nobody answers at home. Kaylee's brother Tyler always drops her off at Jane's on his way to work his shift, so he's at work, and her dad picks her up on his way home, but her mom must be out. When the answering machine comes on, Kaylee says, "Mom, did the siren go off? There's a tornado warning, I hope you're someplace safe. I'm down in Jane's basement till it's over, so don't worry. See you later." Then she rapidly texts *safe in basement @ janes dont worry* and sends that to her mom and dad, then sends *im in janes basement where r u?* to all her best friends at once, Hannah, Tabby, Andrew, Shannon, Jacob, Morgan, Macy, and waits for somebody to text back. It takes her mind off being scared, not that she's all that scared really. There are tornado watches and a few warnings every spring—more and more of them in the last few years—her mom is always complaining, but they've never actually come to anything around Lawrenceburg, though she's seen the TV shots of other places, even in Kentucky, where whole houses got turned into piles of rubble in a few seconds. The worst watches are the night ones, when you can't see what the sky looks like.

While she waits—in the circumstances Jane can hardly object—she gets on Facebook and posts, "I'm in a tornado warning in Jane's basement!"

She's reading Tabby's text—*me + my mom + the twins r in the city hall shelter*—when Jane puts her hand on Kaylee's arm. "Listen. Do you hear that—like a freight train?" Something *does* sound like a freight train, getting louder and louder. She feels a thrill of serious fear, which spikes into panic when Jane says urgently, "Better get down low."

At that instant three more buzzing beeps interrupt the droning radio robot. *A tornado has been sighted on the ground near Glensboro, heading north-northeast at forty miles per hour. If you are in the path of this storm, move to the lowest level of a building or interior room and protect yourself from flying glass.* Kaylee and Jane look at each other; Glensboro is only a couple of miles west of here. *If it stays organized this tornado should pass near Lawrenceburg at 5:45 pm, near Birdie at 5:50 pm, near Alton at 6 o'clock pm, and near Frankfort at 6:15 pm*, the flat voice states.

"Kaylee, get down. Get under the blanket and hold that pillow over your head." Fleece and Roscoe are both whining now; Jane slides out of the low chair onto her knees and stretches herself out on top of Fleece, with her arm tight around Roscoe and terrified Kaylee; she pulls the blanket up over all of them.

The roar becomes deafening. There's pressure in Kaylee's ears, she can feel the floor vibrating. The house blows up.

After the shaking and roaring have stopped, and they've thrown off the blanket, Kaylee can't see anything through the cracked but miraculously unbroken patio doors but a tangle of branches full of new green leaves. The basement has held together, though light is coming through some new cracks in the aboveground foundation block. "Kaylee, let me look at you. Are you okay?" Jane says worriedly.

"I think so." She feels lightheaded with relief that the tornado is over, but nothing hurts when she moves her arms and legs. She automatically checks her SmartBerry, still in her hand, but there are no bars at all. Dismayed, she reports to Jane, "I'm not getting a signal. We can't call anybody."

"I expect the tornado took out the cell tower. Phone line too. Keep the dogs in here with you—I want to check things out, all right?" Holding to the shelter's doorframe, Jane hauls herself up, grimacing, steps carefully out into the basement and looks around. "Looks like we were lucky. The ceiling's still in one piece, far as I can tell." She moves a few cautious steps farther and stops. "The stairs look solid but they're full of junk, I don't think we better try to get out that way. Let's see if the patio doors will open." She goes over and tugs at the sliding door, but it won't budge. "Frame's bent. The window frame may be bent too, but I'll check before we start breaking glass."

Startled, Kaylee says, "You're bleeding! Jane, you're bleeding!" There's a big spreading bloodstain on Jane's shirt and jeans on one side.

"I am? Where?" Jane looks down, sees the blood on her clothes, sees it dripping onto her right boot. "Huh. Now how the dickens did that happen? I must have cut my arm on something." She comes back toward Kaylee. "There's a plastic tub with a lid, see it? Way inside, back where the stairs almost come down to the floor? That's the first-aid stuff; can you pull that out here? Fleece, Roscoe, come. Down. Stay. Get out of Kaylee's way." The dogs, both panting now, slink out of the shelter, very subdued, and slump down on the basement floor by Jane's feet without an argument. Fleece has some blood on her woolly white back but seems unhurt. Apparently the blood is Jane's.

There are three or four plastic tubs with lids back there, all blue. "Which one?"

"The closest one, nearest the door. Just drag it out here." Suddenly Jane leans against the wall, then reaches into the shelter, pulls out the camp chair and sits in it.

Kaylee backs out with a tub. "This one?"

Jane snaps off the lid and looks in. "Yep. Thanks." She rummages around inside, gets out a packet of gauze pads and a pressure bandage, and rips the seal off the packet. She starts unbuttoning her flannel shirt. "Do you faint at the sight of blood? If you don't, maybe you can help me find the cut. The back of my arm is numb, I guess I cut a nerve."

Kaylee isn't crazy about the sight of blood, but this is no time to wimp out. But the cut makes her feel a little sick. It's high up on the back of Jane's left arm, deep and triangular, and thick-looking blood is welling out of it. She can't help sort of gasping through her teeth. "I see it. It's pretty bad. What should I do?"

"Put the pads right on it and apply pressure, don't worry about hurting me. The important thing is to stop the bleeding."

Gingerly, Kaylee presses the pads against the wound, but they're saturated in seconds; the cut is really bleeding. "Do you have anything bigger? These aren't really big enough."

"Use my shirt while I look." She paws through the box. "There's this sling thing, but that's not very absorbent, or very big, come to that. And some cotton balls. I guess we could pack the cut with these."

Kaylee suddenly says "Oh! I know!" and lets go of the shirt, which Jane grabs and tightens with her other hand. "Sorry," says Kaylee, "only I just remembered, I've got some, well, some maxipads in my backpack, because you know, just in case . . . anyway—" she fishes in her pack and pulls out a plastic bag triumphantly.

"Perfect!" Jane says. "Brilliant!"

Kaylee flushes, embarrassed but gratified. She snatches

away the shirt and slaps a pad onto Jane's wound, wrapping it around her arm. Then, showing further initiative, she says, "Hold that like that," and puts another pad on top of the first, and binds them both to Jane's arm with the pressure bandage. "There! Just hold that really tight. If you bleed through the first one there's another one all ready to go."

"I will," Jane says. "Thanks." She looks around. "I need to sit still while this clots. Do you want to see if the window will open? I don't like to have you walking around down here till we know for sure the house isn't going to cave in on that side"—her voice catches and Kaylee thinks for the first time, *Her house is totally wrecked, her perfect little house!*—"but it should be okay. Just pry up the levers and try turning the crank. It kind of sticks. If anything shifts or falls, jump back."

What felt like an explosion turns out to have been a humongous old hickory tree smashing down right on top of the house. The tornado only clipped one corner, peeling back part of the roof and tearing the screened porch off, but it dumped that hickory right in the middle of the crushed roof, where it's hanging with its branches on one side and its roots on top of Jane's car on the other. The car is crushed and plainly undrivable, but even if it could be driven there would be no way to get it down to the road; Jane's steep quarter-mile driveway is completely blocked with downed trees.

In fact, the world has become a half-moonscape. Everything on one side of the house just looks about the way it might look after a really violent windstorm, but everything on the other has been toppled and ripped and broken to pieces. "We must have been right on the very edge," Jane says, holding her wounded arm with her other hand. "And this must have been one hell of a big tornado." There are no trees standing in the creek valley below Jane's house: none. They're all laid down in the same direction, pointing uphill on this side and downhill on the other. The road that follows the creek, the only way there is to get to Jane's house, has completely vanished under a pile of trunks and branches, broken and jagged, piled many feet deep on top of each other.

The sight of this world of leafy destruction has obliterated Kaylee's spurt of competence. She's shaking and crying in little sobs, arms wrapped about herself. "I need to talk to my mom," is all she can think of to say, "I need to find out if she's okay."

Jane says soothingly, "The best thing you can do for your mom and dad right now is just take care of yourself and stay calm. They know where you are, and they know you're with me. Eventually somebody will come looking for us. It might take them a few days—if that twister hit any population centers, all the emergency equipment and personnel are going to be very, very busy for a while. We have to give people time to get things up and running again. But they'll be along."

"But the road's covered with *trees*!"

"I'm betting on a helicopter ride long before they get the road open. The good news is, lots of people know where you are. We just have to hunker down and wait."

Kaylee pictures KY 44 as it looked before the tornado, two lanes, no shoulders, a steep wooded bluff on one side and Indian Creek on the other, with another wooded bluff across the creek. The road follows the creek. If all the trees on both sides of the valley went down the whole way to town, like they did here, she can't imagine how they'll *ever* get the road open again. Worst of all in a way, her wonderful new SmartBerry, her Christmas and birthday presents combined, that keeps her continually connected her to everything that matters, is useless. She's worried to death about her family and friends, and there's no way to find out if they're okay. From being in constant touch with everybody, suddenly she's out of touch with everybody! It makes her feel lonely and frantic, and furious with Jane, because of whom she's stranded in this war zone. "How can you stand living out here all by yourself?" she yells. "Something like this happens and you're stuck, you're just stuck!" When Jane reaches toward her she jerks away and takes off running, crying hard, down the mowed path to the garden where things still look almost normal, away from the wrecked house and jagged devastation in the other direction.

She'd changed out of her sneakers into flip-flops after

visiting the nests. Running in flip-flops on a path grown up thick in clover and scattered with broken branches doesn't work, so she's walking and crying when she gets to the path box, which is down on its side, metal post bent and half up-rooted. It's empty, the baby bluebirds fledged over the week-end, thank goodness. The box in the garden has been knocked over too—but that one's not empty, Kaylee remembers now, there were six new hatchlings in that one this morning. She shakes off the flip-flops and runs to the gate, left open in Jane's haste. The latch on the box popped open when it hit the ground; the nest has fallen out, scattering tiny pink bod-ies and loose feathers on the grass. Quick as she can, Kaylee stands the nest box up and steps on the base with her bare foot, to jam it back into the ground. She picks up the nest, built entirely out of Jane's straw garden mulch—square out-side like the square nest box, a soft lined cup inside—and fits it back in. Then, one by one, with extreme delicacy, she picks up the fragile, weightless baby birds, puts them back in their cradle, and latches the front. She can't tell whether the tiniest are even alive, but a couple of others twitch a little bit when she's handling them. It's a warm day. Now, if the parents come fast, most of them ought to make it.

But then Kaylee thinks, Where *are* the parents? She's never once checked this nest, not while it was being built and not while the eggs were being incubated and not this afternoon, when the parents weren't carrying on something terrible. There's been no sign of them. With a sinking feel-ing she faces the truth: They were almost certainly killed in the tornado.

She hears footsteps swishing through the clover and starts to explain before Jane even gets to the gate: "The garden box was down and the nest fell out, and I was trying to put every-thing back together, but the parents haven't come back—what should we do?"

Jane comes in carrying Kaylee's flip-flops, looks into the box, then scans the sky, then shakes her head. "I doubt the parents survived. These babies won't either unless we hand-raise them, which is a big job under ideal conditions and right now—nature can be ruthless, Kaylee. You did the right thing, and if the parents had come through, they could take over now. But as it is—"

"You said we could hand-raise them? How?"

Jane makes a pained face. "I've never tried it with swallows. With robins or bluebirds you make a nest, using an old bowl or something lined with paper towels. Then you soak dry dog food in water and feed them pinches of that *every forty-five minutes*, for a week or ten days. You have to change the paper towel every time you feed them, because they'll poop on it. When they get bigger—"

"Do we have dog food?" Kaylee says. "I want to try! I'm sorry I behaved like such a creep," she adds contritely. All at once she desperately wants to try to save these morsels of life, helpless and blameless, from the wreckage of the world. How badly she wants this amazes her. She can see Jane thinking about it, wanting to refuse. *"Please!"* Kaylee says. "I'll do everything myself, well, I will as soon as you teach me how. Do we have paper towels? Please, Jane, I just have to try this, I just *have* to."

With a rush of relief she sees Jane make up her mind. "Well—we do have dog food. Very expensive, low-fat dog food. No paper towels, but toilet paper and tissues. We can manage. But Kaylee, listen to me now: even experienced rehabbers commonly lose about half the baby birds they try to rear, more than half when the babies are so young. You can see why, when they've been stressed and banged around, and gotten chilled—I don't want you to set your heart on this without understanding how hard it is to be successful."

Kaylee nods as hard as she can. "I understand! Really, I really do, I won't go to pieces if it doesn't work. Oh, thanks, Jane, thank you, I don't know what I'd have done if you'd said no."

"But if we're going to do this we need to act fast. We'll take the whole nest," she says. "Back to the house. It takes a little while for kibble to soften up, so we'll start with canned; these babies need to get warmed up and fed ASAP."

"How come you've got all this stuff stashed under the stairs?" Kaylee asks Jane, when the little swallows are safely tucked into their artificial nest (Roscoe's bowl, lined with Kleenex).

First she and Jane had to hold the hatchlings in their hands, three apiece, to warm them up enough so they could eat; Jane said little birds can't warm up by themselves when they first hatch out, which is why the mother has to brood them. "Normally we do this with a heating pad or a microwaved towel or something." Then she opened a can of Mill's Wet/Dry Veterinary Diet, under the intense scrutiny of Roscoe and Fleece. "Watch this time, then next time you can help. Their gape response isn't working, but it should come back once we can get a bite or two down the hatch," Jane said. And sure enough, when Jane carefully pried a tiny beak open and pushed a bit of canned food as far back as she could with her little finger, and closed the beak to help the baby swallow, the beak opened again by itself.

Now they had all been fed. (They hadn't pooped, which probably just meant they hadn't eaten since before the tornado.) And Kaylee, yearning over their bowl, thought to ask Jane about the supplies.

Jane sits back in her chair, then stiffens. "Oh!" she says, "*That*'s what I cut myself on, that bracket on the shelf there. Wedged between paint cans. Can you push it back out of the way?" Kaylee gets up, holding the bowl carefully, and tucks the bracket out of sight; she is helpfulness itself. "Last summer," Jane says when Kaylee sits back down on the mat, "after I'd been down here with the dogs three times in about three weeks, I started thinking, What if this was the real deal? All I've got in the way of emergency supplies is six jugs of water!" So I took a weekend and made a list and went shopping. Good thing I did."

"Are we getting more tornadoes than we used to? My mom keeps saying that, but my dad thinks she just doesn't remember."

"I don't think anybody knows for sure. But a lot of information about climate change passes through this house," Jane says, and pauses, and Kaylee can tell she's thinking, *used to pass*, so she hitches forward and looks very interested, and Jane catches herself and goes on: ". . . and I've seen several articles about the effect of climate change on weather lately, and quite a few climate scientists seem to be leaning that way. The argument goes that warmer ocean temperatures mean more storms. Heat is just energy, and heat affects how much moisture there is in the atmosphere."

"So more heat and more moisture in the atmosphere means more tornadoes?"

"It means more frequent and more violent storms in general, apparently. There are computer models that say so, not that that proves anything necessarily. Tornadoes are complex, lots of things affect their formation—but it *is* true that they've been occurring earlier and farther north than they used to. Unusually high temperatures, unusually frequent tornadoes, so the thinking goes, and it does make sense. Though actually," she adds, "there've always been more tornadoes in Kentucky than people think."

"We had something last year in science about Hoosier Alley," Kaylee chimes in. "It was something about a new definition of Tornado Alley—if my SmartBerry was working I could look it up! But anyway, there's still Tornado Alley but now they're talking about Dixie Alley and Hoosier Alley and something else."

"I hadn't heard that." Jane winces and shifts in her chair.

Pleased to think there was anything she knew that Jane didn't, Kaylee says, "Hoosier Alley, that's Indiana and the western two-thirds of Kentucky, and pieces of a couple other states too. So what all do you have here?"

"Besides what you see?" Jane considers. "Mostly food. Cans and PowerBars. Dishes. Spare clothes. Tools. Stuff to clean up with. Also cans and kibble for the dogs—birds too, as it turns out." Kaylee grins happily. "And speaking of birds, before it's time to feed them again, would you mind helping me with this cut? I can't see the darn thing, and I want to pour some peroxide in there to clean it out and bandage it with something less, ah, bulky. It's going to need stitches but we'll let a professional handle that part."

Kaylee *does* mind, quite a lot really, but she takes herself in hand and acts like she doesn't. They climb back out the window—Jane's set a little step stool just outside, to make it easier to come and go—and then Jane takes off the bloody shirt, and the tee shirt too this time, and holds the arm out from her side while Kaylee pours most of a bottle of peroxide into the jagged mouth of the wound, struggling to keep from gagging while pink bubbles froth and fizz there. In nothing but a bra, Jane's back and arm look scrawny and old. She *is* old, Kaylee thinks uncomfortably; and while she's helping apply the clean bandage and wash dried blood off the arm, and helping Jane into a clean shirt from one of the plastic tubs, she's hoping she won't have to do this again. She's not proud of it, but that's how she feels.

When the arm has been dealt with, Jane becomes managerial. Feed the baby swallows. When that's done, get the dogs out by lifting them through the window (Kaylee lifts, Jane directs, protecting her arm). Bring the boxes of supplies outside. The porch above the patio is gone, but they clear the pink insulation batts, tumbled firewood, broken branches, and nameless debris away, and have a firm, level surface to work on. It's also enclosed by fencing which has survived the tornado, making it a good place for the dogs to sleep if it doesn't rain tonight, and in fact the sky has cleared completely and the radio robot says it will stay clear. Roscoe and Fleece can look through the patio doors straight into the shelter.

Amazingly, the outhouse has withstood the storm. A tree right next to it is down, but the little structure is still sitting there a trifle cattywompus on its foundation. "Praise the Lord," Jane says, "at least that's one problem we haven't got." She also says, "It might be a good thing these patio doors won't open. They may be reinforcing the wall. We can stay in here and keep dry till they come to get us, unless there's another storm." Kaylee doesn't want to think about another storm. "Let's make a fire," Jane says. "It'll cheer us up to have something hot. Want to build it, Kaylee?" Kaylee admits she has no earthly idea how to go about building a fire. "Watch and learn, then," Jane says. "Next time it'll be your turn."

The evening has turned chilly; the fire feels good. Kaylee puts down her empty plate and holds her mug of instant hot cider in both hands. She's sitting on a log of firewood, but Jane's chair has been handed through the window and Jane is sitting in that, cleaning up her plate of beans with the shambles of her house around her, as if nothing could be more natural. The dogs, stomachs full and bladders empty, lie peacefully on either side of Jane. There's almost a campfire feeling to the moment, except when Kaylee accidentally looks at the light fixture from which the phoebe nest with its five babies has disappeared without a trace. She looks away quickly, and thinks instead about how deftly Jane built the fire. How she assembled the big sticks, smaller sticks, really tiny twigs, and dry grass Kaylee collected for her—combining them like following a sort of recipe—then lit one match, and hey presto! magicked forth the coals that heated the pots of water and beans. She says, "Where did you learn to build a fire like that? Without even any newspaper? My dad always uses lots of newspaper."

Jane hands her a granola bar and unpeels one for herself. "I usually use paper too, when I'm firing up the wood stove," she says, and then there's another one of those pauses when Kaylee knows she's thinking *But I'll never do that again.* Jane takes a deep breath. "But I always make fires for grilling or whatever without paper. One match, no paper, that's the rule. I can't do the 'one match' thing every single time, especially not if there's any wind, but it seems like a good skill to keep up."

"But *where*? Did your parents teach you?" She bites off the end of the bar.

"I learned in Scouts," Jane says. "I was a Girl Scout from Brownies clear through high school. We did a lot of camping. Then later I was a counselor at different Scout camps for several summers. Primitive camps, these were, with latrines and cold water from a hydrant, and lots of campfire cooking. Plenty of fire-building practice, all in all." In a moment she adds, "I never had any kids, but I always assumed I would, and I always thought that when I did I would teach them certain basic skills. How to swim, was one. How to build a fire with one match and no paper, that was another."

"I wish somebody'd taught *me*."

Jane laughs. "The last time I looked, somebody *was* teaching you! By the time you get home you'll have something to show your dad. But the skills kids need nowadays are so different than they were when I was your age, it's hard to believe. What are you, fourteen, fifteen?"

Kaylee swallows her bite. "Fifteen last month." She takes another.

"You've got so many skills already, at fifteen, that I don't have and never will have. I wouldn't have the faintest idea what to do with that SmartBerry, for instance; I've seen your thumb going lickety-split on that thing and wondered how the dickens you do it!"

Kaylee grins, feeling proud. Then the grin fades. She says slowly, "Right now those skills aren't too useful, are they?"

"We're in a sort of time warp here, just for a couple of days. A natural disaster. When things get back to normal—"

"But you were saying before," Kaylee says, feeling funny, "that there's going to be more and more natural disasters. Because of climate change."

Jane looks at her sharply. "*I* didn't actually say that, you know. What I said was, some scientists think there will be, but we don't know for sure."

It was obvious she was trying to avoid saying anything that would offend Kaylee's parents if it got back to them, but Kaylee wanted to know what she really thought. "We're pretty sure though, right?"

After a moment Jane nods. "Yes, we are. We're pretty damn sure. But it's good to know how to manage whenever a crisis *does* come, nobody could argue with that."

"Right, but what I'm thinking now," Kaylee says, refusing to be deflected from her line of thought, "is that there's something wrong with getting so far away from knowing *how* to manage. I mean, if you weren't here, what would I do? I don't know anything, nobody I know knows anything! My mom would *die* if she had to use an outhouse! Let alone go in the bushes! I mean," she said more quietly, "it's not about outhouses, that's dumb, but it seems like there's just something *wrong*. About everybody getting so far away from, like, the basics."

Now Jane is looking at Kaylee in a new way, more serious, almost more respectful. "It could be argued," she says finally, "that getting so far from the basics is one way of thinking about climate change. Why it's happening. Why people don't want to believe in it, so they won't have to stop doing the things that make it worse."

"My parents sure don't believe in it: they think it's hogwash," Kaylee admitted. "Nobody in my church believes in it. But," she says, "*you* do, you live like this on purpose. Is that why? To stop making things worse?"

Jane stands up carefully and stretches. "Time to feed the babies. When we're done, if you really want to know, I'll tell you about that."

Kaylee lies in the dark, thinking. She and Jane are sleeping in their clothes on the basement floor, in beds put together from a hodgepodge of old porch cushions and blankets. Kaylee has insisted that Jane take the only pillow; her own head rests on a bundle of Jane's spare clothes stuffed in a bag. The dogs are sharing a blanket on the patio. A funky lamp in what looks like a pickle jar, that burns olive oil, is a comforting source of light in the otherwise total darkness.

It turns out you don't have to feed hatchlings every fortyfive minutes all night, only during the daytime. The six babies are asleep too on the work bench, their dog bowl nestled in the hollow of a hot-water bottle, covered by a towel.

Kaylee's thinking about Jane's story. It turns out that living like this—conserving water, composting, recyling everything, ~~composting~~, driving as little as possible, generating some of her own electricity, growing most of her own food, buying most of the rest locally ("Except tea. I could give up tea only if there were none to be had.")—is *consistent* with trying to reduce the impact of people on climate change. But Jane had been living like this long before anyone had thought to worry about global warming. The reason is that when Jane was in college she had met an old couple who were living completely off the grid, except they had an old car they used to go to cultural events sometimes. They had no electricity, no phone or indoor toilet. *Their* cistern was higher than the house, so they didn't need a pump. They would never have even noticed a power outage. "They would have noticed a tornado," Kaylee had said darkly, and Jane had nodded ruefully. "They were lucky. A huge tornado came quite close to their place about forty years ago, but it missed them."

The term for that sort of life was *homesteading*. "They did things I could only dream about—grew and put up *all* their own food, for instance, plus picked berries and nuts and wild greens. And they kept goats for milk and cheese, meat too."

Kaylee is intrigued. "Why don't *you* have goats? You've got plenty of room."

Jane sighs. "I always meant to have some. Tennessee fainting goats—they're a cashmere type. But before I could get that far I broke my wrist, and that's when I found out that you can't have livestock if you live by yourself. Somebody has to be able to take over if you get injured or sick. Orrin had Hannah, you see, that's why it worked for them—plus Orrin was tough as nails. But even he got snakebit once, and Hannah had to go for help."

Their names were Hubbell, Orrin and Hannah Hubbell. Orrin was a landscape painter. He had built the house they were living in, on the Ohio River, and all the furniture. Hannah cooked and put up food on a wood-burning cookstove, Orrin fished and gardened and milked. Jane was nineteen when she met them, five years older than Kaylee, and she had fallen utterly in love with their homestead on the river. "I thought their place was magical, and the life they were living there was magical. I could see it was a lot of work, but the work seemed to keep them, well, you said it yourself: in touch with fundamental things, things they got enormous satisfaction out of. They were old by then, and got tired and cranky sometimes, but underneath there was always this—this deep serenity. It was like—well, as if what they did all day every day was a religious calling, as if they were monks or something, living every moment in the consciousness of a higher purpose."

And *that* was why Jane had chosen to live as she did. "Oh, I compromise in ways they never would have. I've got electricity, though I make as much of it as I can myself, and conserve what I make. I've got gadgets: a washer, a TV, a computer, a landline phone. *Had* gadgets," she corrected herself, and paused again. But then she went on without Kaylee having to prompt her. "The purity of *their* life came at the cost of ignoring society—though society didn't ignore them, people heard about them and were always dropping by. I didn't aspire to go as *far* as they did—they paid no attention to current events, never voted, they basically chose not to be citizens of the world. But if there had been another person or two who wanted the life I wanted, we would have been able to come much closer to the Hubbell's self-sufficiency than I have. Sustainability, that's the word for that."

"But nobody did."

"Nobody did. Not really. Not after they'd tried it for a while, experimentally."

"So you finally just went ahead and did it by yourself."

"Mm-hm. Compromises and all."

"Are you glad?"

Jane thinks a bit. "On the whole," she says finally, "Yes, very glad."

By the third day Jane and Kaylee have developed a routine. They've run out of bottled water for washing and cooking, so Kaylee hauls it a bucket at a time from the cistern—the pump house is gone but the cistern is below grade and is still there, still full—and Jane purifies it with tablets from the first-aid box. They take turns feeding and changing the hatchlings, all six of whom are eating and pooping up a storm, and have grown amazingly on bites of low-fat kibble; they're all-over gray fuzz now, with open eyes and big yellow mouths. Jane and Kaylee don't bother with a fire except at night, when they wash up all the dishes and then themselves with minimal amounts of water from the kettle. (Kaylee washes out her underwear, the only pair she's got, and dries it by the embers.) They take naps after lunch. Kaylee's period starts: no big deal, she's got pads and cramp pills. Kaylee changes the bandage on Jane's arm, which doesn't seem infected and has started to heal, though if it doesn't get stitched up soon she'll have one humongous scar. They've shoved all the loose junk in the basement against the walls, so they have more room in there, and a clear path from the shelter to the window.

On the third afternoon it rains. Their ceiling, which is the upstairs floor, leaks in a few places, so they retreat to the shelter with their bedding and Jane's chair, and bring the dogs back inside. "No fire tonight," Jane prophesies, though they've anticipated rain, and brought some firewood inside to keep it dry. "We'll have one in the morning if it's still raining at dinnertime." Jane breaks out an old board game, Clue, which they play by solar lantern light.

In the middle of the second game the dogs leap up and dash to the open window, barking wildly. A moment later they can both hear it: the deep nasal roar of a helicopter, flying low. Kaylee skins out of shelter, basement, and window in a flash, and jumps up and down in the rain, waving a blanket, yelling, "We're here! We're down here!" They couldn't have actually heard her over the racket, but an amplified voice from heaven thunders, "We see you! Stand by!"

Jane comes carefully through the window too now, wearing a rain jacket, and waves too, and tells the dogs to be quiet. The chopper hovers, then gradually settles in the hayfield next to the garden, and a guy in a yellow rain slicker jumps out and hurries toward them. "Jane Goodman? Kaylee Perry? You ladies all right—any injuries?"

"Jane's got a bad cut," Kaylee says, dancing around in the rain, excited by the suddenness of rescue, "but I'm fine! Are my mom and dad okay?"

"They're just dandy, and they sure do want to see you!" To Jane he says, "The tornado passed west of Lawrenceburg but Frankfort got clobbered. An EF3, they're saying. We been busy." He looks Jane over critically, sees she's not too badly hurt. "Okay, let's get going then," the guy says, turning to head back to the chopper.

Kaylee starts to hurry after him, but stops abruptly. "The hatchlings! Wait, I have to get . . ." she doubles back and pops through the window.

While she's stuffing a few things into her backpack, and putting the bowl of tree swallows into a rainproof plastic bag, she can hear them talking. "Baby birds," Jane's explaining. She'll just be a second. But I've got two dogs here, I can't leave them. I'll stay till we can all be lifted out together. Or till the road's open." Kaylee's mouth falls open; Jane's not coming?

"What about the cut?" says the guy in the slicker, and Jane's voice says, "It'll keep."

"Supplies?"

"Running low, but enough for another day or so."

"We'll drop you a bag of stuff on the next trip out. Should be able to pick you all up tomorrow."

Jane's not coming! Kaylee pops through the window between the dogs, who are barking again because of all the commotion, without the bowl of hatchlings or her backpack. "Jane, listen, if you're not leaving, I'm not either. You need me to change your bandage."

She's the only one not wearing rain gear and she's standing in the rain getting soaked. The adults look at her with surprise and consternation. "Honey, your parents need to see you, I'll be fine here for another day or so."

"We'll be back tomorrow to pick up this lady and the dogs," says the EMS guy. "You need to get on home."

"No," Kaylee says. She backs away from them. "I won't go so don't try to make me. Not till Jane does. As long as my parents know I'm fine, I'm staying here with her."

"I appreciate it, hon, I really do," Jane starts to say, "but—"

"No!" She stamps her foot; why won't they take her seriously? "I'm not leaving you here by yourself!"

The rain stops after all in time for them to have a hot supper, consisting of some of the food the chopper dropped off an hour before. Hot soup. Bacon and cheese sandwiches on fresh bread, mm. Apples. Bananas. Even Ding Dongs. Kaylee got the fire going herself, though not with one match. More like fifteen. "How long do you think it'll take to get your new house built?" she asks now, licking Ding Dong off her lips. She feeds each dog a piece of banana.

Jane is staring into Kaylee's fire. She looks up. "Hm?"

"To replace this one," Kaylee says. "How long?"

"Oh—" Jane sighs heavily. "I don't think . . . it doesn't make much sense, does it? Everybody says I'm nuts anyway, living out here alone in the middle of nowhere. I'm almost seventy, Kaylee. I'd been hoping to hang on a while longer, but maybe the tornado just forced a decision I've been putting off."

Kaylee sits up straight on the log. Her heart starts pounding. "What do you mean?"

"There's a retirement community in Indiana I've been looking at. Maybe it's time."

Stricken, Kaylee says, "But—you have to build a new house *here*! What about the birds, what are they supposed to do if you're not here? What would the *hatchlings* have done?"

Jane smiles. "The birds got along without me before I came. They'll be okay. I gave them a nice boost for a while, that's worth something; and as for the hatchlings, they have you to thank more than me."

Abruptly Kaylee bursts into tears, startling herself and making Jane jump. "What about *me* then? How am *I* gonna learn everything if you go away? What if the *Hubbells* went somewhere, just when you found out you wanted to live like them and be like them, and come see them all the time and help out, and—and feed the goats when they cut their arms or whatever, how would *you* feel?" She wipes her face on her sleeve, but the tears won't stop coming.

"Mercy," Jane says mildly after a minute. "I apologize, Kaylee. I had no idea you felt like that."

"Well, I do," she says, sniffling.

"Well, in that case, I guess I might have to think again. No promises, mind, but I won't decide anything just yet." She smiles. "You came at me out of left field with that one."

Kaylee wipes her sleeve across her eyes and smiles back shakily. "We'll get you a cell phone. Then if something happens, you won't be out here alone in the middle of nowhere 'cause you can call *me*. You wouldn't have to text message or anything."

Mercies

GREGORY BENFORD

Gregory Benford (www.gregorybenford.com) lives in Irvine, California. He is a CEO of several biotech companies devoted to extending longevity using genetic methods. He retains his appointment at UC Irvine as a professor emeritus of physics. He is the author of more than twenty novels, including Jupiter Project, Artifact, Against Infinity, Eater, *and the famous SF classic,* Timescape *(1980). Many of his (typically hard) SF stories are collected in* In Alien Flesh, Matters End *, and* Worlds Vast and Various. *Benford says, "I have just reissued in a new edition my cryonics novel* Chiller, *have out a new short story collection,* Anomalies. *In Fall 2012, I have A Big Smart Object novel out with Larry Niven,* The Bowl of Heaven."*

"Mercies" was published in the original anthology Enginering Infinity, *edited by Jonathan Strahan, the first of two selections from that excellent book we choose to reprint here. This story explores the real meaning of the science fiction cliché of going back in time to kill someone in order to change history. Never mind what you would do to history. If you took it up as a hobby, what would this say about you?*

All scientific work is, of course, based on some conscious or subconscious philosophical attitude.

Werner Heisenberg

He rang the doorbell and heard its buzz echo in the old wooden house. Footsteps. The worn, scarred door eased open half an inch and a narrowed brown eye peered at him.

"Mr. Hanson?" Warren asked in a bland bureaucratic tone, the accent a carefully rehearsed approximation of the flat Midwestern that would arouse no suspicions here.

"Yeah, so?" The mouth jittered, then straightened.

"I need to speak to you about your neighbour. We're doing a security background check."

The eye swept up and down Warren's three-piece suit, dark tie, polished shoes—traditional styles, or as the advertisements of this era said, "timeless." Warren was even sporting a gray fedora with a snap band.

"Which neighbour?"

This he hadn't planned on. Alarm clutched at his throat. Instead of speaking he nodded at the house to his right. Daniel Hanson's eye slid that way, then back, and narrowed some more. "Lemme see ID."

This Warren had expected. He showed an FBI ID in a plastic case, up-to-date and accurate. The single eye studied it and Warren wondered what to do if the door slammed shut. Maybe slide around to the window, try to—

The door jerked open. Hanson was a wiry man with shaggy

hair—a bony framework, all joints and hinges. His angular face jittered with concern and Warren asked, "You are the Hanson who works at Allied Mechanical?"

The hooded eyes jerked again as Warren stepped into the room.

"Uh, yeah, but hey—whassit matter if you're askin' 'bout the neighbour?"

Warren moved to his left to get Hanson away from the windows. "I just need the context in security matters of this sort."

"You're wastin' your time, see, I don't know 'bout—"

Warren opened his briefcase casually and in one fluid move brought the short automatic pistol out. Hanson froze. He fired straight into Hanson's chest. The popping sound was no louder than a dropped glass would make as the silencer soaked up the noise.

Hanson staggered back, his mouth gaping, sucking in air. Warren stepped forward, just as he had practiced, and carefully aimed again. The second shot hit Hanson squarely in the forehead and the man went down backward, thumping on the thin rug.

Warren listened. No sound from outside.

It was done. His first, and just about as he had envisioned it. In the sudden silence he heard his heart hammering.

He had read from the old texts that professional hit men of this era used the 0.22 automatic pistol despite its low calibre, and now he saw why. Little noise, especially with the suppressor, and the gun rode easily in his hand. The silencer would have snagged if he had carried it in a coat pocket. In all, his plans had worked. The pistol was light, strong, and— befitting its mission—a brilliant white.

The dark red pool spreading from Hanson's skull was a clear sign that this man, who would have tortured, hunted, and killed many women, would never get his chance now.

Further, the light 0.22 slug had stayed inside the skull, ricocheting so that it could never be identified as associated with this pistol. This point was also in the old texts, just as had been the detailed blueprints. Making the pistol and ammunition had been simple, using his home replicator machine.

He moved through the old house, floors creaking, and systematically searched Hanson's belongings. Here again the old texts were useful, leading him to the automatic pistol taped under a dresser drawer. No sign yet of the rifle Hanson had used in the open woods, either.

It was amazing, what twenty-first century journals carried, in their sensual fascination with the romantic aura of crime. He found no signs of victim clothing, of photos or mementos—all mementos Hanson had collected in Warren's timeline. Daniel Hanson took his victims into the woods near here, where he would let them loose and then hunt and kill them. His first known killing lay three months ahead of this day. The timestream was quite close, in quantum coordinates, so Warren could be sure that this Hanson was very nearly identical to the Hanson of Warren's timeline. They were adjacent in a sense he did not pretend to understand, beyond the cartoons in popular science books.

Excellent. Warren had averted a dozen deaths. He brimmed with pride.

He needed to get away quickly, back to the transflux cage. With each tick of time the transflux cage's location became more uncertain.

On the street outside he saw faces looking at him through a passing car window, the glass runny with reflected light. But the car just drove on. He made it into the stand of trees and then a kilometre walk took him to the cage. This was as accurate as the quantum flux process made possible during a jogg back through decades. He paused at the entrance hatch, listening. No police sirens. Wind sighed in the boughs. He sucked in the moist air and flashed a supremely happy grin.

He set the coordinates and readied himself. The complex calculations spread on a screen before him and a high tone sounded *screeeee* in his ears. A sickening gyre began. The whirl of space-time made gravity spread outward from him, pulling at his legs and arms as the satin blur of colour swirled past the transparent walls. *Screeeee . . .*

* * *

For Warren the past was a vast sheet of darkness, mired in crimes immemorial, each horror like a shining, vibrant, blood-red bonfire in the gloom, calling to him.

He began to see that at school. History instruction then was a multishow of images, sounds, scents and touches. The past came to the schoolboys as a sensory immersion. Social adjustment policy in those times was clear: only by deep sensing of what the past world was truly like could moral understanding occur. The technologies gave a reasonable immersion in eras, conveying why people thought or did things back then. So he saw the dirty wars, the horrifying ideas, the tragedies and comedies of those eras . . . and longed for them.

They seemed somehow more real. The smart world everyone knew had embedded intelligences throughout, which made it dull, predictable. Warren was always the brightest in his classes, and he got bored.

He was fifteen when he learned of serial killers.

The teacher—Ms. Sheila Weiss, lounged back on her desk with legs crossed, her slanted red mouth and lifted black eyebrows conveying her humour—said that quite precisely, "serials" were those who murdered three or more people over a period of more than thirty days, with a "cooling off" period between each murder. The pattern was quite old, not a mere manifestation of their times, Ms. Weiss said. Some sources suggested that legends such as werewolves and vampires were inspired by medieval serial killers. Through all that history, their motivation for killing was the lure of "psychological gratification"—whatever that meant, Warren thought.

Ms. Weiss went on: Some transfixed by the power of life and death were attracted to medical professions. These "angels of death"—or as they self-described, angels of mercy—were the worst, for they killed so many. One Harold Shipman, an English family doctor, made it seem as though his victims had died of natural causes. Between 1975 and 1998, he murdered at least two hundred and fifteen patients. Ms. Weiss added that he might have murdered two hundred and fifty or more.

The girl in the next seat giggled nervously at all this, and Warren frowned at her. Gratification resonated in him, and he struggled with his own strange excitement. Somehow, he realized as the discussion went on around him, the horror of death coupled with his own desire. This came surging up in him as an inevitable, vibrant truth.

Hesitantly he asked Ms. Weiss, "Do we have them . . . serial killers . . . now?"

She beamed, as she always did when he saw which way her lecture was going. "No, and that is the point. Good for you! Because we have neuro methods, you see. All such symptoms are detected early—the misaligned patterns of mind, the urges outside the norm envelope—and extinguished. They use electro and pharma, too." She paused, eyelids fluttering in a way he found enchanting.

Warren could not take his eyes off her legs as he said, "Does that . . . harm?"

Ms. Weiss eyed him oddly and said, "The procedure— that is, a normalization of character before the fact of any, ah, bad acts—occurs without damage or limitation of freedom of the, um, patient, you understand."

"So we don't have serial killers anymore?"

Ms. Weiss's broad mouth twisted a bit. "No methods are perfect. But our homicide rates from these people are far lower now."

Boyd Carlos said from the back of the class, "Why not just kill 'em?" and got a big laugh.

Warren reddened. Ms. Weiss's beautiful, warm eyes flared with anger, eyebrows arched. "That is the sort of crime our society seeks to avoid," she said primly. "We gave up capital punishment ages ago. It's uncivilized."

Boyd made a clown face at this, and got another laugh. Even the girls joined in this time, the chorus of their high giggles echoing in Warren's ears.

Sweat broke out all over Warren's forehead and he hoped no one would notice. But the girl in the seat across the aisle did, the pretty blonde one named Nancy, whom he had been planning for weeks to approach. She rolled her eyes, gestured to friends. Which made him sweat more.

His chest tightened and he thought furiously, eyes averted from the blonde. Warren ventured, "How about the victims who might die? Killing killers saves lives."

Ms. Weiss frowned. "You mean that executing them prevents murders later?"

Warren spread his hands. "If you imprison them, can't they murder other prisoners?"

Ms. Weiss blinked. "That's a very good argument, Warren, but can you back it up?"

"Uh, I don't—"

"You could research this idea. Look up the death rate in prisons due to murderers serving life sentences. Discover for yourself what fraction of prison murders they cause."

"I'll . . . see." Warren kept his eyes on hers.

Averting her eyes, blinking, Ms. Weiss seemed pleased, bit her lip and moved on to the next study subject.

That ended the argument, but Warren thought about it all through the rest of class. Boyd even came over to him later and said, with the usual shrugs and muttering, "Thanks for backin' me up, man."

Then he sauntered off with Nancy on his arm. A bit later Warren saw Boyd holding forth to his pals, mouth big and grinning, pointing toward Warren and getting more hooting from the crowd. Nancy guffawed too, lips lurid, eyes on Boyd.

That was Warren's sole triumph among the cool set, who afterward went back to ignoring him. But he felt the sting of the class laughing all the same. His talents lay in careful work, not in the zing of classroom jokes. He was methodical, so he should use that.

So he did the research Ms. Weiss had suggested. Indeed, convicted murderers committed the majority of murders in prison. What did they have to lose? Once a killer personality had jumped the bounds of society, what held them back? They were going to serve out their life sentences anyway. And a reputation for settling scores helped them in prison, even gave them weird prestige and power.

These facts simmered in him for decades. He had never forgotten that moment—the lurid lurch of Ms. Sheila Weiss's mouth, the rushing terror and desire lacing through him, the horrible high, shrill giggle from that girl in the next seat. Or the history of humanity's horror, and the strange ideas it summoned up within him.

His next jogg took him further backward in time, as it had to, for reasons he had not bothered to learn. Something about the second law of thermodynamics, he gathered.

He slid sideways in space-time, following the arc of Earth's orbit around the galaxy—this he knew, but it was just more incomprehensible technical detail that was beside his point entirely. He simply commanded the money and influence to make it happen. How it happened was someone else's detail.

Just as was the diagnosis, which he could barely follow, four months before. Useless details. Only the destination mattered; he had three months left now, at best. His stomach spiked with growling aches and he took more of the pills to suppress his symptoms.

In that moment months before, listening to the doctor drone on, he had decided to spend his last days in a long space-time jogg. He could fulfil his dream, sliding backward into eras "nested," as the specialists said, close to his own. Places where he could understand the past, act upon it, and bring about good. The benefits of his actions would come to others, but that was the definition of goodness, wasn't it—to bring joy and life to others.

As he decided this, the vision coming sharp and true, he had felt a surge of purpose. He sensed vaguely that this glorious campaign of his was in some way redemption for his career, far from the rough rub of the world. But he did not inspect his impulses, for that would blunt his impact, diffuse his righteous energies.

He had to keep on.

He came out of the transflux cage in a city park. It was the mid-1970s, before Warren had been born.

His head spun sickly from the flexing gravity of the jogg. Twilight gathered in inky shadows and a recent rain flavoured the air. Warren carefully noted the nearby landmarks. As he walked away through a dense stand of scraggly trees, he turned and looked back at each change of direction. This cemented the return route in his mind.

He saw no one as night fell. With a map he found the cross street he had expected. His clothing was jeans and a light brown jacket, not out of place here in Danville, a small Oklahoma town, although brown mud now spattered his tennis shoes. He wiped them off on grass as he made his way into the street where Frank Clifford lived. The home was an artful Craftsman design, two windows glowing with light. He searched for a sure sign that Clifford lived here. The deviations from his home timeline might be minor, and his prey might have lived somewhere else. But the mailbox had no name on it, just the address. He had to be sure.

He was far enough before Clifford's first known killing, as calculated by his team. Clifford had lived here for over a month, the spotty property tax records said, and his pattern of killings, specializing in nurses, had not emerged in the casebooks. Nor had such stylized killings, with their major themes of bondage in nurse uniforms and long sexual bouts, appeared along Clifford's life history. Until now.

The drapes concealed events inside the house. He caught flickering shadows, though, and prepared his approach. Warren made sure no one from nearby houses was watching him as he angled across the lawn and put his foot on the first step up to the front door.

This had worked for the first three disposals. He had gained confidence in New Haven and Atlanta, editing out killers who got little publicity but killed dozens. Now he felt sure of himself. His only modification was to carry the pistol in his coat pocket, easier to reach. He liked the feel of it, loaded and ready. *Avenging angel*, yes, but preventing as well.

Taking a breath, he started up the steps—and heard a door slam to his right. Light spattered into the driveway. A car door opened. He guessed that Clifford was going to drive away.

Looping back to this space-time coordinate would be impossible, without prior work. He had to do something now, outside the house. Outside his pattern.

An engine nagged into a thrumming idle. Warren walked to the corner of the house and looked around. Headlights flared in a dull-toned Ford. He ducked back, hoping he had not been seen.

The gear engaged and the car started forward, spitting gravel. Warren started to duck, stay out of sight—then took a breath. *No, now.*

He reached out as the car came by and yanked open the rear passenger door. He leaped in, not bothering to pull the door closed, and brought the pistol up. He could see the man only in profile. In the dim light Warren could not tell if the quick profile fit the photos and 3D recreations he had memorized. Was this Clifford?

"Freeze!" he said as the driver's head jerked toward him. Warren pressed the pistol's snub snout into the man's neck. "Or I pull the trigger."

Warren expected the car to stop. Instead, the man stamped on the gas. And said nothing.

They rocked out of the driveway, surged right with squealing tires, and the driver grinned in the streetlamp lights as he gunned the engine loud and hard.

"Slow down!" Warren said, pushing the muzzle into the back of the skull. "You're Clifford, right?"

"Ok, sure I am. Take it easy, man." Clifford said this casually, as if he were in control of the situation. Warren felt confusion leap like sour spit into his throat. But Clifford kept accelerating, tires howling as he turned onto a highway. They were near the edge of town and Warren did not want to get far from his resonance point.

"Slow down, I said!"

"Sure, just let me get away from these lights." Clifford glanced over his right shoulder. "You don't want us out where people can see, do you?"

Warren didn't know what to say. They shot past the last traffic light and hummed down a state highway. There was no other traffic and the land lay level and barren beyond. In the blackness, Warren thought, he could probably walk back into town. But—

"How far you want me to go?"

He had to shake this man's confidence. "Have you killed any women yet, Frank?"

Clifford didn't even blink. "No. Been thinkin' on it. Lots."

This man didn't seem surprised. "You're sure?" Warren asked, to buy time.

"What's the point o' lyin'?"

This threw Warren into even more confusion. Clifford stepped down on the gas again though and Warren felt this slipping out of his control. "Slow down!"

Clifford smiled. "Me and my buddies, back in high school, we had this kinda game. We'd get an old jalopy and run it out here, four of us, and do the survivor thing."

"What—?"

"What you got against me, huh?" Clifford turned and smirked at him.

"I, you—you're going to *murder* those women, that's what—"

"How you know that? You're like that other guy, huh?"

"How can you—wait—other guy—?"

The car surged forward with bursting speed into a flat curve in the highway. Headlights swept across bare fields as the engine roared. Clifford chuckled in a dry, flat tone, and spat out, "Let's see how you like our game, buddy-o."

Clifford slammed the driver's wheel to the left and the Ford lost traction, sliding into a skid. It jumped off the two-lane blacktop and into the flat field beyond. Clifford jerked on the wheel again—

—and in adrenaline-fed slow motion the seat threw Warren into the roof. The car frame groaned like a wounded beast and the wheels left the ground. The transmission shrieked like a band saw cutting tin, as the wheels got free of the road. Warren lifted, smacked against the roof, and it pushed him away as the frame hit the ground—*whomp.* The back window popped into a crystal shower exploding around him. Then the car heaved up, struggling halfway toward the sky again—paused—and crashed back down. Seams twanged, glass shattered, the car rocked. Stopped.

Quiet. Crickets. Wind sighing through the busted windows. Warren crawled out of the wide-flung door. He still clutched the pistol, which had not gone off. On his knees in the ragged weeds he looked around. No motion in the dim quarter-moonlight that washed the twisted Ford. Headlights poked two slanted lances of gray light across the flat fields.

Warren stood up and hobbled—his left leg weak and trembling—through the reek of burnt rubber, to look in the driver's window. It was busted into glittering fragments. Clifford sprawled across the front seat, legs askew. The moonlight showed glazed eyes and a tremor in the open mouth. As he watched a dark bubble formed at the lips and swelled, then burst, and he saw it was blood spraying across the face.

Warren thought a long moment and then turned to walk back into town. Again, quickly finding the transflux cage was crucial. He stayed away from the road in case some car would come searching, but in the whole long walk back, which took a forever that by his timer proved to be nearly an hour, no headlights swept across the forlorn fields.

He had staged a fine celebration when he invented masked inset coding, a flawless quantum logic that secured against deciphering. That brought him wealth beyond mortal dreams, all from encoded 1s and 0s.

That began his long march through the highlands of digital craft. Resources came to him effortlessly. When he acquired control of the largest consortium of advanced research companies, he rejoiced with friends and mistresses. His favourite was a blonde who, he realized late in the night, reminded him of that Nancy, long ago. Nearly fifty years.

The idea came to him in the small hours of that last, sybaritic night. As the pillows of his sofa moved to accommodate him, getting softer where he needed it, supporting his back with the right strength, his unconscious made the connection. He had acquired major stock interest in Advanced Spacetimes. His people managed the R&D program. They could clear the way, discreetly arrange for a "sideslip" as the technicals termed it. The larger world called it a "jogg," to evoke the sensation of trotting blithely across the densely packed quantum spacetimes available.

He thought this through while his smart sofa whispered soft, encouraging tones. His entire world was smart. Venture to jaywalk on a city street and a voice told you to get back, traffic was on the way. Take a wrong turn walking home and your inboards beeped you with directions. In the countryside, trees did not advise you on your best way to the lake. Compared to the tender city, nature was dead, rough, uncaring.

There was no place in the claustrophobic smart world to sense the way the world had been, when men roamed wild and did vile things. No need for that horror, anymore. Still, he longed to right the evils of that untamed past. Warren saw his chance.

Spacetime intervals were wedges of coordinates, access to them paid for by currency flowing seamlessly from accounts, which would never know the use he put their assets to—or care.

He studied in detail that terrible past, noting dates and deaths and the heady ideas they called forth. Assembling his team, he instructed them to work out a trajectory that slid across the braided map of nearby space-times, all generated by quantum processes he could not fathom in the slightest.

Each side-slide brought the transflux passenger to a slightly altered, parallel universe of events. Each held potential victims, awaiting the knife or bludgeon that would end their own timelines forever. Each innocent could be saved. Not in Warren's timeline—too late for that—but in other spacetimes, still yearning for salvation.

The car crash had given him a zinging adrenaline boost, which now faded. As he let the transflux cage's transverse gravity spread his legs and arms, popping joints, he learned from the blunders he had made. Getting in the car and not immediately shoving the snout of the 0.22 into Clifford's neck, pulling the trigger—yes, an error. The thrill of the moment had clouded his judgment, surely.

So he made the next few joggs systematic. Appear, find the target, kill within a few minutes more, then back to the cage. He began to analyse those who fell to his exacting methods.

A catalogue of evil, gained at the expense of the sickness that now beset him at every jogg.

Often, the killers betrayed in their last moments not simple fear, but their own motives. Usually sexual disorders drove them. Their victims, he already knew, had something in common—occupation, race, appearance or age. One man in his thirties would slaughter five librarians, and his walls were covered with photos of brunettes wearing glasses. Such examples fell into what the literature called, in its deadening language, "specific clusters of dysfunctional personality characteristics," along with eye tics, obsessions, a lack of conversational empathy.

These men had no guilt. They blustered when they saw the 0.22 and died wholly self-confident, surprised as the bullets found them. Examining their homes, Warren saw that they followed a distinct set of rigid, self-made rules. He knew that most would keep photo albums of their victims, so was unsurprised to find that they already, before their crimes, had many women's dresses and lingerie crammed into their hiding places, and much pornography. Yet they had appeared to be normal and often quite charming, a thin mask of sanity.

Their childhoods were marked by animal cruelty, obsession with fire setting, and persistent bedwetting past the age of five. They would often lure victims with ploys appealing to the victims' sense of sympathy.

Such monsters should be erased, surely. In his own timeline, the continuing drop in the homicide rate was a puzzle. Now he sensed that at least partly that came from the work of sideslip space-time travellers like himself, who remained invisible in that particular history.

Warren thought on this, as he slipped along the whorl of space-time, seeking his next exit. He would get as many of the vermin as he could, cleansing universes he would never enjoy. He had asked his techs at Advanced Spacetimes if he could go forward in time to an era when someone had cured the odd cancer that beset him. But they said no, that sideslipping joggs could not move into a future undefined, unknown.

He learned to mop up his vomit, quell his roaming aches, grit his teeth and go on.

He waited through a rosy sundown for Ted Bundy to appear. Light slid from the sky and traffic hummed on the streets nearby the apartment Warren knew he used in 1971. People were coming back to their happy homes, the warm domestic glows and satisfactions.

It was not smart to lurk in the area, so he used his lock picks to enter the back of the apartment house, and again on Bundy's door. The mailboxes below had helpfully reassured him that the mass murderer of so many women lived here, months before his crimes began.

To pass the time he found the materials that eventually Bundy would use to put his arm in a fake plaster cast and ask women to help him carry something to his car. Then Bundy would beat them unconscious with a crowbar and carry them away. Bundy had been a particularly organized killer—socially adequate, with friends and lovers. Sometimes such types even had a spouse and children. The histories said such men were those who, when finally captured, were likely to be described by acquaintances as kind and unlikely to hurt anyone. But they were smart and swift and dangerous, at all times.

So when Warren heard the front door open, he slipped into the back bedroom and, to his sudden alarm, heard a female voice. An answering male baritone, joking and light.

They stopped in the kitchen to pour some wine. Bundy was a charmer, his voice warm and mellow, dipping up and down with sincere interest in some story she was telling him. He put on music, soft saxophone jazz, and they moved to the living room.

This went on until Warren began to sweat with anxiety. The transflux cage's position in space-time was subject to some form of uncertainty principle. As it held strictly to this timeline, its position in spatial coordinates became steadily more poorly phased. That meant it would slowly drift in position, in some quantum sense he did not follow. The techs assured him this was a small, unpredictable effect, but cautioned him to minimize his time at any of the jogg points.

If the transflux cage moved enough, he might not find it again in the dark. It was in a dense pine forest and he had memorized the way back, but anxiety began to vex him.

He listened to Bundy's resonant tones romancing the woman as bile leaked upward into his mouth. The cancer was worsening, the pains cramping his belly. It was one of the new, variant cancers that evolved after the supposed victory over the simpler sorts. Even suppressing the symptoms was difficult.

If he vomited he would surely draw Bundy back here. Sweating from the pain and anxiety, Warren inched forward along the carpeted corridor, listening intently. Bundy's voice rose, irritated. The woman's response was hesitant, startled—then beseeching. The music suddenly got louder. Warren quickly moved to the end of the corridor and looked around the corner. Bundy had a baseball bat in his hands, eyes bulging, the woman sitting on the long couch speaking quickly, hands raised, Bundy stepping back—

Warren fished out the pistol and brought it up as Bundy swung. He clipped the woman in the head, a hard smack. Her long hair flew back as she grunted and collapsed. She rolled off the couch, thumping on the floor.

Warren said, "Bastard!" and Bundy turned. "How many have you killed?"

"What the—who are you?"

Warren permitted himself a smile. He had to know if there had been no victims earlier. "An angel. How many, you swine?"

Bundy relaxed, swinging the bat in one hand. He smirked, eyes narrowing as he took in the situation, Warren, his opportunities. "You don't look like any angel to me, buster. Just some nosy neighbour, right?" He smiled. "Watch me bring girls up here, wanted to snoop? Maybe watch us? That why you were hiding in my bedroom?"

Bundy strolled casually forward with an easy, athletic gait as he shrugged, a grin breaking across his handsome face, his left hand spread in a casual so-what gesture, right hand clenched firmly on the bat. "We were just having a little argument here, man. I must've got a little mad, you can see—"

The *splat* of the 0.22 going off was mere rhythm in the jazz that blared from two big speakers. Bundy stepped back and blinked in surprise and looked down at the red stain on his lumberjack shirt. Warren aimed carefully and the second shot hit him square in the nose, splattering blood. Bundy toppled forward, thumping on the carpet.

Warren calculated quickly. The woman must get away clean, that was clear. He didn't want her nailed for a murder. She was out cold, a bruise on the crown of her head. He searched her handbag: Norma Roberts, local address. She appeared in none of the Bundy history. Yet she was going to be his first, clearly. The past was not well documented.

He decided to get away quickly. He got her up and into a shoulder carry, her body limp. He opened the front door, looked both ways down the corridor, and hauled her to the back entrance of the apartment house. There he leaned her into a chair and left her and her coat and handbag. It seemed simpler to let her wake up. She would probably get away by herself. Someone would notice the smell in a week, and find an unsolvable crime scene. It was the best he could do.

The past was not well documented . . . Either Bundy had not acknowledged this first murder, or else Warren had sideslipped into a space-time where Bundy's history was somewhat different. But not different enough—Bundy was clearly an adroit, self-confident killer. He thought on this as he threaded his way into the gathering darkness.

The pains were crippling by then, awful clenching spasms shooting through his belly. He barely got back to the transflux cage before collapsing.

He took time to recover, hovering the cage in the transition zone. Brilliant colours raced around the cage. The walls hummed and rattled and the capsule's processed air took on a sharp, biting edge.

There were other Bundys in other timelines, but he needed to move on to other targets. No one knew how many timelines there were, though they were not infinite. Complex quantum processes generated them and some theorists thought the number might be quite few. If so, Warren could not reach some timelines. Already the cage had refused to go to four target murderers, so perhaps his opportunities were not as large as the hundreds or thousands he had at first dreamed about.

He had already shot Ted Kaczynski, the "Unabomber." That murderer had targeted universities and wrote a manifesto that he distributed to the media, claiming that he wanted society to return to a time when technology was not a threat to its future. Kaczynski had not considered that a future technology would erase his deeds.

Kaczynski's surprised gasp lay behind him now. He decided, since his controls allowed him to choose among the braided timelines, to save as many victims as he could. His own time was growing short.

He scanned through the gallery of mass murder, trying to relax as the flux cage popped and hummed with stresses. Sex was the primary motive of lust killers, whether or not the victims were dead, and fantasy played strongly in their killings. The worst felt that their gratification depended on torture and mutilation, using weapons in close contact with the victims—knives, hammers, or just hands. Such lust killers often had a higher cause they could recite, but as they continued, intervals between killings decreased and the craving for stimulation increased.

He considered Coral Watts, a rural murderer. A surviving victim had described him as "excited and hyper and clappin' and just making noises like he was excited, that this was gonna be fun." Watts killed by slashing, stabbing, hanging, drowning, asphyxiating, and strangling. But when Warren singled out the coordinates for Watts, the software warned him that the target timeline was beyond his energy reserves.

The pain was worse now, shooting searing fingers up into his chest. He braced himself in the acceleration chair and took an injection his doctors had given him, slipping the needle into an elbow vein. It helped a bit, a soothing warmth spreading through him. He put aside the pain and concentrated, lips set in a thin white line.

His team had given him choices in the space-time coordinates. The pain told him that he would not have time enough to visit them all and bring his good work to the souls who had suffered in those realms. Plainly, he should act to cause the greatest good, downstream in time from his intervention.

Ah. There was a desirable target time, much further back, that drew his attention. These killers acted in concert, slaughtering many. But their worst damage had been to the sense of stability and goodwill in their society. That damage had exacted huge costs for decades thereafter. Warren knew, as he reviewed the case file, what justice demanded. He would voyage across the braided timestreams and end his jogg in California, 1969.

He emerged on a bare rock shelf in Chatsworth, north of the valley bordering, the Los Angeles megaplex. He savoured the view as the flux cage relaxed around him, its gravitational ripples easing away. Night in the valley: streaks of actinic boulevard streetlights, crisp dry air flavoured of desert and combustion. The opulence of the era struck him immediately: blaring electric lights lacing everywhere, thundering hordes of automobiles on the highways, the sharp sting of smog, and large homes of glass and wood, poorly insulated. His era termed this the Age of Appetite, and so it was.

But it was the beginning of a time of mercies. The crimes the Manson gang was to commit did not cost the lot of them their lives. California had briefly instituted an interval with no death penalty while the Manson cases wound through their lethargic system. The guilty then received lifelong support, living in comfortable surrounds and watching television and movies, labouring a bit, writing books about their crimes, giving interviews and finally passing away from various diseases. This era thought that a life of constrained ease was the worst punishment it could ethically impose.

Manson and Bundy were small-scale murderers, compared with Hitler, Mao, and others of this slaughterhouse century. But the serial killers Warren could reach and escape undetected. Also, he loathed them with a special rage.

He hiked across a field of enormous boulders in the semi-night of city glow, heading north. Two days ahead in this future, on July 1, 1969, Manson would shoot a black drug dealer named "Lotsapoppa" Crowe at a Hollywood apartment. He would retreat to the rambling farm buildings Warren could make out ahead, the Spahn Ranch in Topanga Canyon. Manson would then turn Spahn Ranch into a defensive camp, with night patrols of armed guards. Now was the last possible moment to end this gathering catastrophe, silence its cultural impact, save its many victims.

Warren approached cautiously, using the rugged rocks as cover. He studied the ramshackle buildings, windows showing pale lighting. His background said this was no longer a functioning ranch, but instead a set for moving pictures. He wondered why anyone would bother making such dramas on location, when computer graphics were much simpler; or was this time so far back that that technology did not exist? The past was a mysterious, unknowingly wealthy land.

Near the wooden barns and stables ahead, a bonfire licked at the sky. Warren moved to his right, going uphill behind a rough rock scree to get a better view. Around the fire were a dozen people sitting, their rapt faces lit in dancing orange firelight, focused on the one figure who stood, the centre of attention.

Warren eased closer to catch the voices. Manson's darting eyes caught the flickering firelight. The circle of faces seemed like moons orbiting the long-haired man.

Warren felt a tap on his shoulder. He whirled, the 0.22 coming naturally into his hand. A small woman held her palms up, shaking her head. Then a finger to her lips, *shhhh.*

He hesitated. They were close enough that a shot might be heard. Warren elected to follow the woman's hand signals, settling down into a crouch beside her.

She whispered into his ear, "No fear. I am here for the same reason."

Warren said, "What reason? Who the hell are you?"

"To prevent the Tate murders. I'm Serafina." Her blonde hair caught the fire glow.

Warren whispered, "You're from—"

"From a time well beyond yours."

"You . . . side-slipped?"

"Following your lead. Your innovation." Her angular features sharpened, eyes alive. "I am here to help you with your greatest mercy."

"How did you—"

"You are famous, of course. Some of us sought to emulate you. To bring mercy to as many timelines as possible."

"Famous?" Warren had kept all this secret, except for his—ah, of course, the team. Once he vanished from his native timeline, they would talk. Perhaps they could track him in his sideslips; they had incredible skills he would never understand. In all this, he had never thought of what would happen once he left his timeline, gone forever.

"You are a legend. The greatest giver of mercies." She smiled, extending a slender hand. "It is an honour."

He managed to take her hand, which seemed impossibly warm. Which meant that he was chilled, blood rushing to his centre, where the pain danced.

"I . . . thank you. Uh, help, you said? How—"

She raised the silencing finger again. "Listen."

They rose a bit on their haunches, and now Warren heard the strong voice of the standing man. Shaggy, bearded, arms spread wide, the fierce eyes showed white.

"We are the *soul* of our time, my people. The *family*. We are in truth a part of the *hole* in the *infinite*. That is our destiny, our *duty*." The rolling cadences, Manson's voice rising on the high notes, had a strange hypnotic ring.

"The blacks will soon *rise up*." Manson forked his arms skyward. "Make no mistake—for the Beatles *themselves* saw this coming. The *White Album* songs say it—in *code*, my friends. John, Paul, George, Ringo—they directed that album at *our Family itself*, for we are the *elect*. Disaster *is* coming."

Warren felt the impact of Manson's voice, seductive: he detested it. In that rolling, powerful chant lay the deaths to come at 10050 Cielo Drive. Sharon Tate, eight and a half months pregnant. Her friend and former lover Jay Sebring. Abigail Folger, heiress to the Folger coffee fortune. Others, too, all innocents. Roman Polanski, one of the great drama makers of this era and Tate's husband, was in London at work on a film project or else he would have shared their fate, with others still—

The thought struck him—what if, in this timeline, Roman Polanski was there at 10050 Cielo Drive? Would he die, too? If so, Warren's mission was even more a mercy for this era.

Manson went on, voice resounding above the flickering flames, hands and eyes working the circle of rapt acolytes. "We'll be movin' soon. *Movin'!* I got a canary-yellow home in Canoga Park for us, not far from here. A great pad. Our family will be submerged beneath the awareness of the outside world"—a pause—"I call it the *Yellow Submarine!*" Gasps, applause from around the campfire.

Manson went on, telling the "family" they might have to show blacks how to start "Helter Skelter," the convulsion that would destroy the power structure and bring Manson to the fore. The circle laughed and yelped and applauded, their voices a joyful babble.

He sat back, acid pain leaking into his mind. In his joggs Warren had seen the direct presence of evil, but nothing like this monster.

Serafina said, "This will be your greatest mercy."

Warren's head spun. "You came to make . . ."

"Make it happen." She pulled from the darkness behind her a long, malicious device. An automatic weapon, Warren saw. Firepower.

"Your 0.22 is not enough. Without me, you will fail."

Warren saw now what must occur. He was not enough against such massed insanity. Slowly he nodded.

She shouldered the long sleek weapon, clicked off the safety. He rose beside her, legs weak.

"You take the first," she said. He nodded and aimed at Manson. The 0.22 was so small and light as he aimed, while crickets chirped and the bile rose up into his dry throat. He concentrated and squeezed off the shot.

The sharp splat didn't have any effect. Warren had missed. Manson turned toward them—

The hammering of her automatic slammed in his ears as

he aimed his paltry 0.22 and picked off the fleeing targets. *Pop! Pop!*

He was thrilled to hit three of them—shadows going down in the firelight. Serafina raged at them, changing clips and yelling. He shouted himself, a high long *ahhhhhh*. The "family" tried to escape the firelight, but the avenging rounds caught them and tossed the murderers-to-be like insects into their own bonfire.

Manson had darted away at Serafina's first burst. The man ran quickly to Warren's left and Warren followed, feet heavy, hands automatically adding rounds to the 0.22 clip. In the dim light beyond the screams and shots Warren tracked the lurching form, framed against the distant city glow. Some around the circle had pistols, too, and they scattered, trying to direct fire against Serafina's quick, short bursts.

Warren trotted into the darkness, feet unsteady, keeping Manson's silhouette in view. He stumbled over outcroppings, but kept going despite the sudden lances of agony creeping down into his legs.

Warren knew he had to save energy, that Manson could outrun him easily. So he stopped at the crest of a rise, settled in against a rock and held the puny 0.22 in his right hand, bracing it with his left. He could see Manson maybe twenty meters away, trotting along, angling toward the ranch's barn. He squeezed off a shot. The *pop* was small against the furious gunfire behind him, but the figure fell. Warren got up and calculated each step as he trudged down the slope. A shadow rose. Manson was getting up. Warren aimed again and fired and knew he had missed. Manson turned and Warren heard a barking explosion—as a sharp slap knocked him backward, tumbling into sharp gravel.

Gasping, he got up against a massive weight. On his feet, rocky, he slogged forward. *Pock pock* gunfire from behind was a few sporadic shots, followed immediately by furious automatic bursts, hammering on and on into the chill night.

Manson was trying to get up. He lurched on one leg, tried to bring his own gun up again, turned—and Warren fired three times into him at a few meters range. The man groaned, crazed eyes looking at Warren and he wheezed out, "Why?"—then toppled.

Warren blinked at the stars straight overhead and realized he must have fallen. The stars were quite beautiful in their crystal majesty.

Serafina loomed above him. He tried to talk but had no breath.

Serafina said softly, "They're all gone. Done. Your triumph."

Acid came up in his throat as he wheezed out, "What . . . next . . ."

Serafina smiled, shook her head. "No next. You were the first, the innovator. We followed you. There have been many others, shadowing you closely on nearby space-time lines, arriving at the murder sites—to savour the reflected glory."

He managed, "Others. Glory?"

Serafina grimaced. "We could tell where you went—we all detected entangled correlations, to track your ethical joggs. Some just followed, witnessed. Some imitated you. They went after lesser serial killers. Used your same simple, elegant methods—minimum tools and weapons, quick and seamless."

Warren blinked. "I thought I *was* alone—"

"You were alone. The first. But the idea spread, later. I come from more than a century after you."

He had never thought of imitators. Cultures changed, one era thinking the death penalty was obscene, another embracing it as a solution. "I tried to get as many—"

"As you could, of course." She stroked his arm, soothing the disquiet that flickered across his face, pinching his mouth. "The number of timelines is only a few hundred—Gupta showed that in my century—so it's not a pointless infinity."

"Back there in Oklahoma—"

"That was Clyde, another jogger. He made a dumb mistake, got there before you. Clyde was going to study the aftermath of that. He backed out as soon as he could. He left Clifford for you."

Warren felt the world lift from him and now he had no weight. Light, airy. "He nearly got me killed, too."

Serafina shrugged. "I know; I've been tagging along behind you, with better transflux gear. I come from further up our shared timestream, see? Still, the continuing drop in the homicide rate comes at least partly from the work of jogg people, like me."

He eyed her suspiciously. "Why did you come here?"

Serafina simply leaned over and hugged him. "You failed here. I wanted to change that. Now you've accomplished your goal here—quick mercy for the unknowing victims."

This puzzled him but of course it didn't matter anymore, none of it. Except—

"Manson . . ."

"He killed you here. But now, in a different timestream—caused by me appearing—you *got* him." Her voice rose happily, eyes bright, teeth flashing in a broad smile.

He tried to take this all in. "Still . . ."

"It's all quantum logic, see?" she said brightly. "So uncertainty applies to time travel. The side-jogg time traveller affects the time stream he goes to. So then later side-slipping people, they have to correct for that."

He shook his head, not really following.

She said softly, "Thing is, we think the irony of all this is delicious. In my time, we're more self-conscious, I guess."

"What . . . ?"

"An ironic chain, we call it. To jogg is to act, and be acted upon." She touched him sympathetically. "You did kill so many. Justice is still the same."

She cocked his own gun, holding it up in the dull sky glow, making sure there was a round in the chamber. She snapped it closed. "Think of it as a mercy." She lowered the muzzle at him and gave him a wonderful smile.

The Education of Junior Number 12

MADELINE ASHBY

Madeline Ashby (www.madelineashby.com) is a science fiction writer and foresight consultant living in Toronto. Her debut novel, vN, is out from Angry Robot Books in 2012. Her stories have been published in Nature, FLURB, Tesseracts, Escape Pod, and elsewhere. She has also blogged for Boing-Boing, WorldChanging, Tor.com, and io9.com.

"The Education of Junior Number 12" appeared online at the website of angryrobotbooks.com at the end of December 2011, and this is perhaps its first appearance in print. About this story, Ashby says, "Javier is a character who appears in vN. He's one of my favorite characters, and this is one of his more sombre stories."

Charlie Jane Anders calls the story, "dark and intense and amazing."

"You're a self-replicating humanoid. vN."

Javier always spoke Spanish the first few days. It was his clade's default setting. "You have polymer-doped memristors in your skin, transmitting signal to the aerogel in your muscles from the graphene coral inside your skeleton. That part's titanium. You with me, so far?"

Junior nodded. He plucked curiously at the clothes Javier had stolen from the balcony of a nearby condo. It took Javier three jumps, but eventually his fingers and toes learned how to grip the grey water piping. He'd take Junior there for practise, after the kid ate more and grew into the clothes. He was only toddler-sized, today. They'd holed up in a swank bamboo tree house positioned over an infinity pool outside La Jolla, and its floor was now littered with the remnants of an old GPS device that Javier had stripped off its plastic. His son sucked on the chipset.

"Your name is Junior," Javier said. "When you grow up, you can call yourself whatever you want. You can name your own iterations however you want."

"Iterations?"

"Babies. It happens if we eat too much. Buggy self-repair cycle—like cancer."

Not for the first time, Javier felt grateful that his children were all born with an extensive vocabulary.

"You're gonna spend the next couple of weeks with me, and I'll show you how to get what you need. I've done this with all your brothers."

"How many brothers?"

"Eleven."

"Where are they now?"

Javier shrugged. "Around. I started in Nicaragua."

"They look like you?"

"Exactly like me. Exactly like you."

"If I see someone like you but he isn't you, he's my brother?"

"Maybe." Javier opened up the last foil packet of vN electrolytes and held it out for Junior. Dutifully, his son began slurping. "There are lots of vN shells, and we all use the same operating system, but the API was distributed differently for each clade. So you'll meet other vN who look like you, but that doesn't mean they're family. They won't have our clade's arboreal plugin."

"You mean the jumping trick?"

"I mean the jumping trick. And this trick, too."

Javier stretched one arm outside the treehouse. His skin fizzed pleasantly. He nodded at Junior to try. Soon his son was grinning and stretching his whole torso out the window and into the light, sticking out his tongue like Javier had seen human kids do with snow during cartoon Christmas specials.

"It's called photosynthesis," Javier told him a moment later. "Only our clade can do it."

Junior nodded. He slowly withdrew the chipset from between his tiny lips. Gold smeared across them; his digestive fluids had made short work of the hardware. Javier would have to find more, soon.

"Why are we here?"

"In this treehouse?"

Junior shook his head. "Here." He frowned. He was only two days old, and finding the right words for more nuanced concepts was still hard. "Alive."

"Why do we exist?"

Junior nodded emphatically.

"Well, our clade was developed to—"

"No!" His son looked surprised at the vehemence of his

own voice. He pushed on anyway. "vN. Why do vN exist at all?"

This latest iteration was definitely an improvement on the others. His other boys usually didn't get to that question until at least a week went by. Javier almost wished this boy were the same. He'd have more time to come up with a better answer. After twelve children, he should have crafted the perfect response. He could have told his son that it was his own job to figure that out. He could have said it was different for everybody. He could have talked about the church, or the lawsuits, or even the failsafe. But the real answer was that they existed for the same reasons all technologies existed. To be used.

"Some very sick people thought the world was going to end," Javier said. "We were supposed to help the humans left behind."

The next day, Javier took him to a park. It was a key part of the training: meeting humans of different shapes, sizes, and colours. Learning how to play with them. Practising English. The human kids liked watching his kid jump. He could make it to the top of the slide in one leap.

"Again!" they cried. "Again!"

When the shadows stretched long and, Junior jumped up into the tree where Javier waited, and said: "I think I'm in love."

Javier nodded at the playground below. "Which one?"

Junior pointed to a redheaded organic girl whose face was an explosion of freckles. She was all by herself under a tree, rolling a scroll reader against her little knee. She kept adjusting her position to get better shade.

"You've got a good eye," Javier said.

As they watched, three older girls wandered over her way. They stood over her and nodded down at the reader. She backed up against the tree and tucked her chin down toward her chest. Way back in Javier's stem code, red flags rose. He shaded Junior's eyes.

"Don't look."

"Hey, give it back!"

"Don't look, don't look—" Javier saw one hand lash out, shut his eyes, curled himself around his struggling son. He heard a gasp for air. He heard crying. He felt sick. Any minute now the failsafe might engage, and his memory would begin to spontaneously self-corrupt. He had to stop their fight, before it killed him and his son.

"D-Dad—"

Javier jumped. His body knew where to go; he landed on the grass to the sound of startled shrieks and fumbled curse words. Slowly, he opened his eyes. One of the older girls still held the scroll reader aloft. Her arm hung there, refusing to come down, even as she started to back away. She looked about ten.

"Do y-you know w-what I am?"

"You're a robot . . ." She sounded like she was going to cry. That was fine; tears didn't set off the failsafe.

"You're damn right I'm a robot." He pointed up into the tree. "And if I don't intervene right now, my kid will die."

"I didn't—"

"Is that what you want? You wanna kill my kid?"

She was really crying now. Her friends had tears in their eyes. She sniffled back a thick clot of snot. "No! We didn't know! We didn't see you!"

"That doesn't matter. We're everywhere, now. Our failsafes go off the moment we see one of you chimps start a fight. It's called a social control mechanism. Look it up. And next time, keep your grubby little paws to yourself."

One of her friends piped up: "You don't have to be so *mean*—"

"*Mean?*" Javier watched her shrink under the weight of his gaze. "*Mean* is getting hit and not being able to fight back. And that's something I've got in common with your little punching bag over here. So why don't you drag your knuckles somewhere else and give that some thought?"

The oldest girl threw the reader toward her victim with a weak underhand. "I don't know why you're acting so hurt," she said, folding her arms and jiggling away. "You don't even have real feelings."

"Yeah, I don't have real fat, either, tubby! Or real acne! Enjoy your teen years, *querida!*"

Behind him, he heard applause. When he turned, he saw a redhaired woman leaning against the tree. She wore business clothes with an incongruous pair of climbing slippers. The fabric of her tights had gone loose and wrinkled down around her ankles, like the skin of an old woman. Her applause died abruptly as the little freckled girl ran up and hugged her fiercely around the waist.

"I'm sorry I'm late," the mother said. She nodded at Javier. "Thanks for looking after her."

"I wasn't."

Javier gestured and Junior slid down out of his tree. Unlike the organic girl, Junior didn't hug him; he jammed his little hands in the pockets of his stolen clothes and looked the older woman over from top to bottom. Her eyebrows rose.

"Well!" She bent down to Junior's height. The kid's eyes darted for the open buttons of her blouse and widened considerably; Javier smothered a smile. "What do you think, little man? Do I pass inspection?"

Junior grinned. *"Eres humana."*

She straightened. Her eyes met Javier's. "I suppose coming from a vN, that's quite the compliment."

"We aim to please," he said.

Moments later, they were in her car.

It started with a meal. It usually did. From silent prison guards in Nicaragua to singing cruise directors in Panama, from American girls dancing in Mexico and now this grown American woman in her own car in her own country, they started it with eating. Humans enjoyed feeding vN. They liked the special wrappers with the cartoon robots on the front. (They folded them into origami unicorns, because they thought that was clever.) They liked asking about whether he could taste. (He could, but his tongue read texture better than flavour.) They liked calculating how much he'd need to iterate again. (A lot.) This time, the food came as a thank-you. But the importance of food in the relationship was almost universal among humans. It was important that Junior learn this, and the other subtleties of organic interaction. Javier's last companion had called their relationship "one big HCI problem." Javier had no idea what that meant, but he suspected that embedding Junior in a human household for a while would help him avoid it.

"We could get delivery," Brigid said. That was her name. She pronounced it with a silent G. *Breed*. Her daughter was Abigail. "I'm not much for going out."

He nodded. "That's fine with us."

He checked the rearview. The kid was doing all right; Abigail was showing him a game. Its glow diffused across their faces and made them, for the moment, the same colour. But Junior's eyes weren't on the game. They were on the little girl's face.

"He's adorable," Brigid said. "How old is he?"

Javier checked the dashboard. "Three days."

The house was a big, fake hacienda with the floors and walls and ceilings all the same vanilla ice cream colour. Javier felt as though he'd stepped into a giant, echoing egg. Light followed Brigid as she entered each room, and now Javier saw bare patches on the plaster and the scratch marks of heavy furniture dragged across pearly tile. Someone had moved out. Probably Abigail's father. Javier's life had just gotten enormously easier.

"I hope you don't mind the Electric Sheep . . ."

Brigid handed him her compact. In it was a menu for a chain specializing in vN food. ("It's the food you've been dreaming of!") Actually, vN items were only half the Sheep's menu; the place was a meat market for organics and synthetics. Javier had eaten there but only a handful of times, mostly at resorts, and mostly with people who wanted to know what he thought of it "from his perspective." He chose a Toaster Party and a Hasta La Vista for himself and Junior. When the orders went through, a little lamb with an extension cord for a collar *baa'd* at him and bounded away across the compact.

"It's good we ran into you," Brigid said. "Abby hasn't

exactly been very social, lately. I think this is the longest conversation she's had with, well, *anybody* in . . ." Brigid's hand fluttered in the air briefly before falling.

Javier nodded like he understood. It was best to interrupt her now, while she still had some story to tell. Otherwise she'd get it out of her system too soon. "I'm sorry, but if you don't mind . . ." He put a hand to his belly. "There's a reason they call it labour, you know?"

Brigid blushed. "Oh my God, of course! Let's get you laid, uh, down somewhere." Her eyes squeezed shut. "I mean, um, that didn't quite come out right—"

Oh, she was so cute.

"It's been a long day—"

She was practically glowing.

"And I normally don't bring strays home, but you were so nice—"

He knew songs that went this way.

"Anyway, we normally use the guest room for storage, I mean I was sleeping in it for a while before everything . . . But if it's just a nap . . ."

He followed her upstairs to the master bedroom. It was silent and cool, and the sheets smelled like new plastic and discount shopping. He woke there hours later, when the food was cold and her body was warm, and both were within easy reach.

The next morning Brigid kept looking at him and giggling. It was like she'd gotten away with something, like she'd spent the night in a club and not in her own bed, like she wasn't the one making the rules she'd apparently just broken. The laughter took ten years off her face. She had creams for the rest, and applied them.

Downstairs, Abigail sat at the kitchen bar with her orange juice and cereal. Her legs swung under her barstool, back and forth, back and forth. She seemed to be rehearsing for a later role as a bored girl in a coffee shop: reading something on her scroll, her chin cradled in the pit of her left hand as she paged through with her right index finger, utterly oblivious to the noise of the display mounted behind her or Junior's enthusiastic responses to the educational show playing there. It was funny—he'd just seen the mother lose ten years, but now he saw the daughter gaining them back. She looked so old this morning, so tired.

"My daddy is going out with a vN, too," Abigail said, not looking up from her reader.

Javier yanked open the fridge. "That so?"

"Yup. He was going out with her *and* my mom for a while, but not any more."

Well, that explained some things. Javier pushed aside the milk and orange juice cartons and found the remainder of the vN food. Best to be as nonchalant with the girl as she'd been with him. "What kind of model? This other vN, I mean."

"I don't know about the clade, but the model was used for nursing in Japan."

He nodded. "They had a problem with old people, there."

"Did you know that Japan has a whole city just for robots? It's called Mecha. Like that place that Muslim people go to sometimes, but with an H instead of a C."

Javier set about preparing a plate for Junior. He made sure the kid got the biggest chunks of rofu. "I know about Mecha," he said. "It's in Nagasaki Harbour. It's the same spot they put the white folks a long time ago. Bigger now, though."

Abigail nodded. "My daddy sent me pictures. He's on a trip there right now. That's why I'm here all week." She quickly sketched a command into her reader with her finger, then shoved the scroll his way. Floating on its soft surface, Javier saw a Japanese-style vN standing beside a curvy white reception-bot with a happy LCD smile and braids sculpted from plastic and enamel. They were both in old-fashioned clothes, the smart robot and the stupid one: the vN wore a lavender kimono with a pink sash, and the receptionist wore "wooden" clogs.

"Don't you think she's pretty?" Abigail asked. "Everybody always says how pretty she is, when I show them the pictures."

"She's all right. She's a vN."

Abigail smiled. "You think my mom is prettier?"

"Your mom is human. Of course I do."

"So you like humans the best?"

She said it like he had a choice. Like he could just shut it off, if he wanted. Which he couldn't. Ever.

"Yeah, I like humans the best."

Abigail's feet stopped swinging. She sipped her orange juice delicately through a curlicued kiddie straw until only bubbles came. "Maybe my daddy should try being a robot."

It wasn't until Brigid and Abigail were gone that Javier decided to debrief his son on what had happened in the park. He had felt sick, he explained, because they were designed to respond quickly to violence against humans. The longer they avoided responding, the worse they felt. It was like an allergy, he said, to human suffering.

Javier made sure to explain this while they watched a channel meant for adult humans. A little clockwork eye kept popping up in the top right corner of the screen just before the violent parts, warning them not to look. "But it's not real," Junior said, in English. "Can't our brains tell the difference?"

"Most of the time. But better safe than sorry."

"So I can't watch TV for grown-ups?"

"Sometimes. You can watch all the cartoon violence you want. It doesn't fall in the Valley at all; there was no human response to simulate when they coded our stems." He slugged electrolytes. While on her lunch break, Brigid had ordered a special delivery of vN groceries. She clearly intended him to stay awhile. "You can still watch porn, though. I mean, they'd never have built us in the first if we couldn't pass *that* little test."

"Porn?"

"Well. Vanilla porn. Not the rough stuff. No blood. Not unless it's a vN getting roughed up. Then you can go to town."

"How will I know the difference?"

"You'll know."

"*How* will I know?"

"If it's a human getting hurt, your cognition will start to jag. You'll stutter."

"Like when somebody tried to hurt Abigail?"

"Like that, yeah."

Junior blinked. "I need to see an example."

Javier nodded. "Sure thing. Hand me that remote."

They found some content. A nice sampler, Javier thought. Javier paused the feed frequently. There was some slang to learn and explain, and some anatomy. He was always careful to give his boys a little lesson on how to find the clitoris. The mega-church whose members had tithed to fund the development of their OS didn't want them hurting any of the sinners left behind to endure God's wrath after the Rapture. Fucking them was still okay.

He had just finished explaining this little feat of theology when Brigid came home early. She shrieked and covered her daughter's eyes. Then she hit Javier. He lay on the couch, unfazed, as she slapped him and called him names. He wondered, briefly, what it would be like to be able to defend himself.

"He's a child!"

"Yeah, he's *my* child," Javier said. "And that makes it *my* decision, not yours."

Brigid folded her arms and paced across the bedroom to retrieve her drink. She'd had the scotch locked up way high in the kitchen and he'd watched her stand on tiptoes on a slender little dining room chair just to get it, her calves doing all sorts of interesting things as she stretched.

"I suppose you show all your children pornography?" She tipped back more of her drink.

"Every last one."

"How many is that?"

"This Junior is the twelfth."

"*Twelve?* Rapid iteration is like a felony in this state!"

This was news to him. Then again, it made a certain kind of sense—humans worked very hard to avoid having children, because theirs were so expensive and annoying and otherwise burdensome. Naturally they had assumed that vN kids were the same.

"I'll be sure to let this Junior know about that."

"*This* Junior? Don't you even *name* them?"

He shrugged. "What's the point? We don't see each other. Let them choose their own name."

"Oh, so in addition to being a pervert, you're an uncaring felonious bastard. That's just great."

Javier had no idea where "caring" came into the equation, but decided to let that slide. "You've been with me. Did I ask you to do anything weird?"

"No—"

"Did I make you feel bad?" He stepped forward. She had very plush carpet, the kind that dug into his toes if he walked slowly enough.

"No . . ."

They were close; he could see where one of her earrings was a little tangled and he reached under her hair to fix it. "Did I make you feel good?"

She sighed through her nose to hide the quirk in her lip. "That's not the point. The *point* is that it's wrong to show that kind of stuff to kids!"

He rubbed her arms. "Human kids, yeah. They tend to run a little slow. They get confused. Junior knows that the vids were just a lesson on the failsafe." He stepped back. "What, do you think I was trying to *turn him on*, or something? Jesus! And you think *I'm* sick?"

"Well, how should *I* know? I come home and you're just sitting there like it's no big deal . . ." She swallowed the last of the drink. "Do you have any *idea* what kinds of ads I'm going to get, now? What kind of commercials I'm going to have to flick past, before Abigail sees them? I don't want that kind of thing attached to my profile, Javier!"

"Give me a break," Javier said. "I'm only three years old."

That stopped her in her tracks. Her mouth hung open. Human women got so uptight about his age. The men handled it much better—they laughed and ruffled his hair and asked if he'd had enough to eat.

He smiled. "What, you've never been with a younger man?"

"That's not funny."

He lay back on the bed, propped up on his elbows. "Of course it's funny. It's hysterical. You're railing at me for teaching my kid how to recognize the smutvids that won't *fry his brain*, and all the while you've been riding a three-year-old."

"Oh, for—"

"And very eagerly, I might add."

Now she looked genuinely angry. "You're a total asshole, you know that? Are you training Junior to be a total asshole, too?"

"He can be whatever he wants to be."

"Well, I'm sure he's finding plenty of good role models in the adult entertainment industry, Javier."

"Lots of vN get rich doing porn. They can do the seriously hardcore stuff." He stretched. "They have to pay a licensing fee to the studio that coded the crying plugin, though. Designers won a lawsuit."

Brigid sank slowly to the very edge of the bed. Her spine folded over her hips. She held her face in her hands. For a moment she became her daughter: shoulders hunched, cowering. She seemed at once very fragile and very heavy. Brigid did not think of herself as beautiful. He knew that from the menagerie of creams in her bathroom. She would never understand the reassurance a vN could find in the solidity of her flesh, or the charm of her unique smiles, or the hundred different sneezes her species seemed to have. She would only know that they melted for humans.

As though sensing his gaze, she peered at him through the spaces between her fingers. "Why did you bother bringing a child into this world, Javier?"

He'd felt this same confusion when Junior asked him about the existence of all vN. He had no real answer. Sometimes, he wondered if his desire to iterate was a holdover from the clade's initial programming as ecological engineers, and he was nothing more than a Johnny Appleseed planting his boys hither and yon. After all, they did sink a lot of carbon.

But nobody ever seemed to ask the humans this question. Their breeding was messy and organic and therefore special, and everybody treated it like some divine right no matter what the consequences were for the planet or the psyche or the body. They'd had the technology to prevent unwanted children for decades, but Javier still met them every day, still listened to them as they talked themselves to sleep about accidents and cycles and late-night family confessions during holiday visits. He thought about Abigail, lonely and defenceless under her tree. Brigid had no right to ask him why he'd bred.

He nodded at her empty glass. "Why did you have yours? Were you drunk?"

Javier spent that night on a futon in the storage room. He lay surrounded by the remnants of Brigid's old life: t-shirts from dive bars that she insisted on keeping; smart lease agreements and test results that she'd carefully organized in Faraday boxes. It was no different from the mounds of clutter he'd found in other homes. Humans seemed to have a thing about holding on to stuff. *Things* held a special meaning for them. That was lucky for him. Javier was a thing, too.

He had moved on to the books when Junior came in to see him. The boy shuffled toward him uncertainly. He had eaten half a box of vN groceries that day. The new inches messed with his posture and gait; he didn't know where to put his newly-enlarged feet.

"Dad, I've got a problem." Junior flopped onto the futon. He hugged his shins. "Are you having a problem, too?"

"A problem?"

Junior nodded at the bedroom.

"Oh, that. Don't worry about that. Humans are like that. They freak out."

"Is she gonna kick us out?" Junior stared directly at Javier. "I know it's my fault and I'm sorry, I didn't mean to mess things up—"

"Shut up."

His son closed his mouth. Junior looked so small just then, all curled in on himself. It was hard to remember that he'd been even tinier only a short time ago. His black curls overshadowed his head, as though the programming for hair had momentarily taken greater priority than the chassis itself. Javier gently pulled the hair away so he could see his son's eyes a little better.

"It's not your fault."

Junior didn't look convinced. ". . . It's not?"

"No. It's not. You can't control how they act. They have systems that we don't—hormones and glands and nerves and who knows what—controlling what they do. You're not responsible for that."

"But, if I hadn't asked to see—"

"Brigid reacted the way she did because she's meat," Javier said. "She couldn't help it. I chose to show you those vids because I thought it was the right thing to do. When you're bigger, you can make those kinds of choices for your own iterations. Until then, I'm running the show. Got it?"

Junior nodded. "Got it."

"Good." Javier stood, stretched, and found a book for them to read. It was thick and old, with a statue on the cover. He settled down on the futon beside Junior. "You said you had a problem?"

Junior nodded. "Abigail doesn't like me. Not the way I want. She wouldn't let me hold hands when we made a fort in her room."

Javier smiled. "That's normal. She won't like you until you're an older boy. That's what they like best, if they like boys. Give it a day or two." He tickled his son's ribs. "We'll make a bad boy of you yet, just you watch."

"Dad . . ."

Javier kept tickling. "Oh yeah. Show me your broody face. Show me angst. They love that."

Junior twisted away and folded his arms. He threw himself against the futon in a very good approximation of huffy irritation. "You're not helping—"

"No, seriously, try to look like a badass. A badass who gets all weepy about girls."

Finally, his son laughed. Then Javier told him it was time to learn about how paper books worked, and he rested an arm across his son's shoulders and read aloud until the boy grew bored and sleepy. And when the lights were all out and the house was quiet and they lay wrapped up in an old quilt, his son said: "Dad, I grew three inches today."

Javier smiled in the dark. He smoothed the curls away from his son's face. "I saw that."

"Did my brothers grow as fast as me?"

And Javier answered as he always did: "No, you're the fastest yet."

It was not a lie. Each time, they seemed to grow just a little bit faster.

Brigid called him the next day from work. "I'm sorry I didn't say goodbye before I left this morning."

"That's okay."

"I just . . . This is sort of new for me, you know? I've met other vN, but not ones Junior's age. I've never seen them in this phase, and—"

He heard people chattering in the background. Vaguely, he wondered what Brigid did for a living. It was probably boring, and she probably didn't want to think about work while she was with him. Doing so tended to mess with human responses.

"—you're trying to train him for everything, and I get them, but have you ever considered slowing things down?"

"And delay the joys of adulthood?"

"Speaking of which," she said, her voice now lowered to a conspiratorial whisper, "what are you doing tonight?"

"What would you like me to do?"

She giggled. He laughed, too. How Brigid could be so shy and so nervous was beyond him. For all their little failings humans were very strong; they felt pain and endured it, and had the types of feelings he would never have. Their faces flushed and their eyes burned and their hearts sometimes skipped a few beats. Or so he had heard. He wondered what having organs would feel like. Would he be constantly conscious of them? Would he notice the slow degradation and deterioration of his neurons, blinking brightly and frantically before dying, like old filament bulbs?

"Have a bath ready for me when I get home," she said.

Brigid liked a lot of bubbles in her bath. She also liked not to be disturbed. "I let Abigail stay at a friend's house tonight."

She stretched backward against Javier. "I wish Junior had friends he could stay with."

Javier raised his eyebrows. "You plan on getting loud?"

She laughed a little. He felt the reverberation all through him. "I think that depends on you."

"Then I hope you have plenty of lozenges," he said. "Your throat's gonna hurt, tomorrow."

"I thought you couldn't hurt me." She grabbed his arms and folded them around herself like the sleeves of an over-sized sweater.

"I can't. Not in the moment. But I'm not responsible for any lingering side-effects."

"Hmm. So no spanking, then?"

"Tragically, no. Why? You been bad?"

She stilled. Slowly, she turned around. She had lit candles, and they illuminated only her silhouette. Her face remained shadowed, unreadable. "In the past," she said. "Sometimes I think I'm a really bad person, Javier."

"Why?"

"Just . . . I'm selfish. And I know it. But I can't stop."

"Selfish how?"

"Well . . ." She walked two fingers down his chest. "I'm terrible at sharing."

He looked down. "Seems there's plenty to go around . . ."

The candles fizzed out when she splashed bubbles in his face.

Later that night, she burrowed up into his chest and said: "You're staying for a while, right?"

"Why wouldn't I? You spoil me."

She flipped over and faced away from him. "You do this a lot, don't you? Hooking up with humans, I mean."

He hated having this conversation. No matter how hard he tried to avoid it, it always popped up sometime. It was like they were programmed to ask the question. "I've had my share of relationships with humans."

"How many others have there been like me?"

"You're unique."

"Bullshit." She turned over to her back. "Tell me. I want to know. How many others?"

He rolled over, too. In the dark, he had a hard time telling where the ceiling was. It was a shadowy void far above him that made his voice echo strangely. He hated the largeness of this house, he realized. It was huge and empty and wasteful. He wanted something small. He wanted the treehouse back.

"I never counted."

"Of course you did. You're a computer. You're telling me you don't index the humans you sleep with? You don't categorize us somewhere? You don't chart us by height and weight and income?"

Javier frowned. "No. I don't."

Brigid sighed. "What happened with the others? Did you leave them or did they leave you?"

"Both."

"Why? Why would they leave you?"

He slapped his belly. It produced a flat sound in the quiet room. "I get fat. Then they stop wanting me."

Brigid snorted. "If you don't want to tell me, that's fine. But at least make up a better lie, okay?"

"No, really! I get very fat. Obese, even."

"You do *not*."

"I do. And then they die below the waist." He folded his hands behind his head. "You humans, you're very shallow."

"Oh, and I suppose you don't give a damn what we look like, right?"

"Of course. I love all humans equally. It's priority programmed."

She scrambled up and sat on him. "So I'm just like the others, huh?"

Her hipbones stuck out just enough to provide good grips for his thumbs. "I said I love you all equally, not that I love you all for the same reasons."

She grabbed his hands and pinned them over his head. "So why'd you hook up with me, huh? Why me, out of all the other meatsacks out there?"

"That's easy." He grinned. "My kid has a crush on yours."

The next day were Junior's jumping lessons. They started in the backyard. It was a nice backyard, mostly slate with very little lawn, the sort of low-maintenance thing that suited Brigid perfectly. He worried a little about damaging the surface, though, so he insisted that Junior jump from the lawn to the roof. It was a forty-five degree jump, and it required confident legs, firm feet, and a sharp eye. Luckily, the sun beating down on them gave them plenty of energy for the task.

"Don't worry," he shouted. "Your body knows how!"

"But, Dad—"

"No buts! Jump!"

"I don't want to hit the windows!"

"Then don't!"

His son gave him the finger. He laughed. Then he watched as the boy took two steps backward, ran, and launched himself skyward. His slender body sailed up, arms and legs flailing uselessly, and he landed clumsily against the eaves. Red ceramic tiles fell down to the patio, disturbed by his questing fingers.

"Dad, I'm slipping!"

"Use your arms. Haul yourself up." The boy had to learn this. It was crucial.

"Dad—"

"Javier? Junior?"

Abigail was home from school. He heard the patio door close. He watched another group of tiles slide free of the roof. Something in him switched over. He jumped down and saw Abigail's frightened face before ushering her backward, out of the way of falling tiles. Behind him, he heard a mighty crash. He turned, and his son was lying on his side surrounded by broken tiles. His left leg had bent completely backward.

"Junior!"

Abigail dashed toward Junior's prone body. She knelt beside him, her face all concern, her hands busy at his sides. His son cast a long look between him and her. She had run to help Junior. She was asking him if it hurt. Javier knew already that it didn't. It couldn't. They didn't suffer, physically. But his son was staring at him like he was actually feeling pain.

"What happened?"

He turned. Brigid was standing there in her office clothes,

minus the shoes. She must have come home early. "I'm sorry about the tiles," Javier said.

But Brigid wasn't looking at the tiles. She was looking at Junior and Abigail. The girl kept fussing over him. She pulled his left arm across her little shoulders and stood up so that he could ease his leg back into place. She didn't let go when his stance was secure. Her stubborn fingers remained tangled in his. "You've gotten bigger," Abigail said quietly. Her ears had turned red.

"Junior kissed me."

It was Saturday. They were at the playground. Brigid had asked for Junior's help washing the car while Javier took Abigail to play, and now he thought he understood why. He watched Abigail's legs swinging above the ground. She took a contemplative sip from her juicebox.

"What kind of kiss?" he asked.

"Nothing fancy," Abigail answered, as though she were a regular judge of kisses. "It was only right here, not on the lips." She pointed at her cheek.

"Did that scare you?"

She frowned and folded her arms. "My daddy kisses me there all the time."

"Ah." Now he understood his son's mistake.

"Junior's grown up really fast," Abigail said. "Now he looks like he's in middle school."

Javier had heard of middle school from organic people's stories. It sounded like a horrible place. "Do you ever wish you could grow up that fast?"

Abigail nodded. "Sometimes. But then I couldn't live with Mom, or my daddy. I'd have to live somewhere else, and get a job, and do everything by myself. I'm not sure it's worth it." She crumpled up her juicebox. "Did you grow up really fast, like Junior?"

"Yeah. Pretty fast."

"Did your daddy teach you the things you're teaching Junior?"

Javier rested his elbows on his knees. "Some of it. And some of it I learned on my own."

"Like what?"

It was funny, he normally only ever had this conversation with adults. "Well, he taught me how to jump really high. And how to climb trees. Do you know how to climb trees?"

Abigail shook her head. "Mom says it's dangerous. And it's harder with palm trees, anyway."

"That's true, it is." At least, he imagined it would be for her. The bark on those trees could cut her skin open. It could cut his open, too, but he wouldn't feel the pain. "Anyway, Dad taught me lots of things: how to talk to people; how to use things like the bus and money and phones and email; how stores work."

"How stores work?"

"Like, how to buy things. How to shop."

"How to shop*lift*?"

He pretended to examine her face. "Hey, you sure you're organic? You sure seem awful smart . . ."

She giggled. "Can you teach *me* how to shoplift?"

"No way!" He stood. "You'd get caught, and they'd haul you off to jail."

Abigail hopped off the bench. "They wouldn't haul a *kid* off to jail, Javier."

"Not an organic one, maybe. But a vN, sure." He turned to leave the playground.

"Have *you* ever been to jail?"

"Sure."

"When?"

They were about to cross a street. Her hand found his. He was careful not to squeeze too hard. "When I was smaller," he said simply. "A long time ago."

"Was it hard?"

"Sometimes."

"But you can't feel it if somebody beats you up, right? It doesn't hurt?"

"No, it doesn't hurt."

In jail they had asked him, at various times, if it hurt yet. And he had blinked and said *No, not yet, not ever.* Throughout, he had believed that his dad might come to help him. It was his dad who had been training him. His dad had seen the *policia* take him in. And Javier had thought that there was a plan, that he would be rescued, that it would end. But there was no plan. It did not end. His dad never showed. And then the humans had turned on each other, in an effort to trigger his failsafe.

"Junior didn't feel any pain, either," Abigail said. "When you let him fall."

The signal changed. They walked forward. The failsafe swam under the waters of his mind, and whispered to him about the presence of ears and the priority of human life.

"What do you mean, he's not here?"

Abigail kept looking from her mother to Javier and back again. "Did Junior go away?"

Brigid looked down at her. "Are you all packed up? Your dad is coming today to get you."

"*And* Momo, Mom. Daddy *and* Momo. They're both coming straight from the airport."

"Yes. I know that. Your dad and Momo. Now can you please check upstairs?"

Abigail didn't budge. "Will Junior be here when I come back next Friday?"

"I don't know, Abigail. Maybe not. He's not just some toy you can leave somewhere."

Abigail's face hardened. "You're mean and I hate you," she said, before marching up the stairs with heavy, decisive stomps.

Javier waited until he heard a door slam before asking: "Where is he, really?"

"I really don't know, Javier. He's your son."

Javier frowned. "Well, did he say anything—"

"No. He didn't. I told him that Abigail would be going back with her dad, and he just up and left."

Javier made for the door. "I should go look for him."

"No!" Brigid slid herself between his body and the door. "I mean, please don't. At least, not until my ex leaves. Okay?"

"Your ex? Why? Are you afraid of him or something?"

Javier tipped her chin up with one finger. "He can't hurt you while his girlfriend's watching. You know that, right?"

She hunched her shoulders. "I know. And I'm not afraid of him hurting me. God. You always leap to the worst possible conclusion. It's just, you know, the way he gloats. About how great his life is now. It hurts."

He deflated. "Fine. I'll wait."

In the end, he didn't have long to wait. They showed up only fifteen minutes later—a little earlier than they were supposed to, which surprised Brigid and made her even angrier for some reason. "He was never on time when *we* were together," she sniffed, as she watched them exit their car. "I guess dating a robot is easier than buying a fucking watch."

"That's a bad word, Mom," Abigail said. "I'm gonna debit your account."

Brigid sighed. She forced a smile. "You're right, honey. I'm sorry. Let's go say hi to your dad."

At the door, Kevin was a round guy with thinning hair and very flashy-looking augmented lenses—the kind usually marketed at much younger humans. He stood on the steps with one arm around a Japanese-model vN wearing an elaborate Restoration costume complete with velvet jacket and perfect black corkscrew curls. They both stepped back a little when Javier greeted them at the door.

"You must be Javier," Kevin said, extending his hand and smiling a dentist smile. "Abigail's told me lots about you."

"You did?" Brigid frowned at her daughter.

"Yeah." Abigail's expression clouded. "Was it supposed to be a surprise?"

Brigid's mouth opened, then closed, then opened again. "Of course not."

The thing about the failsafe was that it made sure his perceptual systems caught every moment of hesitation in voices or faces or movements. Sometimes humans could defeat it, if they believed their own bullshit. But outright lies, especially about the things that hurt—he had reefs of graphene coral devoted to filtering those. Brigid was lying. She had meant for this moment to be a surprise. He could simulate it, now: she would open the door and he would be there and he would make her look good because he looked good, he was way prettier by human standards than she or her ex had any hope of ever being, and for some reason that mattered. Not that he couldn't understand; his own systems were regularly hijacked by his perceptions. He responded to pain; they responded to proportion. He couldn't actually hurt the human man standing in front of him—not with his fists. But his flat stomach and his thick hair and his clear, near-poreless skin: they were doing the job just fine. Javier saw that, now, in the way Kevin kept sizing him up, even when his own daughter danced into his arms. His jetlagged eyes barely spared a second for her. They remained trained on Javier. Beside him, Brigid stood a little taller.

God, Brigid was such a bitch.

"I like your dress, Momo," Abigail said.

This shook Kevin out of his mate-competition trance. "Well that's good news, baby, 'cause we bought a version in your size, too!"

"That's cute," Brigid said. "Now you can both play dress-up."

Kevin shot her a look that was pure hate. Javier was glad suddenly that he'd never asked about why the two of them had split. He didn't want to know. It was clearly too deep and organic and weird for him to understand, much less deal with.

"Well, it was nice meeting you," he said. "I'm sure you're pretty tired after the flight. You probably want to get home and go to sleep, right?"

"Yes, that's right," Momo said. Thank Christ for other robots; they knew how to take a cue.

Kevin pinked considerably. "Uh, right." He reached down, picked up Abigail's bag, and nodded at them. "Call you later, Brigid."

"Sure."

Abigail waved at Javier. She blew him a kiss. He blew one back as the door closed.

"Well, thank goodness that's over." Brigid sagged against the door, her palms flat against its surface, her face lit with a new glow. "We have the house to ourselves."

She was so pathetically obvious. He'd met high-schoolers with more grace. He folded his arms. "Where's my son?"

Brigid frowned. "I don't know, but I'm sure he's fine. You've been training him, haven't you? He has all your skills." Her fingers played with his shiny new belt buckle, the one she had bought for him especially. "Well, most of them. I'm sure there are some things he'll just have to learn on his own."

She knew. She knew exactly where his son was. And when her eyes rose, she knew that he knew. And she smiled.

Javier did not feel fear in any organic way. The math reflected a certain organic sensibility, perhaps, the way his simulation and prediction engines suddenly spun to life, their fractal computations igniting and processing as he calculated what could go wrong and when and how and with whom. How long had it been since he'd last seen Junior? How much did Junior know? Was his English good enough? Were his jumps strong enough? Did he understand the failsafe completely? These were the questions Javier had, instead of a cold sweat. If he were a different kind of man, a man like Kevin or any of the other human men he'd met and enjoyed in his time, he might have felt a desire to grab Brigid or hit her the way she'd hit him earlier, when she thought he was endangering her offspring in some vague, indirect way. They had subroutines for that. They had their own failsafes, the infamous triple-F cascades of adrenaline that gave them bursts of energy for dealing with problems like the one facing him now. They were built to protect their own, and he was not.

So he shrugged and said: "You're right. There are some things you just can't teach."

They went to the bedroom. And he was so good, he'd learned so much in his short years, that Brigid rewarded his technique with knowledge. She told him about taking Junior to the grocery store with her. She told him about the man who had followed them into the parking lot. She told him how, when she had asked Junior what he thought, he had given Javier's exact same shrug.

"He said you'd be fine with it," she said. "He said your dad did something similar. He said it made you stronger. More independent."

Javier shut his eyes. "Independent. Sure."

"He looked so much like you as he said it." Brigid was already half asleep. "I wonder what I'll pass down to my daughter, sometimes. Maybe she'll fall in love with a robot, just like her mommy and daddy."

"Maybe," Javier said. "Maybe her whole generation will. Maybe they won't even bother reproducing."

"Maybe we'll go extinct," Brigid said. "But then who would you have left to love?"

Our Candidate

ROBERT REED

Robert Reed (www.robertreedwriter.com) lives in Lincoln, Nebraska, with his wife and daughter, and is a Nebraska science fiction renaissance of one. He is perhaps the Poul Anderson of his generation. He is certainly the most prolific SF writer of high-quality short fiction writing today. He has had stories appear in at least one of the annual Year's Best *anthologies in every year since 1992. He is perhaps most famous for his Marrow universe, and the novels and stories that take place in that huge, ancient spacefaring environment. A new Marrow book,* Eater of Bone, *collecting four novellas, is out this year. His story collections,* The Dragons of Springplace *(1999) and* The Cukoo's Boys *(2005), skim only some of the cream from his body of work. He is overdue for another substantial collection. He had another excellent year in a long line of them in 2011, and could easily have had three or four stories in this volume.*

"Our Candidate" was published at Tor.com, and this is perhaps its first time in print. It is a story about how the illusion of political participation and democracy can pave the way to fascism. We offer it for what it is worth in an election year during hard times in the U.S.

Their first candidate was a youngish fellow with a list of minor achievements and small qualifications, plus a handsome wife willing to attend some portion of the rallies and fundraising events. He was the brave soldier who stepped forward when the state's less-popular political party couldn't find anybody who might win. The conservative opponent was unbeatable. Even agnostic voters considered the current governor as being Chosen. Once the invisible lieutenant governor, he stepped into the office when his predecessor's Blackhawk went down in a freak hailstorm. Proper words and a few strategic tears at the funeral cemented the man's rule over the sprawling state, and the new chief executive had served twenty-two months without scandal, scrupulously accomplishing nothing that tested his base supporters while avoiding becoming the enemy of those inclined to stand against him.

Wise tongues decided that seventy percent of the vote would be a disappointment, and more importantly, that the governor's mansion was only a way station before becoming the state's next Senator.

Into the slaughter, the liberal soldier pressed on. Little problems came, and in the way of all campaigns, never quite left. But everything could be endured, right up until the wife decided that nothing was as boring as rallies and her smile muscles were awfully, awfully tired. Even worse were matters of finance: a candidate was supposed to generate interest and dollars, and the interest was lacking early and the dollars dried up. His skeletal staff was competent enough to run a compelling student election but nothing more. Then the wife who was no longer on the campaign trail filed for divorce. That's when the campaign died. One hundred days before the election—after half a year of mastering nothing in politics—the candidate released a poorly composed, grammatically questionable press release blaming the lack of party support and certain unspecified threats against his loved ones, leaving him no choice but to pack up and head home early.

His party was appalled. That is, except for quirky souls who saw opportunity in one man's incompetence. Thankfully, an organizational meeting was scheduled for a few days later—the kind of non-event usually controlled by retirees and the most desperate political hacks. A replacement candidate would have to be appointed there. Various names were mentioned and discarded. Wealthy men and one famous widow with liberal tendencies were approached, but none said "yes." That led to a second tier of names and biographies that were scrubbed and analyzed until a suitable candidate was found. But then several discrepancies were found in what seemed like an otherwise fine life story. No, the gentleman had never quite served in Iraq, and he did have more than two DUIs in his past, and the college that he always claimed as his own couldn't find evidence that he was ever on campus, much less kicked the winning field goal in the '98 game against the hated Bulldogs.

The media had gathered, expecting a new face and name, and the state deserved some kind of choice, no matter how uninspired. On that pragmatic note, the powers of the party gathered next to the overchlorinated pool at the Day's Inn, and after a few drinks and some deep gazes into this endless mess, one voice in the back called out, "Okay. Me."

"Me" was Morris Hersh. Quiet and polite and generally presentable, Morris was one of those individuals who leaves a good impression with strangers yet makes very few friends, and who despite a withering intelligence in several fields, can hide his gifts while sitting among half-drunk liberals, knowing the best moment to speak and what voice to use and anticipating which questions would be asked before being led out before a pack of reporters working on deadline.

Morris's candidacy was launched quietly—a few words about persevering through difficult times but winning in the end—and the candidate's first week was little different from the incompetence of his predecessor. Long profiles appeared in the state's surviving newspapers. The retired professor of chemistry was a widower with three grown children and a long history of public action. Past flirtations with splinter parties and odd causes were mentioned and quickly discounted. He was a true believer now, and the liberals were happy to have him, and that's the attitude that reigned until the State Fair and a choreographed not-really-a-debate debate against the reigning governor.

First to speak, the conservative held forth about the state's wonderful residents and their justified suspicions about change and those high-minded, over-educated ideas from Washington and other sorry, ill-informed places. He promised jobs and minimal taxes and a thriving environment for good businesses. Of course he would do everything in his power to maintain agricultural supports from the bureaucrats in Washington. Of course he talked about the sanctity of education and the need to defeat waste. Then, in summation, he stated how much he loved this state and its goodhearted and exceptional, strong-willed and unquestionably honest people.

Standard applause led to polite silence. Morris took a few moments to flip through a towering stack of index cards that he left where he was sitting. Dressed in a suit that had been worn in the high halls of education, the new candidate stepped to the podium, looking out at an audience that nobody else could see. That was the first impression of careful observers. He stared at a place above every head, and he tried to smile at whatever he was seeing. Then the expression flickered and died, and he sighed as if suffering some small pain. Not a bit of nervousness showed. Indeed, he probably had the slowest heartbeat on the stage. One long finger needed to scratch at the white hair above an ear, and again he sighed, and then the other hand took hold of the microphone and he said, "We are in such deep, deep trouble, my friends."

It was a strong, distinctly angry voice.

"Our world is moving into a time of catastrophe and extraordinary danger," he continued. "The life that we believe that we have earned and deserve is about to vanish. Climate change and nuclear proliferation are two of the players in this ongoing tragedy. I'm sure a few of you agree with me on these counts. Blame can be given to overpopulation and wasted resources and carbon dioxide and the simple lack of good manners. But a full accounting of the villains would take too long. Suffice it to say, each of us is guilty. I am guilty and you are all guilty and the governor is culpable as well. We are the agents of change, and we have built this new world, and events will come soon enough that all but the oldest and luckiest of us will discover what misery means and how the universe deals with pests who dare infest one of its pretty blue worlds."

At that point, Morris paused. Everybody needed a deep breath. But the old man didn't give people time to rest, and he certainly didn't wait for applause. Lucid and sober, almost cheerful, he offered up a list of vivid predictions for what would happen in the coming decade or two. Nobody listened to every word. Even the Greenest voter—a college girl who rode her bike halfway across the state to support this man—was numbed by the relentless awfulness of what was being predicted. The earth was wounded. Ice was melting and droughts were looming and millions would soon move toward the high ground blessed with reliable aquifers. "Which is here," he said. "We are living on what will become a promised land." But he also promised tipping points, maybe several at a time, and governments would fail, and even the United States was subject to collapse. "We don't have the money we think we do, and we don't have any time left, and decisions will have to be made on the fly, and our state would be smart to make preparations for when it will have to take care of itself."

Then came another brief pause, another shared breath by the audience.

At that point, Morris paused. But he still had twenty seconds for introductory remarks, which is why he offered a wide smile, thanking the Rotarians for sponsoring this event, and singling out Mrs. Gina Potts for her delicious lemonade.

Throughout the non-debate—with the opening statement and everything that followed—the governor stayed on track. He clung to his marks when he spoke and sat motionless while waiting his turn to speak again, smiling in that vacuous fashion common to people who can compartmentalize every portion of their lives. He wasn't an exceptionally smart fellow. He had a pleasant, not-quite-handsome face made older by the baldness that had begun in his twenties. But he had always been blessed with competence and luck, and his wife was lovely and at least as ambitious as he was. The governor also had a gorgeous golf swing that had served him well in fifteen years of public life. Sitting on a folding chair, listening to the ex-professor's diatribe, he not only understood that he would win the election by a four-to-one edge, but his opponent was doing his cause grave, irreparable harm. And being a considerate church-going person, the governor felt empathy. Taking an old man out of his element and putting him on public display like this . . . it was the kind of mistake he would never make. Governance was the magic done through a multitude of tiny, imperfect steps. If key details could be identified and the worst errors avoided or later denied, then it was possible to do just enough, leaving the world better than it otherwise would have been.

The event was scheduled to last sixty minutes. With ten minutes remaining, Morris threw a hand at the sky, saying, "If lightning strikes and I happen to win this election, there will be no greater champion making this state ready for what is to come. I'll use these final weeks to make clear what is necessary and essential. Changes will be necessary if we are to hold onto a portion of our rights as citizens, retain some sliver of our present wealth, and not lose ourselves to the panic and reflexive violence sure to claim billions of unready, untested souls.

"I don't believe in God," he proclaimed, "but I believe in Laws. The Laws of Nature, the Laws of Cause and Effect.

"And there are no other Gods but Them."

On that peculiar note, Morris Hersh returned to his folding chair and sat on his forgotten note cards.

The moderator took the microphone, but he had no voice. He looked at his watch, discovering the extra time. Not wanting to leave things in this uncomfortable place, he rolled his free hand in the air, inviting the governor to respond—a breach of the rules, but nobody complained.

The governor stood without hurrying.

With a big wink, he convinced half of the audience that he was looking at them, and then he stepped to the podium and smiled, waiting for the perfect response to come to mind.

He settled on a story from his teenage years—detassling corn from four in the morning until dusk every day, for minimum wage. Avoiding mention of his opponent or mental illness or the wild claims that would be splashed across newspapers and web sites for the rest of the week, he spoke only about himself and his ethic of hard work, and by the end of those ten minutes a large portion of the audience nearly forgot about madness and doom. People were smiling for no reason other than to hear how this round-faced golfer once wore his hands raw under a hot July sun. And then the governor sat, smiling at his lovely wife and their three darling children and a certain young aide lurking near the stage. A leader could do only so much. At the end of the day, almost nothing was possible, and very little was planned, and no person could claim total responsibility for the silly and the great decisions that he managed to make, every minute of his life.

Videos of the debate proved a huge embarrassment to one political party and were wildly popular on YouTube. But that changed when Kashmiri separatists raided a military base outside Islamabad, grabbing hostages and claiming possession of nuclear weapons. After a prolonged standoff, three missiles were launched at India. No warheads were onboard, and nobody important panicked. The hoped-for conflagration between old enemies failed to materialize. But those distant events had transformed the crazy candidate into a quirky prophet, and suddenly Morris's appearance was watched closely, and every doomsday utterance caused the Web to spasm and shiver.

World notoriety didn't bring success at home. Fifteen percent approval was his high mark. Voters saw a possible genius and a definite whack-job with no particular talent for managing the smallest limb of government. Morris's backers briefly dreamed of forty percent in the general election—but no, he wouldn't soften his message and refused to be edited, and he warned that if the party tried running television ads that didn't focus on the world's growing miseries, he would use his own savings, paying for spots that would make his earlier speeches seem decidedly bland.

The most rational player in this maelstrom was the governor. He smiled when necessary and shook every hand, and every speech was tailored to the audience of the moment. Mentioning Morris only as "my opponent", he always used a tone of measured, imprecise concern—as if mentioning some neighbor who you worry about but don't feel comfortable discussing in public. Aides pressed him to include national issues in his speeches. The election was won, they argued; why not begin the future senatorial campaign? But instinct told the governor to resist. He didn't quite understand why and didn't bother trying to explain. Sure enough, six weeks away from the election, an alarming rumor surfaced: The state's most liberal billionaire was so alarmed by the deranged Dr. Hersh that he was mulling over the possibility of stepping into this mess.

The same aides pretended to be unconcerned. No newcomer, even one with bottomless pockets, could steal what rightfully belonged to their candidate. They claimed the billionaire might get thirty-five percent, maybe forty. But at this late date, with so much momentum on their side, there was no way a new player could win the contest.

The governor was less sure. Gambling was dangerous, regardless of whose money or reputation was at stake. The surest course to victory was to keep Morris in the race. As it

happened, the governor's wife was good friends with a retired mayor in the other camp. One discreet call brought
news about an emergency meeting of party leaders taking
place in a little city west of the capital. The governor was on
the road within the hour, and at his urging, the state patrol
officer at the wheel covered a hundred miles in a little more
than an hour.

Another swimming pool had been commandeered for
duty—this pool closed for repairs, the contractor home for the
weekend. Twenty tense, irritated political beasts were sitting
around one uncharacteristically quiet candidate. Whatever
had been said just seconds ago was still hanging in the air.
Nobody wanted to look at anybody else. Nobody wanted to
be here, and every person was desperate to find some route
by which they could escape a situation that was only growing worse.

That was the scene that the governor walked into.

He smiled and said, "Hello," and then nodded, success-
fully crafting a face and persona that could not have looked
more ignorant or less dangerous.

It was Morris who acted thrilled to see him. "Hello, sir.
How are you?"

Alarm spread among the others. The meeting had gone
badly, but here was the enemy, grinning like an idiot. It almost made them happy. Almost. A couple of the younger men
stood, as did the ex-mayor, and she shook the governor's
hand first and asked about his wife, feigning ignorance to
camouflage her involvement in his arrival.

The governor spoke to everyone by name.

Then after ninety seconds of intense, utterly empty small
talk, the newcomer asked for a moment or two with their
candidate. It was a matter of state business, he implied. It
was important, he promised. Then he shook half of their
hands as they filed away, and he looked hard at Morris; and
after a very long pause, he said, "If I didn't know better, I
would believe they were trying to figure out some easy way
to have you killed."

"Everything but that," the professor allowed.

"Of course they're all wishing you would die. Natural causes, or whatever."

Morris looked old and pale.

"Are you going to quit?"

"No."

"Then again, they could just dump you as their official man, bringing in the rich capitalist. Your margin would shrink to five percent, if that. And at that point your party might convince itself that this is a campaign."

It was a warm and stuffy room, and Morris shivered.

"Stay," said the governor.

"What?"

"In the race. I don't want you sitting on the sidelines."

"Because you want to win."

"And you want lightning to strike. But you need to ask yourself: 'What would I accept as lightning? What would constitute enough of a blow against the odds and common sense to make this shitty process worthwhile?'"

Morris hunched lower. "Okay. I'm listening."

"You have plans. You claim you do, and I for one believe you." The governor leaned close enough to pat the man on the knee, but he kept his hands to himself. "You have a strategy for when everything goes wrong. When the glaciers turn to steam and zombies hit the streets. There's enough detail in your speeches and the interviews to make me think you've done tons of preparation, that there's some elaborate set of contingencies ready to be unleashed. Like what? When the Federal government starts falling down, the governor grabs special powers for the office?"

"Before that," Morris said.

"Really?"

"The state constitution isn't all that flexible, but there's some old statutes from the Cold War days. Before the national government is in ruins, the governor has to call in the legislature. It's going to take time to make ready. The National Guard is a start, but we'll need a militia and training and officials making informed decisions. There's going to have to be road blocks on every highway, and refugee camps that can be effectively policed, and that's just part of what has to be done."

The governor hid his smile. "All right," he said encouragingly.

"And human labor," Morris blurted. "Backbones and muscle will be essential. Because coal plants are going to be shut down, if only because we won't be able to guarantee the deliveries from Wyoming, and gasoline and fuel oil will have to be rationed, and supply lines maintained, and there's going to have to be a horse-breeding program through the ag school."

"I see."

Morris smiled as if embarrassed, but he couldn't stop talking. "Honestly, this is awful stuff. I try to be kind in my Human Labor chapter . . . but I'm talking about the kinds of servitude left behind in the Dark Ages. Or in Mississippi."

"You have chapters?"

"I have a very big book," Morris said.

"How big?"

"Fifteen hundred pages, plus charts."

"Charts?"

"Several hundred. And a PowerPoint presentation."

The governor wasn't startled or upset, or much of anything. But he took a moment, giving the matter considerable thought before saying, "Okay, this is my offer. My deal. Give me your book. And I want every last copy of your research, too. Then you continue with your campaign, and to keep your associates happy enough, I want you to soften your message. Let's keep the billionaires out of our business. And when this race is over, I promise—I do promise you—I will keep your work as a resource, and I'll even put you on my staff if the nightmare comes. Is that a worthy enough solution to satisfy you, Dr. Hersh?"

Big eyes filled with tears, and laughing sadly, Morris confessed, "You know, I'm about the last person you'd want to be governor."

He didn't need to worry.

And thirteen days after the state's final election, the same Kashmiri separatists drove a heavy truck into Delhi, unleashing a fifty-kiloton device that may or may not have been supplied by elements inside the Pakistani military. The war lasted two weeks, killing millions while injecting soot into the stratosphere, and just as the world situation couldn't appear any worse, a substantial portion of the West Antarctic ice field decided to begin its majestic and inevitable slide into a rapidly rising ocean.

The funeral was held on the highest hill outside the capital. It was an overcast November morning, but a Lakota shaman and a Lutheran minister worked together, convincing the rain to stay away. The tomb was the most splendid and ornate structure built in forty years. For his genius, the Mexican architect was awarded citizenship and five acres of bottomland. Oxen trains carried the granite from Colorado, but every block of limestone was native. State engineers had overseen the project. Estimates varied, but as many as two hundred guest workers died in order to make the target date. Yet the Old Man had rallied, recovering from the cancer. The tomb had to be mothballed until he was eighty-two, and that's when the only autocrat the state had ever known passed away in his sleep.

His body had lain in state for three days. Well-wishers brought dried flowers and religious offerings and prayers, and delicate embroidery intended for the leader's six daughters and two youngest wives. Disgruntled individuals managed a few incidents, but nothing of note. The Land's Militia took charge of security, sweeping the tomb grounds for bombs and poisons. This was to be an enormous day, and to help ensure peace, five thousand individuals were rounded up under the Quarantine Laws. Some twenty thousand chairs and benches were placed on the wet grass, and they weren't enough. Supporters rode bikes from the farthest corners of the state, while neighboring autocrats and strongmen and self-appointed generals traveled to the capital in motor vehicles and several working airplanes. Despite rumors of immortality, the Old Man had died. His rivals were relieved, and they were definitely hungry for opportunity. What mattered was to meet the son who had been given reins to this flush and wet and very green state—a kingdom that by every past measure was poor, and compared with every other corner of the sickly world, was enviably wealthy.

The new governor was thirty-nine and ready. His stride showed the world his measured confidence, and his voice was a booming, masterly instrument. Without break and almost without water, he told the full story of his father, reciting the history of their Free State, including three wars and one famine, and the legendary Eastern Incursion that brought back several nuclear weapons—each traded for gold and seed as well as the race horses that became the basis of the world's best cavalry. Then the young man pulled back the clock to days that few remembered. Of course he repeated the story of his dear father working the fields as a child, wearing his hands bloody doing exactly the same jobs required of every school age boy and girl today. There were twenty stories of sacrifice and toughness, and he told the fake tales with the same sure voice that he used with those that were a little true. Then he concluded by mentioning the Old Man as a golfer—an average-looking fellow underestimated by every opponent, but blessed with a grace and strength that endured until his last day.

That is when the new governor stopped talking.

Five different religious authorities gave appropriate prayers, and the Shadow Riders brought the body and its long wagon up to the tomb. There were more prayers to come, and ceremonies, and the new governor had settled in to endure all of it. But a face caught his eye—a pretty woman that he didn't remember yet felt familiar. He asked for the woman's name. Hersh, was it? Of course he knew who she was. It was the granddaughter—a minor figure in small-town politics out in wheat country.

He made a request and then slipped back into the still-open tomb.

Miss Hersh was brought to him. Flustered but trying to appear brave, she watched him, probably fearing the rumors told about him. But no, he was going to behave, certainly today and in this place. Not that he was superstitious, but the tomb stood around them, and even his voice was more hushed than usual. "I want to show you something," he said. "It's something you might have heard about. Something that will definitely interest you."

"What?" she asked quietly.

Many of the Old Man's effects were to be buried with him, preserved for future historians and whatnot. Inside one steel box were crystals meant to absorb moisture and a single enormous manuscript, plus two flash-drives and the hard-drive that had written the entire work.

"Is that my grandfather's?"

The governor nodded. "Yes, it is."

"It is," she agreed. "This is the template to everything. It is."

He let her dream, and then with a firm, stern voice, he said, "No."

"No?" She looked again. "Why is it still wrapped in plastic? I've heard. My father told me. It was wrapped in plastic when Grandpa gave it to your father, and I think that's his signature there."

"It's never been opened."

"Did the governor use the flash-drives?"

"No."

"What did you say?"

"Never." And the new governor laughed. "I know the myth. But this is the truth: Years ago, my father showed me the sealed manuscript and the drives and everything. 'That poor professor,' he told me. 'Dr. Hersh believed he had something of genuine value.'"

The young woman was trembling, and maybe she was about to cry.

"'Years of work and hard scholarship on his part,' my father said, 'and do you know what it taught that old chemist? It taught him exactly what any good politician knows on Day One. Power and authority are built on many, many little steps.'"

"I don't believe you," she said.

He watched her.

"You're lying," she said. "I know you're lying. My grandfather's plan is what saved our state from falling apart."

The governor said nothing. When neither of them spoke, the tomb was wonderfully silent.

"What are you doing?" she asked.

He had changed his mind.

"Don't touch me," she said.

No, he wasn't superstitious. The next generation was always talking about signs and omens, but to him, this place was nothing but cool and polished limestone that could use a little fun.

Thick Water

KAREN HEULER

Karen Heuler (www.KarenHeuler.com) lives in New York City. She is the author of several novels, including Journey To Bom Goody *(2005),* The Soft Room *(2004), and* The Other Door *(1995). Karen Heuler's stories have appeared in more than sixty literary and speculative journals and anthologies, including several "Best of" collections. She has received an O. Henry Award and has been short-listed for the Iowa Short Fiction Prize, the Bellwether Prize, and the Shirley Jackson award, among others. She's published a short-story collection and three novels. Her latest novel,* The Made-up Man *(2011), is about a woman who sells her soul to the devil to be a man for the rest of her life—with unexpected results.*

"Thick Water," a story on the edge between sf, horror, and surrealism, was published in Albedo One, *the fine SF magazine from Ireland. A crew of four people lands on a Solaris-esque planet. Three of the four go native, but what native turns out to be is very strange indeed.*

The sunset was orange again, strange, beautiful, and serene. It had a saffron edge, then it blended down to yellows, getting milder and milder the farther it spread along the horizon. It hung there slowly, spilling its colors gently across the sky, with a thin dash of red or rose blending then fading.

The ocean was almond-colored, and slow. The biggest problem, Jenks said, was that she couldn't swim in it.

"Like swimming in a pillow," Brute snorted. "No, the biggest problem is we can't drink it. Tired of water rations. I mean, I'm okay with water rations unless I have to look at a whole lot of water all day."

"See, the real problem is, you insist on calling it water. If you stopped calling it water, you'd feel right as rain." This came from Squirrel, who always thought he had the essential point.

"Rain," Brute sighed, and they all stared out at the ocean, observing it. Was it water? It spread out wide against the horizon, as oceans did. But the water was thick and rolled; it was theoretically possible to walk on it, if you shifted your weight in the pockets the water formed and if you didn't go too quickly, which would cause a widespread line of waves, or worse, one of those sinkholes that never even glugged before it covered over.

They hadn't touched it; they still wore suits. But they had a piece of it in a tube in the lab room, and Sibbetts was writing lots of meticulous things about it in her reports. Good for Sibbetts. Brute didn't think they needed the suits any more; the air could be handled with just one of the simpler filters, a light mask over the nose and mouth. But Sibbetts was cautious; Sibbetts said wait.

The trolley wasn't due back for another year. The crew—two men, three women—had a habit of nicknaming everything, and the trolley was their name for the long-range transport.

Jenks, who was head of the exploratory team, said, "Maybe we're in at the beginning—you know, before life evolves."

"There's some kind of seaweed on the rocks," Darcy pointed out. He was polite and gorgeous and well bred, and Jenks—the reader in the group—had named him Darcy.

Their colony of two and a half domes was on the first shelf of a kind of stepped ascent from the beach. Discarded containers and broken equipment were left in the open next to it. There was no wind so they weren't careful about securing it.

They spent half the day outside, just poking around and observing, except for Sibbetts who worked on her own inside. One day they gave themselves the task of examining the smooth, cigar-shaped stones that sat around on the lip of the beach.

It was natural, after handling the stones, to want to wash the dust off their gloves. They went to the sea and cupped their hands and pulled out gobs of thick water. It amused them to carry the water around, and eventually they took some of it back to their collection of rocks. Darcy leaned over too far with his hands full, and he made it into a fake fall and rolled onto his back.

"Now look at that sunset," he said, pointing. His hand, blunted in its dirty tan glove, rose to the horizon.

The sunset was a long line of shadow, a pale hue up in the sky that drove along the surface in a line. It started from one direction and then—unlike an earthly sunset which went down—it shifted around in a 180-degree arc. The light reflected off a series of moons, so it was handed across the horizon from left to right. It took hours. The sunrises were quieter, like pale ribbons. Midday was cream-colored, with hints of salmon along the edges.

"Go get Sibbetts," Jenks said. Squirrel ran inside, but Sibbetts wouldn't come out.

"She said she can see it from inside," Squirrel reported.

Strike one against Sibbetts, Jenks thought.

The rocks seemed smooth, but they must have had an abrasive component to them. Darcy found, one night, a tear in two places on his right glove. He got alcohol and cleaned his hands. Of course, he should report it. He didn't.

Jenks found a tear in her suit, around her knee. She put it in the daily report. They were out of range, now; there was no one to check with, to discuss it with. She didn't want to alarm her junior officers.

Darcy got a new glove and saw within a day that it had shredded along the wrist. Nothing had happened to him after the first hole, so when Brute said, "Damn, my suit's ripped!" he said, "It doesn't matter. Mine ripped a week ago. I'm fine."

They were coming inside. Jenks heard them both. She didn't say anything; she kept thinking about it at dinner. "My suit was torn too," she said finally. "No signs of anything."

"You can't be sure," Sibbetts said. "An alien bacteria, a disease—who says you would know by now? Take some antibiotics, get some new suits."

"We're pretty much already done for, if we're done for," Darcy said.

Sibbetts, always in her lab, could be seen as a figure bending over or lifting things, tapping at her computer or putting something in a jar. They could see her through the plexi window; she never seemed to look for them.

"She's so stuck," Darcy said. "Never tries anything. Never takes a risk. And she calls herself an explorer."

"She calls herself a scientist," Brute said.

"*I'm* the explorer," Squirrel said. The face window on his suit showed a big grin. He lifted his hands and took off the hood.

"Put that back on," Jenks said.

"Look at my hands." Squirrel lifted them up and showed the holes. "The air's been getting in for two weeks, at least. Let me tell you," he said, breathing in deep, his nostrils working, "it's got a strange smell." He sucked in air so hard his chest rose up. "Spicy." His chest relaxed. "Good."

"Oh hell," Brute said, taking off her hood as well. "It's not like I haven't done it already. I've been out sniffing it when no one's looking. I swear, sir, it's harmless." She looked at Jenks and saluted.

Darcy already had his off. "Sir," he said, "the smell gets better at sunset. It has something to do with the colors, I think."

They looked at Jenks, waiting. She considered the facts: they were all exposed anyway. So she took her hood off. The air was moist, which was surprising; the sea never evaporated, it just rolled around. There was never moisture on their suits. But the smell was good, indeed.

"The colors are brighter," Brute said, looking at the sea. Even though it wasn't evening yet, the colors wove into the sky: yellow, saffron, salmon, butter, carnelian, ruby, blood.

They shed their hoods and then they shed their suits. The weather was perfect. There seemed no variation in temperature as they felt it. They did keep on shoes, because the arches of their feet were always tender, but they stripped down to their underwear.

And then they began touching the water.

It was irresistible. "Did you notice the variations?" Brute asked. "The variations of shade. How it runs from almond to cream? How you can watch the colors move?"

"To think I didn't notice it before," Darcy said. "What do you think caused that? The hoods? Maybe it was too subtle to make it through that plastic window of ours."

"Plastic window," Jenks laughed. "I think so. Look at Sibbetts, now, she doesn't notice anything." They turned and looked at Sibbetts, who straightened up and looked out at them, then turned away again.

"See that color there," Squirrel said, pointing. "The way it laps." They came up next to each other, forming a line. They stood very close. They were naked along their arms and legs, and they pulled in close to each other, so their skin touched. "I would hate to leave this place."

"True, it's getting to be more and more like home." This was from Brute, who stepped forward and bent down, scooping up a ball of water. "All the comforts." Her face got a sudden illumination and her eyes narrowed a little and she got a wicked grin. She looked at the ball of water in her hand, said, "Here goes, kids," and neatly split it in two, dropping half and popping the other half in her mouth.

Jenks wasn't fast enough to stop her, and it would have been half-hearted anyway. They understood each other better, so they all knew that they agreed with Brute: test the water. The air had proved to be all right, the temperature was perfect. They had never felt better, never been happier. Sibbetts in her little window looked ridiculous; out here, in the creamy sunlight, near the iridescent sea—out here was a higher order of perfection.

Still, they watched as Brute swallowed and her eyes went internal, tracking the feel of the water going down.

"Brute? What's it like?" Jenks took a step closer.

Brute sighed. "It's good." She looked around, to the sea, the horizon, the rock shelf behind them. "It's very satisfying. I can feel it."

Brute was fine that day and the next and the next. Jenks caught Darcy and Squirrel pulling small rolls of water from the edge, pushing it around in their palms, eating it. She watched in silence.

"Everything's sharper," they said. "Not at the edges, no, in the center. It's hard to describe, but it's great. Don't be afraid."

That was from Darcy, who whispered to her. Jenks was already considering it. She bent down and pulled a bead of water out. It had soft edges, reforming slowly. She took it in her mouth, rolled it on her tongue, and swallowed.

"Well," Darcy said. "Welcome to the club."

The thick water was all they needed—that and the gray sea-weed that formed like a frost along certain rocks; slightly crisp, a small taste that lingered. "You guys are nuts," Sibbetts said tightly when they showed dutifully up for meals. "You don't know what's going to happen, the effects, the long-term significance. You've left me all alone here now. If something happens, I'm the only one who can take care of you."

"You could join us," Brute said, shrugging. "We're not so bad. And you'll have more fun."

"I have work to do," Sibbetts answered, lowering her eyes. She ate her food industriously, chewing vigorously and swallowing carefully. They all watched her.

"Why are you watching me?" she said finally.

"You don't look comfortable with us," Squirrel said.

Sibbetts put down her fork. "You're not wearing clothes. You don't eat. You stare at me when you come in. You eat the water. None of you is acting normal." She looked around the room. They looked at her, all of them, and they were all smiling. One by one, they held their hands out to her. "You should come with us," one of them said. She couldn't tell which one.

The next day Brute came up to the plexi window. Sibbetts didn't see her at first; she was waiting for the centrifuge to stop spinning. She had no hope that anything new would be discovered, but she was thorough. If she did a test once, she did a test twice.

She looked up to relieve her eyes from the fine work. She looked out the plexi window.

And there was Brute, grinning at her through the window, staring and grinning, her lips pulling back more and more from her teeth. Brute's eyelids rose even higher and she moved back as if confounded, then she pushed her head fast against the plexi. Sibbetts could even see the plexi move a little, and she was annoyed.

What if she broke it? Sibbetts stood up, raised her hand, about to yell, when her hand dropped and her mouth opened.

Brute's face was smack against the plexi, yes, and it was entirely flat. Like a balloon against the plexi. Sibbetts stared, her mind slowing down, trying to make it into some trick, when Brute slowly peeled her flat face off the plexi, and Sibbetts watched as the face reshaped itself, back to Brute's face. Even then, she stood frozen, waiting for some explanation to occur to her, something sensible. Brute stared at her, winked at her!

Sibbetts stood there, trying to think, watching Brute wave at the others, who were standing together and watching. They all met together, waving arms gently, bobbing in and out. She could almost feel how much they gravitated together. In the old days, they wouldn't have tolerated that. Everyone had been conscious of personal space.

She spent the afternoon wondering if she had caught some kind of dementia; if she were seeing things. She checked herself and doubted herself and shivered a little, and took some antibiotics.

They ate less and less, yet they seemed healthy. They came to dinner most of the time, arriving together and staying for a while, then drifting away. Drifting. Well, it was hardly drifting with all that laughter. They giggled together, they cast glances together, they squealed with joy when Sibbetts asked if they had done their reports, if they had checked any of the equipment, if they had brought more samples.

"Samples?" Darcy asked. "Samples?" And with that he pulled a hair out of his head. He held it out dramatically and then dropped it into the soup. His cohorts laughed again. Sibbetts could feel herself tense; laughter laughter laughter. They were monsters.

"I don't like that," she said. "That's food. Who knows what contamination—"

"Absolutely none," Jenks said. "You can write that down somewhere."

Sibbetts looked at the captain cautiously. She had gotten thinner, tauter, quicker, but there was a little blurring around the edges. Her chin wasn't exactly the same shape? Could that be possible?

The rest of them all looked at Sibbetts eagerly, as if she might perform. Then they laughed again, their bodies bouncing around. They each rested their right hand on their stomachs, as if the laughing hurt.

Sibbetts lowered her head and ate her soup. When she was finished, she looked around. None of them had eaten and they were all still looking at her, expectantly.

"What?" she said.

"We can see that soup move down your esophagus," Squirrel said. "Like going down a drain."

"No you can't," Sibbetts said.

"We have x-ray vision," Brute said. And she winked.

Sibbetts' heart was racing. "If you guys don't eat, then I'm going to stop cooking for you. We shouldn't waste food. But you have to eat?" She had changed her tone halfway through, careful not to be out of line. The captain was her superior, after all.

"We eat the urden," Jenks said.

"Urden?"

"The seaweed thing. It's delicious. And it takes care of your appetite for hours, maybe days. You don't need much and your whole body feels light and clear."

"You shouldn't eat it!" Sibbetts burst out. "How do you know what it will do to you?"

"We *do* know what it will do to us," Brute said, standing up. "*Because* we've eaten it."

And they stood up smoothly, all together, and faced her. All their faces looked the same, and Sibbetts couldn't be sure if she was looking at Brute or Jenks or Darcy or Squirrel. How could all their faces look the same? She wanted to weep, but she never did that. It was just this sense of total frustration, this sense that it had gotten away from her. Could this be some kind of hallucination?

"I think I'm sick," she said finally. "I keep seeing things that can't be."

"Oh really," the person most on her left said. "Like what?"

"You keep changing. Physically." She lifted her head. "Right now, I can't tell any of you apart."

"You're all cooped up," Brute said (if it was Brute). "That's the problem."

"Come out and play!" Squirrel hooted.

"I'm a scientist," Sibbetts said feebly. "I don't think what you're doing is right. It's untested. We don't know what will happen."

"It's funny. You said 'we.' *We're* the we, now. You're just an I."

Who said that, Sibbetts wondered, squinting a little. Was it Darcy? Or Squirrel?

"Awfully lonely," Jenks said. "Isn't it?"

And with that, they left, like a bunch of puppets. Thank God they slept outside. She cleaned up, wiping down the chairs and the table with antibacterials. They were "off," she was sure of it. They had abandoned their duties, such as they were. They had, really, abandoned her. And she thought, again and again, this is unforgivable. It gave her a small sense of triumph, that she could define their behavior that way. But the sense of anger faded—what good did it do, after all, to blame them for their actions? They had bonded. They had excluded her. Against all the rules. Against advice. How could they do it, do something so fundamentally wrong? Her anger was rising again. Leaving her to face it all alone!

She felt it strongly. She was the one now who had to maintain civilization on this planet. Was that it—had they gone native? What could that mean in a place with no natives? She stared out the plexi, scanning the beach for them. There they were now, knee deep in that thick water. One of them bent down, snaking her arm into the water. From this distance, it looked like the arm became part of the water.

She turned her back on them. It was up to her to do all the work, then. She went back to her office. She would stop preparing food for them. Until they changed their behavior, it was nothing more than an ordeal for her, and a farce if they didn't eat. It would keep them from slipping something in the food, too; that had to be a consideration. If they could drop a contaminated hair in, who knew what else. . . . What if they snuck some of that water in, behind her back?

She would lock them out during mealtimes because, really, they were no longer members of her team. That was true, wasn't it? She stopped and looked out the window.

They weren't there, so she moved into the next dome and looked through that window.

There they were, she realized with a jolt, standing lined up, all facing her. Just standing. And then they all waved at her and walked away.

A feeling of exhaustion overcame her, and a longing for someone to talk to about it. Then she saw them walking into the water, sinking down, and disappearing. No bubbles, no outstretched hand (just as well: what would she do in that case?).

And then they slowly rose again. It was very graceful, but she found herself straining for air long before she could see the tops of their heads slowly begin to surface.

It did look beautiful. They did look happy. She wasn't happy, that much was certain. But she had no inclination to join them, whatever they were doing. If, in some future time, they proved themselves to be right, proved her to be wrong—fine.

The next day, she didn't open the door to let them in for meals. She could hear their voices, now, very dimly, all of them sounding exactly the same. Sometimes they were right outside her window, saying things, as if speaking to her. But the words sounded made-up. She wouldn't put that past them, that they were speaking some language not their own. Or, well, not hers. Too infuriating, really. Like pig-Latin, meant to point out how she didn't fit in.

Each morning she got up and wrote her report and transmitted it although it went nowhere—the planets blocked her words from reaching anyone. It was comforting all the same. In less than a year, some morning not unlike this one, she would hear a blip, a beep, some startled movement on the line. It would be a warm voice, a human voice, a relief after all this weirdness—and maybe this wasn't even the end of it, maybe they would become sand or rock or pellets of water themselves (she couldn't know)—there would be a voice over the line, telling her, You made it. You were right, to seal that door. You are the one who is valuable. You are the one who saved the mission, and we adore you.

And she liked the sound of that so much—the love that was in that voice—that she began to fear that Jenks or Brute or Squirrel or Darcy would knock on the door someday and ask to come in. And she would be uncertain. She would want to open the door because for once they would sound normal. And they would complain they were hungry. How would she be able to withstand that? If they did that? Or if they bumped their foreheads against the plexi, crying, "Sibbetts, Sibbetts, we're sorry, let us in!"

That would be unfair. To endure for almost all the way, and then have them trick her like that at the end. She would have to set up some rules. She would be clear about what they could and could not do. If they wanted food, she would leave it outside. That was reasonable. If they wanted anything else, they could leave her a note.

She found a notebook and pen to give them and suited up. Just because they had survived without a suit didn't mean she would change procedure. Who knew what was growing inside their brains or in their blood vessels, biding its time?

She waited for the air lock to empty, then she stepped outside. Where were they now? They'd been in sight before she suited up. She turned around and bam! something hit her. She dropped the notebook, staggering a little. She still held on to the pen.

Then another strike. Her mind was trying to figure it out. She looked down at her arm and saw something moving down it. Like oil.

It was the thick water, of course. She turned to the left, and another one hit her.

"Can Sibbetts come out and play?" Squirrel called, his voice high and squeaky. He had his own face today, Sibbetts saw.

"Stop it," Sibbetts said. "It isn't funny."

Someone put on a hand on her, from behind. She twisted as best she could in the suit. It was Jenks. "We miss you, Sibbetts. It's hard to command someone who stays inside all day. Don't you feel like you're in prison?"

"I'm not sure who's in prison," Sibbetts answered. "I'm happier inside."

"But I want you out here," Jenks said. "I order you."

"Yes, sir," Sibbetts said, backing up. "Just let me stow my gear and I'll be right back."

Someone laughed. "Fat chance." That was Brute. "Just get her helmet off."

She was close to the door, close enough to get in and slam it.

That was that, then. Her heart was pounding. She went to the clean room. She stood under the spray. When she was done, she took off her suit. One of the clasps for the helmet had been undone. Luckily, they hadn't gotten farther than that.

There really was no reason to go outside anymore. But they knew everything about the domes—could she really keep them from coming in?

If she wanted to survive, she would have to get rid of them. Her hands got very still, she clasped them together in her lap. The idea was horrific. Could she really kill them? No, it was too much. She could never be driven that far. If she stayed inside, and they stayed outside, then there was no reason for it. They would just keep to their own sides of the door.

Late one night, just as she was drifting off, she heard a scratching sound. Something small and rough. Was she imagining it? She took a flashlight and inched her way towards the sound. It was coming from the next dome, but it stopped as she neared it. Of course: she had passed a plexi window; they had seen the light.

They moved around, like mice, nibbling here and there. Were they using their fingernails? Did they still have fingernails? They could be using the rocks to scrape away at the dome, making the walls here and there thinner and thinner, so that one night they might poke their hands through and pull her out.

Maybe she couldn't just sit and wait for rescue; that was too far off. What were they thinking about? What were they planning?

She was a scientist; she could fight them. She thought about how to kill them, now. She reminded herself that they were aliens, they were after her. Sometimes they stood, one at each plexi, just to frighten her, to say she couldn't escape them. Well, she could. She could escape them if they were dead.

She hated having to think this way—and who was responsible for *that*? Who was forcing her to think of *that*?

It would have to be something that got them all together, all at once. That meant an explosion. Yes, blow them up entirely, leave no trace. They were fond of standing together like forks, good.

There was a set of explosives and a remote fuse, two in fact. She took them to the kitchen table and read the instructions. It was easy. She took off the wrappings and stopped.

She sat at the table, her hands shaking.

She began to keep records about their movements. When she rose, she checked all the windows, recording where they were. They were almost always together. Sometimes one or two broke off and went up the rocky inclines. Did they still eliminate, then, and have the need for privacy? Were they mating?

She heard scraping again. In the daytime. So now she had two reasons to go out: to see if they really were trying to scratch through the walls, and to set up the explosives, just in case. She didn't have to use them; it was merely a precaution.

So. Where should she place the explosives? She went back to her log. They liked to appear in her windows, but usually one by one for that. They liked to go as a group to the thick water, but that was too far away, and the water would probably shield them. Occasionally they picked through the rubble of the trash heap and took a scrap of something.

She decided to take out some small objects, to put them along with the explosives, in the trash heap. She decided on a toothbrush, a cup, a candy bar. The candy bar would make it seem like she was trying to see if they still ate; that would satisfy their curiosity.

She watched from the plexi. The first day they didn't go in the water; they merely stood about. The second day only two of them went in. The scratchings continued overnight, like animals pawing at the door to get in. On the third day, she was rewarded.

They all went in the thick water, sliding through it and then sliding down, until their feet vanished, their hips vanished, their heads vanished. Sibbetts suited up, unbolted the door and walked out. She walked around the domes. Yes, there were scratches; there were areas that had been peeled away. She thought maybe it had proved too hard for them, until she circled around to the back, where her lab was. There was a bigger spot here, a more delicate spot. She tapped her foot against it, and it gave slightly. Her heart pounded. They were distracting her, she thought, with scratching at other places so she wouldn't concentrate on this spot.

Her mouth was dry. She looked at the beach and saw that someone's head was showing through the line of the water. She moved quickly to the trash heap and put out the items, hiding the explosives under a bit of trash. She saw that three of them were kicking their way out of the water, pushing themselves to shore. She waved (sarcastically), and went inside.

Let them think what they would.

There was no doubt in her mind that they were about to break in. She went to the lab room, got down on her knees, pressing against the wall until she found the soft spot. It wouldn't take them long. She placed a plastic sheet over it and taped around it. This would protect her against a breach, temporarily at least.

If they stopped scratching at the walls, she would leave them alone. She would give them that chance, one last chance. It was not her decision; it was theirs.

She folded herself into her bed that night, hoping there would be nothing but silence around her. But the scratching started, the little nibblings at the wall; that night, they seemed to be at all the walls from all sides. Had she missed other spots that were just as well worn as the one in the lab?

She bolted upright. She turned the lights on, crouching and running through the domes, listening. The sounds stopped as she drew near, then they started up somewhere else, as if they were tracking her, aware of her every move.

She ran around, and wherever she thought a sound had come from, she pounded her fist just above it (she would not push her hand through a weakened spot, no, she wouldn't be pushed to that kind of error); to the top at first and then over to the right or to the left, she varied it because she didn't want them to work out how she would act.

She did it for hours, skittering around, hating them, for the sounds, for their concentration, for their harmony—they were working in concert against her; if one of them weakened, there was another and she only had her wits and her sense and her logic and her hard, hard determination.

In the afternoon, she blew them up. They finally came to see what she had laid out in the trash heap, picking up the toothbrush, holding up the cup. They came as they usually did, and she pulled the switch and there was a muffled boom! And they were shattered, just like that.

She didn't have the nerve to go out and look, not right away. She waited until she stopped shaking, and then she wrote down, again, her reasons: How they didn't eat, how they drank the water. The way they were breaking in. That they wanted to infect her.

She added to her notes: they would bring the pollution back to earth.

She stayed inside for two days. She was used to being inside, but there was something in her heart, in her mind, somewhere, that wanted her to go outside. To see. Just to check. Something.

Finally she suited up, quite slowly, took the laser guns, and let herself out. She turned around carefully, surveying the area before moving to the blast site. The hole the explosion had made was deeper than she'd thought it would be. There was a glittering along the walls. Metallic ash? She surveyed it warily, some ten yards away. Most of the debris would be plastics, with some metal. There shouldn't be much dust. She moved closer, squinting through the window of her helmet. She was afraid there would be blood, but she couldn't see any blood.

She spun around. For a moment she'd felt that someone was watching her. But there was no one. Of course there was no one.

She was close now, standing at the edge of the blackest part, just looking slowly around, along the ground, checking the bits and pieces of things. She glanced quickly, not knowing what there was she could be afraid of.

A movement. She scanned along the outside wall of the dome. Something, yes, something small. A piece that had stuck to the wall was now, slowly, falling down.

And another. Yes, very small. That's why it was so hard to see, there were drops of things moving down the wall. Her heart lurched but she thought she had to verify it, she would imagine things if she didn't.

She walked up to the wall and bent over slightly, peering at it.

A piece of flesh down at the bottom of the wall, on the ground. How had it survived? She stared at it. Something else slid down the wall. So small, like a drop, and while she watched it fell at the edge of the skin and joined it.

She straightened up suddenly. That glittering—the wall seemed to have a sheen; it wavered a little. She told herself to stop thinking, to stop anticipating. She forced her body to still itself, she made herself stare, unblinking, at the steady, slow accretion of the sheen, so that the thin wet slick of it gathered, getting thicker, until it pooled to a heavy drop. There were drops here and there, small ones that gathered weight from another small one nearby; others that never moved and seemed to be waiting.

Some of them shivered, impatiently. They hovered against the wall until the weight shifted them down to a drop below them, or slightly to the side.

As she watched, she could see the largest one fall down minutely, shifting to the left, heading for the skin on the ground. Then it joined it. Of course it was still small, it was skin, yes, but just a bit of skin.

Sibbetts leaned over it. She bent closer. Another drop found it and it moved, just a little. The tip of a finger. She waited again, without moving, until the silvery, sheeny stuff—thick water, she knew it—formed another drop, and reached it. She could see where the top sliver of the fingernail was just starting to be visible. It was being built in front of her.

Sibbetts sucked in the air inside her helmet. Was there no relief from this kind of horror? They would assemble themselves every day, bit by bit, until she would wake one morning and find a balloon-face pressed against the plexi, or all four of them, touching at the shoulder, just standing together and pointing at her. It was unbearable—the thought that they would be there again, *knowing what she'd done*—she could feel her eyes rolling back in her head. She could hear herself whimper.

And the scratchings would begin again. Her shoulders tightened. She would be inside, listening to them claw their way to her, grinning, nodding, blending, aiming themselves at her. She could see, indeed, that they had turned into a joint organism; organism, yes, not people, and she should dispel any lingering trace of regret or guilt.

She went back to her lab for comfort. She stood and looked around, at the shelves of specimens—mostly the thick water. There were plastic jars and glass jars. They were all sizes, and there was a whole container of more jars in the clean room.

She thought her way through it, and then she assembled her materials the next day—jars, lids, pipettes, scoops, tweezers—and put on her suit. She carried the things carefully to the ruined dome. The wall still glistened faintly, but on the ground there were small staggered movements as globules combined. She took her first plastic cup and ticked her eyes along the ground, evaluating. That finger she had seen the day before was now assembled to the tip of the cuticle. But there was a piece of the top of the head complete with hair, far to the right. Next to that a bone with a scrap of sinew. A piece of beige skin inched towards it. She began to index, in her head, any recognizable thing. An elbow, a rib, a foot nearly complete and flexing hopefully. She bent over, watching. The things moved; they had purpose. "Probably dying to get together again," she thought, and smiled. She could stop that.

She opened jars and took the larger parts, and the moveable parts—she would have none of them wandering away, gathering behind a rock or in the sea, repairing.

Every other day she went out, gathering with her jars and vats, picking out the hearts, the tongues, the scar on Jenks' thigh, two tattoos (was that Squirrel or Darcy?).

The hearts and lungs and guts could wait; they were going nowhere. Feet and hands had to come first, but the heads—no, they would be gathered in pieces. It was too disturbing, even for her analytic bent, her Euclidean eye. It was enough that she would reassemble them in her mind, put the puzzle together, intellectually. Let it remain intellectual—let her surmise that the jar on the top shelf belonged with the jar on the bottom shelf, cheek-by-jowl, brow to chin. They were like lovers who were no good for each other and should be kept apart.

Or, at least, no good for her.

She gathered them, plucking them and sorting them. Would they only truly recognize their own or would they pollinate—making a Brute-Darcy, a Squirrel-Jenks, a Squirrel-Darcy? They had ballooned into each other; they might have the desire to form one interconnected being: eight legs, eight arms, four hearts, one mind.

One brain bloomed and she bottled it, not waiting for the brainpan to find its home. Four brains, each on a shelf. They might have achieved telepathy; she would see.

So, at the end, over the course of two weeks, she spooned them up, in segments or in parts, and jarred them. At first she kept them dry, then she thought—mercifully thought, scientifically thought; or heroically thought: they want the water.

She went down to the sea, and carved out a piece in her bucket, and brought it back, weighted with virtue. And she cut off pieces into each jar, tightening the lids—no hokum from them, delighting in the water—and sealed them tight.

In six months, in five months, in four months, in three—soon, soon, there would be a beep on her screen, the first text from home.

"How are you?" it would ask, and she would sit down, a smile on her face, her hands slightly shaking. The eyes behind her, blinking, the hearts beating, the lungs insisting on their own thick-water breathing—all of them watching, and she would type:

We are well.

The War Artist

TONY BALLANTYNE

Tony Ballantye (tonyballantyne.com) is a British writer living in Oldham, England, with his wife and children, whose works tend to focus on the subject of Artificial Intelligence and robotics. In college he studied mathematics and later became a teacher, first teaching math and, later, Internet technology. He began publishing SF short stories in 1998, mostly in Interzone, *and has since published three idea-rich novels:* Recursion *(2004),* Capacity *(2005), and* Divergence *(2007), which comprise the Recursion trilogy.* Twisted Metal *(2009) and* Blood and Iron *(2010) are two novels in his Robot Wars. If there is such a thing as post-cyberpunk hard SF, that's what he writes.*

"The War Artist" was published in the original anthology Further Conflicts, *edited by Ian Whates. War artists depict war, often creating their images en plein aire, though the scenes are military rather than scenic. There have been both official and unofficial war artists. In both World Wars I and II, the British Ministry of Information appointed or just drafted artists and deployed them to the battlefield to paint and sketch. Ballantyne uses that quirk of history to speculate on a future in which, if this goes on . . .*

My name is Brian Garlick and I carry an easel into battle.

Well, in reality I carry a sketch book and several cameras, but I like to give people a picture of me they can understand.

The sergeant doesn't understand me, though. He's been staring since we boarded the flier in Marseilles. Amongst the nervous conversation of the troops, their high-pitched laughter like spumes of spray on a restless sea, he is a half-submerged rock. He's focussing on me with dark eyes and staring, staring, staring. As the voices fade to leave no sound but the whistle of the wind and the creak of the pink high-visibility straps binding the equipment bundles, he's still staring, and I know he's going to undermine me. I've seen that look before, though less often than you might expect. Most soldiers are interested in what I do, but there are always those who seem to take my presence as an insult to their profession. Here it comes . . .

"I don't get it," he says. "Why do we need a war artist?"

The other soldiers are watching. Eyes wide, their breath fast and shallow, but they've just found something to distract them from the coming fight. Well, I have my audience; it's time to make my pitch to try and get them on my side for the duration of the coming action.

"That's a good question," I reply. I smile, and I start to paint a picture. A picture of the experienced old hand, the unruffled professional.

"Someone once said a good artist paints what can't be painted. Well, that's what a war artist is supposed to do."

"You paint what can't be painted," says the Sergeant. It's

to his credit he doesn't make the obvious joke. For the moment he's intrigued, and I take advantage of the fact.

"They said Breughel could paint the thunder," I say. "You can paint lightning, sure, but can you make the viewer *hear* the thunder? Can you make them *feel* that rumble, deep in their stomach? That's the job of a war artist, to paint what can't be painted. You can photograph the battle, you can show the blood and the explosions, but does that picture tell the full story? I try to capture the excitement, the fear, the terror." I look around the rows of pinched faces, eyes shiny. "I try to show the heroism."

I've composed my picture now, I surreptitiously snap it. That veneer of pride that overlays the hollow fear filling the flier as it travels through the skies.

The sergeant sneers, the mood evaporates.

"What do *you* know about all that?"

I see the bitter smiles of the other soldiers. So I paint another picture. I lean forward and speak in a low voice.

"I've been doing this for six years. I was in Tangiers after the first Denial of Service attack. I was in Barcelona when the entire Spanish banking system was wiped out; I was in Geneva when the Swiss government network locked. I know what we're flying into, I know what it's like to visit a State targeted by hackers."

There are some approving nods at this. Or is it just the swaying of the craft as we jump an air pocket? Either way, the sergeant isn't going to be convinced.

"Maybe you've seen some action," he concedes. "Maybe you've been shot at. That doesn't make you one of us. You take off the fatigues and you're just another civilian. You won't get jostled in the street back home, or refused service in shops. You won't have people calling you a butcher, when all you've tried to do is defend their country."

This gets the troops right back on his side. I see the memory of the taunts and the insults written on their faces. Too many people were against us getting involved in the Eurasian war, numbers that have only grown since the fighting started. There's a cold look in the troops' eyes. But I can calm them, I know what to say.

"That's why the government sent me here. A war artist communicates the emotions their patron chooses. That's why war artists are nearly always to be found acting in an official capacity. I'm here to tell *your* side of the story, to counteract those images you see on the web."

That's the truth, too. Well, almost the truth. It's enough to calm them down. They're on my side. Nearly all of them, anyway. The sergeant is still not convinced, but I don't think he ever will be.

"I don't like it," he says. "You've said it yourself, what you're painting isn't real war . . ."

All that's academic now as the warning lights start to flash: orange sheets of fire engulfing the flier's interior. I photograph the scene, dark bodies lost in the background, faces like flame in the foreground, serious, stern, brave faces, awaiting the coming battle. That's the image I will create, anyway.

"Get ready!" calls the sergeant.

There's a sick feeling in my stomach as we drop towards the battle and I wonder, how can I show that?

A shriek of engines, a surge of deceleration and a jolt and we're down and the rear ramp is falling . . .

We land in a city somewhere in southern Europe. Part of what used to be Italy, I guess. Red bricks, white plaster, green tiles. I hear gunfire, but it's some distance away. I smell smoke, I hear the sound of feet on the metal ramp, the rising howl of the flier's engines as it prepares to lift off again. I see buildings, a narrow road leading uphill to a blue sky and a yellow sun. I smell something amidst the smoke, something that seems incongruous in this battle scene. Something that reminds me of parties and dinners and dates with women. It takes me a moment in all the confusion of movement to realise what it is.

Red wine. It's running down the street. Not a euphemism, there's a lorry at the top of the hill, on its side, the front smashed where it's run into a wall, the driver's arm drooping from the open window, the silver clasp of his watch popped open so it hangs like a bracelet . . . Jewels of broken glass are scattered on the road, diamonds from the windshield, rubies from the truck's lights and emeralds from the broken bottles that are spilling red blood down the street. It's such a striking image that, instinctively, I begin snapping.

The soldiers are flattening themselves against the vine-clad walls that border the street, the chameleon material of their suits changing to dusty white, their guns humming as they autoscan the surrounding area. Their half-seen figures are edging their way up and down the hill, changing colour, becoming the red of doors and the dusty dark of windows. They're sizing up the area, doing their job, just like me, cameras in my hand, in my helmet, at my belt. Sizing up the scene.

The peacefulness of the street is at odds with the tension we feel, and I need to capture that. The lazy smell of the midday heat mixed with wine. Lemons hanging waxy from the trees leaning over the white walls, paint peeling from window frames. A soldier pauses to touch the petals trailing from a hanging basket and I photograph that.

As if in response to my action, someone opens fire from up the street and there is a whipsnap of movement all around. The sergeant shouts something into a communicator, the flier whines into the air, guns rattling, I see thin wisps of cloud emerge from the doorway of a house up the hill. Someone fired upon us, and now the flier's returned the compliment. Incendiaries, I guess, seeing the orange-white sheets that ripple and flicker up the plaster walls of the building.

I snap the picture, but it's not what I'm after: it's too insubstantial. If I were to paint this, the explosion would be much bigger and blooming and orange. It would burst upon the viewer: a heroic response to a cowardly attack.

Then I see the children, and the image I'm forming collapses. Children and women are tumbling from the house. The sound of the flier, the crackle of the flames, they paint a picture in my mind that doesn't involve children. But the truth is unfolding. There were civilians in there! The camera captures their terrified, wide-eyed stares, but it can't capture that weeping, keening noise they make. It can't capture the lurching realisation that someone just made a huge mistake.

I see the look on the sergeant's face, that sheer animal joy, and I turn the camera away. That's not what I'm after, but my hand turns back of its own accord. If I had time, I'd try and sketch it right here and now. There is something about the feelings of the moment, getting them down in pencil.

The sergeant sees me looking at him, and he laughs. "So? Innocents get hurt. That's what happens in war."

I make to answer him, but he's concentrating on his console. The green light of the computer screen illuminates his face.

"That's St Mark's church at the top of the hill," he says. "There's a square beyond it with a town hall facing it. We occupy those two buildings, we have the high ground."

He runs his finger across the screen.

"Big rooms in there, wide corridors. A good place to make our base."

A woman screams. She's pleading for something. I see a child; I see a lot of blood. A medic is running up, and I photograph that. The gallant liberators, aiding the poor civilians. That's the problem with a simple snap. Taken out of context, it can mean anything.

But that's why I'm here. To choose the context.

We make it to the top of the hill without further incident. The cries of pain are receding from my ears and memory. I focus on the scene at hand.

A wide square, littered with the torn canvas and broken bodies of umbrellas that once shaded café patrons. Upturned tables and chairs. Panic spreads fast when people find their mobile phones and computers have stopped working. They've seen the news from other countries; they know that the rioting is not far behind. Across the square, a classic picture: the signs of money and authority, targeted by the mobs. Two banks, their plate glass fronts smashed open, their interiors peeled inside out in streamers of plastic and trampled circuitry.

The town hall is even worse. It looks like a hollow shell; the anger of the mob has torn the guts out of this place, eviscerated it.

This is what happens when a Denial of Service attack hits, wiping out every last byte of data attached to a country, smoothing the memory stores to an endless sequence of 1's.

Everything: pay, bank accounts, mortgages, wiped out completely. The rule of law breaks down, and armies are sent in to help restore order.

That was the official line, anyway.

"Funny," says the woman at my side. "We seem to be more intent on securing militarily advantageous positions than in helping the population."

"Shut up, Friis," snaps the Sergeant.

"Just making an observation, Sergeant." The woman winks at me.

"Tell you what, Friis, you like making observations so much, why don't you head in there and check it out?"

"Sure," she says, and she looks at me with clear blue eyes. "You coming, painter boy?"

"Call me Brian."

"Aren't you afraid he might get hurt?" laughs the Sergeant.

"I'll look after him."

I pat my pockets, checking my cameras, and follow her through the doorway, the glass crunching beneath my feet.

A large entrance hall, the floor strewn with broken chairs. The rioters haven't been able to get at the ceiling though, and I snap the colourful frescoes that look down upon us. The soldier notices none of this; she's scanning the room, calm and professional. She speaks without looking at me.

"I'm Agnetha."

"Pleased to meet you."

She has such a delightful accent. Vaguely Scandinavian. I've heard it before.

I see strands of blonde hair curling from beneath her helmet. Her face is slightly smudged, which makes her look incredibly, sexy.

We move from room to room. Everything is in disarray—this place has been stripped and gutted. There's paper and glass everywhere. Everything that could be broken has been broken.

"Always the same," says Agnetha. "The data goes, and people panic. They have no money to buy food, they can't use the phone. They think only of themselves, looting what they can and then barricading themselves into their houses. They steal from themselves, and then we come in and take their country from them."

"I thought we were here to help!"

She laughs at that, and we continue our reconnaissance.

Eventually, it's done. Agnetha speaks into her radio.

"This place is clear."

I recognise the Sergeant's voice. "Good. We'll move in at once. There are reports of guerrilla activity down at the *Via Baciadonne.*"

"*Baciadonne.*" Agnetha smiles at me. "That means *kisses women.*"

She's clever as well as pretty. I like that.

The area is quickly secured, which is good because outside the random sound of gunfire is becoming more frequent. I feel the excitement of the approaching battle building in my stomach. The flier comes buzzing up over the roofs, turning this way and that, and I watch the soldiers as they go through the building, filling it with equipment bundled in pink tape.

We find a room with two doors that open out onto a balcony with a view over the city beyond. Agnetha opens the doors to get a better field of fire, then leans against the wall opposite, her rifle slung across her knees. She smiles coquettishly at me.

"Why aren't you taking my picture?" she asks.

I point the camera at her and hear it click.

"Are you going to use that?"

"I don't know."

"Keeping it for your private collection?"

She stretches her legs and yawns.

"You don't mind me being attached to your group, then," I say, "not like your sergeant."

She wrinkles her nose.

"He doesn't speak for all of us. I don't agree with everything the government says, either. We're sent out here with insufficient equipment and even less backup, and when we get home we're forgotten about at best. I think it's good that we have people like you here."

She frowns. "So tell me, what *are* you going to paint?"

"Actually, I don't just paint. I use computers, software, all those things. It's all about the final image."

"I understand that. But what *are* you going to paint?"

I can't keep evading the issue. For all my fine words about reflecting the war as it really is, the Sergeant had it right. I'll paint whatever Command wants me to. I like to paint a picture of myself as a bit of a rogue, but, at heart, I know the establishment has me, body and soul.

"I don't know yet. That's why I'm here. I need to experience this place, and then I can try and convey some emotion."

"What emotion?"

"I don't know that, either."

There's a crackle of gunfire, sharp silver, like tins rattling on the floor. I ignore it.

"You're very pretty," I say.

"Thank you." She lowers her eyes in acknowledgement. I like that. She doesn't pretend she isn't pretty; she takes the compliment on its own terms.

"How did you end up in the army?" I ask.

She yawns and stretches.

"I worked in insurance," she says, and that seems all wrong. So drab and everyday. She should have been a model, or a mountaineer, or an artist or something.

"I lost my job when Jutland got hit by the DoS attack. Everything was lost, policies, claims, payroll. The hackers had been feeding us the same worm for months; the backups were totally screwed."

"I'm sorry," I say, and I am. Really sorry. So that's why her accent sounded so familiar. Fortunately, she doesn't seem to notice my reaction.

"Other people had it worse." She shrugs. "We had a garden; we had plenty of canned goods in the house. My mother had the bath filled with water, all the pans and the dishes. We managed okay until your army moved in to restore order."

She seems remarkably unperturbed by the affair.

"So you joined us out of gratitude?" I suggest.

She laughs.

"No, I joined you for security. This way I get to eat and I'm pretty sure that my salary won't be wiped out at the touch of a button. If your army's servers aren't secure, then whose are?"

"Fair enough."

"No, it's not fair. It's just life. Your army wiped out Jutland's data. Just like it did this country's."

I try to look shocked.

"You think that we are responsible for the trouble here?"

"It's an old trick. Create civil unrest and then send in your troops to sort out the problem. You've swallowed up half of Europe that way."

"I don't think it's that well planned," I said, honestly. "I just think that everyone takes whatever opportunity they can when a DoS hits."

As if to underline the point, the staccato rattle of gunfire sounds in the distance.

"Aren't you worried that I will report you?" I ask. "Have you charged with sedition?"

She rises easily to her feet and walks towards me.

"No. I trust you. You have nice eyes."

She's laughing at me.

"Come here," she says. I lean down and she kisses me on the lips. Gently, she pushes my face away. "You're a very handsome man. Maybe later on we can talk properly."

"I'd like that."

She looks back out of the window, checking the area. Little white puffs of cloud drift across the blue sky.

"So, what are you going to paint?" she asks. "The heroic rescuers, making the country safe once more?"

"You're being sarcastic."

"No," she says, and she pushes a strand of blonde hair back up into her helmet. "No. We all do what we must to get by. Tell me, what will you paint?"

"I honestly don't know yet. I'll know it when I see it." I

look down into the square, searching for inspiration. "Look at your flier."

She comes to my side. We look at the concrete-grey craft, a brutalist piece of architecture set amongst the elegant buildings of this city.

"Suppose I were to paint that?" I say. "I have plenty of photos, but I need a context, a setting. I could have it swooping down on the enemy! The smoke, the explosions, the bullets whizzing past."

"That's what the army would like . . ."

"Maybe. How about I paint it with you all seated around the back? That could send a message to the people back home: that even soldiers are human, they sit and chat and relax. Or should I evoke sympathy? Draw the flier all shot up. The mechanics around it, trying to fix it up. One of you being led from the scene, blood seeping from the bandages."

She nods. She understands. Then her radio crackles, and I hear the Sergeant's voice.

"Friis! Get down to the Flier! We need help bringing equipment inside."

"Coming!"

"I'll tag along," I say.

The whine of the Flier is a constant theme; the engines are never turned off. We join the bustle of soldiers around the rear ramp, all busy unloading the pink-bound boxes and carrying them into the surrounding buildings.

"What is all that?" I wonder aloud.

"Servers, terminals, NAS boxes," says Agnetha. "I saw this in Jutland. We're establishing a new government in this place."

"Keep it down, Friis," says the sergeant, but without heat. I notice that no one seems to be denying the charge. The head of the soldier behind him suddenly spouts red blood. I'm photographing the scene before I realise what's happening.

"Sniper!"

Everyone is dropping, looking this way and that.

"Up there," shouts someone.

The Sergeant is looking at his console, the green light of the screen illuminating his face.

"That's the Palazzo Egizio. The Via Fossano runs behind it . . ."

He's thinking.

"Friis, Delgado, Kenton. Head to the far end of the street. See if you can get into that white building there . . ."

I raise my head to get a better look, and I feel someone push me back down. At the same time there are more shots and I hear a scream. I feel a thud of fear inside me.

Agnetha has been shot.

Shot protecting me.

She's coughing up blood.

"Agnetha," I begin . . .

"Get back," yells the Sergeant. "You've caused enough trouble as it is . . ."

Agnetha's trying to speak, but there is too much blood. She holds out her hand and I reach for it, but the sergeant knocks it away.

"Let the medic deal with it," he says. "Let someone who should be here deal with it," he adds, nastily.

The other soldiers have located the sniper now, and I'm left to watch as a man kneels next to Agnetha and takes hold of her arm. She looks at me with those brilliant blue eyes, and I don't see her. For a brief moment I see another picture. Blues and greens. Two soldiers: a man and a woman, standing in front of a flier just like the one behind us. They're surrounded by cheering, smiling civilians. A young child comes forward, carrying a bunch of flowers. A thank you from the grateful liberated.

The picture I painted of Jutland.

I push it from my mind, and I see those brilliant blue eyes are already clouding over.

"We all do what we have to do," I whisper. But is that so true? She joined the army so her family could eat. I'm here simply to build a reputation as an artist.

The medic injects her with something. She closes her eyes. The medic shakes his head. I know what that means. The sergeant looks at me.

"I'm sorry," I say.

"So?" he says. "How's that going to help?" He turns away. The others are already doing the same. Dismissing me.

I take hold of Agnetha's hand, feel the pulse fading.

The picture.

I wonder if Agnetha would approve of what I had done? I suspect not. She was too much of a realist.

I included the flier after all. But not taking off, not swooping down from the skies.

No, this was a different picture.

The point of view is from just outside the cockpit, looking in at the pilot of the craft. And here is where we move beyond the subject matter to the artistic vision, because the person flying the craft is not the pilot, but the sergeant.

His face is there, centred on the picture. He's looking out at the viewer, looking beyond the cockpit.

What can he see? The dead children in the square, sheltered by the bodies of their dead parents? We don't know. But that doesn't matter, because there is a clue in the picture. A clue to the truth. One that I saw all the time, but never noticed. It's written across the sergeant's face. Literally.

A reflection in green from the light of the monitor screen, a tracery of roads and buildings, all picked out in pale green letters. Look closely at his cheek and you can just make out the words *St Mark's Church*. All those names that were supposedly wiped for good by the DoS attack, and yet there they were, still resident in the Sergeant's computer. And none of us found that odd at the time. We could have fed that country's data back to it all along, but we chose not to.

They say a picture paints a thousand words.

For once, those words will be mostly speaking the truth.

The Master of the Aviary

BRUCE STERLING

---

*Bruce Sterling (www.wired.com/beyond_the_beyond/) lives
usually in some exotic place in Europe, from which he continues his lifelong habit of cultural observation and commen-
tary, now mostly online. In 2003 he became Professor of
Internet studies and science fiction at the European Graduate School, where he teaches intensive Summer seminars.
His most recent novel, his eleventh, is SF,* The Caryatids
(2009). His short fiction is collected in Ascendancies: The
Best of Bruce Sterling *(2007). Throughout Sterling's career,
part of his project has been to put us in touch with the larger
world in which we live, giving us glimpses of not only speculative and fantastic realities, but also the bedrock of politics
in human behavior. He says, "Once I got my head around
this idea that 'the future' was bogus, I was able to mess
around with a lot of invisible assumptions." He is drawn to
events and especially people tipping the present over into the
future. His short fiction, now as likely to be fantasy as SF, is
one of the finest bodies of work in the genre over the last three
decades.*

*"The Master of the Aviary" is our second story choice
from* Welcome to the Greenhouse, *a Gene Wolfean story of
the far future that takes place after environmental catastrophe. It involves political intrigues and a scholar who thinks
he's done with that sort of thing. We think it has a fine last
line.*

Every Sunday, Mellow Julian went to the city market to search for birds. Commonly a crowd of his adoring students made his modest outing into a public spectacle.

The timeless questions of youth tortured the cultured young men of the town. "What is a gentleman's proper relationship to his civic duty, and how can he weasel out of it?" Or: "Who is more miserable, the young man whose girl has died, or the young man whose girl will never love him?"

Although Julian had been rude to men in power, he was never rude to his students. He saw each of these young men as something like a book: a hazardous, long-term, difficult project that might never find a proper ending. Julian understood their bumbling need to intrude on his private life. A philosopher didn't have one.

On this particular market Sunday, Julian was being much pestered by Bili, a pale, delicate, round-headed eccentric whose wealthy father owned a glass smelter. The bolder academy students were repelled by Bili's mannerisms, so they hadn't come along. Mellow Julian tolerated Bili's youthful awkwardness. Julian had once been youthful and awkward himself.

Under their maze of parasols, cranes, aqueducts, and archery towers, the finer merchants of Selder sold their fabrics, scissors, fine glass baubles, medications, oils, and herbal liquors. The stony city square held a further maze of humble little shacks, the temporary stalls of the barkers. The barkers were howling about vegetables.

295

"Asparagus! Red lettuce! Celery! Baby bok choy!" Each shouted name had the tang of romance. Selder's greenhouses close-packed the slope of the mountain like so many shining warts. It was for these rare and precious vegetables that foreigners braved the windy mountain passes and the burning plains.

Mellow Julian bought watercress and spinach, because their bright-green spiritual vibrations clarified his liver.

"Maestro, why do you always buy the cheapest, ugliest food in this city?" Bili piped up. "Spinach is awful."

"It's all that I know how to cook," Julian quipped.

"Maestro, why don't you marry? Then your wife could cook."

"That's a rather intrusive question," Julian pointed out. "Nevertheless, I will enlighten you. I don't care to indulge in any marriage ritual. I will never indulge in any bureaucratic ritual in this city, ever again."

"Why don't you just hire a cook?" persisted Bili.

"I'd have to give him all his orders! I might as well simply cook for myself."

"I know that I'm not very bright," said Bili humbly. "But a profound thinker like you, a man of such exemplary virtue . . . Everybody knows you're the finest scribe in our city. Which is to say, the whole world! Yet you live alone in that little house, fussing with your diet and putting on plays in your backyard."

"I know people talk about me," shrugged Julian. "People chatter and cackle like chickens."

Bili said nothing for a while. He knew he had revealed a sore spot.

Mellow Julian examined the sprawling straw mat of a foreign vendor. All the women of Selder adored seashells, because seashells were delicate, pretty, and exotic. Mellow Julian shared that interest, so he had a close look at the wares.

The shell vendor was a scarred, bristle-bearded sea pirate. His so-called rare seashells were painted plaster fakes.

Julian put away his magnifying lens. He nodded shortly and retreated. "Since you were born almost yesterday, Bili," he said, glancing over his shoulder, "I would urge you to have a good look at that wild, hard-bitten character. This marketplace has never lacked for crooks, but this brute may be a spy."

Bili pointed. "There's even worse to be seen there, maestro."

Huddled under a torn cotton tarp were five dirty refugees: black-haired, yellow-skinned people in travel-torn rags. One of the refugees was not starving. He was the owner or boss of the other four, who visibly were.

"They shouldn't let wretches like those through the gates," said Bili. "My father says they carry disease."

"Every mortal being carries *some* disease," Julian allowed. He edged nearer to the unwholesome scene. The exhausted refugees couldn't even glance up from the cobblestones. "Well," said Julian, "no need to flee these wild invaders. My guess would be that somebody invaded them."

"They're some 'curious specimens,' as you always put it, maestro."

"Indeed, they most certainly are."

"They must have come from very far away."

"You are staring at them, Bili, but you are not observing them," said Julian. "This man is in the ruins of a uniform, and he has a military bearing. This younger brute must be his son. This boy and girl are a brother and sister. And this older woman, whom he has dragged along from the wreck of their fortunes . . . Look at her hands. Those hands still have the marks of rings."

The ruined soldier rose in his tattered boots and stuck out his callused mitt. *"Money, water, food, house! Shelter! Fish! Vegetable!"*

"I understand you," Julian told him, in a fluent Old Proper English. *"I'm touched that you've taken the trouble to learn so many nouns. So. What is your name, sir? My friends call me Mellow Julian Nebraska."*

"You give me money for her," the soldier demanded, pointing. *"You take her away, I buy shelter, water, food, fish, vegetable!"*

"I have some money," offered Bili.

"Don't get hasty, Bili."

"But I think I understand what this foreigner is saying!" said Bili. "Listen! I want to try out my Old Proper English on him. *I buy this woman. You take my money. You eat your fish and vegetables.*" Bili pointed at the boy and girl. *"You feed these children. You wash your clothes. You comb your hair."* He glanced at Julian. "That's the right English word, isn't it? *Comb?*"

"It is," Julian allowed.

"You wash yourself in the public bath," Bili persisted. *"You stink lesser!"* He turned to Julian triumphantly. "Just look at him! Look at his eyes! He really does understand me! My lessons in the Academy of Selder . . . That dead language is practical! I can't wait to tell my dad!"

"You should no longer call this city 'Selder,' Bili. The true name of your city is 'Shelter.' 'The Resilient, Survivable, Sustainable Shelter,' to list all her antique titles. If your ancestors could see you speaking like this—in their own streets, in their own language—they'd say you were a civilized man."

"Thank you, maestro," said Bili, with a blush to his pale, beardless cheeks. "From you, that means everything."

"We must never forget that we descend from a great people. They made their mistakes—we all do—but someday, we'll surpass them."

"I'm going to buy this woman," Bili decided. "I can afford her. The Selder Academy doesn't cost all *that* much."

"You can't just buy some woman here in the public street!" said Julian. "Not sight unseen, for heaven's sake!"

Julian untied the mouth of his scholar's bag and rustled through the dense jumble within it—his watercress, spinach, scarf, pipe, scissors, string, keys, wax tablet, and magnifying glass. He pulled out one ancient silver dime.

Julian crouched beside the cowering woman and placed the time-worn coin into her blistered hand. "Here," he said, "this coin is for you. Now, stay still, for I'm going to examine you. I won't hurt you. Stick out your tongue."

She gripped the coin feverishly, but she understood not one word.

"Stick out your tongue," commanded Julian, suiting action to words.

He examined her teeth with the magnifying glass.

Then he plucked back the slanted folds of her eyelids. He touched both her ears—pierced, but no jewels left there, not anymore. He thumped at her chest until she coughed. He smelled her breath. He closely examined her hands and feet.

"She's well over forty years old," he said. "She's lost three teeth, she's starving, and she's been walking barefoot for a month. These two youngsters are not her children. I dare say a woman of her years had children once, but these are not them. This brute here with the leather belt, which he used on her legs . . . He's not her husband. She was a lady once. A civilized woman. Before whatever happened, happened."

"How much should I pay for her?" said Bili.

"I have no idea. This is no regular auction. The Godfather is a decent man, he prohibited all that slave-auction mischief years ago. You'd better ask your father how much he thinks a house-servant like her is worth. Not very much, I'd be guessing."

"I'm not buying her for my house," said Bili. "I'm buying her for *your* house."

A moment passed.

"Bili—," Julian said severely, "have I taught you nothing with my lectures, or from the example of my life? I devote myself to sustainable simplicity! Our ancestors never had slaves! Or rather, yes they did, strictly speaking—but they rid themselves of that vice, and built machines instead. We all know how *that* ugly habit turned out! Why would I burden myself with her?"

Bili smiled sheepishly. "Because she is so much like a pet bird?"

"She is rather like a bird," Julian admitted. "More like a bird than a woman. Because she is starving, poor thing."

"Maestro, please accept this woman into your house. Please. People talk about you all the time, they gossip about you. You don't mind that, because you are a philosopher. But maestro, they talk about *me*! They gossip about *me*, because

I follow you everywhere, and I adore you! I'd rather kneel at your feet than drill with the men-at-arms! Can't you do me this one favor, and accept a gift from me? You know I have no other gifts. I have no other gifts that even interest you."

After Mellow Julian accepted Bili's gift, Bili became even more of the obnoxious class pet. Bili insisted on being addressed by his antique pseudonym Dandy William Idaho, and sashayed around Selder in a ludicrous antique costume he had faked up, involving "blue jeans." Bili asked impertinent, look-at-me questions during the lectures. He hammed it up after class in amateur theatricals.

However, Bili also applied himself to his language studies. Bili had suddenly come to understand that Old Proper English was the language of the world. Old Proper English was the language of laws, rituals, boundary treaties, water rights, finance arrangements, and marriage dowries. The language of civilization.

That was why a wise and caring Godfather took good care to see that his secretaries wrote an elegant and refined Old Proper English. A scribe with such abilities could risk some personal eccentricities.

Julian named his new servant House Sparrow Oregon. Enquiries around the court made it clear that she was likely from Oregon. War and plague—they were commonly the same event—had expelled many of her kind from their distant homeland.

Deprived of food and shelter, they had dwindled quickly in the cruelties of the weather.

Sometimes, when spared by the storms, refugees found the old grassy highways, and traveled incredible distances. Vagrants came from the West Coast, and savages from the East Coast. Pirates came from the North Coast, where there had once been nothing but ice. The South was a vast baking desert that nobody dared to explore.

Once a teenage boy named Juli had left a village in Nebraska. Julian had suffered the frightening, dangerous trip to Selder, because the people in Selder still knew about the old things. And they did know them—some of them. They knew that the world was round, and that it went around the sun. They knew that the universe was thirteen thousand, seven hundreds of millions of years old. They knew that men were descended from apes, although apes were probably mythical.

They had also built the only city in the known world that was not patched-up from the scraps of a fallen city. Created at the sunset of a more enlightened age, Selder was a thousand years old. Yet it was the only city that had grown during the long dark ages.

The court of the Godfather was a place of sustainable order. The council-of-forty, the Men in Red, were its educated, literate officials. They held the authority to record facts of state. They knew what was meet and proper to write, and what was of advantage to teach, and what should be censored. They had taught Julian, and he had worked for them. He had come to know everything about what they did with language. He was no longer overly fond of what they did.

House Sparrow Oregon had no language that Julian understood. To test her, Julian inscribed the classic letters of antiquity into his wax tablet: THE QUICK BROWN FOX JUMPS OVER THE LAZY DOG. PACK MY BOX WITH FIVE DOZEN LIQUOR JUGS.

In response, Sparrow timidly made a few little scrapes with the stylus. Crooked little symbols, with tops and bottoms. They were very odd, but she knew only ten of them. Sparrow was nobody's scholar.

Julian was patient. Every child who ever entered a school was a small barbarian. To beat them, to shout at them, to point out their obvious shortcomings . . . what did that ever avail? What new students needed were clear and simple rules.

This aging, frightened, wounded woman was heartsick. She had lost all roles, all rules, and all meaning. She was terrified of almost everything in Selder, including him.

So: it was about a small demonstration, and then a patient silence: the wait for her response. So that Sparrow's dark eyes lost their cast of horror and bewilderment. So that she observed the world, no longer mutely gazing on it.

So: This is the water. Here, drink it from this cup. It's good, isn't it? Yes, fresh water is good! The good life is all about simple things like clear water.

Now, this is our bucket in which we bring the water home. Come with me, to observe this. There is nothing to fear in this street. Yes, come along. They respect me, they will not harm you.

You see this? Every stranger living in Selder must learn this right away. This is our most basic civic duty, performed by every able-bodied adult, from the Godfather himself to the girl of twelve. These waterworks look complex and frightening, but you can see how I do this myself. This is a water-lever. It holds that great leather bucket at one end, and this stone weight here at our end.

We dip the great bucket so as to lift the dirty water, so that it slowly flows in many locks and channels, high back up the hillside. We recycle all the water of this city. We never spill it, or lose its rich, fertile, and rather malodorous nutrients. We can spill our own blood in full measure here, but we will never break our water cycle. This is why we have sustained ourselves.

After we heave this great bucket of the dirty civic water—and not before!—then we are allowed to tap one small bucket of clean water, over here, for our private selves.

Now you can try.

Don't let those stupid housewives hurt your feelings. We all look comical at first, before we learn. Yes, you are a foreigner, and you are a curious specimen. That is all right. In the House of Mellow Julian Nebraska, we embrace curiosity. Our door is always open to those who make honest inquiries. We house many things that are strange, as well as you.

Now for the important moral lesson of the birds. Yes, I own many birds. I own too many. Some are oddly shaped, and special, and inbred, and rather sickly. Quite often they die for mysterious reasons. I cannot help that: It is my fate to be the master of an aviary.

Yes, the name I gave you is Sparrow, just like that smallest bird hopping there. These are my pigeons, these are my chickens, these are my ducks. In antiquity there were many other birds, but these are the surviving species.

One can see that to care for these birds suits your proclivities. When you chirp at them in your native language, they hear you and respond to you. As Sparrow the birdkeeper, you have found new purpose in the world. We will have one small drink to celebrate that. It's pretty good, isn't it? It isn't pure clean water, but a moderate amount of sophistication has its place in life.

Now that you have become the trusted mistress of the aviary, it is time for you to learn about this cabinet of curiosities. Being a scholar of advanced and thoughtful habits, I own a large number of these inexplicable objects. Old drawings, fossil bones, seashells, coins and medals, and, especially, many arcane bits of antique machinery. Some are rare. Most are quite horribly old. They all need to be cleaned and dusted. They break easily. Be tender, cautious, and respectful. Above all, do not peel off the labels.

My curiosities are not mere treasures. Instead, they are wonders. Watch with the students, and you will see.

Students, dear friends of learning and the academy: Tonight we study the justly famous "external combustion engine." Tonight we will make one small venture in applied philosophy, revive this engine from its ancient slumbers, and cause it to work before your very eyes.

And what does it do? you may well ask me. What is its just and useful purpose? Nobody knows. No one will ever know. No one has known that for three thousand years.

Now my trusted assistant Sparrow will light the fire beneath the engine's cauldron. Nothing sinister about that, a child could do it, an illiterate, a helpless alien, yes, her. Please give her a round of applause, for she is shy. That was good, Sparrow. You may sit and watch with the others now.

Now see what marvels the world has, to show to a patient observer. Steam is boiling. Steam travels up these pipes. Angry steam flows out of these bent nozzles. This round metal bulb with the nozzles begins to spin. Slowly at first, as you observe. Then more rapidly. At greater speed, greater speed yet: tremendous, headlong, urgent, whizzing speed!

This item from my cabinet, which seemed so humble and obscure: This is the fastest object in the whole world!

Why does it spin so fast? Nobody knows.

It is sufficient to know, young gentlemen, that our ancestors built fire-powered steaming devices of this kind, and they wrecked everything. *They utterly wrecked the entire world.* They wrecked the world so completely that we, their heirs so long after, can scarcely guess at the colossal shape of the world that they wrecked.

You see as well, little Sparrow? Now you know what a wonder can do. When it spins and flashes, in its rapid, senseless, glittering way, you smile and clap your hands.

In the summer, a long and severe heat came. The wisdom of the founders of Selder was proven once again.

Every generation, some venturesome fool would state the obvious—why don't we grow our crops outside of these glass houses? Without those pergolas, sunshades, reflectors, straw blankets, pipes, drips, pumps, filters, cranes, aqueducts, and the Cistern. That would be a hundred times cheaper and easier!

So that error might well be attempted, and then disaster would strike. The exposed crops were shriveled by heat waves, leveled by storm gusts, eaten by airborne hordes of locusts and vast brown crawling waves of teeming mice. In endless drenching rains, the tilled soil would wash straight down the mountainside.

In the long run, all that was not sustainable was not sustained.

Brown dust-lightning split the angry summer sky. Roiling gray clouds blew in from the southern deserts and their dust gently settled on the shining glass of Selder. There were no more pleasant, boozy, poetic star-viewing parties. People retreated into the stony cool of the seed vaults. When they ventured out, they wore hats and goggles and wet, clinging, towel-like robes. They grumbled a great deal about this.

Mellow Julian Nebraska made no such complaint. In times of civic adversity, it pleased him to appear serene. Despite this unwholesome heat and filth, we dwell in a city of shining glass! We may well sweat, but there is no real risk that we will starve! Let us take pride in our community's unique character! We are the only city of the world not perched like a ghost within the sprawling ruin of some city of antiquity! Fortitude and a smiling countenance shall be the watchwords of our day!

Julian sheltered his tender birds from the exigencies of the sky. He made much use of parasols, misting-drips, and clepsydra. The professor's villa was modest, but its features were well considered.

Dirt fell lavishly from the stricken sky, but Sparrow had learned the secret of soap, that mystic potion of lye, lard, ashes, and bleach. Sparrow spoke a little now, but not one word of the vulgar tongue: only comical scraps of the finest Old Proper English. Sparrow wore the clean and simple white robes that her master wore, with a sash around her waist to show that she was a woman, and a scarf around her hair to show that she was a servant. Sparrow would never look normal, but she had come to look neat and dainty.

Julian's enemies—and he had made some—said dark things about the controversial philosopher and his mute exotic concubine. Julian's friends—and he had made many—affected a cosmopolitan tolerance about the whole arrangement. It was not entirely decent, they agreed, but it was, they opined, very like him.

Julian was not a wealthy man, but he could reward his friends. His small garden was cool in the stifling heat, and Sparrow had learned to cook. Sparrow cooked highly alarming meals, with vegetables cut in fragments, and fried in a metal bowl. This was the only Selder food that Sparrow could eat without obvious pangs of disgust.

His students ate these weird concoctions cheerily, because healthy young men ate anything. Then they ran home in darkness to boast that they had devoured marvels.

The wicked summer heat roiled on. It was the policy of the finer folk of the court to dine on meat: mostly rabbit, guinea pig, and mice. Meat spoiled quickly.

When he fell ill, there were rumors that the Godfather had been poisoned. No autocrat ever died without such claims.

But no autocrat could live forever, either. So the old God-father perished.

On the very day of the old man's death, the dusty heat wave broke. Vast torrential rains scoured the mountains. Everyone remarked on this fatal omen.

It was time for the Godfather's cabal to retire into the secret seed vaults, don their robes and masks, and elect the successor.

Julian's students had never seen a succession ritual. It was a sad and sobering time. Men who had never sought out a philosopher asked for some moral guidance.

What on earth are we to do now? Console the grieving, feed the living, and lower the dead man into the Cistern.

What will history say of Godfather Jimi the Seventh? That the warlike spirit of his youth had matured into a wise custodianship of the arts and crafts of peace.

Then there were others with a darker question: What about the power?

There Mellow Julian held his peace. He could guess well enough what would happen. There would be some jostling confusion among the forty masked Men in Red, but realistically, there were only two candidates for the Godfather's palace. First, there was the Favorite. He was the much-preened and beloved nephew of the former Godfather, a well-meaning idiot never tested by adversity.

There was the Other Man, who had known nothing but adversity. He had spent his career in uniform, repressing the city's barbarian enemies. His supporters were hungry and ambitious and vulgar. He would not hesitate to grasp power by any means fair or foul. His own wife and children feared him. He was stubborn and bold, as Julian knew, because he had once been Julian's classmate.

Who would complain if a professor, in a time of trouble, retired into his private life? No rude brawling for the thinking man, no street marches, no shouted threats and vulgar slogans. No intrigues: instead, civility. The cleanly example of the good life. Food, drink, friends, and study. Simplicity and clarity. Humanity.

Humanity.

* * *

"Tonight," said Mellow Julian, in his finest Old Proper English, "as scholars assembled in civil society, we shall study together. The general theme of our seminars is remote from all earthly strife. Because she is shining, she is gorgeous, she is lovely, she is the planet Venus. In all her many attributes."

Hoots and cheers and claps.

"Young men," said Julian, "I do not merely speak to you of the carnal Venus. You will recall that your ancestors sent *flying machines* to Venus. *Electrical* machines, gentleman, and they had *virtual* qualities. The people of antiquity *observed* Venus. And Mercury. And Mars. And Jupiter, Saturn, and Neptune. It is written that they sent their machines to observe moons and planets that we can no longer see."

Respectful silence.

"We do not deny that Venus has her venereal aspects," said Julian. "What we want to assert—as civic philosophers—is a solid framework for systematic understanding! What is a man, what is his role in the universe, under the planets and stars?

"Consider this. If a man has a soul, then Venus must touch that soul. We all know that. But how, why? It is not enough to meander dully through our lives, vaguely thinking: 'Venus is the brightest planet in the heavens, so surely she must have something to do with me.' Of course the vibrations of Venus affect a man! Can any man among you deny that we live through the vibrations of the sun? Raise your hand."

Being used to rhetorical questions, they knew better than to raise their hands.

"Certain students of our Academy," said Julian, "have chosen not to attend this course of Venusian seminars. They felt that they needed to be together with their families in this difficult season . . . In this perilous moment in the long life of our city. Yet when we, as scholars, by deliberate policy . . . when we remove ourselves from the unseemly dust and mud of our civil strife . . . from all that hurly-burly . . ."

A hand shot up in the audience.

"Yes, Practical Jeffrey of Colorado? You have a question?"

"Maestro, what is *hurly-burly*? Is that even a word? *Hurly-burly* doesn't sound very Old Proper English."

"You make a good point as usual, Practical Jeffrey. *Hurly-burly* is an onomatopoeic term. That word directly arises from the sonic vibrations of the natural universe. Are there other questions about *onomatopoeia*, or the general persistence of some few words of Truly Ancient Greek within the structure of Old Proper English?"

There were no such questions.

Julian gestured beyond the row of chairs. Sparrow rose at once from her cross-legged seat on her mat.

"You gentlemen have never witnessed a device remotely like this one," said Julian, "for very few have. So let me frame this awful business within its rhetorical context. How did our ancestors observe Venus? As is well known to everyone, our ancestors tamed the lightning. On top of the wires in which they confined that lightning, they built yet another mystic structure, fantastic, occult, and exceedingly powerful. Their electrical wires, we can dig up in any ruin. No traces of that virtual structure remain: only certain mystical hints.

"So we know, we must admit, very little about antique virtuality. But we do know that virtuality moved vibrations: It moved images, and light, and sound, and numbers. Tonight, for the first time in your lives, you will be seeing a projected image. Tomorrow night—if you see fit to return here—you will see that image *moving. With sounds.*"

Sparrow bent her attention to the magic lantern. Julian arranged the makeshift stage. It was a taut sheet of white cotton, behind a flooring of bricks.

Then Julian ventured through the small crowd to the aviary, where he had seen an ominous figure lurking.

This unsought guest wore a red robe, with a faceless red hood. Everyone was cordially pretending to ignore the Man in Red. Even the youngest students knew that this was how things were done.

"Thank you for gracing us with your presence tonight," murmured Julian.

"I haven't seen that magic lantern in forty years," said the Man in Red.

"It consumes a very special oil, with a bright limestone powder . . . rare and difficult," said Julian.

"Are you willing," said the Man in Red, "to pay the rare and difficult price for your failure to engage with the world?"

"If you're referring to the cogent matter of the succession," said Julian cordially, "I've made it the policy at these civil seminars to discuss that not at all."

"If the Other Man takes command of the Palace," said the Man in Red, "he will attack you. Yes, you academics. Not that you have done anything subversive or decadent! No, I wouldn't allege that! But because your weakness invites attack. Since you are so weak, he can make an example of you."

Julian now had a quite good idea who the Man in Red was, but Julian gave no sign to show that. "I refuse to despair," he said, smiling. "This is merely a change of regime. The world is not ending, sir. The world already ended a thousand years ago."

"Our world," said the Man in Red, "this world we both enjoyed under the bounty of the previous Godfather, does not have to end. It's true that the Other Man has the force of numbers on his side—because he's forged an ignoble alliance of the greedy and the stupid. But it's not too late for a small, bold group to preempt him."

"If there is trouble," said Julian, "my students will come to harm. Because my students are brave. And bold. And idealistic. And exceedingly violent. You can start a brawl like that. Do you think you can end it?"

"You could rally your students. These young men of fine families . . . Many about to lose their sinecures from the old man's court . . . They trust your counsel. They adore you. Some of them more than they should, perhaps."

"Oh," said Julian, "I don't doubt I could find you one bold, bright, expendable young fool with a cloak and a dagger! But may I tell you something? Quite honestly? I spit on your cynical palace intrigues. I do. I despise them. They repel me."

"You quarreled with the old regime, Julian. The next regime might be kinder to you."

"I live simply. You have nothing that I want."

"I can tolerate a man of integrity," said the Man in Red, "because the innocent men are all fools. But a man who re-asserts his integrity—after what you did?—that is a bit more difficult to tolerate."

"Don't let me be difficult," said Julian. "You must have many pressing errands elsewhere."

"To tell the truth, I envy you," admitted the Man in Red, with a muffled note of sadness behind his red fabric mouth-hole. "All of us envy you. We all tell each other that we would love to do just as you did: put aside the pen, take off the robes, and retire to a life of the mind. Oh yes, you do make that sound mild and humble, but this private dreamworld of yours, with these sweet little birdcages . . . It's much more exciting and pleasurable than our grim, sworn duties. Your life merely seems lighthearted and self-indulgent. You have found a gen-uinely different way of life."

"My friend, yes I have, and I believe . . . I know that all of life could be different. Despite the darkness of the world it ruined, humanity could still transform itself. Yes, humanity could."

"You even have found yourself some creature comforts, lately. One of your minions bought you a mistress. I'm not sure I understand the appeal of that—for you."

"I rather doubt I'd understand the appeal of your mistress, either."

"I don't understand that myself," sighed the Man in Red. "A man imagines he's cavorting like a rooster, while all the time he's merely bleeding wealth. A mistress who cares noth-ing for you is an enemy in your bed. A mistress who does care for you is your hostage to fortune. A pity that my warnings were so useless. Good evening, sir."

The Man in Red left, with serene and measured step. The crowd parted silently before him as he approached, and it surged behind him as he left.

Julian filtered through the crowd to Sparrow, where she knelt by the lantern, cautiously unwrapping fragile slides of painted glass.

He gripped her by the arm and dragged her to her feet. "Sparrow will sing tonight!" he announced, pulling her toward the stage. "Sparrow will sing her very best song for you! It's very curious and unusual and antique! I believe it maybe the oldest song in the whole world." He lowered his trembling voice. "Go on, Sparrow. Sing it, sing . . ."

Sparrow was in an agony of reluctance and stage fright.

Julian could not urge her to be brave, because he was very afraid. "This is the oldest song in the whole world!" he repeated. "Gentlemen, please try to encourage her . . ."

In her thready, nasal voice, Sparrow began to choke out her mournful little wail. Although her words meant nothing to anyone who listened, it was clearly and simply a very sad song. It was something like a sad lover's song, but much worse. It was a cosmic sadness that came from a cold grave in the basement of the place where lovers were sad.

The lament of a mother who had lost her child. Of a child who could find no mother. A heartbreaking chasm in the natural order of being. A collapse, a break, a fall, a decay, a loss, and a lasting darkness. It was that sad.

Sparrow could not complete her song. She panicked, hid her face in her wrinkled hands and fled into a corner of the house.

Julian set to work on the magic lantern.

His student Practical Jeffrey came to his side. Jef spoke casually, in the local vulgar tongue. "Maestro, what was that little episode about? That was the worst stage performance that I've ever seen."

"That was the oldest song in the whole world, Jef. And now, you have heard it."

"I couldn't understand one line of that lousy dirge! She's a terrible singer, too. She's not even pretty. If she were young and pretty, that might have been tolerable."

"Don't let me interfere with your pressing quest for a young and pretty girl, Jef."

"I know that I didn't understand all that," Jef persisted, "but I know that something has changed. Not just that the old man is finally dead, or that the antique world is so rotten. We have to force the world to rise again in some other shape . . . For me, this was enough of that. I'm leaving you, maestro. I'm leaving your academy for good. I've had enough of all your teaching and your preaching, sir. Thank you for your efforts to improve me. I have to get to work now."

Julian glanced up. He was not much surprised by Jef's news. "You should stay to see this magic lantern, Jef. Projected images are extremely dramatic. They are very compelling. Really, if you've never seen one, they are absolutely wondrous. People have been known to faint."

"I'm sure your phantoms are marvelous," said Jef, pretending to yawn. "I'm going back to the Palace now, I have a family meeting . . . You stay well."

Jef did not appear for the next night of the Venus seminar. Julian's house and yard were densely packed, because word had gotten out about the magic lantern and its stunning effects. The little house roiled and surged with metalsmiths, sculptors, mural painters, orators, men of medicine, men of the law . . . Even a few women had dared to show up, with their brothers or husbands as escorts.

Practical Jeffrey had sent his apology for leaving the school, written in his sturdy, workmanlike calligraphy. He'd also shipped along a handsome banquet, and, as a topper, a wooden keg of the finest long-aged corn liquor. All the other students were hugely impressed by Jef's farewell gesture. Everyone toasted him and agreed that, despite his singular absence from the proceedings, Practical Jeffrey was a gentleman of high style.

So the second night started lively and, lavishly lubricated by Jef's magnanimity, it got livelier yet.

This night, the students put on a series of dramatic skits, performed in Old Proper English. These episodes involved the myths and heroes of remote antiquity: the Man who walked on the Moon, the Man who flew alone across the ocean, the Man who flew around without any machines at all, and was made of steel, and fought crime (he was always popular).

These theatricals were an unprecedented success, because the crowd was so dense, and so drunk, and because the graceless Dandy William Idaho was not there to overact and spoil anything.

Three of the masked Men in Red graced the scene with their presence, which made life three times more dangerous than life had been the night before. Julian watched them, smiling in his best mellow fashion, to hide his pride and his dread.

All his glamorous, shining young men, striking their poses on the tiny stage, with their young, strong, beautiful bodies . . . Maybe it could be said that Julian had saved them from deadly danger. It might also be said that he was fiddling as the city burned.

Julian knew that a settling of accounts was near. A time of such tension needed only one provocation. An obscure clash by night, a sudden insult offered, an insult stingingly returned, and Dandy William Idaho had been beaten senseless in the street. Bili was crushed, spurned, trampled on, and spat upon. Bili had never been the kind of kid you could hit just once.

Then the troubles started. Bitter quarrels, flung stones near glass houses . . . The police restored order through the simple pretext of attacking the foreigners. Everybody knew that the foreigners in the city were thieves, because so many had been forced to be thieves. No one of good sense and property was going to defend any thieves.

The police richly enjoyed the luscious irony of the police robbing thieves. So the police kicked in the doors of some of the wealthier foreigners, and seized everything they had.

Julian spent the night of that seminar activating an electrical generator. Electrical generators had been true fetish objects for the remote founders of Selder. Periodically, as a gesture of respect to antiquity, some scholar would disinter an old generator and rebuild another new generator in the same shape. So Julian owned a generator, packed in its moldering, filthy grease. It had elaborate, hand-etched schematics to explain how to work it.

This electrical night was not nearly so successful as the earlier seminar nights. After much cursing and honest puzzlement, the students managed to get the generator assembled. They even managed to crank it. It featured some spots of bare metal that stung the bare hand with a serpent's bite. Other than that, it was merely an ugly curio. The generator did not create any visible mystical powers or spiritual transcendence. Society did not advance to a higher plane of being.

Next day, the emboldened police repressed some of the darker elements of the old regime. These arrogant time-servers were notorious for their corruption. So the police beat the fancy crooks like dogs and kicked them out the door, and the crowd cheered that action, too.

People spoke quite openly of who would be serving in the Other Man's new regime, and what kind of posts they would hold.

The Favorite for the post of Godfather acted the fine gentleman: He urged calm, made dignified noises, and temporized. In the meantime, the gate guards had been bribed. Exiles poured into the city. The sentence of exile had been the merciful punishment of the late Godfather's later years. Now it became clear that the Godfather had merely exported resentments to a future date. These exiles—those among them who survived—had become hard, weathered men. They knew what they had lost. They also knew what they had to regain.

So there were more clashes, this time with gangs of hardened cutthroats. The Favorite pulled up his stakes and fled in terror.

Julian spent that night explaining how to use electricity and virtuality to connect the soul of Man with the planet Venus.

There was a large crowd for his last hermetic ceremony, and not because it was such an interesting topic. People had fled to Julian's refuge because the city was convulsed with fear.

It had always been said of the people of Selder that they would shed their own blood rather than lose one drop of water. Like many clichés, that was true. The smothered resentments of a long, peaceful reign were all exposed to the open air. That meant beatings, break-ins, and back-alley backstabbings.

The elections were held in conditions of desperate haste, because only one man was fit to restore order.

To his credit, the new Godfather took prompt action. He

averted anarchy through the simple tactic of purging all his opponents.

Julian surrendered peaceably. He had rather imagined that he might have to. The grass that bent before the wind would stand upright again, he reasoned. The world was still scarred with the windblown wrecks of long-dead forests.

Prison was dark, damp, and dirty. The time in prison weighed heavily on a man's soul. Julian had nothing to write with, nothing to read. He never felt the sun, or breathed any fresh air.

Julian's best friends in the underground cell were small insects. Over a passage of ten centuries, cave insects had somehow found the many wet passages beneath the city. Most of these wild denizens were smaller than lice, pale, long-legged, and eyeless. Julian had never realized there were so many different breeds of them. The humble life sheltered within the earth had suffered much less than the life exposed to mankind on its surface.

At length—at great length—Julian had a prison visitor.

"You will forgive Us," stated the Godfather, "for trying a philosopher's well-known patience. There were certain disorders consequent on Our accession, and a great press of necessary public business. Word has reached Our ears, however, that you have been shouting and pleading with your jailers. Weeping and begging like a hysterical woman, they tell Us."

"I'm not a well man now, your eminence. I cannot thrive without the vibrations of the sun, the stars, and planets."

"Surely you didn't imagine that We would ever forget a classmate."

"No, sir."

"They tell Us you have been requesting—no, sobbing and pleading—for some literary material," said the Godfather. He nodded at his silent bodyguard, who passed a sheaf of manuscripts through the carved stone pillars of the cell. "You will find these documents of interest. These are the signed confessions of your fellow conspirators."

Julian leafed through the warrants. "It's good to see that my friends kept up their skills in calligraphy."

"We took the liberty of paging through the archives of our predecessor, as well," said the Godfather. He produced a set of older documents. "You will recognize the striking eloquence of these death sentences. You were in top form back then. These documents of state are so grandiloquent, so closely argued, and in such exquisite English. They killed certain members of my own family—but as legal court documents, they were second to none."

Julian sighed. "I just couldn't do that any longer."

"You won't have to do it," the Godfather allowed. "You wrote such sustainable classics here that We won't need any new death sentences. We can simply reuse your fine, sturdy documents, over and over."

"It was my duty to write sentences," said Julian. "Sentences are a necessity of statecraft. Let me formally express my remorse."

"You express your remorse now," remarked the Godfather. "At the time, you were taking great pride in your superb ability to compose a sentence."

"I admit my misdeeds, sir. I am contrite."

"More recently, you and your friends were plotting against Our election," said the Godfather patiently. "As a further patent insult to Our dignity, you had yourself crowned as the 'President of the United States.' There are witnesses to that event."

"That was a diversion," said Julian. "That was part of a magic ceremony. To help me electrically reach the virtual image of the planet Venus."

"Juli, have you become a heretic, or just a maniac? You should read the allegations in these confessions! They are fantastic. Your fellow conspirators say that you believe that men can still fly. That you conjured living phantoms in public. We don't know whether to laugh or cry."

"People talk," said Julian. "In a cage, people will sing."

"You dressed your slave as a golden goddess and you made people worship her."

"That was her costume," said Julian. "She enjoyed that. I think it was the only time I've ever seen her happy."

"Juli, We are not your classmate any more. We have become your Godfather. It is unclear to Us what you thought you were gaining by this charade. In any case, that will go on no longer. Your cabal has been arrested. Your house, and all that eerie rubbish inside it, has been seized. In times this dark and troubled, We have no need for epicene displays. Is that understood?"

"Yes, sir."

"Now tell Us what We are supposed to do with you."

"Let me go," said Julian, sweating in the stony chill. "Release me, and I will sing your praises. Some day history will speak of you. You will want history to say something noble and decent about you."

"That is a tempting offer," mused the Godfather. "I would like history to say this of me: that I was an iron disciplinarian who scourged corruption, and struck his enemies with hammer blows. Can you arrange that?"

"I can teach rhetoric. Someone will say that for you, and they'll need great skill."

"I hate a subtle insult," said the Godfather. "I can forgive an enemy soldier who flings a spear straight at me, but a thing like that is just vile."

"I don't want to die here in this stone cage!" screeched Julian. "I can write a much better groveling confession than these other wretches! A man of your insight knows that confessions are nothing but rhetoric! Of course they all chose to indict me! How could they not? They are men with families to consider, while I am foreign-born and I have no one! We're all intelligent men! We all know that if someone must die, then I'm the best to die. I'm one against four! But surely you must know better!"

"Of course I know better," said the Godfather. "You imagined that, as men of letters, you were free of the healthy atmosphere of general fear so fit for everyone else. That is not true. Men of letters have to obey Us, they have to serve Us loyally, and they have to know that their lives are forfeit. Just like everyone else."

" 'Uneasy lies the head that wears the hood,' " said Julian.

"You always had a fertile mind for an apposite quote. We are inclined to spare you."

Light bloomed in the dampest corner of Julian's mind. "Yes, of course, of course I should be spared! Why should I die? I never raised my hand against you. I never even raised my voice."

"Like the others, you must write your full and complete confession. It will be read aloud to the assembled court. Then, a year in the field with the army will toughen you up. You're much too timid to fight, but Our army needs its political observers. We need clearly written reports from the field. And the better my officers, the worse they seem to write!"

"Is there a war? Who has attacked us?"

"There is no war just as yet," said the Godfather. "But of course they will attack Us, unless We prove to them that they dare not attack. So, we plan a small campaign to commence Our reign. One insolent village, leveled. You'll be in no great danger."

"I'm not a coward."

"Yes, in fact, you are a coward, Julian. You happened to live in a time when you could play-act otherwise. Those decadent times have passed. You're a coward, and you always were. So, make a clean breast of your many failings. We pledge that you too will be spared. You might as well write your own confessions, for your sins are many and you know them better than anyone."

"Once I do that for you, you'll spare my friends."

"We will. We don't say they will suck the blood of the taxpayer anymore, but yes, they will be spared."

"You'll spare my students."

"Fine young men. They were led astray. Young men of good family are natural officer material."

"You'll give me back my house and my servant."

"Oh, you won't need any house, and as for your wicked witch . . . You should read the thunderation that rings around her little head! Your friends denounced you—but in their wisdom, they denounced her much, much more violently. They all tell Us that this lamentable situation is not your fault at all. They proclaim that she seduced you to it, that she turned your head. She drove you mad, she drugged you. She used all the wicked wiles of a foreign courtesan. She descended to female depths of evil that no mere man can plumb."

Julian sat on his stony bench for a moment. Then he rose again and put his hands around the bars. "Permit me to beg for her life."

"To spare her is not possible. We can't publish these many eloquent confessions without having her drowned in the Cistern right away. It would be madness to let a malignant creature like that walk in daylight for even an hour."

"She did nothing except what I trained her to do! She's completely harmless and timid. She's the meekest creature alive. You are sacrificing an innocent for political expediency. It's a shame."

"Should We spare this meek creature and execute you, and four friends? She was a lost whore, and the lowest of the low, as soon as her own soldiers failed to protect her from the world. You want to blame someone for the cold facts? Blame yourself, professor. Let this be a good lesson to you."

"You are breaking a bird on an anvil here. That's easy for you to do, but it's a cruelty. You'll be remembered for that. It will weigh on your conscience."

"It will not," said the Godfather. "Because We will kindly offer to spare the witch's life. Then We will watch your friends in a yapping frenzy to have her killed. Your noble scholars will do everything they can to have her vilified, lynched, dumped into the Cistern, and forgotten forever. They will blame her lavishly in order to absolve themselves. Then, when you meet each other again, you men with a cause, you literati—that's when the conscience will sting."

"So," said Julian, "it's not enough that we're fools, or that we're cowards, or that we failed to defend ourselves. We also have to be evil."

"You are evil. Truly, you are fraudulent and wicked men. We should wash you from the fabric of society in a cleansing bath of blood. But We won't do that. Do you know why? Because We understand necessity. We are responsible. We know what the state requires. We think these things through."

"You could still spare us. You could forgive us for the things we wrote and thought. You could be courageous and generous. That is within your great power."

The Godfather sighed. "That is so easy for a meager creature like you to say, and so difficult for Us to do. We will tell you a little parable about that. Soon, this cell door will open. Now: When this door is opened, place your right hand in this doorframe. We will have this husky bodyguard slam this iron door on your fingers. You will never scribble one mischievous word again. If you do that, Julian, that would be 'courageous and generous.' That would be the bravest act of your life. We will spare the life of your mystic witch for that noble act."

Julian said nothing.

"You're not volunteering to be so courageous and generous? You can marry her: You have Our blessing. We will perform that ceremony Ourselves."

"You are right. I don't want her," said Julian. "I have no further need for her. Let her be strangled in all due haste and thrown down the well. Let the hungry fish nibble her flesh, let her body be turned into soup and poured through the greenhouses. She came to me half-dead, and every day I gave to her was some day she would never have seen! Let me see that sunlight she will never see again. I hate this cage. Let me out of here."

After his release from darkness, very little happened to Julian that he found of any interest. After two years of service, Julian managed to desert the army of Selder. There had been no chance of that at first, because the army was so eager, bold, and well disciplined.

However, after two years of unalloyed successes, the army suffered a sharp reverse at the walls of Buena Vista. The hardscrabble villagers there were too stubborn, or perhaps too stupid, to be cowed by such a fine army. To the last man, woman, and child, they put up a lethal resistance. So the village was left in ruins, but so was the shining reputation of the Godfather and his troops.

Julian fled that fiery scene by night, losing any pursuers

in the vast wild thickets of cactus and casuarina. Soon afterward, he was captured by the peasants of Denver. There was little enough left of that haunted place. However, the Denver peasants sold him to a regional court with a stony stronghold in the heights of Vale.

Julian was able to convince the scowling peers of that realm that they would manage better with tax records and literate official proclamations. That was true: They did improve with a gloss of civility. They never let him leave, but they let him live.

After a course of further indifferent years, word arrived in Vale that the Godfather of Selder had perished in his own turn. He had died of sickness in a war camp, plague and war being much the same thing. There were certain claims that he had been poisoned.

After some further tiresome passage of years, the reviving realm of Selder began to distribute traders, bankers, and ambassadors. They were a newer and younger-spirited people. They were better dressed and brighter-eyed. They wrote everything down. They observed new opportunities in places where nothing had happened for ages. They had grand plans for those places, and the ability to carry them out.

These new men of Selder seemed to revel in being a hundred things at once. Not just poets, but also architects. Not just artists, but also engineers. Not just bankers, but gourmands and art collectors. Even their women were astonishing.

Julian had no desire to return to the damp glassy shadows of Selder. He had come to realize that a Sustainable City that could never forget its past could become an object of terror to simpler people. Also, he had grown white-haired and old.

But he was not allowed to ignore a velvet invitation—a polite command, really—from Godfather Magnanimous Jef the First. Practical Jeffrey had outlasted his city's woes with the stolid grace that was his trademark. Jef's shrewd rise to power had cost him a brother and two bodyguards, but once in command, he never set his neatly shod foot wrong.

In his reign, men and women breathed a new air of magnificence, refinement, and vivacity. Troubles that would have crushed a lesser folk were made jest of, simply taken in stride.

Men even claimed that the climate was improving. This was delusional, for nothing would ever make the climate any better. But the climate within the hearts of men was better. Men were clearly and simply a better kind of man.

Julian had never written a book, for he had always said that his students were his books. And with the passage of years, Julian's students had indeed become his books. They were erudite like books, complex like books, long-lasting like books. His students had become great men. Their generation was accomplishing feats that the ancients themselves had never dreamt of. Air wells, ice-ponds and aqueducts. Glass palaces of colored light. Peak-flashing heliographs and giant projection machines. Carnivals and pageants. Among these men, greatness was common as dirt.

It was required, somehow, that the teacher of such men should himself be a great man. So the great men delighted in honoring Julian. He was housed in a room in one of their palaces, and stuffed with creature comforts like a fattened capon. His only duty was to play the sage for his successors, to cackle wise inanities for them. To sing the praises of the golden present, and make the darkest secrets of a dark age more tenaciously obscure.

Futurity could never allow the past to betray it again.

Home Sweet Bi'Ome

PAT MacEWEN

Pat MacEwen is a physical anthropologist by trade with more than a decade's worth of experience as a crime scene investigator. "My central field of research, however, is genocide," she says. "I've also worked on war crimes investigations in the former Republic of Yugoslavia (now the independent nation of Kosovo) for the International Criminal Tribunal. I'm deeply interested in global warming, which I think is likely to spawn more genocides, and I'm something of a science geek." She has published short fiction in several genres: fantasy, sf, horror, and mystery. A new sf novelet, "Taking the Low Road," is out in 2012. Her forensic/urban-fantasy trilogy, Rough Magic, is forthcoming, with the first volume, The Fallen, *out in 2012. Likewise, a YA series about a crippled boy who can't talk to people but finds out he can talk to dragons. The first volume in that series,* The Dragon's Kiss, *is also out in 2012.*

"Home Sweet Bi'Ome" was published in F&SF. It is an amusing story about future allergies, biotech solutions, and more. MacEwen says in an interview, "as for the story itself, I dreamed it. A friend of mine has a daughter living in a stripped-down cabin on the slopes of Mt. Shasta because she has hyperallergic syndrome and can't tolerate the synthetic side of modern life . . . my subconscious made hay with it."

I woke up feeling itchy, and started to scratch my face before I'd quite gotten my eyes open.

Oh, no. As soon as I was conscious, I balled my hand up and made a fist. It's a trained reflex, one I've acquired through long practice. You can't scratch an itch with a fist. You can rub hard, but your knuckles don't set off the histamine complexes, making them worse than they already are. You won't tear open tender skin and start off all those nasty secondary infections.

I sat up and balled the other fist. I was itching, all right. All over. But I didn't have a rash. Wonder of wonders, when I took a look at myself, my skin was a nice even pink everywhere. There were faint welts where I'd begun to scratch, but nothing more.

What on Earth?

As I examined myself, the itch intensified. It traveled. Into my mouth. My ears. My . . . well, never mind where. Let's just say that all of my mucosal tissues were staging a riot, and for no apparent reason.

Not knowing what else to do, I got up. Tea, I told myself. Chamomile. Or white. White tea is soothing, and there's nothing in it that sets me off. I get mine from a guy in Sri Lanka, who grows the stuff without pesticides. He packs the tea in plain old-fashioned wax paper, inside a tin. No plastics, no dyes or preservatives. No excess packaging, covered with ink and shellac and God knows what else.

I padded through the house, careful to keep my hands off

my hide. Just walking, however, set off a fresh round of itching, this time on the balls of my feet. Couldn't quite keep myself from doing a circular Sufi dance across the coarse black fur that serves as a carpet, letting the friction of skin against wiry hair turn the prickling heat into definite inflammation.

The cold enamel tooth-tiles on the kitchen floor calmed it down some but there was no denying the fact that I was having some kind of allergic reaction. To what? There was no nylon in the house. No plastic of any kind. No paint. No fragrance. No synthetic anything. That's the whole point of a Bi'Ome. Everything is totally organic and completely familiar to me, or at least to my immune system.

Nervously, I checked my fingers. When I get the hives, it shows up first in my hands. I get ugly red blotches (what doctors call urticaria). Then my fingers swell up like stubby pink sausages. My lips, too. I start looking like a Ubangi, except there's no clay saucer stretching my mouth out of shape. Just oedema. Good old Mother Nature. And when it gets bad, well, my throat closes up. Or I pass out. Then my throat closes up. Where had all my EpiPens gone?

I reached out, grabbed the edge of a pouch underneath the nearest kitchen counter, and felt my fingers slide across half a dozen small hard bumps. Like Braille, only bigger.

I looked down. The rash was an odd one, the bumps looking weirdly transparent and delicate rather than small, hard, and red. Whatever. It speckled half the cabinets, the walls, the ceiling, and most of the pouches I use for drawers.

I spat, "Son of a bug-eater!"

It wasn't *me* that had the rash. It was my house.

It took them five hours to send me an EMT—three solid hours to find the clown and another two to get his sorry ass up the mountain. You know how long that is, when you're fighting a desperate need to scratch where it itches?

Then, when he did show up, he didn't even have a truck. What he had was all these piercings and implants and crap. He even had a LoJack locked into his skull right behind his left ear. Swear to God, the guy looked like a Borg who'd mated with a mess of fishing tackle. Worse than that, he had a uniform on, a polyester mix. I could tell as soon as the tech climbed off his freakin' motorcycle. Worse than *that*, even. Aftershave.

Oh my God. One whiff and my throat closed up.

Not that he noticed. The goof came rambling up to my front door just like some demented encyclopedia salesman, all smiling, eyebrow-beringed, and happy-faced.

I met him with a loaded crossbow.

Seeing that, he stopped dead. Both hands flew up, aerating armpits awash with some kind of deodorant. Fresh Scent, Extra Dry something or other. I started wheezing, fell to my knees, and found myself aiming at the point directly in front of me, which happened to be his crotch.

He definitely noticed *that*.

"Hey, take it easy." He turned his hips sideways, acting like he didn't know he'd just threatened my life.

"Don't you come any closer," I gasped.

"I won't! But you . . . you called for a tech, right?"

I stared up at him over the length of the quarrel. "*You're* it? Where's Chen? Or Fredo? Or Saylah?"

I got a sheepish smile this time, along with a shrug. "All the regular guys are tied up. If you wanna wait—"

"No! I can't!"

"Okay, then." He gathered up some confidence and pulled out a business card, which I did not even think of accepting. After a moment's embarrassment, he let his hand drop. He introduced himself. "I'm Rey Fox. R-E-Y. Short for Reynard. It's kind of a joke. See, Moms was French."

My crossbow wobbled a bit but I did my best to keep it centered on his private parts while I checked his company ID card. Reynard, indeed.

" 'Fox' Fox?" I couldn't help asking, though I didn't have much air to spare.

The doofus nodded, his smile spreading out like my getting the stupid joke made everything okay between us.

"You see the signs?" I demanded. Hack. Wheeze.

"Uh . . . signs?"

I rolled my eyes, which were nearly as itchy as everything

else. "The *No Trespassing* signs. I have them posted all over the place."

"Oh. Um, I didn't look. On the bike, I get kinda . . . well. . . ." He gave me that same silly shrug again. "Curvy mountain roads and me, I kind of get into it."

Great. Just great.

"Well, what about your work order? Didn't that say anything?"

"About what?"

Oh, Lord. I started coughing up a lung. I guess it sounded pretty bad. He peered at me, and in the process he took a step nearer.

I nearly shot him, right then and there.

"About hyperallergic syndrome!" I wheezed, as soon as the coughing jag eased up. Waving the point of the quarrel at three of the signs, I read them for him. "Do not approach if you are wearing any kind of perfume or fragrance. NO PLASTIC! NO NYLON!"

His dark eyes flicked back and forth.

"Why d'you think I live up here on the mountain?" I asked him. "Why do you think I bought a Bi'Ome? You idiot! I'm allergic. To practically everything."

"But I—"

"You're wearing plastic," I told him. "If I let you into my house, if I touch your shirt, I could go into anaphylactic shock." Pant. Wheeze. "I could die."

His mouth fell open. His lower lip flapped in the breeze, amid a faint jangle of the six chromed rings looping around its middle reaches.

"All that stinkum on you—Good God, I'm that close to choking on that shit alone. From here. What on *Earth* were you thinking?"

He shook his head, the lower lip still flapping. "They, uh, they said it was an emergency."

"*It is*, you moron! Just look at my house!"

Only then did I let go of the crossbow with one hand and wave at the pink skin/wall behind me, the rosy expanse that would normally be turning golden green this time of year, as the sunshine of early spring spurred tanning as well as some serious photosynthetic power generation. Instead, the whole eastern side was covered with spots. I could barely restrain myself from reaching out to touch them, to rub them . . . to scratch.

Again, he took a step forward. I brought the crossbow back up to bear on his family jewels.

He raised a hand, Indian powwow style, but he didn't say, "How." Instead, he quietly told me, "Ma'am, I *need* a closer look."

Ma'am. That made me feel older than shit, on top of everything else. But I was the one who'd yelled for help, wasn't I? Sourly, congested and starting to wheeze again, I backed off and closed the door. Then I watched through the corneal window set into it while Reynard the Fox peered and poked at my wall. While he fetched a small med kit out of the bike's saddlebags and took swabs off the affected surfaces. While he stuck a giant hypodermic into my siding. That gave me a twinge, so I turned away rather than watch him take his biopsy samples. When he was done, he knocked on the door and backed away a careful ten paces.

"How long will it take?" I demanded as soon as I'd opened the door, still on the defensive although I'd left the crossbow sitting on the kitchen table.

"I'm not done yet. I need to see what's going on inside."

"The hell you say!"

He won, of course. But he also went back to the bike and pulled on a cleansuit—a pure white cotton and silk blend with breathing apparatus, a full hood, gloves and booties, the outfit he should have been wearing before he came anywhere near me.

Grudgingly, still trying hard not to inhale when a breeze wafted past him, I let Fox enter.

By now, the whole living room, ceiling and walls and a patch of the floor, was adorned with the rash. The inflamed bit of flooring intrigued him the most. He stroked the wiry black hair with a gloved hand, and smiled when nearly half the room developed goose bumps in response. "Living carpet," he said. "That's so cool. But it's not scalp hair, is it? Too dark." He glanced up at my dirty-blond mane.

I was already breathless and frozen in place by my own sudden onslaught of gooseflesh. But then, catching up with his question, I flushed a hot scarlet that would have put a full-blown case of strep A to shame. Wheezing, wide-eyed, I sputtered, "No! No, it's, uh, pubic. It stands up better . . . to wear and tear."

To my surprise, he did not bust a gut over that one. Just nodded at me, looking owlish. "Yeah, that makes sense. As long as your hair growth is dense enough."

Density, I thought, just might be the problem here. But not with the carpet.

"Is that itching too?" he asked, pointing at a hair-free slightly swollen strip of bare floor that served as a threshold, a lip between the inner and outer surfaces of the house.

Just thinking about it set off a furious prickling in the corresponding reaches of my anatomy. "Yes!" I snapped, forbidding my hands to go anywhere near the relevant body part. "What is it? And why is it making *me* itch? I don't have the freakin' rash!"

"A sympathetic reaction. Your nervous system is picking up on the symptoms affecting your better half."

"My *what*?"

"The house."

I planted my fists on my hips. "I think you'd better explain yourself, mister. I'm not *married* to this house."

He grinned. "Oh, no. Your relationship is way closer than that." Then, as he took in my unhappy reaction, he sobered up. "Look, you do know that this house was grown from your own stem cells, right?"

I nodded.

"We had to tweak the growth and development genes pretty hard. But underneath all that . . . the house is your twin. The DNA is the same. The nervous system—all the same. So, yeah, there have been some cases where Bi'Omes and their, uh, sources, have turned out to be just a little too sympatico."

"*That* was not disclosed," I told him. "Not when I bought mine."

"Well, there's still a big hairy argument. . . ." He broke off, flushing, trying real hard not to look at the carpet while his brain caught up with his mouth. "Uh, begging your pardon, ma'am, no pun intended—"

Impatience swept over me like a tidal wave. "Get on with it!" I nearly shouted. "What argument?!"

"Um, well, about whether the side effects are, ah, real, or, uh, psychosomatic."

I glared at him, then barely managed to whisper the word, I was so stinking mad. *"Psychosomatic?"*

He nodded, bobbing his head up and down like a fifties-style hula girl off somebody's dashboard.

"Are you aware that hyperallergic syndrome has, itself, been called psychosomatic?"

"Yeah, sure. I mean, after all, you people do have . . . a lot of . . . neuroses."

It was like watching a train wreck in slow motion—him realizing what he was about to say, and yet not quite able to stop himself.

" 'You *people*,' " I repeated, feeling dangerous. "Neuroses?"

"I didn't mean it like that," he said.

"Didn't you? Listen, I think you'd better leave."

He didn't argue, just gathered up all his stuff and walked out the door. I slammed it behind him, threw the lock, and went to check on my supply of oatmeal soap. A soothing bath might calm my skin down enough to let me think.

I was lolling in the tub, enjoying some blessed relief from the itching while I used a deep-breathing exercise to try and get my lungs back under control. I was just getting into the zone when I heard a knock on the front door. For Christ's sake. He'd only been gone half an hour, so *now* what?

Pulling a robe on, I padded out to the foyer to confront Fox. *"Yes?"* I inquired.

He just stood there, staring at me while his faceplate steamed up.

"What?"

"Uh. . . ."

Whoops. I hadn't bothered to towel off all of the oatmeal. The robe was stuck to me here and there. I pulled it tighter, which was the wrong thing to do. Made his eyes bug out.

I snapped my fingers in front of his faceplate. "Hey! Fox! What . . . Do . . . You . . . Want?"

"Ma'am, if I tell you that . . . I'm afraid you're gonna shoot me."

Which is as close to a compliment as I've had in the last seven years, up here on the mountain. Yeah, so I glanced at the crossbow. I'll admit that, but just for a second. Then I sighed. "I promise. I will not shoot you. Okay?"

Bozo nodded, but needed another half-minute or so to get back to the point. "Um, sorry to bother you."

"Which you did because . . . ?"

"Oh. I, uh, I got a prelim diagnosis. On the house."

"And?"

He had to yank his gaze upward to meet my eyes, but he managed it. "It's . . . not an allergy."

"Okay. What is it, then?"

"Well, um, listen. I took a look at the specs on this house. You may remember that Bi'Ome had to alter the house's immune system."

I nodded. "Yeah, so it wouldn't react so strongly to all the things that make *me* sick."

"That's right. They, ah, we had to selectively cripple the antigen-recognition system, so that it wouldn't react to . . . well, all sorts of things. Especially the man-made stuff—plastics and paints, and perfumes, insecticides—"

"Of course," I said, getting a little impatient, I do admit. I mean, the man *was* standing there in a silk and cotton moonsuit, just so that *he* wouldn't set me off.

"Well, that meant reducing the immunities that you'd already acquired to certain natural . . . *biological* hazards."

"What are you talking about?" I demanded. "Has my house been poisoned?"

"Technically, no!" Reynard answered.

"Then what the devil *is* wrong?"

"The house is infected."

What? I stared at him. He mostly stared at the floor. Despite the faceplate, I could see how red he was. Like *he* was sick.

"Infected with . . . what?"

Reynard flicked a glance upward, then fled my gaze again. "At first, I thought it might be a herpes virus—"

"Herpes?!"

He jumped when I hit high C, but I just couldn't help it. I screeched at the man. "Are you trying to tell me my house has a *social disease*? My house has *never* had sex!"

"I, uh, well, I wouldn't be too sure of that," answered Reynard, "but, um, that's not exactly the virus I'm talking about."

Huh? But . . . a thin shred of memory fled through my mind. What I'd thought was a dream. Erotic, sensual—surely that hadn't been *real*?

Paralyzed by the sudden suspicion that my house might have more of a social life than I did, I glared at Reynard. I spoke softly, for fear of cutting my own throat with the razor's edge of anger slicing at me from the inside out. "So what *are* you talking about?"

"Varicella zoster."

Zoster? I'd heard that before. But I couldn't quite make it click. "Vari-what?"

"It's a childhood disease. Used to be. Hardly anyone gets it these days because most kids are immunized."

"Most kids," I repeated, arms akimbo. I found myself leaning forward. With reckless daring, I went right on leaning, ignoring the fact that my robe had flapped open. In fact, I took a giant step closer before I demanded, "What about houses?"

Reynard licked his lips. "We, uh, we didn't think there would be any need. The odds against exposure, up here—"

Right. "Exposure—To—*What*?"

Then the Latin words clicked, somewhere deep down in my memory. Oh, no. I backed off again, staring at him. I threw wild glances at every wall. Every pale, red-speckled, minutely blistered wall.

"Dewdrop on a rose petal" . . . that's how my mother's medical books had described the rash. I rounded on Reynard. "My house has . . . *chicken pox*?"

He shrugged again. "There's, um, a blood test we can run. To make sure."

I shook my head, willing my hands to stay put on my hips, to remain fisted. I would *not* give in, not to the itchiness or to the need to slap the living shit out of this so-called tech aide. "Don't bother. Just treat it."

"Well, I, um . . ."

"Honest to God, I can't take much more of this," I told him, squirming. The oatmeal solution on my skin was drying up. My bathrobe was stuck to the stuff, so my every move tugged at it, making everything itch all the more. "Do something!" I pleaded.

"I can't."

"But—"

"The only treatment available is an antiviral—acyclovir, but it has to be started within the first twenty-four hours after exposure. Three or four days ago it might have done you some good. But it's too late now."

"Too . . . late?"

The white hood nodded. "The virus has already multiplied. It's everywhere. All we can do now is—"

"Oh, *God*," I whimpered and sat down, right there on the floor. The furry rug and my behind were both so inflamed, I began to rotate, pushing myself around in a circle with all four hands and feet. The wiry fur did a wonderful job of scrubbing my arse, but it didn't help one bit overall. The resulting friction just made the house and me itch even more. I began to weep. "Go away, will you? Just *go away*."

Ever so quietly, he did.

When he was gone, I made myself get up again. I could hardly walk for the need to bend over and scratch the floor with my fingernails. But that would only make things worse, so I tottered toward the lavatory, randomly raking the walls as I went, intending to dive right back into my warm oatmeal bath.

Never made it, though.

Whoop! Whoop! Whoop!

The freaking house alarm went off. It scared me half to

death. I fell over, then rolled around on the carpet as that set off more of my skin and I tried in vain to scratch everything at once. What with the frenzied boogaloo going on, I didn't realize what had happened, not till I noticed the flashing lights. Oh, boy. The whole friggin' wall screen had lit up, the background crimson, the space taken up by a single word:

QUARANTINE!

It was a notice from the Health Department, putting me and mine under full quarantine for ten days. As if I *could* leave.

I goggled. I crawled toward it. I slapped at buttons and entered the reset codes, and then sysop codes, and got nowhere. My house's smartnet was no longer mine to command. The county had taken control of it, of *everything*. Swearing, I got up all over again and staggered toward the front door. "That little son of a bitch! The nerve!"

I flung the front door open, groping for my crossbow as whiffets of cold air threw last year's leaves in my face. I peered through the fingers of one hand, trying to take aim, intending to plant one in his tiny heinie, but stopped when I saw even more flashing lights on my front gate. On his bike, too. His hazard lights were flashing, and so were his headlights. Likewise, something on his bike's handlebars pulsed in lurid scarlet. Then his horn started beeping.

He bent over, staring at some kind of screen on the bike, oblivious to me and *my* outrage. Then, ripping his cleansuit's helmet off, he flung it down. He swore at the bike, ran three steps forward, and kicked the helmet a full forty yards down the driveway.

Bad Idea. As the helmet sailed past the gate, more flashing lights appeared. "Warning!" the house cried. "Perimeter armed! Do not pass posted limits! This house is now under quarantine!"

As if to underline the point, a red laser beam hit the helmet. It flew ten more feet down the drive and sat there staring back at us, a smoking hole dead-center in the faceplate.

"What the . . . ?" Fox started toward it, but stopped when I yelled at him.

"Don't! It'll shoot you too!"

He turned, glared at me in disbelief, looked at the hole again, and demanded, "What kind of burglar alarm is *that*?!"

Excessive, of course, because that's what I had to have.

"Look, I'm all alone up here," I tried to explain. "And people . . . they don't read the signs. Or they think it's a Gingerbread House and they try to cut chunks off."

I'd caught some picnickers back in October, attempting to barbecue one of my red window shutters. For lunch, the fucking cannibals.

"Well, shut it off!"

"I can't."

His face darkened, matching the lowering sky behind him. "Look, lady, I've gotta get the fuck out of here! I've got a date tonight!"

"You think this was *my* idea?"

Rather than answer me, he slung his leg over the bike and attempted to start it up. When the ignition key failed him, he used his boot to flip out a bar on one side of the motor. He tried to kick-start the machine. My God, did he think a crotch rocket could outrun a laser?

No go, in any case.

I heard a voice. Not his. From his bike, from the console. Don't know what it told him, but he began swearing all over again, only louder this time. Then he jumped off the bike, kicked the front tire, and snarled as the bike shuddered once and the kickstand gave way. Ever so slowly, it fell over onto its side.

Oh, boy. Had to weigh, what? Five hundred pounds?

Apparently, he'd run out of cuss words. He fell silent. His shoulders sagged. Eventually, he turned to face me. "They say *they* disabled the bike. I'm fucking *stuck* here."

Which would have pissed me off even more if he weren't quite so hangdog about it. I stared at him, not even itching for one blessed moment. "What?"

He gazed at the ground. He licked his lip rings. "They, uh, they said they don't know yet if this is the same strain as regular chicken pox, so they're worried I'm going to catch it. Or give it to somebody else. So I've been quarantined too."

I rolled my eyes toward the swiftly darkening sky. "Well,

shit oh dear. I'm *so* friggin' sorry to hear that. Best of luck, Fox." I turned back toward the house.

"Hey!"

I stopped.

"What am I s'posed to do now?"

"How should I know?" I demanded. "Go put up a pup tent or something."

"Lady!? I don't *have* a freakin' tent. I don't have any camping gear. And look at that sky. There's an effing snow storm blowing in. I'll freeze to death out here."

"If I let you bring all *that* inside," I made a squiggly hand gesture meant to encompass the whole of his sartorial splendor, "*I'll* die. You can't come back inside unless you're wearing a clean suit."

We both cast a glance at his ruined helmet, now well beyond our reach even if it had still been intact.

In the end, we compromised.

Well, that's my word for it. He has another one I won't mention here.

I did let him in, but first I made him shuck the clean suit altogether. Then all his clothes and his jewelry. Then all his implants. When he was done, he stood there, using his hands to cover up the empty jacks instead of his groin. Apparently he felt more naked without the machinery than he did without his clothes.

I was firm, however, refusing to turn my back on him until he'd bundled it all up and stashed it in one of his bike's saddlebags.

He made even more noise when I threw a bar of soap his way and made him scrub down with it on the spot, twice, me squirting him with the hose.

Well, it was pretty cold, I suppose, but what was I gonna do? Let him walk right in wearing hair gel and aftershave? The bodywash? Antiperspirant? And whatever the doofus had used to turn *his* pubic hair pink and purple?!

If I could, I'd have made him take off the tattoos as well. He had two of the new interactive type, with glowing colors that swirled when he touched them. The one on his chest, a mandala, spun with his every breath. Since it was sealed in by his epidermis, however, I'd have to flay him to get it off.

A tempting thought, I admit. Or maybe I could get *him* to skin *me*. Anything to stop the itching!

While I fought for self-control, he dove through the front door. I followed, having to fight the wind just to close the door again. There really was quite a storm blowing in.

Once inside, Fox didn't seem to know what to do.

That made two of us. I edged my way past him, tossed him a couple of all-cotton towels, then dug out an old shirt and pants made of unbleached madras, the stretchy stuff. He was only an inch or two taller than me, and slender too, so I thought they'd fit well enough for the moment. The house, thank God, was running a slight fever anyway, giving us both a good chance to warm up.

I spent the next two hours yelling at people, and getting nowhere. The county would not bend an inch, and the company barely responded at all. Even when their man Fox called them, they didn't have time to chat. They were up to their corporate necks in what was clearly an epidemic. Unless I needed acute care, meaning hospitalization, they weren't letting either of us out of there.

By the time I gave up, I was hoarse from shouting, and coughing again. I didn't hear the *whop whop* outside right away.

Fox did. "What's that?" he asked.

A helicopter—it hovered about forty feet off the ground, whipping snowflakes into my eyes as I tried to get them to land. They weren't having it. Instead, in silence except for the noise of the chopper's engines and rotors, they lowered a cargo net full of five gallon buckets. Then they simply released the net, winched up the cable, and left again.

"What the . . . where are they going?" I yelled at Fox.

He shrugged, and shivered. The wind had a real bite to it by then, so we grabbed a bucket and lugged it indoors.

The canister was metal, and a bitch to pry open. When we did, I shared a puzzled look with my uninvited guest. Pepto-Bismol? Then the odor reached out to me. I backed away, beginning to panic before I recognized the smell. Not Pepto. Calamine lotion.

The net, when we looked, had some all-organic paint-brushes, rollers, trays, and extension handles stuffed into the meshwork too. We hauled it all inside, and got busy.

The calamine lotion worked wonders. I can't really use it myself because I react somewhat to one of the chemicals in it, but the house didn't mind. Anyway, I was careful to wear gloves and slippers. I let Fox paint the ceiling, too, not wanting the stuff to drip into my hair or my face. It was still quite a job. The house has four major rooms, a laundry, and a bathroom, and we had to paint it all, everything but the tile-work.

You have any idea how much calamine lotion that takes?

By the time we were done, it was late. I was wiped. I guess Fox was, too.

"So, ah . . . where do I sleep?" he inquired.

The couch was more of a love seat, and not long enough to accommodate him. Besides, we'd been forced to paint that too, and both of the armchairs, since they'd all developed a rash. I wasn't about to suggest he try sleeping on the floor either. Nestled in my pubic hair? I don't think so! But if we were going to be stuck here together for several days, then I'd have to do something. All things considered, it was sure to be something well outside my comfort zone.

Get over it, I told myself. That didn't make it easy.

"Well, uh, there's m . . . my room," I stammered. "You can come . . . take a look."

Given my behavior earlier with the crossbow, I guess he had a right to look askance at me, to wonder about my hesitation. So I bit my lip and led him toward the one room I'd painted all by myself. As we went, I reminded him, "As you've seen, the furniture is all part of the house. So pretty much everything in here is . . . me."

He nodded as he glanced through the arching doorway. Then he froze, and frankly gaped.

I knew what he was looking at. The beds. A pair of rounded mounds, each had a single dark brown cushion at one end that rose about six inches higher than everything else if you stroked them a little. Softly wrinkled, the pillowy masses were circled by smooth brown areolas and there was simply no mistaking what part of the body they'd been derived from.

To give him credit for having *some* sense, he didn't comment on that. Instead, he inquired, "No blankets?"

"I've never needed them," I said. Which was true. The beds were as warm as my own skin. They *were* my own skin. Normally, I didn't bother with PJs either. Tonight, I decided, was different. I'd sleep in my clothes. I dug out a comforter for him, and we both more or less collapsed.

I woke in the dark, still exhausted, not quite certain what had roused me. Then I heard it—a slurping sound of mumbled contentment.

Sitting up, I peered at my unwanted roommate.

He was sleeping peacefully, sprawled on the other bed. His head had slipped off the cushion, however, and he'd wrapped an arm around it. In his sleep, he nuzzled it. As I watched, the nippillow grew firmer, rising, and so did its counterparts, on my own bed, on my chest. It's hard to describe the sensation. Electric yet ghostly, unlike anything I'd felt before. I found myself stretching out, reaching out, longing for something I couldn't name.

But even that much movement set off my skin. I wasn't used to wearing clothes at night. They clung to me, the wrinkles leaving welts, rasping at my neck and my shoulders and hips, and I couldn't help wrapping my arms around myself and digging in. Pretty soon, I was a ball of misery, tears rolling down my face. Every part of me that I could reach lay next to a piece that I couldn't. I was so freakin' miserable, I didn't even know I was whimpering. I never heard him get up either. He was just suddenly there, beside me.

I sobbed. "I can't stand it!" I dug in again, but he stopped me.

"Easy, now," he murmured and called up the room lights. He slowly forced my hands down into my lap. He lifted my face, frowning as he caught sight of the multiple tracheotomy scars on my throat. He rubbed one thumb across them.

Then he got behind me and began rubbing my back. My shoulders. My hips. And when the cloth got in his way, he eased the shirt off me and worked on my bare skin. It wasn't the kind of massage you'd get at the spa, like I was a loaf of bread being kneaded. This was more like being stroked, over and over again. He did it just hard enough to move blood through my skin but without any hard edges. Slowly, the itching subsided, becoming a layer of heat, as if the whole outermost inch of me was slowly combusting.

Laying me down, he continued his work, down each arm and leg and back up again.

"You have such beautiful skin," he said, breathing the words at my bare shoulder. "Beautiful. . . ."

"Yeah, sure. As long as I stay clear of plastic," I whispered. Last time I wore rayon, I looked like a leper for most of a week, and Rick . . . well, Rick seemed to think he might catch it. When I reacted to his aftershave as well . . . I shuddered, trying to shake off the memory. "History," I told myself.

Fox didn't notice. He was too busy caressing the sensitive skin at the base of my spine, where tiny hairs had begun to tremble.

So long, I thought, since anyone touched me.

I sat up, turning to face him. He smiled. He'd taken off his borrowed shirt somewhere along the way. His mandala glowed, gently spinning. His hands kept on moving, caressing my thighs.

I looked down at the tent in his borrowed trousers. "Rub me all *over*," I insisted.

The next time I woke, it was nearly dawn. I felt . . . human. I lay on my side and the warmth at my back wasn't welts. It was Fox, his body spooned around mine. He was snoring, each breath ever so faintly stirring the hair on the nape of my neck.

I marveled, refusing to move. I wanted that moment to last. It might have to, the way things were going. My desensitization treatments had all failed. Unless and until something new came through, I'd be living like this the rest of my life.

At least I wasn't allergic to *him*.

I smiled. With Rey, it was like bedding a virgin. I guess he was so used to having the piercings, the implants and such . . . well, for one thing, he had to be *careful*. Those things can tear skin off. But when he had to do without them, it seemed to throw him off his rhythm. His tentative moves were incredibly gentle, however, and I couldn't help but respond in kind. His attitude, too, was so sweet. He was almost childlike about his discoveries. Lying there, I started feeling vaguely guilty about the whole thing, as if somehow I were taking advantage of him and his innocence.

A disturbing thought. It was interrupted by a tickle, then a sneeze. Then another. Monster sneezes. I wound up on the floor, with Rey's arm around me as I convulsed again and again. As my Mexican yaya would say, *"¡Que romantico!"*

"What is it? You need something? Cortisone? Huh? Do you have an inhaler?" He was in full panic mode, ready to start mouth to mouth. "Is it . . . is it me?"

I shook my head. "No." I was wheezing a bit, but it wasn't because of congestion, which it would be if this were a chemical thing. It was more of a physical prickling, way up inside my nose somewhere. I blew my nose, hard, and got no relief at all. That's when I remembered my skin itching so badly, all on account of the Bi'Ome's infection.

What was happening this time? And where?

We found a good eighteen inches of snow on the ground when we tumbled out the front door. No fair. The snow should have been rain, this late in the season.

The drifts had nearly buried Rey's bike, though the sky above us was perfectly clear by then. In the east, I could see dawn's light edging the Sierra Nevada with an ethereal white lacework of fresh powder. Beautiful—almost beyond words.

Until, that is, something fluttered right into my face, grabbing at me with tiny claws. I flailed at it, knocking the thing off my nose. Then another one came at me.

What were they, owls? Bugs?

I snatched up Rey's discarded, now frozen, towels and

swung them at the pesky creatures, trying to keep them at bay. Not so, Rey. He climbed up on the porch railing, peering at the roofline as more of them fluttered around the house.

"What are they?" I whispered, half-afraid I'd draw them my way again if I spoke any louder. I could hear faint squeaking as it was, like tiny fingernails on a blackboard.

"Stay there," answered Rey.

What?

He swung off the porch and climbed up the access ladder built into the siding. That took him up to a vent near the roof, a triangle opening into the attic space. Like so much of the house, the vent resembled its organ of origin—my nose. While I watched, the small fluttering forms flew at it. They folded up into smaller shapes as they reached its nostrils. Then they vanished altogether.

Scritch scritch . . . *Achoo!!*

I sneezed so hard, I blew one of the little airborn devils backward by nearly a yard. *That* finally scared the buggers off! They veered away from me and joined their fellows upstairs.

Rey climbed back down again. He was grinning.

I demanded, aloud this time, *"What?"*

He laughed, not exactly *at* me, but I still didn't take it well. "Love," he said, "you've got bats in your belfry. Your sinuses, anyway!"

I didn't buy it at first, but when daylight arrived, Rey went back up the ladder and opened the vent's screen. He reached inside and plucked one of them off its roost. When he brought it back down, I was startled to see just how small it was, bodily. With the wings all folded up, it was mouse-size. A baby mouse.

"See that chipmunk stripe down its back?" Rey said. "That's not a natural species. It's a nu-bat. They're gene-gineered, like the house. They've had some human alleles added so they're resistant to white-nose fungus, and rabies too. Replacements for what's gone extinct."

"But . . . but . . . what is it doing *here*?"

He grinned. "My guess is, they found a nice, warm, comfy cave in the attic that literally smells like them, like home. You have a whole colony of them," Rey told me. "It's easy to fix, though. All you need is screens with a smaller mesh size."

I nodded, thinking dire thoughts about bat guano. No wonder my sinuses felt congested so much of the time, in spite of my living way up here.

Then revelation dawned.

"How 'human' are they?" I asked Rey. "Could they catch *other* viruses? Like, say, chicken pox?"

The company rep tried to pooh-pooh the notion, but Rey sent in bat samples, using a sterilized trap/container they lowered to us the same way as the calamine lotion. A couple days later, there was no doubt. My bats had the chicken pox, all right. And nu-bats were clearly the vector that had spread it throughout almost all of the Bi'Omes in northern California. That led to the mass eviction of nu-bats by means of a saline sinus wash and some speedy replacement of natural filters with metal jobs, at least until they could tweak the Bi'Omes' phenotypes. The nu-bats' too, for all I know.

In another week's time, the rash faded away, healing almost as rapidly as it had bloomed. I reveled in my relief from both itching and sinus congestion. My major concern by then was the fast-approaching end of our quarantine.

Rey couldn't wait for a chance at a steak dinner. I couldn't quite make myself say farewell. When the day came, though, he seemed reluctant to go.

"It's been . . . interesting," he told me. "I never imagined . . . ," he started to say, but then stopped, blushing so furiously, his mandala's colors began to fade in comparison.

"Haven't you ever done it *au naturel*?" I asked gently.

He frowned. Slowly, thoughtfully, he said, "I got my first piercing when I was twelve. My first implant. . . ." He shut himself off, then said, simply, "No."

So I gave him a rueful smile. "You know those things were only meant to help people when they have problems. Or when they want to synchronize things exactly. For a treat? But two normal, wholly organic and natural people don't need enhancement. They don't really need anything but each other, and. . . ."

My petite sermon was cut short by Rey's lips attaching themselves to my earlobe. When we came back up for air, an hour later, he told me, "You shouldn't be so alone up here."

All I could do was shrug.

"What about online support groups?" Rey asked.

I shrugged again. "Who needs 'em? What? Do they make it all better? Make everything go away? Make things like they were before?"

"No, but—"

"Whining about it is useless," I blurted, unable to shut off the tap once the seal was cracked. "I've dealt with it, okay? I've got my Bi'Ome. I've rebuilt my life. Now I've got to get on with it. I've just got to go on. . . ."

I fell silent, but not from exhaustion. I was suddenly, acutely aware of how empty my Bi'Ome was. There were no bowling trophies, no Niagara Falls souvenirs, no clutter of toys. No family photos hung from my soft pink walls. Well, why look at what you can't have? I demanded, but Self wasn't fooled for a moment. The walls, and the rooms, and the shelves were all empty of everything I'd walked away from.

To save yourself, I told me sharply.

Yeah, right, Self answered. You're saving yourself . . . for what?

Rey stroked my hair. "Do you . . . d'you think you'd mind a visitor? Y'know, prob'ly just on weekends or holidays. I couldn't—"

I answered him with a kiss. By the time all new business was concluded, I'd offered to build him a bath house, outside the Bi'Ome, with heaters and hot water, towels and slippers, and pure cotton clothes he could wear in the house. If he wanted to wear anything at all.

He laughed. "I think I'd better take this one step at a time."

I couldn't agree more, though I didn't say so. All choked up, I simply clung to him. Finally, though, we sealed the deal with one last lingering smooch. Then I *had* to let him go. It should have been a simple matter of opening my front door. But it wasn't. The doorknob fought back.

So I tried again. No go.

I took a step backward, and finally noticed the bright

salmon-pink flush adorning the wall. An odd distortion on either side of the door jamb made the whole wall panel curve outward. Bulge, in fact.

Cautiously, I reached out and traced the curve on the right side with my fingertips. Hot. Fever-hot. Sore, too. I could *feel* it, an unpleasant ache/tickle on either side of my own throat.

Oh, no.

I turned and stared at Reynard.

He queried the smartnet. Didn't take long. A good thing, since I'd just about quit breathing under the onslaught of sympathy symptoms.

He shook his head, and gave me this sad, sheepish sort of a smile. "I, uh . . . I can't be sure, but it looks like the house might—"

"What?" I demanded. "What is it *this* time?"

Rey waved at the swollen door glands. He shrugged helplessly. "Mumps."

Oh my *god!*

For I Have Lain Me Down on the Stone of Loneliness and I'll Not Be Back Again

MICHAEL SWANWICK

Michael Swanwick (www.michaelswanwick.com) lives in Philadelphia, Pennsylvania. His seventh novel, The Dragons of Babel *(2008), was a sequel to his fantasy novel* The Iron Dragon's Daughter *(1993). His eighth novel,* Dancing with Bears: The Postutopian Adventures of Darger & Surplus, *was published in 2011. His eighth fiction collection,* The Best of Michael Swanwick, *appeared in 2008—there are seven previous story collections, and he continues to publish several stories each year, often more than one good enough to be reprinted in* Year's Best *volumes. In other words, he's still a pretty hot writer, and one of the finest conscious craftsmen in genre fiction today.*

"For I Have Lain Me Down on the Stone of Loneliness and I'll Not Be Back Again" was published in Asimov's. *The protagonist is a young Irish American eager to find his future in space, which alien conquerors have made possible. He's visiting Ireland to take a last look at his world. And he is unknowingly in danger of being trapped by the past, politics and sentiment and all.*

Ich am of Irlaunde,
And of the holy londe
Of Irlande.
Gode sire, pray ich the,
For of saynte chairité
Come ant daunce with me
In Irlaunde.

(anon.)

The bullet scars were still visible on the pillars of the General Post Office in Dublin, almost two centuries after the 1916 uprising. That moved me more than I had expected. But what moved me even more was standing at the exact same spot, not two blocks away, where my great-great-grandfather saw Gerry Adams strolling down O'Connell Street on Easter morning of '96, the eightieth anniversary of that event, returning from a political rally with a single bodyguard to one side of him and a local politico to the other. It gave me a direct and simple connection to the tangled history of that tragic land.

I never knew my great-great-grandfather, but my grandfather told me that story once and I've never forgotten it, though my grandfather died when I was still a boy. If I squeeze my eyes tight shut, I can see his face, liquid and wavy as if glimpsed through candle flames, as he lay dying under a great feather comforter in his New York City railroad flat, his smile weak and his hair forming a halo around him as

347

white as a dandelion waiting for the wind to purse its lips and blow.

"It was doomed from the start," Mary told me later. "The German guns had been intercepted and the republicans were outnumbered fourteen to one. The British cannons fired on Dublin indiscriminately. The city was afire and there was no food to be had. The survivors were booed as they were marched off to prison and execution, for the common folk did not support them. By any conventional standard it was a fiasco. But once it happened, our independence was assured. We lose and we lose and we lose, but because we never accept it, every defeat and humiliation only leads us closer to victory."

Her eyes *blazed*.

I suppose I should tell you about Mary's eyes, if you're to understand this story. But if I'm to tell you about her eyes, first I have to tell you about the holy well.

There is a holy well in the Burren that, according to superstition, will cure a toothache. The Burren is a great upwelling of limestone in the west of County Clare, and it is unlike anyplace else on Earth. There is almost no soil. The ground is stony and the stone is weathered in a network of fissures and cracks, called grykes, within which grow a province of plants you will not find in such abundance elsewhere. There are caves in great number to the south and the east, and like everywhere else in that beautiful land, a plenitude of cairns and other antiquities to be found.

The holy well is one such antiquity, though it is only a round hole, perhaps a foot across, filled with water and bright green algae. The altar over it is of recent construction, built by unknown hands from the long slender stones formed by the natural weathering of the limestone between the grykes, which makes the local stone walls so distinctive and the walking so treacherous. You could tear it down and scatter its component parts and never hear a word spoken about your deed. But if you returned a year later you'd find it rebuilt and your vandalism unmade as if it had never happened. People have been visiting the well for a long, long time. The Christian overlay—the holy medals and broken statues of saints that are sometimes left as offerings, along with the prescription bottles, nails, and coins—is a recent and perhaps a transient phenomenon.

But the important thing to know, and the reason people keep coming back to it, is that the holy well works. Some holy wells don't. You can locate them on old maps, but when you go to have a look, there aren't any offerings there. Something happened long ago—they were cursed by a saint or defiled by a sinner or simply ran out of mojo—and the magic stopped happening, and the believers went away and never returned. This well, however, is charged with holy power. It gives you shivers just to stand by it.

Mary's eyes were like that. As green as the water in that well, and as full of dangerous magic.

I knew about the holy well because I'd won big and gotten a ticket off-planet, and so before I went, I took a year off in order to see all the places on Earth I would never return to, ending up with a final month to spend wandering about the land of my ancestors. It was my first time in Ireland and I loved everything about it, and I couldn't help fantasizing that maybe I'd do so well in the Outsider worlds that someday I'd be rich enough to return and maybe retire there.

I was a fool and, worse, I didn't know it.

We met in the Fiddler's Elbow, a pub in that part of the West which the Bord Failte calls Yeats Country. I hadn't come in for music but only to get out of the rain and have a hot whiskey. I was sitting by a small peat fire, savoring the warmth and the sweet smell of it, when somebody opened a door at the back of the room and started collecting admission. There was a sudden rush of people into the pub and so I carried my glass to the bar and asked, "What's going on?"

"It's Maire na Raghallach," the publican said, pronouncing the last name like Reilly. "At the end of a tour she likes to pop in someplace small and give an unadvertised concert. You want to hear, you'd best buy a ticket now. They're not going to last."

I didn't know Maire na Raghallach from Eve. But I'd seen the posters around town and I figured what the hell. I paid and went in.

* * *

Maire na Raghallach sang without a backup band and only an amp-and-finger-rings air guitar for instrumentation. Her music was . . . well, either you've heard her and know or you haven't and if you haven't, words won't help. But I was mesmerized, ravished, rapt. So much so that midway through the concert, as she was singing "Deirdre's Lament," my head swam and a buzzing sensation lifted me up out of my body into a waking dream or hallucination, or maybe vision is the word I'm looking for. All the world went away. There were only the two of us facing each other across a vast plain of bones. The sky was black and the bones were white as chalk. The wind was icy cold. We stared at each other. Her eyes pierced me like a spear. They looked right through me, and I was lost, lost, lost. I must have been half in love with her already. All it took was her noticing my existence to send me right over the edge.

Her lips moved. She was saying something and somehow I knew it was vastly important. But the wind whipped her words away unheard. It was howling like a banshee with all the follies of the world laid out before it. It screamed like an electric guitar. When I tried to walk toward her, I discovered I was paralyzed. Though I strained every muscle until I thought I would splinter my bones trying to get closer, trying to hear, I could not move nor make out the least fraction of what she was telling me.

Then I was myself again, panting and sweating and filled with terror. Up on the low stage, Mary (as I later learned to call her) was talking between songs. She grinned cockily and with a nod toward me said, "This one's for the American in the front row."

And then, as I trembled in shock and bewilderment, she launched into what I later learned was one of her own songs, "Come Home, the Wild Geese." The Wild Geese were originally the soldiers who left Ireland, which could no longer support them, to fight for foreign masters in foreign armies everywhere. But over the centuries the term came to be applied to everyone of Irish descent living elsewhere, the children and grandchildren and great-great-great-grandchildren of those unhappy emigrants whose luck was so bad they couldn't even manage to hold onto their own country and who had passed the guilt of that down through the generations, to be cherished and brooded over by their descendants forever.

"This one's for the American," she'd said.

But how had she known?

The thing was that, shortly after hitting the island, I'd bought a new set of clothes locally and dumped all my American things in a charity recycling device. Plus, I'd bought one of those cheap neuroprogramming pendants that actors use to temporarily redo their accents. Because I'd quickly learned that in Ireland, as soon as you're pegged for an American, the question comes out: "Looking for your roots, then, are ye?"

"No, it's just that this is such a beautiful country and I wanted to see it."

Skeptically, then: "But you do have Irish ancestors, surely?"

"Well, yes, but . . ."

"Ahhhh." Hoisting a pint preparatory to draining its lees. "You're looking for your roots, then. I thought as much."

But if there's one thing I *wasn't* looking for, it was my fucking roots. I was eighth-generation American Irish and my roots were all about old men in dark little Boston pubs killing themselves a shot glass at a time, and the ladies of Noraid goose-stepping down the street on Saint Patrick's Day in short black skirts, their heels crashing against the street, a terrifying irruption of fascism into a day that was otherwise all kitsch and false sentiment, and corrupt cops, and young thugs who loved sports and hated school and blamed the blacks and affirmative action for the lousy construction-worker jobs they never managed to keep long. I'd come to this country to get away from all that, and a thousand things more that the Irish didn't know a scrap about. The cartoon leprechauns and the sentimental songs and the cute sayings printed on cheap tea towels somehow all adding up to a sense that you've lost before you've even begun, that it doesn't matter what you do or who you become, because you'll never achieve or amount to shit. The thing that sits like a demon in the dark pit of the soul. That Irish darkness.

So how had she known I was an American?

Maybe it was only an excuse to meet her. If so, it was as good an excuse as any. I hung around after the show, waiting for Mary to emerge from whatever dingy space they'd given her for a dressing room, so I could ask.

When she finally emerged and saw me waiting for her, her mouth turned up in a way that as good as said, "Gotcha!" Without waiting for the question, she said, "I had only to look at you to see that you had prenatal genework. The Outsiders shared it with the States first, for siding with them in the war. There's no way a young man your age with everything about you perfect could be anything else."

Then she took me by the arm and led me away to her room.

We were together how long? Three weeks? Forever?

Time enough for Mary to take me everywhere in that green and haunted island. She had the entirety of its history at her fingertips, and she told me all and showed me everything and I, in turn, learned nothing. One day we visited the Portcoon sea cave, a gothic wave-thunderous place that was once òccupied by a hermit who had vowed to fast and pray there for the rest of his life and never accept food from human hands. Women swam in on the tides, offering him sustenance, but he refused it. "Or so the story goes," Mary said. As he was dying, a seal brought him fish and, the seal not being human and having no hands, he ate. Every day it returned and so kept him alive for years. "But what the truth may be," Mary concluded, "is anyone's guess."

Afterward, we walked ten minutes up the coast to the Giant's Causeway. There we found a pale blue, four-armed alien in a cotton smock and wide straw hat painting a watercolor of the basalt columns rising and falling like stairs into the air and down to the sea. She held a brush in one right hand and another in a left hand, and plied them simultaneously.

"Soft day," Mary said pleasantly.

"Oh! Hello!" The alien put down her brushes, turned from her one-legged easel. She did not offer her name, which in her kind—I recognized the species—was never spoken aloud. "Are you local?"

I started to shake my head but, "That we be," Mary said. It seemed to me that her brogue was much more pronounced than it had been. "Enjoying our island, are ye?"

"Oh, yes. This is such a beautiful country. I've never seen such greens!" The alien gestured widely with all four arms. "So many shades of green, and all so intense they make one's eyes ache."

"It's a lovely land," Mary agreed. "But it can be a dirty one as well. You've taken in all the sights, then?"

"I've been everywhere—to Tara, and the Cliffs of Moher, and Newgrange, and the Ring of Kerry. I've even kissed the Blarney Stone." The alien lowered her voice and made a complicated gesture that I'm guessing was the equivalent of a giggle. "I was hoping to see one of the little people. But maybe it's just as well I didn't. It might have carried me off to a fairy mound and then after a night of feasting and music I'd emerge to find that centuries had gone by and everybody I knew was dead."

I stiffened, knowing that Mary found this kind of thing offensive. But she only smiled and said, "It's not the wee folk you have to worry about. It's the boys."

"The boys?"

"Aye. Ireland is a hotbed of nativist resistance, you know. During the day, it's safe enough. But the night belongs to the boys." She touched her lips to indicate that she wouldn't speak the organization's name out loud. "They'll target a lone Outsider to be killed as an example to others. The landlord gives them the key to her room. They have ropes and guns and filthy big knives. Then it's a short jaunt out to the bogs, and what happens there . . . Well, they're simple, brutal men. It's all over by dawn and there are never any witnesses. Nobody sees a thing."

The alien's arms thrashed. "The tourist officials didn't say anything about this!"

"Well, they wouldn't, would they?"

"What do you mean?" the alien asked.

Mary said nothing. She only stood there, staring insolently, waiting for the alien to catch on to what she was saying.

After a time, the alien folded all four of her arms protectively against her thorax. When she did, Mary spoke at last. "Sometimes they'll give you a warning. A friendly local will come up to you and suggest that the climate is less healthy than you thought, and you might want to leave before nightfall."

Very carefully, the alien said, "Is that what's happening here?"

"No, of course not." Mary's face was hard and unreadable. "Only, I hear Australia's lovely this time of year."

Abruptly, she whirled about and strode away so rapidly that I had to run to catch up to her. When we were well out of earshot of the alien, I grabbed her arm and angrily said, "What the fuck did you do *that* for?"

"I really don't think it's any of your business."

"Let's just pretend that it is. Why?"

"To spread fear among the Outsiders," she said, quiet and fierce. "To remind them that Earth is sacred ground to us and always will be. To let them know that while they may temporarily hold the whip, this isn't their planet and never will be."

Then, out of nowhere, she laughed. "Did you see the expression on that skinny blue bitch's face? She practically turned green!"

"Who are you, Mary O'Reilly?" I asked her that night, when we were lying naked and sweaty among the tangled sheets. I'd spent the day thinking, and realized how little she'd told me about herself. I knew her body far better than I did her mind. "What are your likes and dislikes? What do you hope and what do you fear? What made you a musician, and what do you want to be when you grow up?" I was trying to keep it light, seriously though I meant it all.

"I always had the music, and thank God for that. Music was my salvation."

"How so?"

"My parents died in the last days of the war. I was only an infant, so they put me in an orphanage. The orphanages were funded with American and Outsider money, part of the campaign to win the hearts and minds of the conquered peoples. We were raised to be denationalized citizens of the universe. Not a word of Irish touched our ears, nor any hint of our history or culture. It was all Greece and Rome and the Aldebaran Unity. Thank Christ for our music! They couldn't keep that out, though they tried hard to convince us it was all harmless deedle-deedle jigs and reels. But we knew it was subversive. We knew it carried truth. Our minds escaped long before our bodies could."

We, she'd said, and *us* and *our*. "That's not who you are, Mary. That's a political speech. I want to know what you're really like. As a person, I mean."

Her face was like stone. "I'm what I am. An Irishwoman. A musician. A patriot. Cooze for an American playboy."

I kept my smile, though I felt as if she'd slapped me. "That's unfair."

It's an evil thing to have a naked woman look at you the way Mary did me. "Is it? Are you not abandoning your planet in two days? Maybe you're thinking of taking me along. Tell me, exactly how does that work?"

I reached for the whiskey bottle on the table by the bed. We'd drunk it almost empty, but there was still a little left. "If we're not close, then how is that my fault? You've known from the start that I'm mad about you. But you won't even—oh, fuck it!" I drained the bottle. "Just what the hell do you want from me? Tell me! I don't think you can."

Mary grabbed me angrily by the arms and I dropped the bottle and broke her hold and seized her by the wrists. She bit my shoulder so hard it bled and when I tried to push her away, toppled me over on my back and clambered up on top of me.

We did not so much resolve our argument as fuck it into oblivion.

It took me forever to fall asleep that night. Not Mary. She simply decided to sleep and sleep came at her bidding. I, however, sat up for hours staring at her face in the moonlight. It was all hard planes and determination. A strong face but not one given to compromise. I'd definitely fallen in love with the wrong woman. Worse, I was leaving for distant worlds the day after tomorrow. All my life had been shaped toward that end. I had no Plan B.

In the little time I had left, I could never sort out my feelings for Mary, much less hers for me. I loved her, of course, that went without saying. But I hated her bullying ways, her hectoring manner of speech, her arrogant assurance that I would do whatever she wanted me to do. Much as I desired her, I wanted nothing more than to never see her again. I had all the wealth and wonders of the universe ahead of me. My future was guaranteed.

And, God help me, if she'd only asked me to stay, I would have thrown it all away for her in an instant.

In the morning, we took a hyperrapid to Galway and toured its vitrified ruins. "Resistance was stiffest in the West," Mary said. "One by one all the nations of the Earth sued for peace, and even in Dublin there was talk of accommodation. Yet we fought on. So the Outsiders hung a warship in geostationary orbit and turned their strange weapons on us. This beautiful port city was turned to glass. The ships were blown against the shore and broke on the cobbles. The cathedral collapsed under its own weight. Nobody has lived here since."

The rain spattered to a stop and there was a brief respite from the squalls which in that part of the country come off the Atlantic in waves. The sun dazzled from a hundred crystalline planes. The sudden silence was like a heavy hand laid unexpectedly upon my shoulder. "At least they didn't kill anyone," I said weakly. I was of a generation that saw the occupation of the Outsiders as being, ultimately, a good thing. We were healthier, richer, happier, than our parents had been. Nobody worried about environmental degradation or running out of resources anymore. There was no denying we were physically better off for their intervention.

"It was a false mercy that spared the citizens of Galway from immediate death and sent them out into the countryside with no more than the clothes on their backs. How were they supposed to survive? They were doctors and lawyers and accountants. Some of them reverted to brigandry and violence, to be sure. But most simply kept walking until they lay down by the side of the road and died. I can show you as many thousand hours of recordings of the Great Starvation as you can bring yourself to stomach. There was no food to be had, but thanks to the trinkets the Outsiders had used to collapse the economy, everybody had cameras feeding right off their optic nerves, saving all the golden memories of watching their children die."

Mary was being unfair—the economic troubles hadn't been the Outsiders' doing. I knew because I'd taken economics in college. History, too, so I also knew that the war had, in part, been forced upon them. But though I wanted to, I could not adequately answer her. I had no passion that was the equal of hers.

"Things have gotten better," I said weakly. "Look at all they've done for . . ."

"The benevolence of the conqueror, scattering coins for the peasants to scrabble in the dust after. They're all smiles when we're down on our knees before them. But see what happens if one of us stands up on his hind legs and tells them to sod off."

We stopped in a pub for lunch and then took a hopper to Gartan Lough. There we bicycled into the countryside. Mary led me deep into land that had never been greatly populated and was still dotted with the ruins of houses abandoned a quarter-century before. The roads were poorly paved or else dirt, and the land was so beautiful as to make you weep. It was a perfect afternoon, all blue skies and fluffy clouds. We labored up a hillside to a small stone chapel that had lost its roof centuries ago. It was surrounded by graves, untended and overgrown with wildflowers.

Lying on the ground by the entrance to the graveyard was the Stone of Loneliness.

The Stone of Loneliness was a fallen menhir or standing stone, something not at all uncommon throughout the British Isles. They'd been reared by unknown people in Megalithic times for reasons still not understood, sometimes arranged in circles, and other times as solitary monuments. There were faded cup-and-ring lines carved into what had been the stone's upper end. And it was broad enough that a grown man could lie down on it. "What should I do?" I asked.

"Lie down on it," Mary said.

So I did.

I lay down upon the Stone of Loneliness and closed my eyes. Bees hummed lazily in the air. And, standing at a distance, Mary began to sing:

> *The lions of the hills are gone*
> *And I am left alone, alone . . .*

It was "Deirdre's Lament," which I'd first heard her sing in the Fiddler's Elbow. In Irish legend, Deirdre was promised from infancy to Conchubar, the king of Ulster. But, as happens, she fell in love with and married another, younger man. Naoise, her husband, and his brothers Ardan and Ainnle, the sons of Uisnech, fled with her to Scotland, where they lived in contentment. But the humiliated and vengeful old king lured them back to Ireland with promises of amnesty. Once they were in his hands, he treacherously killed the three sons of Uisnech and took Deirdre to his bed.

> *The falcons of the wood are flown*
> *And I am left alone, alone . . .*

Deirdre of the Sorrows, as she is often called, has become a symbol for Ireland herself—beautiful, suffering from injustice, and possessed of a happy past that looks likely to never return. Of the real Deirdre, the living and breathing woman upon whom the stories were piled like so many stones on a cairn, we know nothing. The legendary Deirdre's story, however, does not end with her suicide, for in the aftermath of Conchubar's treachery wars were fought, the injustices of which led to further wars. Which wars continue to this very day. It all fits together suspiciously tidily.

It was no coincidence that Deirdre's father was the king's storyteller.

The dragons of the rock are sleeping
Sleep that wakes not for our weeping . . .

All this, however, I tell you after the fact. At the time, I was not thinking of the legend at all. For the instant I lay down upon the cold stone, I felt all the misery of Ireland flowing into my body. The Stone of Loneliness was charmed, like the well in the Burren. Sleeping on it was said to be a cure for homesickness. So, during the Famine, emigrants would spend their last night atop it before leaving Ireland forever. It seemed to me, prone upon the menhir, that all the sorrow they had shed was flowing into my body. I felt each loss as if it were my own. Helplessly, I started to sob and then to weep openly. I lost track of what Mary was singing, though her voice went on and on. Until finally she sang

Dig the grave both wide and deep
Sick I am, and fain would sleep
Dig the grave and make it ready
Lay me on my true Love's body

and stopped. Leaving a silence that echoed on and on forever.

Then Mary said, "There's someone I think you're ready to meet."

Mary took me to a nondescript cinder-block building, the location of which I will take with me to the grave. She led the way in. I followed nervously. The interior was so dim I stumbled on the threshold. Then my eyes adjusted, and I saw that I was in a bar. Not a pub, which is a warm and welcoming public space where families gather to socialize, the adults over a pint and the kiddies drinking their soft drinks, but a bar—a place where men go to get drunk. It smelled of potcheen and stale beer. Somebody had ripped the door to the bog off its hinges and no one had bothered to replace it. Presumably Mary was the only woman to set foot in the place for a long, long time.

There were three or four men sitting at small tables in the gloom, their backs to the door, and a lean man with a bad complexion at the bar. "Here you are then," he said without enthusiasm.

"Don't mind Liam," Mary said to me. Then, to Liam, "Have you anything fit for drinking?"

"No."

"Well, that's not why we came anyway." Mary jerked her head toward me. "Here's the recruit."

"He doesn't look like much."

"Recruit for what?" I said. It struck me suddenly that Liam was keeping his hands below the bar, out of sight. Down where a hard man will keep a weapon, such as a cudgel or a gun.

"Don't let his American teeth put you off. They're part of the reason we wanted him in the first place."

"So you're a patriot, are you, lad?" Liam said in a voice that indicated he knew good and well that I was not.

"I have no idea what you're talking about."

Liam glanced quickly at Mary and curled his lip in a sneer. "Ahh, he's just in it for the crack." In Irish *craic* means "fun" or "kicks." But the filthy pun was obviously intended. My face hardened and I balled up my fists. Liam didn't look concerned.

"Hush, you!" Mary said. Then, turning to me, "And I'll thank you to control yourself as well. This is serious business. Liam, I'll vouch for the man. Give him the package."

Liam's hands appeared at last. They held something the size of a biscuit tin. It was wrapped in white paper and tied up with string. He slid it across the bar.

"What's this?"

"It's a device," Liam said. "Properly deployed, it can implode the entire administrative complex at Shannon Starport without harming a single civilian."

My flesh ran cold.

"So you want me to plant this in the 'port, do yez?" I said. For the first time in weeks, I became aware of the falseness of my accent. Impulsively, I pulled the neuropendant from beneath my shirt, dropped it on the floor, and stepped on it. Whatever I said here, I would say it as myself. "You want me to go in there and fucking *blow myself up*?"

"No, of course not," Mary said. "We have a soldier in place for that. But he—"

"Or she," Liam amended.

"—or she isn't in a position to smuggle this in. Human employees aren't allowed to bring in so much as a pencil. That's how little the Outsiders think of us. You, however, can. Just take the device through their machines—it's rigged to read as a box of cigars—in your carry-on. Once you're inside, somebody will come up to you and ask if you remembered to bring something for granny. Hand it over."

"That's all," Liam said.

"You'll be halfway to Jupiter before anything happens."

They both looked at me steadily. "Forget it," I said. "I'm not killing any innocent people for you."

"Not people. Aliens."

"They're still innocent."

"They wouldn't be here if they hadn't seized the planet. So they're not innocent."

"You're a nation of fucking werewolves!" I cried. Thinking that would put an end to the conversation.

But Mary wasn't fazed. "That we are," she agreed. "Day by day, we present our harmless, domestic selves to the world, until one night the beast comes out to feed. But at least we're not sheep, bleating complacently in the face of the butcher's knife. Which are you, my heart's beloved? A sheep? Or could there be a wolf lurking deep within?"

"He can't do the job," Liam said. "He's as weak as watered milk."

"Shut it. You have no idea what you're talking about." Mary fixed me with those amazing eyes of hers, as green as the living heart of Ireland, and I was helpless before them. "It's not weakness that makes you hesitate," she said, "but a foolish and misinformed conscience. I've thought about this far longer than you have, my treasure. I've thought about it all my life. It's a holy and noble thing that I'm asking of you."

"I—"

"Night after night, you've sworn you'd do anything for me—not with words, I'll grant you, but with looks, with murmurs, with your soul. Did you think I could not hear the words you dared not say aloud? Now I'm calling you on all those unspoken promises. Do this one thing—if not for the sake of your planet, then for me."

All the time we'd been talking, the men sitting at their little tables hadn't made a noise. Nor had any of them turned to face us. They simply sat hunched in place—not drinking, not smoking, not speaking. Just listening. It came to me then how large they were, and how still. How alert. It came to me then that if I turned Mary down, I'd not leave this room alive.

So, really, I had no choice.

"I'll do it," I said. "And God damn you for asking me to."

Mary went to hug me and I pushed her roughly away. "No! I'm doing this thing for you, and that puts us quits. I never want to see you or think of you again."

For a long, still moment, Mary studied me calmly. I was lying, for I'd never wanted her so much as I did in that instant. I could see that she knew I was lying, too. If she'd let the least sign of that knowledge show, I believe I would have hit her. But she did not. "Very well," she said. "So long as you keep your word."

She turned and left and I knew I would never see her again.

Liam walked me to the door. "Be careful with the package outside in the rain," he said, handing me an umbrella. "It won't work if you let it get damp."

I was standing in Shannon Starport, when Homeworld Security closed in on me. Two burly men in ITSA uniforms appeared to my either side and their alien superior said, "Would you please come with us, sir." It was not a question.

Oh, Mary, I thought sadly. You have a traitor in your organization. Other than me, I meant. "Can I bring my bag?"

"We'll see to that, sir."

I was taken to their interrogation room.

Five hours later I got onto the lighter. They couldn't hold me because there wasn't anything illegal in my possession. I'd soaked the package Liam gave me in the hotel room sink overnight and then gotten up early and booted it down a storm drain when no one was looking. It was a quick trip to orbit where there waited a ship larger than a skyscraper and rarer than almost anything you could name, for it wouldn't return to this planet for centuries. I floated on board knowing that for me there'd be no turning back. Earth would be a story I told my children, and a pack of sentimental lies they would tell theirs.

My homeworld shrank behind me and disappeared. I looked out the great black glass walls into a universe thronged with stars and galaxies and had no idea where I was or where I thought I was going. It seemed to me then that we were each and every one of us ships without a harbor, sailors lost on land.

I used to say that only Ireland and my family could make me cry. I cried when my mother died and I cried when Dad had his heart attack the very next year. My baby sister failed to survive the same birth that killed my mother, so some of my tears were for her as well. Then my brother Bill was hit by a drunk driver and I cried and that was the end of my family. Now there's only Ireland.

But that's enough.

The Ki-anna

GWYNETH JONES

Gwyneth Jones (homepage.ntlworld.com/gwynethann) lives in Brighton, in the UK. She writes both intellectually ambitious SF novels under her real name, as well as books for young adults under the name Anne Halam. She writes aesthetically ambitious, feminist intellectual science fiction and fantasy, for which she has won lots of awards. In a recent interview, she said, "I'm frequently identified as a feminist writer, but just as frequently rejected by feminists." "My most recent book is called Spirit," *she says, "a retelling of The Count of Monte Cristo. In the world of* Spirit *it's against the law for an AI to be embodied in human form, with the exception of sex workers and street-level police officers. These two jobs are thought to be too psychologically and physically dangerous for human beings, and yet best conducted in human-shaped form. So there are bots . . . fully sentient software agents, temporarily inhabiting human-shaped machines." Make that humanoid aliens and you have something like the setup for "The Ki-anna."*

"The Ki-anna" is a murder mystery that appeared in Jonathan Strahan's anthology Engineering Infinity. *It takes place in the established Buonarotti SF future of many other Jones stories and novels. It is about dualized predator-prey relationships among aliens: the protagonist's twin sister has died. How did it happen?*

If he'd been at home, he'd have thought *Dump Plant Injuries*. In the socially unbalanced, pioneer cities of the Equatorial Ring, little scavengers tangled with the recycling machinery. They needed premium, Earth-atmosphere-and-pressure nursing or the flesh would not regenerate—which they didn't get. The gouges and dents would be permanent: skinned over, like the scars on her forearms. Visible through thin clothing, like the depressions in her thighs. But this wasn't Mars, and she wasn't human, she was a Ki. He guessed, uneasily, at a more horrifying childhood poverty.

She seemed very young for her post: hardly more than a girl. She could almost have *been* a human girl with gene-mods. Could have chosen to adopt that fine pelt of silky bronze, glimmering against the bare skin of her palms, her throat and face. Chosen those eyes, like drops of black dew; the hint of a mischievous animal muzzle. Her name was Kianna, she represented the KiAn authorities. Her partner, a Shet called Roaaat Bhvaaan, his heavy uniform making no concession to the warmth of the space-habitat, was from Interplanetary Affairs, and represented Speranza. The Shet looked far more alien: a head like a grey boulder, naked wrinkled hide hooding his eyes.

Patrice didn't expect them to be on his side, this odd couple, polite and sympathetic as they seemed. He must be careful, he must remember that his mind and body were reeling from the Buonarotti Transit—two instantaneous interstellar transits in two days, the first in his life. He'd never even *seen* a non-human sentient biped, in person, this time last week: and here he was in a stark police interview room with two of them.

"You learned of your sister's death a Martian year ago?"

"Her disappearance. Yes."

Ki-anna watched, Bhvaaan questioned: he wished it were the other way round. Patrice dreaded the Speranza mindset. Anyone who lives on a planet is a lesser form of life, of course we're going to ignore your appeals, but it's more fun to ignore them slowly, very, very slowly—

"We can agree she disappeared," muttered the Shet, what looked like mordant humour tugging the lipless trap of his mouth. "Yet, aah, you didn't voice your concerns at once?"

"Lione is, was, my twin. We were close, however far . . . When the notification of death came it was very brief, I didn't take it in. A few days later I collapsed at work, I had to take compassionate leave."

At first he'd accepted the official story. She's dead, Lione is dead. She went into danger, it shouldn't have happened but it did, on a suffering war-torn planet unimaginably far away . . .

The Shet rolled his neckless head, possibly in sympathy.

"You're, aah a Social Knowledge Officer. Thap must be a demanding job. No blame if a loss to your family caused you to crash-out."

"I recovered. I examined the material that had arrived while I was ill: everything about my sister's last expedition, and the 'investigation.' I knew there was something wrong. I couldn't achieve anything at a distance. I had to get to Speranza, I had to get myself *here*—"

"Quite right, child. Can't do anything at long distance, aah."

"I had to apply for financial support, the system is slow. The Buonarotti Transit network isn't for people like me—" He wished he'd bitten that back. "I mean, it's for officials, diplomats, not civilian planet-dwellers."

"Unless they're idle super-rich," rumbled the Shet. "Or refugees getting shipped out of a hellhole, maybe. Well, you persisted. Your sister was Martian too. What was she doing here?"

Patrice looked at the very slim file on the table. No way of telling if that tablet held a ton of documents or a single page.

"Don't you know?"

"Explain it to us," said Ki-anna. Her voice was sibilant, a hint of a lisp.

"Lione was a troposphere engineer. She was working on the KiAn Atmosphere Recovery Project. But you *must* know . . ." They waited, silently. "All right. The KiAn war practically flayed this planet. The atmosphere's being repaired, it's a major Speranza project. Out here it's macro-engineering. They've created a—a membrane, like a casting mould, of magnetically charged particles. They're shepherding small water ice asteroids, other debris with useful constituents, through it. Controlled annihilation releases the gases, bonding and venting propagates the right mix. We pioneered the technique. We've enriched the Martian atmosphere the same way . . . nothing like the scale of this. The job also has to be done from the bottom up. The troposphere, the lowest level of the inner atmosphere, is alive. It's a saturated fluid full of viruses, fragments of DNA and RNA, amino acids, metabolising mineral traces, pre-biotic chemistry. The configuration is unique to a living planet, and it's like the mycorrhizal systems in the soil, back on Earth. If it isn't there, or it's not *right*, nothing will thrive."

He couldn't tell if they knew it all, or didn't understand a word.

"Lione knew the tropo reconstruction wasn't going well. She found out there was an area of the surface, under the An-lalhar Lakes, where the living layer might be undamaged. This—where we are now—is the Orbital Refuge Habitat for that region. She came here, determined to get permission from the Ruling An to collect samples—"

Ki-anna interrupted softly. "Isn't the surviving troposphere remotely sampled by the Project automats, all over the planet?"

"Yes, but that obviously wasn't good enough. That was Lione. If it was her responsibility, she had to do *everything in her power* to get the job done."

"Aah. Raarpht . . . Your sister befriended the Ruling An,

she gained permission, she went down, and she stepped on a landmine. You understand that there was no body to be recovered? That she was vaporised?"

"So I was told."

Ki-anna rubbed her scarred forearms, the Shet studied Patrice. The interview room was haunted by meaning, shadowy with intent—

"Aap. You need to make a 'pilgrimage.' A memorial journey?"

"*No*, it's not like that. There's something *wrong*."

The shadows tightened, but were they for him or against him?

"Lione disappeared. I don't speak any KiAn language, I didn't have to, the reports were in English: when I hunted for more detail there are translator bots. I haven't missed anything. A vaporised body doesn't *vanish*. All that tissue, blood, and bone leaves forensic traces. None. No samples recovered. She was there to *collect* samples, don't tell me it was forbidden . . . She didn't come back, that's all. Something happened to her, something other than a warzone accident—"

"Are you saying your sister was murdered, Patrice?"

"I need to go down there."

"I can see you'd feel thap way. You realise KiAn is uninhabitable?"

"A lot of places on Mars are called 'uninhabitable.' My work takes me to the worst-off regions. I can handle myself."

"Aap. How do you feel about the KiAn issue, Messer Ferringhi?"

Patrice opened his mouth, and shut it. He didn't have a prepared answer for that one. "I don't know enough."

The Shet and the Ki looked at each other, for the first time. He felt they'd been through the motions, and they were agreeing to quit.

"As you know," rumbled Bhvaaan, "the Ruling An must give permission. The An-he will see you?"

"I have an appointment."

"Then thap's all for now. Enjoy your transit hangover in peace."

Patrice Ferringhi took a moment, looking puzzled, before he realised he could go. He stood, hesitated, gave an odd little bow and left the room.

The Shet and the Ki relaxed somewhat.

"Collapsed at work," said Roaaat Bhvaaan. "Thap's not good."

"We can't all be made of stone, Shet."

"Aaah well. Cross fingers, Chief."

They were resigned to strange English figures of speech. The language of Speranza, of diplomacy, was also the language of interplanetary policing. You became fluent, or you relied on unreliable transaid: and you screwed up.

"And all my toes," said the Ki.

On his way to his cabin, Patrice found an ob-bay. He stared into a hollow sphere, permeated by the star-pricked darkness of KiAn system space: the limb of the planet obscured, the mainstar and the blue "daystar" out of sight. Knurled objects flew around, suddenly making endless field-beams visible. One lump rushed straight at him, growing huge: seemed to miss the ob-bay by centimetres, with a roar like monstrous thunder. The big impacts could be close enough to make this Refuge shake. He'd felt that, already. Like the Gods throwing giant furniture about—

He could not get over the fact that nothing was real. Everything had been translated here by the Buonarotti Torus, as pure data. This habitat, this shipboard jumper he wore, this *body*. All made over again, out of local elements, as if in a 3D scanner . . . The scarred Ki woman fascinated him, he hardly knew why. The portent he felt in their meeting (had he really *met* her?) was what they call a "transit hangover." He must sleep it off.

The Ki-anna was rated Chief of Police, but she walked the beat most days. All her officers above nightstick grade were seconded from the Ruling An's Household Guard: she didn't like to impose on them. The Ki—natural street-dwellers, if ever life was natural again—melted indoors as she approached. Her uniform, backed by Speranza, should have made the refugees feel safe: but none of them trusted her. The only people she could talk to were the habitual criminals. *They* appreciated the Ruling An's strange appointment.

She made her rounds, visiting the nests where law-abiding people better stay away. The gangsters knew a human had "joined the station."

They were very curious. She sniffed the wind and lounged with the idlers, giving up Patrice Ferringhi in scraps, a resource to be conserved. The pressure of the human's strange eyes was still with her—

No one ought to look at her scars like that, it was indecent. But he was an alien, he didn't know how to behave.

She didn't remember being chosen for the treatment that would render her flesh delectable, while ensuring that what happened wouldn't kill her. She only knew she'd been sold (tradition called it an honour) so that her littermates could live. She would always wonder, why *me*? What was wrong with *me*? We were very poor, I understand that, but why *me*? It had all been for nothing, anyway. Her parents and her littermates were dead, along with everyone else. So few survivors! A handful of die-hards on the surface. A token number of Ki taken away to Speranza, in the staggeringly distant Blue System. Would they ever return? The Ki-anna thought not . . . Six Refuge Habitats in orbit. And of course some of the Heaven-born, who'd seen what was coming before the war, and escaped to Balas or to Shet.

At curfew she filed a routine report, and retired to her quarters in the Curtain Wall. Roaaat, who was sharing her living space, was already at home. It was fortunate that Shet didn't normally like to sit in Speranza-style "chairs": he'd have broken a hole in her ceiling. His bulk, as he lay at ease, dwarfed her largest room. They compared notes.

"All the Refuges have problems," said the Ki-anna. "But I get the feeling I have more than my share. Extortion, intimidation, theft and violence—"

"We can *grease the wheels*," said Roaat. "Strictly off the record, we can pay your villains off. It's distasteful, not the way to do police work."

"But expedient."

"Aap . . . He seemed very taken with you," said Roaaat.

"The human? I don't know how you make that out."

"Thap handsome Blue, yaas. I could smell pheromones."

"He isn't a 'Blue,' " said the Ki-anna. "The almighty Blues rule Speranza. The humans left behind on Earth, or 'Mars'— What is 'Mars'? Is it a moon?"

"Noope. A smaller planet in the Blue system."

"Well, they aren't Blues, they're just ordinary aliens."

"I shall give up matchmaking. You don't appreciate my help . . . Let's hope the An-he finds your *ordinary alien* more attractive."

The Ki-anna shivered. "I think he will. He's a simple soul."

Roaaat was an undemanding guest, despite his size. They shared a meal, based on "culturally neutral" Speranza Food Aid. The Shet spread his bedding. The Ki-anna groomed herself, crouched by a screen that showed views of the Warrens. Nothing untoward stirred, in the simulated night. She pressed knuckle-fur to her mouth. Sometimes the pain of living, haunted by the uncounted dead, became very hard to bear. Waking from every sleep to remember afresh that there was *nothing left*.

"I might yet back out, Officer Bhvaaan. What if we only succeed in feeding the monsters, and make bad worse?"

She unfolded her nest, and settled behind him.

He patted her side with his clubbed fist—it felt like being clobbered by a kindly rock. "See how it goes. You can back out later."

The Ki-anna lay sleepless, the bulk of her unacknowledged bodyguard between her and the teeth of the An, wondering about Patrice Ferringhi.

When his appointment with alien royalty came around, Patrice was glad he'd had a breathing space. The world was solid again, he felt in control of himself. He donned his new transaid, settling the pickup against his skull, and set out for the high-security bulkhead gate that led to the Refuge Habitat itself.

Armoured guards, intimidatingly tall, were waiting on the other side. They bent their heads, exhaled breath loudly—and indicated that he was to get into a kind of floating palanquin. Probably they knew no English.

The guards jogged around him in a hollow square: between their bodies he glimpsed the approach to an actual *castle*, like something in a fantasy game. Like a recreation of Mediaeval Europe or Japan, rising from a mass of basic living modules. It was amazing. He'd never been inside a big space-station before, not counting a few hours in Speranza Transit Port. The false horizon, the lilac sky, arcing far above the castle's bannered towers, would have fooled him completely, if he hadn't known.

He met the An-he in a windowless, antique chamber hung with tapestries (at least, *tapestries* seemed like the right word). Sleekly upholstered couches were scattered over the floor. The guard who'd escorted him backed out, snorting. Patrice looked around, vaguely bothered by an overly-warm indoor breeze. He saw someone almost human, loose-limbed and handsome in Speranza tailoring, reclining on a couch— large, wide-spaced eyes alight with curiosity—and realised he was alone with the king.

"Excuse my steward," said the An. "He doesn't speak English well, and doesn't like to embarrass himself by trying. Please, be at home."

"Thank you for seeing me," said Patrice. "Your, er, Majesty—?"

The An-he grinned. "You are Patrice. I am the An, let's just talk."

The young co-ruler was charming and direct. He asked about the police: Patrice noted, disappointed, that *Ki-anna* was a title, *the Ki-she*, or something. He wondered what you had to do to learn their personal names.

"It was a brief interview," he admitted, ruefully. "I got the impression they weren't very interested."

"Well, I *am* interested. Lione was a great friend to my people. To *both* my peoples. I'm not sure I understand, were you partners, or litter-mates?"

"We were twins, that means litter-mates, but 'partners' too, though our careers took different directions."

He needed to get *partner* into the conversation. The An

partnership wasn't sexual, but it was lifelong, and the closest social and emotional bond they knew. A lost partner justified his appeal.

The An-he touched the clip on the side of his head (he was using a transaid, too) reflexively. "A double loss, poor Patrice. Please do confide in me, it will help enormously if you are completely frank—"

In this pairing, the An-she was the senior. She made the decisions, but Patrice couldn't meet her, she was too important. He could only work on the An-he, who would (hopefully) promote his cause . . . He had the eerie thought that he *was* doing exactly what Lione had done—trying to make a good impression on this alien aristocrat, maybe in this very room. The tapestries (if that was the word) swam and rippled in the moving air, drawing his attention to scenes he really didn't want to examine. Brightly dressed lords and ladies gathered for the hunt. The game was driven onto the guns. The butchery, the bustling kitchen scenes, the *banquet*—

He realised, horrified, that his host had asked him something about his work on Mars, and he hadn't heard the question.

"Oh," said the An-he, easily. "I see what you're looking at. Don't be offended, it's all in the past, and priceless, marvellous art. Recreated, sadly. The originals were destroyed, along with the original of this castle. But still, our heritage! Don't you Blues love ancient battle scenes, heaps of painted slaughter? And by the way, aren't you closely related, limb for limb and bone for bone, to the beings that *you* traditionally kill and eat?"

"Not on Mars."

"There, you are sundered from your web of life. At home on Earth, the natural humans do it all the time, I assure you."

"I don't know what to say."

Notoriously, the Ki and the An had *both* been affronted when they were identified, by other sentient bipeds, as a single species. Of course they knew, but an indecent topic! In ways, the most disturbing aspect of "the KiAn issue" was not the genocidal war, in which the oppressed had risen up, savagely, against the oppressors. It was the fact that some highly respected Ki leaders actually *defended* "the traditional diet of the An."

The An-he showed his bright white teeth. "Then you have an open mind, my dear Patrice! It gives me hope that you'll come to understand us." He stretched, and exhaled noisily. "Enough. All I can tell you today is that your request is under consideration. You're a valuable person, and it's dangerous down there! We don't want to lose you. Now, I suppose you'd like to see your sister's rooms? She stayed with us, you know: here in the castle."

"Would that be possible?"

"Certainly! I'll get some people to take you."

More guards—or servants in military-looking uniform— led him along winding, irregular corridors, all plagued by that insistent breeze, and opened a round plug of a doorway. The An-he's face appeared, on a display screen emblazoned on a guard's tunic.

"Take as long as you like, dear Patrice. Don't be afraid of disturbing the evidence! The police took anything they thought was useful, ages ago."

The guards gave him privacy, which he had not expected: they shut the door and stayed outside. He was alone, in his sister's space. The aeons he'd crossed, the unthinkable interstellar distance, vanished. Lione was *here*. He could feel her, all around him. The warm air, suddenly still, seemed full of images: glimpses of his sister, rushing into his mind—

"Recreation" was skin-deep here. Essentially the room was identical to his cabin. A bed-shelf with a puffy mattress; storage space beneath. A desk, a closet bathroom, stripped of fittings. Her effects had been returned to Mars, couriered as data. The police had been and gone "ages ago." What could this empty box tell him? Nothing, but he had to try.

Was he under surveillance? He decided he didn't care.

He searched swiftly, efficiently studying the floor, running his hands over the walls and closet space, checking the seals on the mattress. The screen above the desk was set in an ornate decorative frame. He probed around it, and his fingertips brushed something that had slipped behind. Carefully, patiently, he teased out a corner of the object, and drew it from hiding.

Lione, he whispered.

He tucked his prize inside the breast of his shipboard jumper, and went to knock on the round door. It opened, *and* the guards were there.

"I'm ready to leave now."

The An-he looked out of the tunic display again. "By all means! But don't be a stranger. Come and see me again, come often!"

That evening he searched the little tablet's drive for his own name, for a message. He tried every password of theirs he could remember: found nothing, and was heartbroken. He barely noted the contents, except that it wasn't about her work. Next day, to his great surprise, he was recalled to the castle. He met the An-he as before, and learned that the Ruling An would like to approve his mission, but the police were making difficulties.

"Speranza doesn't mind having a tragedy associated with their showcase Project," said the young king. "A scandal would be much worse, so they want to bury this. My partner and I feel you have a right to investigate, but we have met with resistance."

There was nothing Patrice could do . . . and it wasn't a refusal. If the alien royals were on his side, the police would probably be helpless in the end. Back in his cabin he examined the tablet again and realised that Lionc had been keeping a private record of her encounter with "the KiAn issue."

KiAn isn't like other worlds of the Diaspora: they didn't have a Conventional Space Age before First Contact. But they weren't primitives when "we" found them, nor even Mediaeval. The An of today are the remnant of a planetary superpower. They were always the Great Nation, and the many nations of the Ki were treated as inferior, through millennia of civilisation. But it was no more than fifteen hundred standard years ago, when, in a time of famine, the An or "Heaven Born" first began to hunt and eat the "Earth Born" Ki. They don't do that anymore. They have painless processing plants (or did). They have retail packaging—

Cannibalism happens. It's known in every sentient and pre-sentient biped species. What developed on KiAn is different, and the so-called "atavists" are not really atavist. This isn't the survival, as some on Speranza would like to believe, of an ancient prehistoric symbiosis. The An weren't animals, when this "stable genocide" began. They were people, who could think and feel. People, like us.

The entry was text-only, but he heard his sister's voice: forthright, uncompromising. She must have forced herself to be more tactful with the An-he! The next was video. Lione, talking to him. Living and breathing.

Inside the slim case, when he opened it, he'd found pressed fragments of a moss, or lichen. Shards of it clung to his fingers: it smelled odd, but not unpleasant. He sniffed his fingertips and turned pages, painfully happy.

Days passed, in a rhythm of light and darkness that belonged to the planet "below." Patrice shuttled between the "station visitors quarters," where he was the only guest, and the An castle. He didn't dare refuse a summons, although he politely declined all dinner invitations which made the An laugh.

The odd couple showed no interest in Patrice at all, and did not return his calls. He might have tried harder to get their attention, but there was Lione's journal. He didn't want to hand it over; or to lie about it either.

Once, as they walked in the castle's galleries, the insistent breeze nagging at him as usual, Patrice felt he was being watched. He looked up. From a high, curtained balcony a wide-eyed, narrow face was looking down intently. "*That* was the An-she," murmured his companion, stooping to exhale the words in Patrice's ear. "She likes you, or she wouldn't have let you glimpse her . . . I tell her all about you."

"I didn't really see anything," said Patrice, wary of causing offence. "The breeze is so strong, tossing the curtains about."

"I'm afraid we're obsessed with air circulation, due to the crowded accommodation. There are aliens about, who don't always smell very nice."

"I'm very sorry! I had no idea!"

"Oh no, Patrice, not you. You smell fresh and sweet."

The entries in Lione's journal weren't dated, but they charted a progress. At first he was afraid he'd find Lione actually defending industrial cannibalism. That never happened. But as he immersed himself, reviewing every entry over and over, he knew Lione was asking him to understand. Not to accept, but to *understand* the unthinkable—

Compare chattel slavery. We look on the buying and selling of sentient bipeds, as if they were livestock, with revulsion. Who could question that? Then think of the intense bond between a beloved master, or mistress, and a beloved servant. A revered commanding officer and devoted troops. Must this go too? The An and the Ki accept that their way of life *must* change. But there is a deep equality in that exchange of being, which we "democratic individualists" can't recognise—

Patrice thought of the Ki-Anna's scars.

The "deep equality" entry was almost the last.

The journal ended abruptly, with no sense of closure.

Lione's incense—he'd decided the "lichen" was a kind of KiAn incense, perhaps a present from the An-he—filled his cabin with a subtle perfume. He closed the tablet, murmuring the words he knew by heart, *a deep equality in that exchange of being*, and decided to turn in. In his tiny bathroom, for a piercing moment it was Lione he saw in the mirror. A dark-skinned, light-eyed, serious young woman, with the aquiline bones of their North African ancestry. His other self, who had left him so far behind—

The whole journal was a message. It called him to follow her, and he didn't yet know where his passionate journey would end.

* * *

When he learned that permission to visit the surface was granted, but the Ki-anna and the Interplanetary Affairs officer were coming too, he knew that the Ruling An had been forced to make this concession—and the bargaining was over. He just wished he knew *why* the police had insisted on escorting him. To help Patrice discover the truth? Or to prevent him?

He didn't meet the odd couple until they embarked together. They were all in full protective gear: skin sealed with quarantine film, under soft-shell life-support suits. The noisy shuttle bay put a damper on conversation, and the flight was no more sociable. Patrice spent it encased in an escape capsule and breathing tanked air: the police insisted on this. He saw nothing of KiAn until he was crunching across the seared rubble of their landing field.

The landscape was dry tundra, like Martian desert colourshifted into shades of grey and green. Armed Green Belts were waiting, with a landship and all-terrain hardsuits for the visitors.

"The An-he offered me a military escort," said Patrice, freedom of speech restored by helmet radio. "What was wrong with that?"

"Sorry," grunted Bhvaaan. "Couldn't be allowed."

The Ki-anna said nothing. He remembered, vividly, the way he'd felt at their meeting. There had been a connection, on her side too: he knew it. Now she was just another bulky Speranza doll, on a smaller scale than her partner. As if she'd read his thoughts, she cleared her faceplate and looked out at him, curiously. He wanted to tell her that he understood KiAn, better than she could imagine . . . but not with Bhvaaan around.

"You've been keeping yourself to yourself, Messer Ferringhi."

"I could say the same of you two, Officer Bhvaaan."

"Aap. But you made friends with the An-he."

"The Ruling An were very willing to help me."

"We've been working in your interest too," said the Ki-anna. She pivoted her suit to look through the windowband in the landship's flank. "Far below this plateau, back that way, was the regional capital. *Were* fertile plains, rich forests, rich forests, towns and fields and parklands. The 'roof of Heaven' was never beautiful. It's strange, this part hardly seems much changed—"

"Except that one dare not breathe," she added, sadly.

On the shore of the largest ice sheet, the Lake of Heaven, the odd couple and Patrice disembarked. The Ki-anna led the way to a great low arch of rock-embedded ice. The Green Belts had stayed in the ship.

Everything was livid mist.

"We're going under An-lalhar Lake alone?"

"The Green Belts'll be on call. It's not their jurisdiction down there. It's a precious enclave where the Ki and the An are stubbornly dying together." Bhvaaan peered at him. "It's not our jurisdiction either, Messer Ferringhi. If we meet with violence we can protect you, but that's after the event and it might not save your life. The people under the Lake don't have a lot to lose and their mood is volatile. Bear that in mind."

"I could have had an escort they'd respect."

"You're better off with us."

They descended the tunnel. The light never grew less; on the contrary, it grew brighter. When they emerged, the Heaven Lake was above them: a mass of blue-white radiance, indigo shadowed, shot through with rainbow refractions. It was extraordinarily beautiful. It seemed impossible that the ice had captured so much light from the poisoned smog. Far off, in the centre of the glacial depression, geothermal vents made a glowing, spiderweb pattern of fire and snowy steam. Patrice checked his telltales, and eagerly began to release his helmet. The Shet dropped a gauntleted fist on his arm.

"Don't do it, child. Look at your *rads*."

"A moment won't kill me. I want to *feel* KiAn—"

The odd couple, hidden in their gear, seemed to look at him strangely.

"Maybe later," said the Ki-anna, soothingly. "It's safer in the Grottos, where your sister was headed."

"How do we get there?"

"We walk," rumbled Bhvaaan. "No vehicles. There's not

much growing but it's still a sacred park. Let your suit do the work; keep up your fluids."

"Thanks, I know how to handle a hard shell."

They walked in file. The desolation, the ruined beauty that had been revered by both "races," caught at Patrice's heart. His helmet display counted rads, paces, heart rate: counted down the metres. Thirty kilometres to the place where Lione had last been seen alive.

"Which faction mined the Lake of Heaven parkland?"

"To our knowledge? Nobody did, child."

It was a question he'd asked over and over, long ago when he thought he could get answers. Now he asked and didn't care. He followed the Shet, the Ki-anna behind him. His pace was steady, yet the display said his body was pumping adrenaline; not from fear, he knew, but in the grip of intense excitement. He sucked on glucose and tried to calm himself.

As the radiance above them dimmed, they reached the Grotto domain. Rugged rocky pillars seemed to hold up the roof of ice, widely spaced at first, clustering towards a centre that could not be seen. There was a Ki community, surviving in rad-proofed modules. The Ki-anna went inside. Patrice and the Shet waited, in the darkening blighted landscape. She emerged after an hour or so.

"We can't go on without guides, and we can't have guides until tomorrow. At the earliest. They have to think it over."

"They weren't expecting us?"

"They were. They know all about it, but they may have had fresh instructions. They're in full communication with the castle: there's some sophisticated kit in there. We'll just have to wait."

"Do they remember Lione?" demanded Patrice. "I have transaid, I want to talk to someone."

"Not now. I'll ask tomorrow."

"Can we sleep indoors?" asked the Shet.

"No."

The Shet and the Ki-anna made camp in the ruins of the former village, using their suits to clear ground and construct a shelter. Patrice moved over to a heap of boulders where he'd noticed patches of lichen. He had fragments of

Lione's incense in the sleeve pocket of his inner, in a First Aid pouch. The police were fully occupied: furtively he opened the arm of his hardshell, and fished the pouch out. He was right, it was the same—

Lione had stood here. The incense was not a gift, she had gathered it. She had been *standing right here*. His need was irresistible. He released his face-plate, stripped his gauntlets, rubbed away quarantine film.

KiAn rushed in on him, cold and harsh in his throat, intoxicating—

"What is that?"

The Ki-anna was behind him. "A lichen sample," said Patrice, caught out. "Or that's what I'd call it at home. It was in my sister's room, in the An Castle. Look, they're the same."

"Not quite," said the Ki-anna. "Yours is a cultivated variety."

He thought she'd be angry, maybe accuse him of concealing evidence. To his astonishment she took his bared hand, and bowed over it until her cheek brushed the vulnerable inner skin of his wrist. Her touch was a huge shock, sweet and profoundly sexual. She made him dizzy.

This can't be happening, he thought. *I'm here for Lione*—

"I don't know your name."

"We don't do that," she whispered.

"I felt, I can't describe it, the moment I met you—"

"I'd better keep this. You must get your gloves and helmet back on."

"But I want *KiAn*—"

Gently, she let go of his hand. "You've had enough."

The shelter was a snug fit. Sealed inside, they shared rations and drank fresh water they'd brought from the Habitat. They would sleep in their suits, for warmth and security. Patrice lay down at once, to escape their questions and to be alone with his confusion. He was here for Lione, he was here to *join* Lione. How could he and the Ki-anna suddenly feel this way?

"Were you getting romantic, with Patrice, over by those rocks?" asked Bhvaaan. "Sniffing his pheromones?"

"No," said the Ki-anna, grimly. "Something else."

She showed him the First Aid pouch and its contents.

"Mighty Void!"

"He *says* it was in the room Lione used, in the castle."

"I don't think so! We took that cabin apart." The Shet's delicates unfolded from his club of a fist. He turned the clear pouch around, probing her find with sensitive tentacles. "So *that's* how, so *that's* how—"

"So that's how the cookie was crumbled," agreed the Ki-anna.

"What do we do, Chief? Abort this, and run away very quickly?"

"Not without back-up. If we run, and they have heavy weaponry, we're at their mercy. I see what it looks like, but we should show no alarm."

"I *have* had thoughts about him," she murmured, looking at the dark outline of Patrice Ferringhi. "Don't know why. It's something in his eyes."

"Thaap's the way it starts," said the Shet. "Thoughts. Then wondering if anything can come of them. They say sentient bipeds are attracted to each other like . . . like brothers and sisters, long separated. Well, I'll talk to the Greenies. And you and I had better not sleep."

The suit was a house the shape of her body. She sat in it, wondering about sexual pleasure: pleasure with *Patrice*. What would it be like? She had only one strange comparison, but that didn't frighten her . . . What Roaaat Bhvaaan offered was far more disturbing.

She glimpsed the abyss, and fell into oblivion.

Patrice dreamed he was in a strolling crowd, among bronze and purple trees, with branches that swayed in the breeze. He knew where he was, he was in the KiAn Orientation, a virtual reality. But there was something sinister going on, the crowd pressed too close, the beautiful trees hid what he ought to see. Then Lione came running up and *bit* him.

He yelled, and shook her off.

She came back and bit his thigh, but now he was in the dark, cold and sore. Lione was gone, he was being hunted by fierce hungry animals—

Suddenly he knew he was not asleep.

He was completely naked. *Where was his suit? Where was he?*

He had no idea. The air was freezing, the darkness almost complete. He stumbled towards a gleam ahead, and entered a rocky cave. There was ice underfoot, icy stalactites hanging down. A lamp burned incense-scented oil, set on the ground next to a heap of something—

That's a body, he thought. He went over and knelt down. It was a human body, freeze-dried. She was curled on her side, turned away from him, but he knew he'd found Lione. She was naked too.

Why was she naked?

He lifted the lamp and saw where flesh had been cut away, not by teeth, as in his dream, but by sharp knives. Lione had been butchered. He tried to turn her: the body moved all of a piece. Her face was recognisable, smooth and calm in death, the eyes sunken, the skin like cured leather. Was she *smiling*? Oh, Lione—

But why am I naked?, he thought. *Who brought me here?*

The Ki entered the cave, and surrounded Patrice and his sister. They had brought more lights. One of them was carrying, reverently, a flattened spherical object, dull grey-green, the size of Patrice's fist. It had a seam around the centre, a bevelled cap. *That's a vapor mine*, he though shaken by an explosion of understanding. Then the An came. The Ki made no attempt to interfere with the banquet. They were here to witness. Patrice screamed. He fought the knives with his bare hands, kicked out with his bare feet. The An, outraged, kept yelling at him in scraps of English to *keep still, be easy Blue, you want this, what's wrong with you?*

The Ki-anna and the Shet had ditched their hard shells, to search the narrow passages. They arrived armed but badly outnumbered and they couldn't get near Patrice. *"I was the Earth In Heaven!"* shouted the Chief of Police. *"I say that flesh is not sacred, not yours to take. Let the stranger go!"*

She held the fanatics at bay, uncertain because of her former status, until the Green Belts joined the party. Luckily

Bhvaaan had summoned them, before he and the Ki-anna followed Patrice into that drugged sleep.

Patrice's injuries were not dangerous. As soon as he was allowed he signed himself out of medical care. He had to talk to the police again. He met the odd couple in the same bare interview room as before.

"I'm sorry, I need to withdraw my statement. I can't press charges."

If the next of kin didn't press charges, KiAn law made it difficult for Interplanetary Affairs to prosecute. He knew that, but he had no choice.

"I realise the tablet I found in Lione's room was planted on me. I know her words, if some of them were genuinely hers, had been rearranged to fool me into accepting atavism. It doesn't matter. My sister *wanted* to die that way. She gave herself, her body. It was a ritual sacrifice, for peace. She was my twin, I can't explain, I have to respect her wishes."

"A beautiful, consensual ritual," remarked the Shet. "Yaap. That's what the cannibal die-hards always say. But if you scratch any of these halfway 'respectable' atavists, such as our Ruling An here—"

"You find the meat-packing industry," said the Ki-anna.

Patrice heard the blinkered, Speranza mindset.

"My sister was *willing*."

"I believe she was." To his confusion, the Ki-anna reached out, took his injured hand and held his wrist, where the blood ran, to her face. The same sweet, intimate gesture as on KiAn. "So are you, a little. It'll wear off."

She drew back, and placed an evidence bag, containing his First Aid pouch and the scraps of lichen, on the table.

"In English, the common name of this herb, or lichen, would be 'Willingness.' It grows naturally only under the Lake of Heaven. Long ago it was known as a powerful aphrodisiac: the labwork kind has another use. It's given to a child chosen to be the Ki-anna, which means sold to the An as living meat. It's a refined form of cannibalism, practiced in my region. A drugged child, a willing victim, with a strong resistance to infection and trauma, is eaten alive, by degrees.

If one of these children survives to adulthood, they are free, the debt is paid."

The Ki-anna showed her teeth. "I made it, as you see; but I haven't forgotten that scent. When I smelled your flesh, under the Lake, I knew you'd been treated for butchery—and I understood. They drugged Lione until she was delirious with joy to be eaten, and they sent her to the atavist fanatics under *An-lalhar*. Then they tried the same trick on you."

Bhvaaan tapped the casefile tablet with his delicates. "Your sister died too quickly, that was the problem."

"What—?"

"We couldn't prove it, but we knew they'd killed Lione, Messer Ferringhi. We could even show, thanks to the Chief here, who was pulling the strings, and how they got the prohibited ordnance into the Grottos. Your sister fell into a trap. She had to get under the Heaven Lake and that suited the atavists just fine. It would have been a powerful message. A Speranza scientist ritually eaten, then consumed by the very air of KiAn—"

"Controlled annihilation," whispered Patrice. "That's what I *saw*, in the cave. Something they would understand—"

"Thap was the idea. The atavists are planning to bring back the meat factories, once their planet has an atmosphere again. Your sister was going to help them: except something didn't work out. You were right about the tropo sampling: there's also stringent military activity monitoring. If a mine had gone off under the Lake, we'd know. If a human-sized body had been atomised, there'd have been a spike. So we knew the 'consummation' hadn't happened, and we couldn't figure it out. We think we know the answer now: she died too quickly. She had to be vaporised alive, a dead body can't be *willing*. But she wasn't a Ki, and they hit an artery or something."

Patrice had gone grey in the face.

"You going to crash out, child—?"

"No, go on—"

The Shet rearranged his bulk on the inadequate office chair. "The autopsy'll tell us the details. Then you came along, Patrice. We saw a chance to get ourselves to the crime scene, and wasted Diaspora funds pushing on an open door. And you nearly died, because we drank the nice fresh water from this Habitat. Which happened to be doped—"

"The atavists thought the *willingness* they'd cooked up for Lione would work on you," explained the Ki-anna. "They've never heard of 'fraternal twins.' Ki litter-mates can be of any sex, but otherwise they are identical. You were begging to be lured to the Grottos, it was perfect, you would replace Dr Ferringhi. Luckily, you and your sister *weren't* clones. You were affected, but you weren't ready to be butchered. You fought for your life."

"You see, Messer Ferringhi," said Bhvaaan, "what really happened here is that a pair of murdering atavist bastards thought they'd appoint themselves as Chief of Police a child *who had been eaten.* A girl like that, they thought, will never dare to do us any damage. Instead they found they had a tiger by the tail . . ." He opened the casefile tablet, and pushed it over to Patrice. "They're glamorous, the Atavist An. But your sister would never have fallen for them in her right mind, from what I've learned of her. Still want to withdraw this?"

Patrice was silent, eyes down. The Ki-anna saw him shedding the exaltation of the drug; quietly taking in everything he'd been told. A new firmness in the lines of his face, a deep sadness as he said farewell to Lione. The human felt her eyes. He looked up and she saw another farewell, sad but final, to something that had barely begun—

"No," he said. "But I should go through it again. Can we do that now?"

The Ki-anna returned to her quarters.

Roaaat joined her in a while. She sat by her window on the streets, small chin on her silky paws, and didn't look round when he came in.

"He'll be fine. What will you do? You'll have to leave, after this."

"I know. Leave or get killed, and I must not get killed."

"You could go with Patrice, see what Mars is like."

"I don't think so. The pheromones are no more, now that

he knows what making love to the Ki-anna is supposed to be like."

"I've no idea what making love to you is supposed to be like. But you're a damned fine investigator. Why don't you come to Speranza?"

Yes, she thought. I knew all along what *you* were offering.

Banishment, not just from my own world, but from all the worlds. Never to be a planet-dweller any more. And again I want to ask, *Why me? What did I do?* But you believe it is an honour and I think you are sincere.

"Maybe I will."

Eliot Wrote

NANCY KRESS

Nancy Kress (www.sff.net/people/nankress/) lives in Seattle, Washington, with her husband, Jack Skillingstead. She is the author of twenty-six books: sixteen science fiction novels, three fantasy novels, four short story collections, and three books on writing. Her stories are rich in texture and psychological insight, and have been collected in Trinity and Other Stories *(1985),* The Aliens of Earth *(1993), and* Beaker's Dozen *(1998). She has won two Nebulas and two Hugos for them, and been nominated for a dozen more of these awards. Published in 2010 were* Nano Comes to Clifford Falls and Other Stories, *her fourth collection, and* Dogs, *a bio-thriller. She published several fine new stories in 2011, and her novella,* After the Fall, Before the Fall, During the Fall, *is out as a chapbook in 2012.*

"Eliot Wrote" was published online at Lightspeed. It is a story about the powerlessness of a fiercely intelligent fifteen-year-old kid who has lost his mother and is now losing his hospitalized father, whom he loves and needs, and who uses revisions of his high-school writing assignment on metaphor to explore his feelings. It is a story that interrogates ageism.

*Not only is the universe stranger than we imagine, it
is stranger than we can imagine.*

J.B.S. Haldane

Eliot wrote: *Picture your brain as a room. The major
functions are like furniture. Each in its own place, and you
can move from sofa to chair to ottoman, or even lie across
more than one piece of furniture at the same time. Memory
is like air in the room, dispersed everywhere. Musical ability is a specific accessory, like a vase on the mantel. Anger
is a Doberman pinscher halfway out of the door from the
kitchen. Algebra just fell down the heat duct. Love of your
sibling is a water spill that evaporated three weeks ago.*

Well, maybe not accurate, Eliot thought, and hit DE-
LETE. Or maybe too accurate for his asshole English class.
What kind of writing assignment was "Explain something
important using an extended metaphor"?

He closed his school tablet and paced around the room.
Cold, cheerless, bereft—or was that his own fault? Partly
his own fault, he admitted; Eliot prided himself on self-
honesty. He could turn up the heat, pick up the pizza boxes,
open the curtains to the May sunshine. He did none of these
things. Cold and cheerless matched bereft, and there was
nothing to do about bereft. Well, one thing. He went to the
fireplace (cold ashes, months old) and from the mantel
plucked the ceramic pig and threw it as hard as he could onto
the stone hearth. It shattered into pink shards.

Then he left the apartment and caught the bus to the hospital.

Eliot's father had been entered into Ononeida Psychiatric Hospital ten days ago, for a religious conversion in which he saw the clear image of Zeus on a strawberry toaster pastry.

Ononeida, named for an Indian tribe that had once occupied Marthorn City, was accustomed to religious visions, and Carl Tremling was a mathematician, a group known for being eccentric. Ordinarily the hospital would not have admitted him at all. But Dr. Tremling had reacted to the toaster pastry with some violence, flinging furniture out of the apartment window and sobbing that there was dice being played with the universe after all, and that the center would not hold. A flung end-table, imitation Queen Anne, had hit the mailman, who was not seriously injured but was considerably perturbed. Carl Tremling was deemed a danger to others and possibly himself.

A brain scan had failed to find temporal lobe epilepsy, the usual cause of religious visions. Dr. Tremling had continued to sob and to fling whatever furniture the orderlies were not quick enough to defend. Also, the psychiatrist on intake duty, who had recognized both the Einstein and Yeats quotes, was puzzled over the choice of Zeus as the toaster-pastry image. The usual thing was either Christ or the Virgin Mary.

The commitment papers had been signed by Dr. Tremling's sister, a sweet, dim, easily frightened woman who had never been comfortable with her brilliant brother but who was fond of Eliot. She was leaving the hospital as her nephew arrived.

"Eliot! Are you alone?"

"Yes, Aunt Sue." In Susan Tremling Fisher's mind, Eliot was perpetually nine instead of sixteen, and should not be riding buses alone. "How is he?"

"The same." She sighed. "Only they want to—he wants to—Eliot, are you eating enough? You look thinner."

"I'm fine."

"You shouldn't stay in that apartment alone. Anything

could happen! Please come and stay with Uncle Ned and me, you know we'd love to have you and I hate to think of you alone in that big apartment without—"

If Eliot didn't stop her, she would start her Poor Motherless Lamb speech. "What does Dad want to do?"

"What?"

"You said 'They want to—he wants to'—so what do the doctors want to do?"

She sighed again. "I wish I had your memory, Eliot. You get it from poor Carl. That doctor with the mustache, he wants to try some new procedure on Carl."

"What new procedure?"

"I can't recall the name . . ." She fumbled in her purse as if the name might be among the tissues and supermarket coupons.

"Was it Selective Memory Obliteration Neural Re-Routing?"

"Yes! The very words! Your *memory*, Eliot, I swear, your mother would have been so proud of—"

Eliot grabbed her arm. "Are you going to let them operate? *Are you?*"

"Why, Eliot! You're hurting me!"

He let go. "I'm sorry. But—you are going to let them operate, aren't you?"

Aunt Sue looked at him. She had small eyes of no particular color, and a little mouth that was pursing and unpursing in distress. But she was a Tremling. Into those small eyes came stubbornness, an unthinking but resolute stubbornness and yet somehow murky, like a muddy pool over bedrock. She said gently, "I couldn't do that."

"Aunt Sue—"

"Carl will come to himself eventually, Eliot. He's had spells before, you know—why, just consider that time he shut himself up in my spare room for six days and wouldn't even come out to eat! I had to bring him meals on a tray!"

"He was working on his big breakthrough on the topography of knots!"

"Not only would he not eat, he wouldn't even wash. I had to

air that room out for two days afterward, and in *February*. But Carl came out of that spell and he'll come out of this one, too. You just wait and see."

"It's not the same! Don't you understand, his whole mental construct has been turned upside down!"

"That's exactly what he said when he came out of my spare room with those knot numbers," she said triumphantly. "Knots! But even as a boy Carl took fits, why I remember when he was just eight years old and he found out that somebody named Girdle proved there were things you couldn't prove, why that doesn't even make common sense to—"

"Aunt Sue! You have to sign the papers allowing this operation!"

"No. I won't. Eliot, you listen to me. I went online last night and read about this Memory Obligation Whatever. It's new and it's dangerous because the doctors don't really know what they're doing yet. In one case, after the operation a woman didn't even remember who she was, or recognize her own children, or anything! In another case, a man could no longer read and—get this!—he couldn't relearn how to do it, either! Something had just gone missing in his brain as a result of the operation. Imagine Carl unable to read! We can't risk—"

Eliot was no longer listening. He'd known Aunt Sue all his life; she wasn't going to budge. He barreled down the hall and rattled the door to the ward, which was of course locked. An orderly wielding a mop peered at him through the reinforced glass and pantomimed pressing the call button.

"Yes?" said the disembodied voice of a nurse. Eliot recognized it.

"Mary, I want to see Dr. Tallman!"

"Oh, Eliot, I'm glad you came just now, your father is quiet and—"

"I don't want to see my father! I want to see Dr. Tallman!".

"He's not here, dear. I'll just buzz you in."

Mary came out of the nurse's station to meet him. Middle-aged, kind, motherly, she radiated the kind of brisk competence that Eliot admired, and had seen so little of in his own disordered household. Or at least he would have admired it if it weren't for the motherliness. She saw him not as the intellectual he knew himself to be, but rather as the skinny, short, floppy-haired kid he seemed to be. He was smarter than Mary, smarter than Aunt Sue, smarter than most of the world, so why the hell couldn't the world notice that?

"I want to see Dr. Tallman!"

"He's not on the ward, dear."

"Call him!"

"I'm afraid I can't do that. Eliot, you seem upset."

"I *am* upset! Isn't my father going to have SMON-R? Because my aunt wouldn't sign the papers?"

Motherliness gave way to professionalism. "You know I can't discuss this with you."

No one would discuss anything with Eliot. He didn't count. The rational world didn't count, not in here. Eliot glared at Mary, who gazed calmly back. He said, "I'll sign them! I will!"

"You're underage, Eliot. And your father is non compos mentis. Did you come to visit? He's in the day room. But if you're going to upset him, it might be better if you chose another time to visit."

Eliot bolted past her and ran into the day room.

His father was not flinging furniture. He slumped inert in a chair, staring at the TV, which showed a rerun of *Jeopardy.* Eliot groaned. His father had published papers in scientific journals, developed algorithms for high-resolution space imagery, had a promising lead on actually solving the Riemann Hypothesis. He did not watch *Jeopardy.* This was the anti-psychotic drugs, not the real Carl Tremling. Everything the hospital was doing was just making the situation worse.

"Hey, Dad."

"Hey, Eliot."

Alex Trebek said, "The tendency of an object in motion to remain in motion, or an object at rest to remain at rest, unless acted upon by an outside force."

"How are you doing?"

"Just fine." But he frowned. "Only I can't quite . . . there was something . . ."

Something. There were a lot of somethings. There was rational thought, and logical progressions, and the need to restore a man's proper intellect.

Someone on the TV said, "What is 'inertia'?"

"Zeus," Dr. Tremling brought out triumphantly. "Who would have believed—" All at once his face sagged from underneath, like a pie crust cooling. "Who would have believed . . ." His face crumpled and he clutched Eliot's sleeve. "It's real, Eliot! It's loose in the world and nothing that I thought was true—"

"It was a *toaster pastry*, Dad!"

Three patients slowly swiveled their heads at Eliot's raised voice. He lowered it. "Listen to me. Please listen to me. The doctors want to do a procedure on you called Selective Memory Obliteration Neural Re-Routing. It will remove the memory of the . . . the incident from your mind. Only Aunt Sue—"

"Where's the pig?" Dr. Tremling said.

Eliot rocked back and forth with frustration. "Even if Aunt Sue won't sign the papers, if you can seem reasonably lucid—in compos mentis—then—"

"I asked you to bring the pig!"

"It's broken!"

Dr. Tremling stared at Eliot. Then he threw back his head and howled at the ceiling. Two orderlies, a nurse, and four patients sprang to attention. Dr. Tremling rose, overcoming the inertia of his drugs, and picked up his chair. His face was a mask of grief. "It isn't true. Nothing I believed is true! The universe—Zeus—dice—"

Eliot shouted, "It was just a fucking toaster pastry!"

"I needed that pig!" He flung the chair at the wall. Orderlies rushed forward.

Nurse Mary grabbed Eliot and hustled him out of the room. "I told you not to upset him!"

"I didn't upset him, *you* did, by not giving him what he needs! Do you know how finely balanced a mathematician's brain is, how prone to obsessions already, and it needs to be clear to—you're refusing to remove a tumor from his brain!"

"Your father does not have a brain tumor, and you need to leave now," Mary said, hustling him down the hallway.

A male voice said, "I'll take scientific terms for 400, Alex."

"It's his brain!" Eliot shouted. He meant: *My brain*, and he knew it, and the knowledge made him even angrier.

Mary got him to the door of the ward, keyed in a code to unlock it, and waved him through. As he stalked off, she called after him, "Eliot? Dear? Do you have enough money for the bus home?"

Eliot's parents had met at college, where both studied mathematics. Even though Eliot's mother was not beautiful, there were few girls in the graduate math program, and she was sought after by every mathematician with enough social skills to approach her, including two of the professors. Her own social skills lacked coherence, but something in Carl Tremling appealed to her. She emailed her bewildered mother, "There is a boy here I think I like. He's interested in nothing but algorithms and pigs." Carl, who had grown up in farm country, had a theory that pigs were much smarter than other animals and deserved respect.

Fuming on the bus, Eliot wondered why his father had wanted the ceramic pig. Did he have a premonition that in its artificial pink wrinkles he might see Hermes, god of mathematics? Aphrodite? His dead wife? How could his mind have so betrayed Carl Tremling? Eliot wanted his father back, and in his own mind.

Eliot's mind was so much like his father's. Everybody said so.

"Fuck," he said aloud, which caused a man to glare at him across the bus aisle and a woman to change her seat. Embarrassed, Eliot pulled out his school tablet.

Memory, he wrote, *is a bridge between what you are today and what you were for all the days before that. All your life you go back and forth across that bridge, extending and reinforcing it. You add a new strut. You hang flower pots on the railing. You lay down kitty litter during icy weather. You chase away the kids who are smoking pot on top of the pilings and under the roadway. Then one day, a section of the bridge gives way. When that happens, it is criminal to not repair it. An unrepaired bridge is like a deep pothole on a dark road and—*

Two metaphors. This was not working. And it was due Tuesday.

The man across the aisle was still watching him. Probably thought that Eliot was some sort of gang-affiliated punk. Well, no, not that, not with his build and clothing. A crazy, then. The man thought Eliot might be a gun-toting, cheerleader-loathing shooter who would court death to kill everybody on the bus, perhaps because school shooting was now such a risk, what with all the metal detectors and guards and lock-down protocols.

I am not a shooter, Eliot silently told the man. He was a rationalist and an intellectual, and he just wanted his father back, whole, the way he had been before.

He got off the bus at his Aunt Sue's building.

The building was depressing because it was so smug. It looked as if nothing bad could ever happen here as long as the stoop was swept clean and the curtains were a bright color and the flower boxes were watered. Nothing bad! Wanna bet? Inside, his aunt's apartment was even worse. Her decorating style was country-mystic, with wreaths of dried flowers and tapestries of unicorns and small ceramic plaques that said things like "LET A SMILE BE YOUR UMBRELLA."

"Aunt Sue, I have to tell you things I didn't get a chance to say at the hospital. Please listen to me."

"Of course, Eliot. Don't I always?"

Almost never. But he composed himself and arranged his arguments. "I was online last night, too. Those two cases you mentioned, the man who couldn't read again and the woman who didn't recognize her kids, were anomalies. Selective Memory Obliteration Neural Re-Routing is new, yes, but it passed clinical trials and FDA approval and it has an eighty-nine percent success rate, with a one percent confidence level. Of the remaining eleven percent, two-thirds were neither better nor worse after the operation. That leaves only three-point-eight percent and when you take into account those with only minor—"

"No."

"You're not listening!"

"I *am* listening. Nobody is going to cut into Carl's brain."

"But he believes he saw a defunct Greek god in a toaster pastry!"

"Eliot, is that so bad?"

"It's not true!"

"Well, it's true that Carl *saw* it, anyway, or he wouldn't be so upset. He'll come out of whatever spell he's having about it, he always does. And anyway, I don't understand Carl's reaction. Would it be so bad to believe this Zeus-god is around?"

"That's the part that's not true!"

She shrugged. "Are you so sure you know what's true?"

"Yes!" Eliot shouted. "Mathematics is true! Physics is true! Memory can play us false, there's a ton of research on that, nobody can be sure if their memories are accurate—" He stopped, no longer sure what he was saying.

Aunt Sue said calmly, "Well, if memory is playing Carl false, then he's all the more likely to get over it, isn't he?"

"No! It isn't—I didn't mean—"

"Wouldn't you like some walnut cake, Eliot? I baked it fresh this morning."

Hopeless. They came from two different planets. And she—this kind, stupid woman who inexplicably shared one-quarter of his genes—held the power. In a truly rational world, that couldn't have been true.

"Cream-cheese icing," she said brightly, and caressed his cheek.

Eliot wrote: *Memory is like a corn stalk. Corn blight can wreck any entire economy, starve an entire nation, but it responds to science. Find the bad gene, cut it out, replace it with a genetically engineered Bt gene that fights blight because it allows the use of strong pesticides and voila! Memory functions again! Science triumphs!*

Possibly the worst writing he had ever done. He hit DE-LETE.

His father's liquor cabinet still held three inches of Scotch. Eliot poured himself two fingers' worth, so he could sleep.

The next morning, just as he was leaving to catch the bus for school, the hospital called.

"The answer," his father said, "is obvious."

It wasn't obvious to Eliot. His father sat in the day room, out of his bathrobe and dressed in his ordinary baggy khakis and badly-pilled sweater. Dr. Tremling had shaved. He looked just as he once did, and Eliot would have felt hopeful if he hadn't felt so bewildered, or if the new twitch at the corner of his father's left eye wasn't beating madly and irregularly as a malfunctioning metronome.

"I did see what I thought I saw," his father said carefully. "I *know* so, in a way that, although it defies explanation, is so incontrovertible that—"

"Dad," Eliot said, equally carefully—if only that twitch would stop! "You can't actually 'know' that for certain. Surely you're aware that all our minds can play tricks on us that—"

"Not this time," Dr. Tremling said simply. "I saw it. And I know it was true, not just an aberration of pastry. I know, too, that mathematics, the whole rational underpinning of the universe, is also true. The dichotomy was . . . upsetting me."

Upsetting him. Eliot glanced around at the mental hospital, the orderlies watchful in the corners of the room, the barred window. His father had always had a gift for understatement, which was in part what had made this whole thing so . . . so upsetting.

"What I failed to see," Dr. Tremling said, "was that this is a gift. I have just been handed my life's work."

"I thought the topography of knots was your life's work?"

"It was, yes. But now my life's work is to find the rational and mathematical underpinnings for this new phenomenon."

"For Zeus? In a toaster pastry?"

The twitch beat faster, even more irregularly. "I concede that it is a big job."

"Dad—"

"There must be a larger consciousness, Eliot. If so, it is a physical entity, made up of energy and matter, *must* be a physical entity. And a physical entity can be described mathematically, possibly through a system that does not yet exist, possibly based on non-local quantum physics."

Eliot managed to say, "You aren't a quantum physicist."

"I can learn." Twitch *twitch* TWITCH. "Do you remember what Werner Heisenberg said about belief systems? 'What we observe is not nature itself, but nature exposed to our method of questioning.' I need a new method of questioning to lead toward a new mathematics."

"Well, that's a—"

"They're letting me have my laptop back, with controlled wifi access, until I go home."

"Have they said when that might be?"

"Possibly in a few more weeks."

Dr. Tremling beamed, twitching. Eliot tried to beam, too. He was getting what he'd wanted—his father back home, working on mathematics. Only—"a new mathematics"? His father was not Godel or Einstein or Heisenberg. He wasn't even an endowed chair.

Eliot burst out, before he knew he was going to say anything, "There's no evidence for any larger consciousness! It's mystical wish-fulfillment, a non-rational delusion! There's just no evidence!"

"I'm the evidence. Son, I don't think I actually told you what I experienced." He leaned closer; involuntarily Eliot leaned back. "It *was* Zeus, but it was also Odin, was Christ, was . . . oh, let me think . . . was Isis and Sedna and Bumba and Quetzalcoatl. It was all of them and none of them because the images were in my mind. Of course they were, where else could they possibly be? But here's the thing—the images are unimportant. They're just metaphors, and not very good ones—arrows pointing to something that has neither image nor words, but just *is*. That thing is—how can I explain this?—the world behind the world. Didn't you ever feel in childhood that all at once you sort of glimpsed a flash of a great mystery underlying everything, a bright meaning to it all? I know you did because everybody does. Then we grow up and lose that. But it's still there, bright and shining as solid as . . . as an end table, or a pig. I saw it and now I know it exists in a way that goes beyond any need to question its existence—the way I know, for instance, that prime numbers are infinite. It's the world beyond the world, the space filled with shining light, the mystery. Do you see?"

"No!"

"Well, that's because you didn't experience it. But if I can find the right mathematics, that's a better arrow than verbal metaphors can ever be."

Eliot saw in his father's eyes the gleam of fanaticism. "Dad!" he cried, in pure anguish, but Dr. Tremling only put his hand on Eliot's knee, a startlingly rare gesture of affection, and said, "Wait, son. Just wait."

Eliot couldn't wait. His English assignment was due by third period, which began, with the logic of high school scheduling, at 10:34 a.m. No late assignments were accepted. His tablet on his knees on the crowded bus, Eliot wrote: *Memory is not a room or a bridge or a corn stalk with blight. Memory is not a metaphor because nothing is a metaphor. Metaphors are constructions of a fanciful imagination, not reality. In reality everything is what it is, and that is—or certainly should be!—enough for anybody!*

The little boy sitting next to him said, "Hey, man, you hit that thing so hard, you gonna break it."

"Shut up," Eliot said.

"Get fucked," the kid answered.

But Eliot already was.

Dr. Tremling came home three weeks later. He was required to see a therapist three times a week. Aunt Sue bustled over, cooked for two days straight, and stocked the freezer with meals. When Eliot and his father sat down to eat, Dr. Tremling's eye twitched convulsively. Meals were the only time they met. His father chewed absently and spoke little, but then, that had always been true. The rest of the time he stayed in his study, working. Eliot did not ask on what. He didn't want to know.

Everything felt suspended. Eliot went to school, took his AP classes, expressed scorn for the jocks and goths who teased him, felt superior to his teachers, read obsessively—all normal. And yet not. One day, when his father was at a therapy session, Eliot slid into Dr. Tremling's study and looked at his notebooks and, to the extent he could find them amid such sloppy electronic housekeeping, his computer files. There didn't seem to be much notation, and what there was, Eliot couldn't follow. He wasn't a mathematician, after all. And his father appeared to have invented a new symbol for something, a sort of Olympic thunderbolt that seemed to have left- and right-handed versions. Eliot groaned and closed the file.

Only once did Eliot ask, "So how's it going, Dad?"

"It's difficult," Dr. Tremling said.

No shit. "Have you had any more . . . uh . . . incidents?"

"That's irrelevant, son. I only needed one." But his face twitched harder than ever.

Three weeks after he came home, Dr. Tremling gave up. He hadn't slept for a few nights and his face sagged like a bloodhound's. But he was calm when he said to Eliot, "I'm going to have the operation."

"You are?" Eliot's heart leapt and then, inexplicably, sank. "Why? When?"

His father answered with something of his old precision. "Because there is no mathematics of a larger conscious entity. On Tuesday at eight in the morning. Dr. Tallman certified me able to sign my own papers."

"Oh." For a long terrible moment Eliot thought he had nothing more to say. But then he managed, "I'm sorry about the pig."

"It's not important," Dr. Tremling said, which should have been the first clue.

On Tuesday Eliot rose at 5:00 a.m., and took a cab to the hospital. He sat with his father in Pre-Op, in a vibrantly and mistakenly orange waiting room during the operation, and beside his father's bed in Post-Op. Dr. Tremling recovered well and came home a week later. He was quiet, subdued. When the new term started, he resumed teaching at the university. He read the professional journals, weeded the garden, fended off his sister. Nobody mentioned the incident, and Dr. Tremling never did, either, since hospital tests had verified that it was gone from his memory. Everything back to normal.

But not really. Something had gone missing, Eliot thought—some part of his father that, though inarticulate, had made his eyes shine at a breakthough in mathematics. That had made him love pigs. That had led him, in passion, to fling bad student problem sets and blockhead professional papers across the room, as later he would fling furniture. Something was definitely missing.

"Isn't it wonderful that Carl is exactly the way he used to be?" enthused Aunt Sue. "Modern medicine is just amazing!"

Eliot didn't answer her. On the way home from school, he got off the bus one stop early. He ducked into the Safeway as if planning to rob it, carrying out his purchase more secretively than he'd ever carried out the Trojans he never got to use. In his room, he locked the door, opened the grocery boxes, and spread out their contents on the bed.

On the dresser.

On the desk, beside his calculus homework.

On the computer keyboard.

When there were no other surfaces left, on the not-very-clean carpet.

Then, hoping, he stared at the toaster pastries until his head ached and his eyes crossed from strain.

Eliot wrote, "Metaphor is all we have." But the assignment had been due weeks ago, and his teacher refused to alter his grade.

The Nearest Thing

GENEVIEVE VALENTINE

Genevieve Valentine (www.genevievevalentine.com) lives in New York City. Like most writers, she has been writing all her life, she says, but she began writing for publication in 2007, when her first story appeared in Strange Horizons. *She is a prolific writer, and more than thirty of her short stories have appeared or are forthcoming in magazines such as* Clarkesworld *and* Fantasy, *and in the anthologies* The Living Dead II, Teeth, *and* Running with the Pack. *She is what Jeff VanderMeer terms an "emerging" writer. Her first novel,* Mechanique: A Tale of the Circus Tresaulti, *about a mechanical circus in a post-apocalyptic world, was published late in 2011. She enjoys working within and across all genres of speculative fiction (and finding period films in which anyone wears anything remotely accurate). She has a few novels "in various stages of completion."*

"The Nearest Thing" was published online by Lightspeed, *and this is perhaps its first print publication. Mason is a coding genius and socially awkward. He works for/is owned by a corporation that makes personalized "memorial dolls," robotic duplicates of individuals with artificial pseudo-personalities. He has been shifted to a development team led by Paul, a charismatic wonder-boy; the project is to develop an AI, "the nearest thing" to human.*

CALENDAR REMINDER: STOCKHOLDER DINNER, 8PM.

THIS MESSAGE SENT FROM MORI: LOOKING TO THE FUTURE, LOOKING OUT FOR YOU.

The Mori Annual Stockholder Dinner is a little slice of hell that employees are encouraged to attend, for morale.

Mori's made Mason rich enough that he owns a bespoke tux and drives to the Dinner in a car whose property tax is more than his father made in a year; of course he goes.

(He skipped one year because he was sick, and two Officers from HR came to his door with a company doctor to confirm it. He hasn't missed a party since.)

He's done enough high-profile work that Mori wants him to actually mingle, and he spends the cocktail hour being pushed from one group to another, shaking hands, telling the same three inoffensive anecdotes over and over.

They go fine; he's been practicing.

People chuckle politely just before he finishes the punch line.

Memorial dolls take a second longer, because they have to process the little cognitive disconnect of humor, and because they're programmed to think that interrupting is rude.

(He'll hand it to the Aesthetics department—it's getting harder to tell the difference between people with plastic surgery and the dolls.)

"I hear you're starting a new project," says Harris. He hugs Mrs. Harris closer, and after too long, she smiles.

(Mason will never know why anyone brings their doll out in public like this. The point is to ease the grieving process, not to provide arm candy. It's embarrassing. He wishes stockholders were a little less enthusiastic about showing support for the company.)

This new project is news to him, too, but he doesn't think stockholders want to hear that.

"I might be," he says. "I obviously can't say, but—"

Mr. Harris grins. "Paul Whitcover already told us—" (Mason thinks, *Who?*) "—and it sounds like a marvelous idea. I hope it does great things for the company; it's been a while since we had a new version."

Mason's heart stutters that he's been picked to spearhead a new version.

It sinks when he remembers Whitcover. He's one of the second-generation creative guys who gets his picture taken with some starlet on his arm, as newscasters talk about what good news it would be for Mori's stock if he were to marry a studio-contracted actress.

Mrs. Harris is smiling into middle space, waiting to be addressed, or for a keyword to come up.

Mason met Mrs. Harris several Dinners ago. She had more to say than this, and he worked on some of the conversation software in her generation; she can handle a party. Harris must have turned her cognitives down to keep her pleasant.

There's a burst of laughter across the room, and when Mason looks over it's some guy in a motorcycle jacket, surrounded by tuxes and gowns.

"Who's that?" he asks, but he knows, he knows, this is how his life goes, and he's already sighing when Mr. Harris says, "Paul."

Since he got Compliance Contracted to Mori at fifteen, Mason has come to terms with a lot of things.

He's come to terms with the fact that, for the money he makes, he can't make noise about his purpose. He worked for a year on an impact-sensor chip for Mori's downmarket Prosthetic Division; you go where you're told.

(He's come to terms with the fact that the more Annual Stockholder Dinners you attend, the less time you spend in a cubicle in Prosthetics.)

He has come to terms with the fact that sometimes you will hate the people you work with, and there is nothing you can do.

(Mason suspects he hates everyone, and that the reasons why are the only things that change.)

The thing is, Mason doesn't hate Paul because Paul is a Creative heading an R&D project. Mason will write what they tell him to, under whatever creative-team asshole they send him. He's not picky.

Sure, he resents someone who introduces himself to other adults as, "Just Paul, don't worry about it, good to meet you," and he resents someone whose dad was a Creative Consultant and who's never once gone hungry, and he resents the adoring looks from stockholders as Paul claims Mori is really Going Places This Year, but things like this don't keep him up at night, either.

He's pretty sure he starts to hate Paul the moment Paul introduces him to Nadia.

At Mori, we know you care.

We know you love your family. We know you worry about leaving them behind. And we know you've asked for more information about us, which means you're thinking about giving your family the greatest gift of all:

You.

Medical studies have shown the devastating impact grief has on family bonds and mental health. The departure of someone beloved is a tragedy without a proper name.

Could you let the people you love live without you?

A memorial doll from Mori maps the most important aspects of your memory, your speech patterns, and even your personality into a synthetic reproduction.

The process is painstaking—our technology is exceeded only by our artistry—and it leaves behind a version of you that, while it can never replace you, can comfort those who have lost you.

Imagine knowing your parents never have to say good-bye. Imagine knowing you can still read bedtime stories to your children, no matter what may happen.

A memorial doll from Mori is a gift you give to everyone who loves you.

Nadia holds perfectly still.

Her nametag reads "Aesthetic Consultant," which means Paul brought his model girlfriend to the meeting.

She's pretty, in a cat's-eye way, but Mason doesn't give her much thought. It takes a lot for Mason to really notice a woman, and she's nowhere near the actresses Paul dates.

(Mason's been reading up. He doesn't think much of Paul, but the man can find a camera at a hundred paces.)

Paul brings Nadia to the first brainstorming meeting for the Vestige project. He introduces her to Mason and the two guys from Marketing ("Just Nadia, don't worry about it"), and they're ten minutes into the meeting before Mason realizes she had never said a word.

It takes Mason until then to realize how still she is. Only her eyes move—to him, with a hard expression like she can read his mind and doesn't like what she sees.

Not that he cares. He just wonders where she came from, suddenly.

"So we have to think about a new market," Paul is saying. "There's a diminishing return on memorial dolls, unless we want to drop the price point to expand opportunities and popularize the brand—"

The two Marketing guys make appalled sounds at the idea of Mori going downmarket.

"—or, we develop something that will redefine the company," Paul finishes. "Something new. Something we build in-house from the ground up."

A Marketing guy says, "What do you have in mind?"

"A memorial that can conquer Death itself," says Paul.

(Nadia's eyes slide to Paul, never move.)

"How so?" asks the other marketing guy.

Paul grins, leans forward; Mason sees the switch flip.

Then Paul is magic.

He uses every catchphrase Mason's ever heard in a pitch, and some phrases he swears are from Mori's own pamphlets. Paul makes a lot of eye contact, frowns soulfully. The Marketing guys get glassy and slack-jawed, like they're watching a swimming pool fill up with doubloons. Paul smiles, one fist clenched to keep his amazing ideas from flying away.

Mason waits for a single concept concrete enough to hang some code on. He waits a long time.

(The nice thing about programs is that you deal in absolutes—yes, or no.)

"We'll be working together," and Paul encompasses Mason in his gesture. "Andrew Mason has a reputation for outthinking computers. Together, we'll give the Vestige model a self-sustaining critical-thinking initiative no other developer has tried—and no consumer base has ever seen. It won't be human, but it will be the nearest thing."

The Marketing guys light up.

"Self-sustaining critical-thinking" triggers ideas about circuit maps and command-decision algorithms, and for a second Mason is absorbed in the idea.

He comes back when Paul says, "Oh, he definitely has ideas." He flashes a smile at the Marketing guys—it wobbles when he looks at Nadia, but he recovers well enough that the smile is back by the time it gets to Mason.

"Mason, want to give us tech dummies a rundown of what you've been brainstorming?"

Mason glances back from Nadia to Paul, doesn't answer.

Paul frowns. "Do you have questions about the project?"

Mason shrugs. "I just think maybe we shouldn't be discussing confidential R&D with some stranger in the room."

(Compliance sets up stings sometimes, just to make sure employees are serious about confidentiality. Maybe that's why she hasn't said a thing.)

Nadia actually turns her head to look at him (her eyes skittering past Paul), and Paul drops the act and snaps, "She's not some stranger," like she saved him from an assassination attempt.

It's the wrong thing to say.

It makes Mason wonder what the relationship between Paul and Nadia really is.

That afternoon, Officer Wilcox from HR stops by Mason's office.

"This is just a random check," she says. "Your happiness is important to the company."

What she means is, Paul ratted him out, and they're making sure he's not thinking of leaking information about the kind of project you build a market-wide stock repurchase on.

"I'm very happy here," Mason says, and it's what you always say to HR, but it's true enough; they pulled him from that shitty school and gave him a future. Now he has more money than he knows what to do with, and the company dentist isn't half bad.

He likes his work, and they leave him alone, and things have always been fine, until now.

(He imagines Paul, his face a mask of concern, saying, "It's not that I think he's up to anything, it's just he seems so unhappy, and he wouldn't answer me when I asked him something.")

"Will Nadia be part of the development team?" Mason asks, for no real reason.

"Undetermined," says Officer Wilcox. "Have a good weekend. Come back rested and ready to work on Vestige."

She hands him a coupon for a social club where dinner costs a week's pay and private hostesses are twice that.

She says, "The company really appreciates your work."

He goes home, opens his personal program.

Most of it is still just illustrations from old maps, but places he's been are recreated as close as he can get. Buildings, animals, dirt, people.

They're customizable down to fingerprints; he recreated his home city with people he remembers, and calibrated their personality traits as much as possible. It's a nice reminder of home, when he needs it.

(He needs it less and less; home is far away.)

This game has been his work since the first non-Mori computer he bought—with cash, on the black market, so he had something to use that was his alone.

Now there are real-time personality components and physical impossibility safeguards so you can't pull nonsense. It's not connected to a network, to keep Mori from prying. It stands alone, and he's prouder of it than anything he's done.

(The Memento model is a pale shadow of this; this is what Paul wants for Vestige, if Mason feels like sharing.)

He builds Nadia in minutes—he must have been watching her more than he thought—and gives her the personality traits he knows she has (self-possessed, grudging, uncomfortable), her relationship with Paul, how long he's known her.

He doesn't make any guesses about what he doesn't know for sure. It hurts the game to guess.

He puts Nadia in the Mori offices. (He can't put her in his apartment, because a self-possessed, grudging, uncomfortable person who hasn't known him long wouldn't go. His game is strict.) He makes them both tired from a long night of work.

He inputs Paul, too, finally—the scene won't start until he does, given what it knows about her—and is pleased to see Paul in his own office, sleeping under his motorcycle jacket, useless and out of the way.

Nadia tries every locked door in R&D systematically. Then she goes into the library, stands in place.

Mason watches his avatar working on invisible code so long he starts to drift off.

When he opens his eyes, Nadia's avatar is in the doorway of his office, where his avatar has rested his head in his hands, looking tired and upset and wishing he was the kind of person who could give up on something.

(His program is spooky, when he does it right.)

He holds his breath until Nadia's avatar turns around.

She finds the open door to Paul's office (of course it's open), stands and looks at him, too.

He wonders if her avatar wants to kiss Paul's.

Nadia's avatar leaves Paul's doorway, too, goes to the balcony overlooking the impressive lobby. She stands at the railing for a while, like his avatars used to do before he had perfected their physical limits so they wouldn't keep trying to walk through walls.

Then she jumps.

He blanks out for a second.

He restarts.

(It's not how life goes, it's a cheat, but without it he'd never have been able to understand a thing about how people work.)

He starts again, again.

She jumps every time.

His observations are faulty, he decides. There's not enough to go on, since he knows so little about her. His own fault for putting her into the system too soon.

He closes up shop; his hands are shaking.

Then he takes the Mori coupon off his dining table.

The hostess is pretty, in a cat-eye way.

She makes small talk, pours expensive wine. He lets her because he's done this rarely enough that it's still awkward, and because Mori is picking up the tab, and because something is scraping at him that he can't define.

Later she asks him, "What can I do for you?"

He says, "Hold as still as you can."

It must be a creepy request; she freezes.

It's very still. It's as still as Nadia holds.

Monday morning, Paul shows up in his office.

"Okay," Paul says, rubbing his hands together like he's about to carve a bird, "let's brainstorm how we can get these dolls to brainstorm for themselves."

"Where's Nadia?" Mason asks.

Paul says, "Don't worry about it."

Mason hates Paul.

* * *

The first week is mostly Mason trying to get Paul to tell him what they're doing ("What you're doing now," Paul says, "just bigger and better, we'll figure things out, don't worry about it.") and how much money they have to work with.

("Forget the budget," Paul says, "we're just thinking about software, the prototype is taken care of."

Mason wonders how long Paul has been working on this, acquiring entire prototypes off the record, keeping under the radar of a company that taps your phones, and the hair on his neck stands up.)

"I have a baseline ready for implantation," Paul admits on Thursday, and it feels like a victory for Mason. "We can use that as a jumping-off point to test things, if you don't want to use simulators."

"You don't use simulators until you have a mock-up ready. The baseline is unimportant while we're still working on components." Then he thinks about it. "Where did you get a baseline with no R&D approval?"

Paul grins. "Black market," he says.

It's the first time Mason's ever suspected Paul might actually care about what they're doing.

It changes a lot of things.

On Friday, Mason brings in a few of his program's parameters for structuring a sympathy algorithm, and when Paul shows up he says, "I had some ideas."

Paul bends to look, his motorcycle jacket squeaking against Mason's chair, his face tinted blue by the screen.

Mason watches Paul skim it twice. He's a quick reader.

"Fantastic," Paul says, in a way that makes Mason wonder if Paul knows more about specifics than he'd admit. "See what you can build me from this."

"I can build whatever you need," Mason says.

Paul looks down at him; his grin fills Mason's vision.

Monday morning, Paul brings Nadia.

She sits in the back of the office, reading a book, glancing up when Mason says something that's either on the right track or particularly stupid.

(When he catches her doing it her eyes are deep and dark, and she's always just shy of pulling a face.)

Paul never says why he brought her, but Mason is pretty sure Nadia's not a plant—not even Paul could risk that. More likely she's his girlfriend. (Maybe she is an actress. He should start watching the news.)

Most of the time she has her nose in a book, so steady that Mason knows when she's looking at them if it's been too long between page-turns.

Once when they're arguing about infinite loops Paul turns and asks her, "Would that really be a problem?"

"I guess we'll find out," she says.

It's the first time she's spoken, and Mason twists to look at her.

She hasn't glanced up from her book, hasn't moved at all, but still Mason watches, waiting for something, until Paul catches his eye.

For someone who brings his girlfriend the unofficial consultant to the office every day, Paul seems unhappy about Mason looking.

Nadia doesn't seem to notice; her reflection in Mason's monitor doesn't look up, not once.

(Not that it matters if she does or not. He has no idea what he was waiting for.)

Mason figures out what they're doing pretty quickly. Not that Paul told him, but when Mason said, "Are we trying to create emotional capacity?" Paul said, "Don't worry about it," grinning like he had at Mason's first lines of code, and that was Mason's answer.

There's only one reason you create algorithms for this level of critical thinking, and it's not for use as secretaries.

Mason is making an A.I. that can understand as well as respond, an A.I. that can grow an organic personality beyond its programming, that has an imagination; one that can really live.

(Sometimes, when he's too tired to help it, he gets romantic about work.)

For a second-gen creative guy, Paul picks up fast.

"But by basing preference on a pre-programmed moral scale, they'll always prefer people who make the right decisions on a binary," Mason says. "Stockholders might not like free will that favors the morally upstanding."

Paul nods, thinks it over.

"See if you can make an algorithm that develops a preference based on the reliability of someone's responses to problems," Paul says. "People are easy to predict. Easier than making them moral."

There's no reason for Paul to look at Nadia right then, but he does, and for a second his whole face falters.

For a second, Nadia's does, too.

Mason can't sleep that night, thinking about it.

TO: ANDREW MASON

FROM: HR—HEALTH/WELFARE

Your caffeine intake from the cafeteria today is 40% above normal. Your health is of great importance to us.

If you would like to renegotiate a project timeline, please contact Management to arrange a meeting. If you are physically fatigued, please contact a company doctor. If there is a personal issue, a company therapist is standing by for consult.

If any of these apply, please let us know what actions you have taken, so we may update your records.

If this is a dietary anomaly, please disregard.

The company appreciates your work.

They test some of the components on a simulator.

(Mason tells Paul they're marking signs of understanding. Really, he wants to see if the simulation prefers one of them without a logical basis. That's what humans do.)

He pulls up a baseline, several traits mixed at random from reoccurring types in the Archives, just to keep you from using someone's remnant. (The company frowns on that.)

Under the ID field, Mason types in GALATEA.

"Acronym?" Paul asks.

"Allusion," says Nadia.

Her reflection is looking at the main monitor, her brows drawn in an expression too stricken to be a frown.

Galatea runs diagnostics (a long wait—the text-interface version passed four sentience screenings in anonymous testing last month, and something that sophisticated takes a lot of code). She recognizes the camera, nodding at Mason and Paul in turn.

Then her eyes go flat, refocus to find Nadia.

It makes sense, Nadia's further away, but Mason still gets the creeps. Someone needs to work on the naturalism of these simulators. This isn't some second-rate date booth; they have a reputation to uphold.

"Be charming," Mason says.

Paul cracks up.

"Okay," he says, "Galatea, good to meet you, I'm Paul, and I'll try to be charming tonight."

Galatea prefers Paul in under ten minutes.

Mason would burn the place down if he wasn't so proud of himself.

"Galatea," Mason asks, "what is the content of Paul's last sentence?"

"That his work is going well."

It wasn't what Paul really said—it had as little content as most of Paul's sentences that aren't about code—which means Galatea was inferring the best meaning, because she favored him.

"Read this," Mason says, scrawls a note.

Paul reads, "During a shift in market paradigms, it's imperative that we leverage our synergy to reevaluate paradigm structure."

It's some line of shit Paul gave him the first day they worked together. Paul doesn't even have the shame to recognize it.

"Galatea, act on that sentence," Mason says.

"I cannot," Galatea says, but her camera lens is focused square on Paul's face, which is Mason's real answer.

"Installing this software has compromised your baseline personality system and altered your preferences," he says. "Can you identify the overwrites?"

There's a tiny pause.

"No," she says, sounds surprised.

He looks up at Paul, grinning, but Paul's jaw is set like a guilty man, and his eyes are focused on the wall ahead of him, his hands in fists on the desk.

(Reflected in his monitor: Nadia, her book abandoned, sitting a little forward in her chair, lips parted, watching it all like she's seen a ghost.)

At the holiday party, Paul and Nadia show up together.

Paul has his arm around her, and after months of seeing them together Mason still can't decide if they're dating.

(He only sees how Paul holds out his hand to her as they leave every day, how she looks at him too long before she takes it, the story he's already telling her, his smile of someone desperate to please.)

The way Paul manages a party is supernatural. His tux is artfully rumpled, his hand on Nadia's waist, and he looks right at everyone he meets.

It's too smooth to be instinctive; his father must have trained him up young.

Maybe that's it—maybe they're like brother and sister, if you ignore the way Paul looks at her sometimes when she's in profile, like he wouldn't mind a shot but he's not holding his breath.

(He envies Paul his shot with her; he envies them both for having someone to be a sibling with.)

"Why do you keep watching me?"

She's not coy, either, he thinks as he turns, and something about her makes him feel like being honest.

He says, "I find you interesting."

"Because of how I look." Delivered like the conclusion of a scientific paper whose results surprised everyone.

"Because of how you look at everyone else."

It must shake her; she tilts her head, and for an instant her eyes go empty and flat as she pulls her face into a different expression.

It's so fast that most people wouldn't notice, but Mason is suspicious enough by now to be watching for some small tic that marks her as other than human.

Now he knows why she looks so steadily into her book, if that's what happens every time someone surprises her.

Doesn't stop him from going cold.

(He can't process it. It's one thing to be suspicious, another thing to know.)

It must show on his face; she looks at him like she doesn't know what he's going to do.

It's not how she used to look at him.

He goes colder.

Her eyes go terrified, as terrified as any human eyes.

She's the most beautiful machine he's ever seen.

He opens his mouth.

"Don't," she starts.

Then Paul is there, smiling, asking, "You remember how to dance, right?", lacing his fingers in her fingers and pulling her with him a fraction too fast to be casual.

She watches Mason over her shoulder all the way to the dance floor.

He stands where he is a long time, watching the golden boy of Mori dancing with his handmade Vestige prototype.

He spends the weekend wondering if he has a friend in Aesthetics who could tell him where Nadia's face really came from, or one in Archives who would back him up about a personality Paul Whitcover's been saving for a special occasion.

It's tempting. It wouldn't stop the project, but it would certainly shut Paul up, and with something that big he might be able to renegotiate his contract right up to Freelance. (No one taps your home network when you're Freelance.)

He needs to tell someone, soon. If he doesn't, and someone finds out down the line they were keeping secrets, Mason will end up in Quality Control for the rest of his life, monitored 24/7 and living in the subterranean company apartments.

If he doesn't tell, and Paul does, Paul will get Freelance and Mason will just be put down.

He has to make the call. He has to tell Compliance.

But whenever he's on the verge of doing something, he remembers her face after he'd found her out and she feared the worst from him, how she'd let Paul take her hand, but watched him over her shoulder as long as she dared.

It's not a very flattering memory, but somehow it keeps him from making a move.

(Just as well; turns out he doesn't have a lot of friends.)

Monday morning Paul comes in alone, shuts the door behind him, and doesn't say a word.

It's such a delightful change that Mason savors the quiet for a while before he turns around.

Paul has his arms crossed, his face a set of wary lines. (He looks like Nadia.)

Mason says, "Who is she?"

He's hardly slept all weekend, thinking about it. He'd imagined tragic first love, or some unattainable socialite Paul was just praying would get personality-mapped.

Once or twice he imagined Paul had tried to reincarnate Daddy, but that was too weird even for him.

Paul shakes his head, tightly. "No one."

"Come on," says Mason, "if I haven't called HR by now I'm not going to. Who?"

Paul sits down, rakes his hair back with his hands.

"I didn't want to get in trouble if they found out I was making one," he says. "It's one thing to fuck around with some company components, but if you take a customer's remnant—" He shakes his head. "I couldn't risk it. I had them put in a standard template for her."

Mason thinks about Paul's black-market baseline, wonders how Paul would have known what was there before he installed the chip and woke her.

"She's not standard any more," he settles on.

Nadia should be here; Mason would really feel better about this whole conversation if she were here.

(But Paul wouldn't be talking about it if she were; he knows that much about Paul by now.)

"No," says Paul, a sad smile crossing his face. "I tried a couple of our early patches, before we were working on the full. I couldn't believe how well they took."

Of course they did, thinks Mason, they're mine, but he keeps his mouth shut.

Paul looks as close to wonderment as guys like him can get. "When we announce Vestige, it's going to change the world. You know that, right?"

He knows. It's one of the reasons he can't sleep.

"What happens to Nadia, then?" he asks.

(That's the other reason he can't sleep.)

"I don't know," Paul says, shaking his head. "She knows what she is—I mean, she knows she's A.I.—she understands what might happen. I told her that from the very beginning. At first I thought we could use her as a tester. I had no idea how much I would—" He falters as his feelings get the better of him.

"Not human, but the nearest thing?" Mason says, and it comes out vicious.

Paul has the decency to flinch, but it doesn't last.

"She knows I care about her," he goes on. "I'm planning for better things. Hopefully Mori will be so impressed by the product that they'll let me—that they'll be all right with Nadia."

He means, *That they'll let me keep her.*

"What if they want her as the prototype?"

"I haven't lied to her," Paul says. "Not ever. She knows she might have to get the upgrade to preserve herself, that she might end up belonging to the company. She accepts it. I thought I had, too, but I didn't think she'd be so—I mean, I didn't think I would come to—in the beginning, she really was no one."

Mason remembers the first time Nadia ever looked at him; he knows it isn't true.

They sit quietly for a long time, Paul looking wracked as

to how he fell in love with something he made, like someone who never thought to look up Galatea.

She's waiting in the library, and it surprises him before he admits that of course he'd look for her here; he had a map.

He doesn't make any noise, and she doesn't look up from her console, but after a second she says, "Some of these have never even been accessed." A castigation.

He says, "These are just reference books." He doesn't say, I don't need them. He needs to try not being an asshole sometimes.

She glances up, then. (He looks for code behind her eyes, feels worse than Paul.)

"I love books," she says. "At first I didn't, but now I understand them better. Now I love them."

(She means, *Are you going to give me away?*)

He wonders if this is just her, or if this is his algorithm working, and something new is trying to get out.

"I have a library at home," he says. (He means, *No.*)

She blinks, relaxes. "What do you read?"

"Pulp, mostly," he says, thinks about his collection of detective novels, wonders if she thinks that's poor taste.

She says, "They're all pulp."

It's a sly joke (he doesn't think it's anything of his), and she has such a smile he gets distracted, and when he pulls himself together she's leaving.

"I'll walk you somewhere," he says. "Paul and I won't be done for a while."

Clearly Paul told her not to trust him before he went in to spill his guts, but after a second she says, "Tell me more about your books," and he falls into step beside her.

He tells her about the library that used to be the guest bedroom before he realized he didn't have guests and there was no point in it. He explains why there are no windows and special light bulbs and a fancy dehumidifier to make sure mold doesn't get into the books.

(It's also lined in lead, which keeps Mori from getting a look at his computer. Some things are private.)

Her expression keeps changing, so subtle he'd swear she was human if he didn't know better.

She talks about the library at Alexandria, an odd combination of a machine programmed to access information and someone with enough imagination she might as well have been there.

(Maybe this is immortality, as far as it goes.)

She mentions the Dewey Decimal system, and he says, "That's how I shelve mine."

"That explains your code," she says. When he raises his eyebrows, she says, "It's . . . thorough."

(Diplomacy. Also not his.)

"It has to be," he says. "I want Vestige to be perfect."

He doesn't say, *You.*

"I know," she says, in a way he doesn't like, but by then they're standing in front of Paul's office, and she's closing the door.

This floor has a balcony overlooking the atrium.

He sticks close to the wall all the way back.

He goes home and erases her avatar from his program.

(Not like he cares what she thinks, but there's no harm in cleaning house.)

Marketing calls them in for a meeting about the press announcement.

They talk a lot about advertising and luxury markets and consumer interest and the company's planned stock reissue and how the Patents team is standing by any time they want to hand over code.

"Aesthetics has done some really amazing work," Marketing says, and Mason fakes polite interest as hard as he can so he doesn't stare at the photo.

(It's not quite Nadia; it's close enough that Mason's throat goes tight, but it's a polished, prettier version, the kind of body you'd use if you wanted to immortalize your greyhound in a way society would accept.)

"Gorgeous," Paul says, and then with a smile, "is she single?" and the Marketing guys crack up.

(One of them says, "Now now, Paul, we're still hoping you can make a studio match—HR would be pleased," and Paul looks admirably amenable for a guy who's in love with a woman he thinks he made.)

It's only Paul on the schedule to present, of course—Mason's not a guy you put in front of a camera—and it's far enough away that they'll have time to polish the code.

"Naturally, you should have the prototype presentable ASAP," the Marketing VP says. "We need a pretty face for the ads, and we need her to have her personality installed by then. Aesthetics seems to think it's already in place, in some form?"

The VP's face is just bland enough not to mean anything by it, if their consciences don't get the better of them.

Don't you dare, Mason thinks, don't you dare tell them for a chance to keep her, second-gen or not, it's a trap, not one word, think about what will happen to her.

(She's still a doll, he thinks, deeper, ruthlessly; something will happen to her eventually.)

"I don't know a thing about the particulars, I'm afraid," Paul says, and having thus absolved himself he throws a casual look at Mason.

Mason thinks, *You asshole.* He thinks, *Here's where I rat him out.*

He grits his teeth and smiles.

"We've been running tests," he says. "Would you like to see Galatea?" Then, in his best Paul impression, "She has a crush on Paul, of course."

The Marketing guys laugh, and Mason pulls up Galatea on his pad, and as the lights go down he catches Paul glancing gratefully in his direction.

He hates how strange it feels to have someone be grateful to him; he hates that it's Paul.

Paul walks out with the Marketing guys, grinning and charming and empty, and from the plans they're making for the announcement and the new projects they're already asking him about, Mason suspects that's the last time he'll ever see Paul.

It's so lonely in his office he thinks about turning on Galatea, just for company.

(He's no better than some.)

LiveScribe: MORI PRESS CONFERENCE—VESTIGE, PT 1.

SEARCH PARAMETERS—BEGIN: 10:05:27, END: 10:08:43

PAUL WHITCOVER: From the company that brought you Memento, which has not only pioneered the Alpha series real-time response interface, but has also brought comfort to grieving families across the world.

It's this focus on the humanity behind the technology that is Mori's greatest achievement, and it is what has made possible what I am about to show you. Ladies and gentlemen, may I present: Galatea.

[MORIVESTIGE00001.img available through LiveSketch link]

[APPLAUSE, CALLS, SHOUTS]

PAUL WHITCOVER: Galatea isn't human, but she's the nearest thing. She's the prototype of our Vestige model, which shifts the paradigm of robotics in ways we have only begun to guess—if you can tear your eyes away from her long enough.

[LAUGHTER, APPLAUSE]

PAUL WHITCOVER: Each Vestige features critical-thinking initiatives so advanced it not only sustains the initial personality, but allows the processor to learn from new stimuli, to form attachments—to grow in the same way the human mind does. This Vestige is built on a donor actress—anonymous, for now, though I suspect some in the audience will know who she is as soon as you talk to her.

[LAUGHTER]

In seriousness, I would like to honor everyone at Mori who participated in the development of such a remarkable thing. The stock market will tell you that this is an achievement of great technical merit, and that's true. However, those who have honored loved ones with a Memento doll will tell you that this is a triumph over the grieving heart, and it's this that means the most to Mori.

Understandably, due to the difficulty of crafting each doll, the Vestige is a very limited product. However, our engineers are already developing alternate uses for this technology that you will soon see more of—and that might yet change your world.

Ladies and gentlemen, thank you so much for being here today. It is not only my honor, but my privilege.

[APPLAUSE]

Small-group interviews with Vestige will be offered to members of the press. Check your entrance ticket. Thank you again, everyone, really, this is such a thrill, I'm glad you could be here. If you'd—

The phone call comes from some internal extension he's never seen, but he's too distracted by the streaming press-conference footage to screen it.

Paul is made for television; he can practically see the HR people arranging for his transfer to Public Relations.

(He can't believe Paul carried through with Nadia the Aesthetic Consultant. He can absolutely believe Paul named her Galatea.)

"This is Mason."

There's nothing on the other end, but he knows it's her.

He hangs up, runs for the elevator.

Nadia's on the floor in the library, twitching like she got fifty thousand volts, and he drops to his knees and pulls the connecting cable out of her skull.

"We have to get you to a hospital," he says, which is the stupidest thing that's ever come out of his mouth (he watches too many movies). What she needs is an antivirus screen in one of the SysTech labs.

Maybe it's for her sake he says it, so they can keep pretending she's real until she tells him otherwise.

"It's the baseline," she says, and he can't imagine what she was doing in there.

He says, "I'll get you to an Anti-V, hang on."

"No," she manages.

Then her eyes go blank and flat, and something inside her makes an awful little click.

He scoops her up without thinking, moves to the elevator as fast as he can.

He has to get her home.

He makes it in seven minutes (he'll be paying a lot of tickets later), carries her through the loft. She's stopped twitching, and he doesn't know if that's better or worse.

He assumes she's tougher than she looks—God knows how many upgrades Paul's put her through—but you never know. She's light enough in his arms that he wonders how she was ever expected to last.

He sets her on one of the chaises the Mori designer insisted mimicked the lines of the living room, drags it through the doorway to his study.

He finds the socket (behind one ear), the same place as Memento; rich people don't care for visible flaws.

He plugs her into his program.

It feels slimy, like he's showing her into his bedroom, but at least Mori won't monitor the process.

Her head is limp, her eyes half-lidded and unseeing.

"Hold on," he says, like some asshole, pulls up his program.

(Now he's sorry he deleted her avatar; he could help her faster if he had any framework ready to go.)

The code scans. Some of it is over his head—some parts of her baseline Paul got from the black market. (Black-market programmers can do amazing work. If he gets out of this alive, he might join up with them.)

He recognizes a few lines of his own code that have integrated, feels prouder than he should.

He recognizes some ID stamps that make his whole chest go tight, and his eyes ache.

Paul's an idiot, he thinks, wants to punch something.

Then he sees the first corruption, and his work begins.

He's never worked with a whole system. It's always been lines of code sent to points unknown; Galatea was the first time he'd worked with anything close to a final product.

Now Nadia is staring at the ceiling with those awful empty eyes, and his fingers shake.

If he thinks of this as surgery he's going to be ill. He turns so he can't see her.

After a while he hits a stride; it takes him back to being twelve, recreating their apartment in a few thousand lines of code, down to the squeak in the hall.

("That's very . . . specific," his mother said, and that was when he began to suspect his imagination was wanting.)

When he finishes the last line, the code flickers, and he's terrified that it will be nothing but a string of zeros like a flatline.

But it cycles again, faster than he can read it, and then there's a boot file like Galatea's, and he thinks, *Fuck, I did it.*

Then her irises stutter, and she wakes up.

She makes an awful, hollow noise, and he reaches for her hand, stops—maybe that's the last thing you need when you're having a panic reboot.

She looks at him, focuses.

"You should check the code," he says. "I'm not sure if I got it all."

There's a brief pause.

"You did," she says, and when her eyes close he realizes she's gone to sleep and not shorted out. After some debate he carries her to the bed, feeling like a total idiot. He didn't realize they slept.

(Maybe it was Paul's doing, to make her more human; he had planned for better things.)

He sits in front of his computer for a long time, looking at the code with his finger on the Save button, deciding what kind of guy he is.

(That's the nice thing about programs, he always thought; you only ever deal in absolutes—yes, or no.)

When he finally turns in his chair, she's in the doorway, watching him.

"I erased it," he says.

She says, "I know," in a tone that makes him wonder how long she's been standing there.

She sits on the edge of the chaise, rolls one shoulder like she's human and it hurts.

"Were you trying to kill yourself?" he asks.

She pulls a face.

He flushes. "No, not that I want—I just, have a game I play, and in the game you jumped. I've always been worried."

It sounds exactly as creepy as it is, and he's grateful she looks at his computer and doesn't ask what else he did with her besides watch her jump.

I would have jumped if I were you and knew what I was in for, he thinks, *but some people take the easy way out.*

Nadia sits like a human gathering her thoughts. Mason watches her face (can't help it), wonders how long she has.

The prototype is live; pretty soon, someone at Mori will realize how much Vestige acts like Nadia.

Maybe they won't deactivate her. Paul's smart enough to leverage his success for some lenience; he can get what he wants out of them, maybe.

(To keep her, Mason thinks, wonders why there's no way for Nadia to win.)

"Galatea doesn't remember her baseline," Nadia says, after a long time. "She thinks that's who she always was. Paul said I started with a random template, like her, and I thought I had kept track of what you changed."

Mason thinks about her fondness for libraries; he thinks how she sat in his office for months, listening to them talk about what was going to happen to her next.

She pauses where a human would take a breath. She's the most beautiful machine in the world.

"But the new Vestige prototype was based on a remnant,"

she says. "All the others will be based on just one person. I had to know if I started as someone else."

Mason's heart is in his throat. "And?"

She looks at him. "I didn't get that far."

She means, *You must have.*

He shrugs. "I'll tell you whatever you want to know," he says. "I'm not Paul."

"I didn't call Paul," she says.

(She had called him; she knew how he would respond to a problem. People are easy to predict. It's how you build preferences.)

If he were a worse man, he'd take it as a declaration of love.

Instead he says, "Paul thought you were standard. He got your baseline from the black market, to keep Mori out, and they told him it was."

He stops, wonders how to go on.

"Who was I?" she says, finally.

"They didn't use a real name for her," he says. "There's no knowing."

(The black-market programmer was also a sucker for stories; he'd tagged her remnant "Galatea." Mason will take that with him to the grave.)

She looks at him.

He thinks about the first look she ever gave him, wary and hard in an expression he never saw again, and the way she looked as Galatea fell in love with Paul, realizing she had lost herself but with no way of knowing how much.

He thinks about her avatar leaping over the balcony and disappearing.

He'd leave with her tonight, take his chances working on the black market, if she wanted him to. He'd cover for her as long as he could, if she wanted to go alone.

(God, he wants her to live.)

"I can erase what we did," he says. "Leave you the way you were when Paul woke you."

(Paul won't notice; he loves her too much to see her at all.)

Her whole body looks betrayed; her eyes are fixed in middle space, and she curls her fingers around the edge of the chair like she's bracing for the worst, like at any moment she'll give in.

He's reminded for a second of Kim Parker, who followed him to the Spanish Steps one morning during the Mori Academy study trip to Rome when he was fifteen. He sat beside her for a long time, waiting for a sign to kiss her that never came.

He'd felt stupid that whole time, and lonely, and exhilarated, and the whole time they were sitting together part of him was memorizing all the color codes he would need to build the Steps back, later, in his program.

Nadia is blinking from time to time, thinking it over.

The room is quiet—only one of them is breathing—and it's the loneliest he's felt in a long time, but he'll wait as long as it takes.

He knows how to wait for a yes or a no; people like them deal in absolutes.

A Vector Alphabet of Interstellar Travel

YOON HA LEE

Yoon Ha Lee (pegasus.cityofveils.com) lives in Baton Rouge, Louisiana. She has a degree in mathematics. On her blog, she says, "if I am doing my job correctly as a writer, I am structuring my story around a series of ambushes and trying to deliver as much punishment as possible. Especially by punishing bad assumptions that the reader makes. This is probably a hostile and adversarial stance to take toward the reader, but if I try to conceive of it the collaborative way I get bored and wander off." She has been publishing her carefully crafted stories in the genre for about ten years. Her fiction has appeared in Fantasy & Science Fiction, Lady Churchill's Rosebud Wristlet, Ideomancer, *and* Shadows of Saturn, *among others.*

"A Vector Alphabet of Interstellar Travel" was published at Tor.com, *which maintained its prominent position as a publisher of short fiction in 2011. This story is a compressed, Stapledonian vision of huge vistas of time and space.*

The Conflagration

Among the universe's civilizations, some conceive of the journey between stars as the sailing of bright ships, and others as tunneling through the crevices of night. Some look upon their far-voyaging as a migratory imperative, and name their vessels after birds or butterflies.

The people of a certain red star no longer speak its name in any of their hundreds of languages, although they paint alien skies with its whorled light and scorch its spectral lines into the sides of their vessels.

Their most common cult, although by no means a universal one, is that of many-cornered Mrithaya, Mother of the Conflagration. Mrithaya is commonly conceived of as the god of catastrophe and disease, impartial in the injuries she deals out. Any gifts she bestows are incidental, and usually come with sharp edges. The stardrive was invented by one of her worshipers.

Her priests believe that she is completely indifferent to worship, existing in the serenity of her own disinterest. A philosopher once said that you leave offerings of bitter ash and aleatory wine at her dank altars not because she will heed them, but because it is important to acknowledge the truth of the universe's workings. Naturally, this does not stop some of her petitioners from trying, and it is through their largesse that the priests are able to thrive as they do.

Mrithaya is depicted as an eyeless woman of her people,

small of stature, but with a shadow scarring the world. (Her people's iconography has never been subtle.) She leans upon a crooked staff with words of poison scratched into it. In poetry, she is signified by smoke-wind and nausea, the sudden fall sideways into loss.

Mrithaya's people, perhaps not surprisingly, think of their travels as the outbreak of a terrible disease, a conflagration that they have limited power to contain; that the civilizations they visit will learn how to build Mrithaya's stardrive, and be infected by its workings. A not insignificant faction holds that they should hide on their candled worlds so as to prevent Mrithaya's terrible eyeless gaze from afflicting other civilizations, that all interstellar travel should be interdicted. And yet the pilgrims—Mrithaya's get, they are called—always find a way.

Certain poets write in terror of the day that all extant civilizations will be touched by this terrible technological conflagration, and become subject to Mrithaya's whims.

Alphabets

In linear algebra, the basis of a vector space is an alphabet in which all vectors can be expressed uniquely. The thing to remember is that there are many such alphabets.

In the peregrinations of civilizations grand and subtle, each mode of transport is an alphabet expressing their understandings of the universe's one-way knell. One assumes that the underlying universe is the same in each case.

Codices

The Iothal are a people who treasure chronicles of all kinds. From early on in their history, they bound forest chronicles by pressing leaves together and listening to their secrets of turning worm and wheeling sun; they read hymns to the transient things of the world in chronicles of footprints upon rocky soil, of foam upon restive sea. They wrote their alphabets forward and backward and upside down into reflected cloudlight, and divined the poetry of time receding in the earth's cracked strata.

As a corollary, the Iothal compile vast libraries. On the worlds they inhabit, even the motes of air are subject to having indices written on them in stuttering quantum ink. Some of their visionaries speak of a surfeit of knowledge, when it will be impossible to move or breathe without imbibing some unexpected fact, from the number of neutrons in a certain meadow to the habits of aestivating snails. Surely the end product will be a society of enlightened beings, each crowned with some unique mixture of facts and heady fictions.

The underside of this obsession is the society's driving terror. One day all their cities will be unordered dust, one day all their books will be scattered like leaves, one day no one will know the things they knew. One day the rotting remains of their libraries will disintegrate so completely that they will be indistinguishable from the world's wrack of stray eddies and meaningless scribbles, the untide of heat death.

The Iothal do not call their starships ships, but rather codices. They have devoted untold ages to this ongoing archival work. Although they had developed earlier stardrives—indeed, with their predilection for knowledge, it was impossible not to—their scientists refused to rest until they devised one that drank in information and, as its ordinary mode of operation, tattooed it upon the universe's subtle skin.

Each time the Iothal build a codex, they furnish it with a carefully selected compilation of their chronicles, written in a format that the stardrive will find nourishing. Then its crew takes it out into the universe to carry out the act of inscription. Iothal codices have very little care for destination, as it is merely the fact of travel that matters, although they make a point of avoiding potentially hostile aliens.

When each codex has accomplished its task, it loses all vitality and drifts inertly wherever it ends up. The Iothal are very long-lived, but even they do not always survive to this fate.

Distant civilizations are well accustomed to the phenomenon of drifting Iothal vessels, but so far none of them have deciphered the trail of knowledge that the Iothal have been at such pains to lay down.

The Dancers

To most of their near neighbors, they are known as the dancers. It is not the case that their societies are more interested in dance than the norm. True, they have their dances of metal harvest, and dances of dream descending, and dances of efflorescent death. They have their high rituals and their low chants, their festivals where water-of-suffusement flows freely for all who would drink, where bells with spangled clappers toll the hours by antique calendars. But then, these customs differ from their neighbors' in detail rather than in essential nature.

Rather, their historians like to tell the story of how, not so long ago, they went to war with aliens from a distant cluster. No one can agree on the nature of the offense that precipitated the whole affair, and it seems likely that it was a mundane squabble over excavation rights at a particular rumor pit.

The aliens were young when it came to interstellar war, and they struggled greatly with the conventions expected of them. In order to understand their enemy better, they charged their masters of etiquette with the task of interpreting the dancers' behavior. For it was the case that the dancers began each of their battles in the starry deeps with the same maneuvers, and often retreated from battle—those times they had cause to retreat—with other maneuvers, carried out with great precision. The etiquette masters became fascinated by the pirouettes and helices and rolls, and speculated that the dancers' society was constricted by strict rules of engagement. Their fabulists wrote witty and extravagant tales about the dancers' dinner parties, the dancers' sacrificial exchanges, the dancers' effervescent arrangements of glass splinters and their varied meanings.

It was not until late in the war that the aliens realized that the stylized maneuvers of the dancers' ships had nothing to do with courtesy. Rather, they were an effect of the stardrive's ordinary functioning, without which the ships could not move. The aliens could have exploited this knowledge and pushed for a total victory, but by then their culture was so enchanted by their self-dreamed vision of the dancers that the two came instead to a fruitful truce.

These days, the dancers themselves often speak admiringly of the tales that the aliens wrote about them. Among the younger generation in particular, there are those who emulate the elegant and mannered society depicted in the aliens' fables. As time goes on, it is likely that this fantasy will displace the dancers' native culture.

The Profit Motive

Although the Kiatti have their share of sculptors, engineers, and mercenaries, they are perhaps best known as traders. Kiatti vessels are welcome in many places, for they bring delightfully disruptive theories of government, fossilized musical instruments, and fine surgical tools; they bring cold-eyed guns that whisper of sleep impending and sugared atrocities. If you can describe it, so they say, there is a Kiatti who is willing to sell it to you.

In the ordinary course of things, the Kiatti accept barter for payment. They claim that it is a language that even the universe understands. Their sages spend a great deal of time attempting to justify the profit motive in view of conservation laws. Most of them converge comfortably on the position that profit is the civilized response to entropy. The traders themselves vary, as you might expect, in the rapacity of their bargains. But then, as they often say, value is contextual.

The Kiatti do have a currency of sorts. It is their stardrives, and all aliens' stardrives are rated in comparison with their own. The Kiatti produce a number of them, which encompass a logarithmic scale of utility.

When the Kiatti determine that it is necessary to pay or

be paid in this currency, they will spend months—sometimes years—refitting their vessels as necessary. Thus every trader is also an engineer. The drives' designers made some attempt to make the drives modular, but this was a haphazard enterprise at best.

One Kiatti visionary wrote of commerce between universes, which would require the greatest stardrive of all. The Kiatti do not see any reason they can't bargain with the universe itself, and are slowly accumulating their wealth toward the time when they can trade their smaller coins for one that will take them to this new goal. They rarely speak of this with outsiders, but most of them are confident that no one else will be able to outbid them.

The Inescapable Experiment

One small civilization claims to have invented a stardrive that kills everyone who uses it. One moment the ship is *here*, with everyone alive and well, or as well as they ever were; the next moment, it is *there*, and carries only corpses. The records, transmitted over great expanses against the microwave hiss, are persuasive. Observers in differently equipped ships have sometimes accompanied these suicide vessels, and they corroborate the reports.

Most of their neighbors are mystified by their fixation with this morbid discovery. It would be one thing, they say, if these people were set upon finding a way to fix this terrible flaw, but that does not appear to be the case. A small but reliable number of them volunteers to test each new iteration of the deathdrive, and they are rarely under any illusions about their fate. For that matter, some of the neighbors, out of pity or curiosity, have offered this people some of their own old but reliable technology, asking only a token sum to allow them to preserve their pride, but they always decline politely. After all, they possess safe stardrive technology of their own; the barrier is not knowledge.

Occasionally, volunteers from other peoples come to test it themselves, on the premise that there has to exist some species that won't be affected by the stardrive's peculiar radiance. (The drive's murderousness does not appear to have any lasting effect on the ship's structure.) So far, the claim has stood. One imagines it will stand as long as there are people to test it.

One Final Constant

Then there are the civilizations that invent keener and more nimble stardrives solely to further their wars, but that's an old story and you already know how it ends.

FOR SAM KABO ASHWELL

The Ice Owl

CAROLYN IVES GILMAN

Carolyn Ives Gilman lives in St. Louis, Missouri, and is an internationally recognized historian specializing in eighteenth- and early nineteenth-century North American history, particularly frontier and Native history. Her most recent non-fiction book is Lewis and Clark: Across the Divide. *She is currently working on a history of the American Revolution on the frontier, to be published by Yale in 2013. She has published seventeen or more SF stories since 1986, and one novel,* Halfway Human *(1998). She is a writer in the tradition of Ursula K. Le Guin.* Aliens of the Heart *(2007) is a collection of short fiction. Her novella* Candle in a Bottle *appeared in 2006, and her novella* Arkfall *in 2009. Gilman's latest novel is in two volumes,* Isles of the Forsaken *and* Ison of the Isles, *and is a fantasy about culture clash and revolution in an enchantment-shrouded island nation.*

"The Ice Owl" was published in F&SF. *It is a dense, complex far future sf story. Gilman says it is set in the same universe as her novella* Arkfall, *"but it's also the same universe as a number of other stories I've written. My novel* Halfway Human *is set in this universe, and the ice owl comes from the planet where "The Honeycrafters" takes place. I've started calling this universe the Twenty Planets." Thorn's school has been burned down by a Taliban-like political movement. She seeks out a tutor, who turns out to be a secret art dealer with a complex hidden life.*

Twice a day, stillness settled over the iron city of Glory to God as the citizens turned west and waited for the world to ring. For a few moments the motionless red sun on the horizon, half-concealed by the western mountains, lit every face in the city: the just-born and the dying, the prisoners and the veiled, the devout and the profane. The sound started so low it could only be heard by the bones; but as the moments passed the metal city itself began to ring in sympathetic harmony, till the sound resolved into a note—The Note, priests said, sung by the heart of God to set creation going. Its vibratory mathematics embodied all structure; its pitch implied all scales and chords; its beauty was the ovum of all devotion and all faithlessness. Nothing more than a note was needed to extrapolate the universe.

The Note came regular as clockwork, the only timebound thing in a city of perpetual sunset.

On a ledge outside a window in the rustiest part of town, crouched one of the ominous cast-iron gargoyles fancied by the architects of Glory to God—or so it seemed until it moved. Then it resolved into an adolescent girl dressed all in black. Her face was turned west, her eyes closed in a look of private exaltation as The Note reverberated through her. It was a face that had just recently lost the chubbiness of childhood, so that the clean-boned adult was beginning to show through. Her name, also a recent development, was Thorn. She had chosen it because it evoked suffering and redemption.

As the bell tones whispered away, Thorn opened her eyes. The city before her was a composition in red and black: red of the sun and the dust-plain outside the girders of the dome; black of the shadows and the works of mankind. Glory to God was built against the cliff of an old crater and rose in stair steps of fluted pillars and wrought arches till the towers of the Protectorate grazed the underside of the dome where it met the cliff face. Behind the distant, glowing windows of the palaces, twined with iron ivy, the priest-magistrates and executives lived unimaginable lives—though Thorn still pictured them looking down on all the rest of the city, on the smelteries and temples, the warring neighborhoods ruled by militias, the veiled women, and at the very bottom, befitting its status, the Waster enclave where unrepentent immigrants like Thorn and her mother lived, sunk in a bath of sin. The Waste was not truly of the city, except as a perennial itch in its flesh. The Godly said it was the sin, not the oxygen, that rusted everything in the Waste. A man who came home with a red smudge on his clothes might as well have been branded with the address.

Thorn's objection to her neighborhood lay not in its sin, which did not live up to its reputation, but its inauthenticity. From her rooftop perch she looked down on its twisted warrens full of coffee shops, underground publishers, money launderers, embassies, tattoo parlors, and art galleries. This was the ninth planet she had lived on in her short life, but in truth she had never left her native culture, for on every planet the Waster enclaves were the same. They were always a mother lode of contraband ideas. Everywhere, the expatriate intellectuals of the Waste were regarded as exotic and dangerous, the vectors of infectious transgalactic ideas—but lately, Thorn had begun to find them pretentious and phony. They were rooted nowhere, pieces of cultural bricolage. Nothing reached to the core; it was all veneer, just like the rust.

Outside, now—she looked past the spiked gates into Glory to God proper—there lay dark desires and age-old hatreds, belief so unexamined it permeated every tissue like a marinade. The natives had not chosen their beliefs; they had inherited them, breathed them in with the iron dust in their first breath. Their struggles were authentic ones.

Her eyes narrowed as she spotted movement near the gate. She was, after all, on lookout duty. There seemed to be more than the usual traffic this afternote, and the cluster of young men by the gate did not look furtive enough to belong. She studied them through her pocket binoculars and saw a telltale flash of white beneath one long coat. White, the color of the uncorrupted.

She slipped back through the gable window into her attic room, then down the iron spiral staircase at the core of the vertical tower apartment. Past the fifth-floor closets and the fourth-floor bedrooms she went, to the third-floor offices. There she knocked sharply on one of the molded sheet-iron doors. Within, there was a thump, and in a moment Maya cracked it open enough to show one eye.

"There's a troop of Incorruptibles by the gate," Thorn said.

Inside the office, a woman's voice gave a frightened exclamation. Thorn's mother turned and said in her fractured version of the local tongue, "Worry not yourself. We make safely go." She then said to Thorn, "Make sure the bottom door is locked. If they come, stall them."

Thorn spun down the stair like a black tornado, past the living rooms to the kitchen on street level. The door was locked, but she unlocked it to peer out. The alarm was spreading down the street. She watched signs being snatched from windows, awnings rolled up, and metal grills rumbling down across storefronts. The crowds that always pressed from curb to curb this time of day had vanished. Soon the stillness of impending storm settled over the street. Then Thorn heard the faraway chanting, like premonitory thunder. She closed and locked the door.

Maya showed up, looking rumpled, her lovely honey-gold hair in ringlets. Thorn said, "Did you get her out?" Maya nodded. One of the main appeals of this apartment had been the hidden escape route for smuggling out Maya's clients in emergencies like this.

On this planet, as on the eight before, Maya earned her living in the risky profession of providing reproductive services.

Every planet was different, it seemed, except that on all of them women wanted something that was forbidden. What they wanted varied: here, it was babies. Maya did a brisk business in contraband semen and embryos for women who needed to become pregnant without their infertile husbands guessing how it had been accomplished.

The chanting grew louder, harsh male voices in unison. They watched together out the small kitchen window. Soon they could see the approaching wall of men dressed in white, marching in lockstep. The army of righteousness came even with the door, then passed by. Thorn and Maya exchanged a look of mutual congratulation and locked little fingers in their secret handshake. Once again, they had escaped.

Thorn opened the door and looked after the army. An assortment of children was tagging after them, so Maya said, "Go see what they're up to."

The Incorruptibles had passed half a dozen potential targets by now: the bank, the musical instrument store, the news service, the sex shop. They didn't pause until they came to the small park that lay in the center of an intersection. Then the phalanx lined up opposite the school. With military precision, some of them broke the bottom windows and others lit incendiary bombs and tossed them in. They waited to make sure the blaze was started, then gave a simultaneous shout and marched away, taking a different route back to the gate.

They had barely left when the Protectorate fire service came roaring down the street to put out the blaze. This was not, Thorn knew, out of respect for the school or for the Waste, which could have gone up in flame wholesale for all the authorities cared; it was simply that in a domed city, a fire anywhere was a fire everywhere. Even the palaces would have to smell the smoke and clean up soot if it were not doused quickly. Setting a fire was as much a defiance of the Protectorate as of the Wasters.

Thorn watched long enough to know that the conflagration would not spread, and then walked back home. When she arrived, three women were sitting with Maya at the kitchen table. Two of them Thorn knew: Clarity and Bick, interstellar wanderers whose paths had crossed Thorn's and Maya's on two previous planets. The first time, they had been feckless coeds; the second time, seasoned adventurers. They were past middle age now, and had become the most sensible people Thorn had ever met. She had seen them face insurrection and exile with genial good humor and a canister of tea.

Right now their teapot was filling the kitchen with a smoky aroma, so Thorn fished a mug out of the sink to help herself. Maya said, "So what were the Incorruptibles doing?"

"Burning the school," Thorn said in a seen-it-all-before tone. She glanced at the third visitor, a stranger. The woman had a look of timeshock that gave her away as a recent arrival in Glory to God via lightbeam from another planet. She was still suffering from the temporal whiplash of waking up ten or twenty years from the time she had last drawn breath.

"Annick, this is Thorn, Maya's daughter," Clarity said. She was the talkative, energetic one of the pair; Bick was the silent, steady one.

"Hi," Thorn said. "Welcome to the site of Creation."

"Why were they burning the school?" Annick said, clearly distressed by the idea. She had pale eyes and a soft, gentle face. Thorn made a snap judgment: Annick was not going to last long here.

"Because it's a vector of degeneracy," Thorn said. She had learned the phrase from Maya's current boyfriend, Hunter.

"What has happened to this planet?" Annick said. "When I set out it was isolated, but not regressive."

They all made sympathetic noises, because everyone at the table had experienced something similar. Lightbeam travel was as fast as the universe allowed, but even the speed of light had a limit. Planets inevitably changed during transit, not always for the better. "Waster's luck," Maya said fatalistically.

Clarity said, "The Incorruptibles are actually a pretty new movement. It started among the conservative academics and their students, but they have a large following now. They stand against the graft and nepotism of the Protectorate.

People in the city are really fed up with being harrassed by policemen looking for bribes, and corrupt officials who make up new fees for everything. So they support a movement that promises to kick the grafters out and give them a little harsh justice. Only it's bad news for us."

"Why?" Annick said. "Wouldn't an honest government benefit everyone?"

"You'd think so. But honest governments are always more intrusive. You can buy toleration and personal freedom from a corrupt government. The Protectorate leaves this Waster enclave alone because it brings them profit. If the Incorruptibles came into power, they'd have to bow to public opinion and exile us, or make us conform. The general populace is pretty isolationist. They think our sin industry is helping keep the Protectorate in power. They're right, actually."

"What a Devil's bargain," Annick said.

They all nodded. Waster life was full of irony.

"What's Thorn going to do for schooling now?" Clarity asked Maya.

Maya clearly hadn't thought about it. "They'll figure something out," she said vaguely.

Just then Thorn heard Hunter's footsteps on the iron stairs, and she said to annoy him, "I could help Hunter."

"Help me do what?" Hunter said as he descended into the kitchen. He was a lean and angle-faced man with square glasses and a small goatee. He always dressed in black and could not speak without sounding sarcastic. Thorn thought he was a poser.

"Help you find Gmintas, of course," Thorn said. "That's what you do."

He went over to the Turkish coffee machine to brew some of the bitter, hyperstimulant liquid he was addicted to. "Why can't you go to school?" he said.

"They burned it down."

"Who did?"

"The Incorruptibles. Didn't you hear them chanting?"

"I was in my office."

He was always in his office. It was a mystery to Thorn

how he was going to locate any Gminta criminals when he disdained going out and mingling with people. She had once asked Maya, "Has he ever actually caught a Gminta?" and Maya had answered, "I hope not."

All in all, though, he was an improvement over Maya's last boyfriend, who had absconded with every penny of savings they had. Hunter at least had money, though where it came from was a mystery.

"I could be your field agent," Thorn said.

"You need an education, Thorn," Clarity said.

"Yes," Hunter agreed. "If you knew something, you might be a little less annoying."

"People like you give education a bad name," Thorn retorted.

"Stop being a brat, Tuppence," Maya said.

"That's not my name anymore!"

"If you act like a baby, I'll call you by your baby name."

"You always take his side."

"You could find her a tutor," Clarity said. She was not going to give up.

"Right," Hunter said, sipping inky liquid from a tiny cup. "Why don't you ask one of those old fellows who play chess in the park?"

"They're probably all pedophiles!" Thorn said in disgust.

"On second thought, maybe it's better to keep her ignorant," Hunter said, heading up the stairs again.

"I'll ask around and see who's doing tutoring," Clarity offered.

"Sure, okay," Maya said noncommittally.

Thorn got up, glowering at their lack of respect for her independence and self-determination. "I am captain of my own destiny," she announced, then made a strategic withdrawal to her room.

The next forenote Thorn came down from her room in the face-masking veil that women of Glory to God all wore, outside the Waste. When Maya saw her, she said, "Where are you going in that getup?"

"Out," Thorn said.

In a tone diluted with real worry, Maya said, "I don't want you going into the city, Tup."

Thorn was icily silent till Maya said, "Sorry—Thorn. But I still don't want you going into the city."

"I won't," Thorn said.

"Then what are you wearing that veil for? It's a symbol of bondage."

"Bondage to God," Thorn said loftily.

"You don't believe in God."

Right then Thorn decided that she would.

When she left the house and turned toward the park, the triviality of her home and family fell away like lint. After a block, she felt transformed. Putting on the veil had started as a simple act of rebellion, but out in the street it became far more. Catching her reflection in a shop window, she felt disguised in mystery. The veil intensified the imagined face it concealed, while exoticizing the eyes it revealed. She had become something shadowy, hidden. The Wasters all around her were obsessed with their own surfaces, with manipulating what they *seemed* to be. All depth, all that was earnest, withered in the acid of their inauthenticity. But with the veil on, Thorn *had* no surface, so she was immune. What lay behind the veil was negotiated, contingent, rendered deep by suggestion.

In the tiny triangular park in front of the blackened shell of the school, life went on as if nothing had changed. The tower fans turned lazily, creating a pleasant breeze tinged a little with soot. Under their strutwork shadows, two people walked little dogs on leashes, and the old men bent over their chessboards. Thorn scanned the scene through the slit in her veil, then walked toward a bench where an old man sat reading from an electronic slate.

She sat down on the bench. The old man did not acknowledge her presence, though a watchful twitch of his eyebrow told her he knew she was there. She had often seen him in the park, dressed impeccably in threadbare suits of a style long gone. He had an oblong, drooping face and big hands that looked as if they might once have done clever things. Thorn sat considering what to say.

"Well?" the old man said without looking up from his book. "What is it you want?"

Thorn could think of nothing intelligent to say, so she said, "Are you a historian?"

He lowered the slate. "Only in the sense that we all are, us Wasters. Why do you want to know?"

"My school burned down," Thorn said. "I need to find a tutor."

"I don't teach children," the old man said, turning back to his book.

"I'm not a child!" Thorn said, offended.

He didn't look up. "Really? I thought that's what you were trying to hide, behind that veil."

She took it off. At first he paid no attention. Then at last he glanced up indifferently, but saw something that made him frown. "You are the child that lives with the Gminta hunter."

His cold tone made her feel defensive on Hunter's behalf. "He doesn't hunt all Gmintas," she said, "just the wicked ones who committed the Holocide. The ones who deserve to be hunted."

"What do you know about the Gmintan Holocide?" the old man said with withering dismissal.

Thorn smiled triumphantly. "I was there."

He stopped pretending to read and looked at her with bristly disapproval. "How could you have been there?" he said. "It happened 141 years ago."

"I'm 145 years old, sequential time," Thorn said. "I was 37 when I was five, and 98 when I was seven, and 126 when I was twelve." She enjoyed shocking people with this litany.

"Why have you moved so much?"

"My mother got pregnant without my father's consent, and when she refused to have an abortion he sued her for copyright infringement. She'd made unauthorized use of his genes, you see. So she ducked out to avoid paying royalties, and we've been on the lam ever since. If he ever caught us, I could be arrested for having bootleg genes."

"Who told you that story?" he said, obviously skeptical.

"Maya did. It sounds like something one of her boyfriends

would do. She has really bad taste in men. That's another reason we have to move so much."

Shaking his head slightly, he said, "I should think you would get cognitive dysplasia."

"I'm used to it," Thorn said.

"Do you like it?"

No one had ever asked her that before, as if she was capable of deciding for herself. In fact, she had known for a while that she *didn't* like it much. With every jump between planets she had grown more and more reluctant to leave sequential time behind. She said, "The worst thing is, there's no way of going back. Once you leave, the place you've stepped out of is gone forever. When I was eight I learned about pepcies, that you can use them to communicate instantaneously, and I asked Maya if we could call up my best friend on the last planet, and Maya said, 'She'll be middle-aged by now.' Everyone else had changed, and I hadn't. For a while I had dreams that the world was dissolving behind my back whenever I looked away."

The old man was listening thoughtfully, studying her. "How did you get away from Gmintagad?" he asked.

"We had Capellan passports," Thorn said. "I don't remember much about it; I was just four years old. I remember drooping cypress trees and rushing to get out. I didn't understand what was happening."

He was staring into the distance, focused on something invisible. Suddenly, he got up as if something had bitten him and started to walk away.

"Wait!" Thorn called. "What's the matter?"

He stopped, his whole body tense, then turned back. "Meet me here at four hours forenote tomorrow, if you want lessons," he said. "Bring a slate. I won't wait for you." He turned away again.

"Stop!" Thorn said. "What's your name?"

With a forbidding frown, he said, "Soren Pregaldin. You may call me Magister."

"Yes, Magister," Thorn said, trying not to let her glee show. She could hardly wait to tell Hunter that she had followed his advice, and succeeded.

What she wouldn't tell him, she decided as she watched Magister Pregaldin stalk away across the park, was her suspicion that this man knew something about the Holocide. Otherwise, how would he have known it was exactly 141 years ago? Another person would have said 140, or something else vague. She would not mention her suspicion to Hunter until she was sure. She would investigate carefully, like a competent field agent should. Thinking about it, a thrill ran through her. What if she were able to catch a Gminta? How impressed Hunter would be! The truth was, she wanted to impress Hunter. For all his mordant manner, he was by far the smartest boyfriend Maya had taken up with, the only one with a profession Thorn had ever been able to admire.

She fastened the veil over her face again before going home, so no one would see her grinning.

Magister Pregaldin turned out to be the most demanding teacher Thorn had ever known. Always before, she had coasted through school, easily able to stay ahead of the indigenous students around her, always waiting in boredom for them to catch up. With Magister Pregaldin there was no one else to wait for, and he pushed her mercilessly to the edge of her abilities. For the first time in her life, she wondered if she were smart enough.

He was an exacting drillmaster in mathematics. Once, when she complained at how useless it was, he pointed out beyond the iron gridwork of the dome to a round black hill that was conspicuous on the red plain of the crater bed. "Tell me how far away the Creeping Ingot is."

The Creeping Ingot had first come across the horizon almost a hundred years before, slowly moving toward Glory to God. It was a near-pure lump of iron the size of a small mountain. In the Waste, the reigning theory was that it was molten underneath, and moving like a drop of water skitters across a hot frying pan. In the city above them, it was regarded as a sign of divine wrath: a visible, unstoppable Armageddon. Religious tourists came from all over the planet to see it, and its ever-shrinking distance was posted on the public sites. Thorn turned to her slate to look it up, but Magister Pregaldin made her put it down. "No," he said, "I want you to figure it out."

"How can I?" she said. "They bounce lasers off it or something to find out where it is."

"There is an easier way, using tools you already have."

"The *easiest* way is to look it up!"

"No, that is the lazy way." His face looked severe. "Relying too much on free information makes you as vulnerable as relying too much on technology. You should always know how to figure it out yourself, because information can be falsified, or taken away. You should never trust it."

So he was some sort of information survivalist. "Next you'll want me to use flint to make fire," she grumbled.

"Thinking for yourself is not obsolete. Now, how are you going to find out? I will give you a hint: you don't have enough information right now. Where are you going to get it?"

She thought a while. It had to use mathematics, because that was what they had been talking about. At last she said, "I'll need a tape measure."

"Right."

"And a protractor."

"Good. Now go do it."

It took her the rest of forenote to assemble her tools, and the first part of afternote to observe the ingot from two spots on opposite ends of the park. Then she got one of the refuse-picker children to help her measure the distance between her observation posts. Armed with two angles and a length, the trigonometry was simple. When Magister Pregaldin let her check her answer, it was more accurate than she had expected.

He didn't let on, but she could tell that he was, if anything, even more pleased with her success than she was herself. "Good," he said. "Now, if you measured more carefully and still got an answer different from the official one, you would have to ask yourself whether the Protectorate had a reason for falsifying the Ingot's distance."

She could see now what he meant.

"That old Vind must be a wizard," Hunter said when he

found Thorn toiling over a math problem at the kitchen table. "He's figured out some way of motivating you."

"Why do you think he's a Vind?" Thorn said.

Hunter gave a caustic laugh. "Just look at him."

She silently added that to her mental dossier on her tutor. Not a Gminta, then. A Vind—one of the secretive race of aristocrat intellectuals who could be found in government, finance, and academic posts on almost every one of the Twenty Planets. All her life Thorn had heard whispers about a Vind conspiracy to infiltrate positions of power under the guise of public service. She had heard about the secret Vind sodality of interplanetary financiers who siphoned off the wealth of whole planets to fund their hegemony. She knew Maya scoffed at all of it. Certainly, if Magister Pregaldin was an example, the Vind conspiracy was not working very well. He seemed as penniless as any other Waster.

But being Vind did not rule out his involvement in the Holocide—it just meant he was more likely to have been a refugee than a perpetrator. Like most planets, Gmintagad had had a small, elite Vind community, regarded with suspicion by the indigenes. The massacres had targeted the Vinds as well as the Alloes. People didn't talk as much about the Vinds, perhaps because the Vinds didn't talk about it themselves.

Inevitably, Thorn's daily lessons in the park drew attention. One day they were conducting experiments in aerodynamics with paper airplanes when a man approached them. He had a braided beard strung with ceramic beads that clacked as he walked. Magister Pregaldin saw him first, and his face went blank and inscrutable.

The clatter of beads came to rest against the visitor's silk kameez. He cleared his throat. Thorn's tutor stood and touched his earlobes in respect, as people did on this planet. "Your worship's presence makes my body glad," he said formally.

The man made no effort to be courteous in return. "Do you have a license for this activity?"

"Which activity, your worship?"

"Teaching in a public place."

Magister Pregaldin hesitated. "I had no idea my conversations could be construed as teaching."

It was the wrong answer. Even Thorn, watching silently, could see that the proper response would have been to ask how much a license cost. The man was obviously fishing for a bribe. His face grew stern. "Our blessed Protectorate levies just fines on those who flout its laws."

"I obey all the laws, honorable sir. I will cease to give offense immediately."

The magister picked up his battered old electronic slate and, without a glance at Thorn, walked away. The man from the Protectorate considered Thorn, but evidently concluded he couldn't extract anything from her, and so he left.

Thorn waited till the official couldn't see her anymore, then sprinted after Magister Pregaldin. He had disappeared into Weezer Alley, a crooked passageway that Thorn ordinarily avoided because it was the epicenter of depravity in the Waste. She plunged into it now, searching for the tall, patrician silhouette of her tutor. It was still forenote, and the denizens of Weezer Alley were just beginning to rise from catering to the debaucheries of yesternote's customers. Thorn hurried past a shop where the owner was beginning to lay out an array of embarrassingly explicit sex toys; she tried not to look. A little beyond, she squeamishly skirted a spot where a shopkeeper was scattering red dirt on a half-dried pool of vomit. Several dogleg turns into the heart of the sin warren, she came to the infamous Garden of Delights, where live musicians were said to perform. No one from the Protectorate cared much about prostitution, since that was mentioned in their holy book, but music was absolutely forbidden.

The gate into the Garden of Delights was twined about with iron snakes. On either side of it stood a pedestal where dancers gyrated during open hours. Now a sleepy she-man lounged on one of them, stark naked except for a bikini that didn't hide much. Hisher smooth skin was almost completely covered with the vinelike and paisley patterns of the decorative skin fungus *mycochromoderm*. Once injected, it was impossible to remove. It grew as long as its host lived, in bright scrolls and branching patterns. It had been a Waster fad once.

The dancer regarded Thorn from lizardlike eye slits in a face forested over with green and red tendrils. "You looking for the professor?" heshe asked.

Thorn was a little shocked that her cultivated tutor was known to such an exhibitionist creature as this, but she nodded. The she-man gestured languidly at a second-story window across the street. "Tell him to come visit me," heshe said, and bared startlingly white teeth.

Thorn found the narrow doorway almost hidden behind an awning and climbed the staircase past peeling tin panels that once had shown houris carrying a huge feather fan. When she knocked on the door at the top, there was no response at first, so she called out, "Magister?"

The door flew open and Magister Pregaldin took her by the arm and yanked her in, looking to make sure she had not been followed. "What are you doing here?" he demanded.

"No one saw me," she said. "Well, except for that . . . that. . . ." She gestured across the street.

Magister Pregaldin went to the window and looked out. "Oh, Ginko," he said.

"Why do you live here?" Thorn said. "There are lots better places."

The magister gave a brief, grim little smile. "Early warning system," he said. "As long as the Garden is allowed to stay in business, no one is going to care about the likes of me." He frowned sternly. "Unless you get me in trouble."

"Why didn't you bribe him? He would have gone away."

"I have to save my bribes for better causes," he said. "One can't become known to the bottom-feeders, or they get greedy." He glanced out the window again. "You have to leave now."

"Why?" she said. "All he said was you need a license to teach in public. He didn't say anything about teaching in private."

Magister Pregaldin regarded her with a complex expression, as if he were trying to quantify the risk she represented.

At last he gave a nervous shrug. "You must promise not to tell anyone. I am serious. This is not a game."

"I promise," Thorn said.

She had a chance then to look around. Up to now, her impression had been of a place so cluttered that only narrow lanes were left to move about the room. Now she saw that the teetering stacks all around her were constructed of wondrous things. There were crystal globes on ormolu stands, hand-knotted silk rugs piled ten high, clocks with malachite cases stacked atop towers of leather-and-gilt books. There was a copper orrery of nested bands and onyx horses rearing on their back legs, and a theremin in a case of brushed aluminum. A cloisonné ewer as tall as Thorn occupied one corner. In the middle hung a chandelier that dripped topaz swags and bangles, positioned so that Magister Pregaldin had to duck whenever he crossed the room.

"Is all this stuff yours?" Thorn said, dazzled with so much wonder.

"Temporarily," he said. "I am an art dealer. I make sure things of beauty get from those who do not appreciate them to those who do. I am a matchmaker, in a way." As he spoke, his fingers lightly caressed a sculpture made from an ammonite fossil with a human face emerging from the shell. It was a delicate gesture, full of reverence, even love. Thorn had a sudden, vivid feeling that this was where Magister Pregaldin's soul rested—with his things of beauty.

"If you are to come here, you must never break anything," he said.

"I won't touch," Thorn said.

"No, that's not what I meant. One *must* touch things, and hold them, and work them. Mere looking is never enough. But touch them as they wish to be touched." He handed her the ammonite fossil. Its curve fit perfectly in her hand. The face looked surprised when she held it up before her, and she laughed.

Most of the walls were as crowded as the floor, with paintings hung against overlapping tapestries and guidons. But one wall was empty except for a painting that hung alone, as if in a place of honor. As Thorn walked toward it, it seemed to shift and change colors with every change of angle. It showed a young girl with long black hair and a serious expression, about Thorn's age but far more beautiful and fragile.

Seeing where she was looking, Magister Pregaldin said, "The portrait is made of butterfly wings. It is a type of artwork from Vindahar."

"Is that the home world of the Vind?"

"Yes."

"Do you know who she is?"

"Yes," he said hesitantly. "But it would mean nothing to you. She died a long time ago."

There was something in his voice—was it pain? No, Thorn decided, something less acute, like the memory of pain. It lay in the air after he stopped speaking, till even he heard it.

"That is enough art history for today," he said briskly. "We were speaking of airplanes."

That afternote, Hunter was out on one of his inscrutable errands. Thorn waited till Maya was talking to one of her friends and crept up to Hunter's office. He had a better library than anyone she had ever met, a necessary thing on this planet where there were almost no public sources of knowledge. Thorn was quite certain she had seen some art books in his collection. She scanned the shelves of disks and finally took down one that looked like an art encyclopedia. She inserted it into the reader and typed in "butterfly" and "Vindahar."

There was a short article from which she learned that the art of butterfly-wing painting had been highly admired, but was no longer practiced because the butterflies had gone extinct. She went on to the illustrations—and there it was. The very same painting she had seen earlier that day, except lit differently, so that the colors were far brighter and the girl's expression even sadder than it had seemed.

Portrait of Jemma Diwali, the caption said. *An acknowledged masterpiece of technique, this painting was lost in GM 862, when it was looted from one of the homes of the Diwali family. According to Almasy, the representational*

formalism of the subject is subtly circumvented by the trans-
formational perspective, which creates an abstractionist
counter-layer of imagery. It anticipates the "chaos art" of
Dunleavy. . . . It went on about the painting as if it had no
connection to anything but art theory. But all Thorn cared
about was the first sentence. GM 862—the year of the
Gmintan Holocide.

Jemma was staring at her gravely, as if there were some
implied expectation on her mind. Thorn went back to the
shelves, this time for a history of the Holocide. It seemed
like there were hundreds of them. At last she picked one almost at random and typed in "Diwali." There were uninfor-
mative references to the name scattered throughout the
book. From the first two, she gathered that the Diwalis had
been a Vind family associated with the government on Gmintagad. There were no mentions of Jemma.

She had left the door ajar and now heard the sounds of
Hunter returning downstairs. Quickly she re-cased the books
and erased her trail from the reader. She did not want him to
find out just yet. This was her mystery to solve.

There wasn't another chance to sneak into Hunter's office
before she returned to Magister Pregaldin's apartment on
Weezer Alley. She found that he had cleared a table for them
to work at, directly underneath the stuffed head of a creature
with curling copper-colored horns. As he checked over the
work she had done the note before, her eyes were drawn ir-
resistibly to the portrait of Jemma across the room.

At last he caught her staring at it, and their eyes met. She
blurted out, "Did you know that painting comes from Gmintagad?"

A shadow of frost crossed his face. But it passed quickly,
and his voice was low and even when he said, "Yes."

"It was looted," Thorn said. "Everyone thought it was lost."

"Yes, I know," he said.

Accusatory thoughts were bombarding her. He must have
seen them, for he said calmly, "I collect art from the Holocide."

"That's macabre," she said.

"A great deal of significant art was looted in the Holocide.

In the years after, it was scattered, and entered the black markets of a dozen planets. Much of it was lost. I am reassembling a small portion of it, whatever I can rescue. It is very slow work."

This explanation altered the picture Thorn had been creating in her head. Before, she had seen him as a scavenger feeding on the remains of a tragedy. Now he seemed more like a memorialist acting in tribute to the dead. Regretting what she had been thinking, she said, "Where do you find it?"

"In curio shops, import stores, estate sales. Most people don't recognize it. There are dealers who specialize in it, but I don't talk to them."

"Don't you think it should go back to the families that owned it?"

He hesitated a fraction of a second, then said, "Yes, I do." He glanced over his shoulder at Jemma's portrait. "If one of them existed, I would give it back."

"You mean they're *all* dead? Every one of them?"

"So far as I can find out."

That gave the artwork a new quality. To its delicacy, its frozen-flower beauty, was added an iron frame of absolute mortality. An entire family, vanished. Thorn got up to go look at it, unable to stay away.

"The butterflies are all gone, too," she said.

Magister Pregaldin came up behind her, looking at the painting as well. "Yes," he said. "The butterflies, the girl, the family, the world, all gone. It can never be replicated."

There was something exquisitely poignant about the painting now. The only surviving thing to prove that they had all existed. She looked up at Magister Pregaldin. "Were you there?"

He shook his head slowly. "No. It was before my time. I have always been interested in it, that's all."

"Her name was Jemma," Thorn said. "Jemma Diwali."

"How did you find that out?" he asked.

"It was in a book. A stupid book. It was all about abstractionist counter-layers and things. Nothing that really explained the painting."

"I'll show you what it was talking about," the magister

said. "Stand right there." He positioned her about four feet from the painting, then took the lamp and moved it to one side. As the light moved, the image of Jemma Diwali disappeared, and in its place was an abstract design of interlocking spirals, spinning pinwheels of purple and blue.

Thorn gave an exclamation of astonishment. "How did that happen?"

"It is in the microscopic structure of the butterfly wings," Magister Pregaldin explained. "Later, I will show you one under magnification. From most angles they reflect certain wavelengths of light, but from this one, they reflect another. The skill in the painting was assembling them so they would show both images. Most people think it was just a feat of technical virtuosity, without any meaning."

She looked at him. "But that's not what you think."

"No," he said. "You have to understand, Vind art is all about hidden messages, layers of meaning, riddles to be solved. Since I have had the painting here, I have been studying it, and I have identified this pattern. It was not chosen randomly." He went to his terminal and called up a file. A simple algebraic equation flashed onto the screen. "You solve this equation using any random number for X, then take the solution and use it as X to solve the equation again, then take *that* number and use it to solve the equation again, and so forth. Then you graph all the solutions on an X and Y axis, and this is what you get." He hit a key and an empty graph appeared on the screen. As the machine started to solve the equation, little dots of blue began appearing in random locations on the screen. There appeared to be no pattern at all, and Thorn frowned in perplexity.

"I'll speed it up now," Magister Pregaldin said. The dots started appearing rapidly, like sleet against a window or sand scattered on the floor. "It is like graphing the result of a thousand dice throws, sometimes lucky, sometimes outside the limits of reality, just like the choices of a life. You spend the first years buffeted by randomness, pulled this way by parents, that way by friends, all the variables squabbling and nudging, quarreling till you can't hear your own mind. And then, patterns start to appear."

On the screen, the dots had started to show a tendency to cluster. Thorn could see the hazy outlines of spiral swirls. As more and more dots appeared in seemingly random locations, the pattern became clearer and clearer.

Magister Pregaldin said, "As the pattern fills in, you begin to see that the individual dots were actually the pointillist elements of something beautiful: a snowflake, or a spiral, or concentric ripples. There is a pattern to our lives; we just experience it out of order, and don't have enough data at first to see the design. Our path forward is determined by this invisible artwork, the creation of a lifetime of events."

"You mean, like fate?" Thorn said.

"That is the question." Her tutor nodded gravely, staring at the screen. The light made his face look planar and secretive. "Does the pattern exist before us? Is our underlying equation predetermined, or is it generated by the results of our first random choice for the value of X? I can't answer that."

The pattern on the screen was clear now; it was the same one hidden under the portrait. Thorn glanced from one to the other. "What does this have to do with Jemma?"

"Another good question," Magister Pregaldin said thoughtfully. "I don't know. Perhaps it was a message to her from the artist, or a prediction—one that never had a chance to come true, because she died before she could find her pattern."

Thorn was silent a moment, thinking of that other girl. "Did she die in the Holocide?"

"Yes."

"Did you know her?"

"I told you, I wasn't there."

She didn't believe him for a second. He *had* been there, she was sure of it now. Not only had he been there, he was still there, and would always be there.

Several days later Thorn stepped out of the front door on her way to classes, and instantly sensed something wrong. There was a hush; tension or expectation had stretched the air tight. Too few people were on the street, and they were casting glances up at the city. She looked up toward where the

Corkscrew rose, a black sheet-iron spiral that looked poised to drill a hole through the sky. There was a low, rhythmic sound coming from around it.

"Bick!" she cried out when she saw the Waster heading home laden down with groceries, as if for a siege. "What's going on?"

"You haven't heard?" Bick said.

"No."

In a low voice, Bick said, "The Protector was assassinated last note."

"Oh. Is that good or bad?"

Bick shrugged. "It depends on who they blame."

As Bick hurried on her way, Thorn stood, balanced between going home and going on to warn Magister Pregaldin. The sound from above grew more distinct, as of slow drumming. Deciding abruptly, Thorn dashed on.

The denizens of Weezer Alley had become accustomed to the sight of Thorn passing through to her lessons. Few of them were abroad this forenote, but she nearly collided with one coming out of the tobacco shop. It was a renegade priest from Glory to God who had adopted the Waster lifestyle as if it were his own. Everyone called him Father Sin.

"Ah, girl!" he exclaimed. "So eager for knowledge you knock down old men?"

"Father Sin, what's that sound?" she asked.

"They are beating the doorways of their houses in grief," he said. "It is tragic, what has happened."

She dashed on. The sound had become a ringing by the time she reached Magister Pregaldin's doorway, like an unnatural Note. She had to wait several seconds after knocking before the door opened.

"Ah, Thorn! I am glad you are here," Magister Pregaldin said when he saw her. "I have something I need to. . . ." He stopped, seeing her expression. "What is wrong?"

"Haven't you heard the news, Magister?"

"What news?"

"The Protector is dead. Assassinated. That's what the ringing is about."

He listened as if noticing it for the first time, then quickly went to his terminal to look up the news. There was a stark announcement from the Protectorate, blaming "Enemies of God," but of course no news. He shut it off and stood thinking. Then he seemed to come to a decision.

"This should not alter my plans," he said. "In fact, it may help." He turned to Thorn, calm and austere as usual. "I need to make a short journey. I will be away for two days, three at most. But if it takes me any longer, I will need you to check on my apartment, and make sure everything is in order. Will you do that?"

"Of course," Thorn said. "Where are you going?"

"I'm taking the wayport to one of the other city-states." He began then to show her two plants that would need watering, and a bucket under a leaky pipe that would need to be emptied. He paused at the entrance to his bedroom, then finally gestured her in. It was just as cluttered as the other rooms. He took a rug off a box, and she saw that it was actually a small refrigerator unit with a temperature gauge on the front showing that the interior was well below freezing.

"This needs to remain cold," he said. "If the electricity should go out, it will be fine for up to three days. But if I am delayed getting back, and the inside temperature starts rising, you will need to go out and get some dry ice to cool it again. Here is the lock. Do you remember the recursive equation I showed you?"

"You mean Jemma's equation?"

He hesitated in surprise, then said, "Yes. If you take twenty-seven for the first value of X, then solve it five times, that will give you the combination. That should be child's play for you."

"What's in it?" Thorn asked.

At first he seemed reluctant to answer, but then realized he had just given her the combination, so he knelt and pecked it out on the keypad. A light changed to green. He undid several latches and opened the top, then removed an ice pack and stood back for her to see. Thorn peered in and saw nested in ice a ball of white feathers.

"It's a bird," she said in puzzlement.

"You have seen birds, have you?"

"Yes. They don't have them here. Why are you keeping a dead bird?"

"It's not dead," he said. "It's sleeping. It is from a species they call ice owls, the only birds known to hibernate. They are native to a planet called Ping, where the winters last a century or more. The owls burrow into the ice to wait out the winter. Their bodies actually freeze solid. Then when spring comes, they revive and rise up to mate and produce the next generation."

The temperature gauge had gone yellow, so he fitted the ice pack back in place and latched the top. The refrigerator hummed, restoring the chest to its previous temperature.

"There was a . . . I suppose you would call it a fad, once, for keeping ice owls. When another person came along with a suitable owl, the owners would allow them both to thaw so they could come back to life and mate. It was a long time ago, though. I don't know whether there are still any freezer owls alive but this one."

Another thing that might be the last of its kind. This apartment was full of reminders of extinction, as if Magister Pregaldin could not free his mind of the thought.

But this one struck Thorn differently, because the final tragedy had not taken place. There was still a hope of life. "I'll keep it safe," she promised gravely.

He smiled at her. It made him look strangely sad. "You are a little like an owl yourself," he said kindly. "Older than the years you have lived."

She thought, but did not say, that he was also like an owl—frozen for 141 years.

They left the apartment together, she heading for home and he with a backpack over his shoulder, bound for the waystation.

Thorn did not wait two days to revisit the apartment alone to do some true detective work.

It was the day of the Protector's funeral, and Glory to God was holding its breath in pious suspension. All businesses were closed, even in the Waste, while the mourning rituals went on. Whatever repercussions would come from the assassination, they would not occur this day. Still, Thorn wore the veil when she went out, because it gave her a feeling of invisibility.

The magister's apartment was very quiet and motionless when she let herself in. She checked on the plants and emptied the pail in order to give her presence the appearance of legitimacy. She then went into the magister's bedroom, ostensibly to check the freezer, but really to look around, for she had only been in there the one time. She studied the art-encrusted walls, the shaving mirror supported by mythical beasts, the armoire full of clothes that had once been fine but now were shabby and outmoded. As she was about to leave she spotted a large box—a hexagonal column about three feet tall—on a table in a corner. It was clearly an off-world artifact because it was made of wood. Many sorts of wood, actually: the surface was an inlaid honeycomb design. But there were no drawers, no cabinets, no way inside at all. Thorn immediately realized that it must be a puzzle box—and she wanted to get inside.

She felt all around it for sliding panels, levers, or springs, but could not find any, so she brought over a lamp to study it. The surface was a parquet of hexagons, but the colors were not arranged in a regular pattern. Most tiles were made from a blond-colored wood and a reddish wood, interrupted at irregular intervals by hexagons of chocolate, caramel, and black. It gave her the strong impression of a code or diagram, but she could not imagine what sort.

It occurred to her that perhaps she was making this more complex than necessary, and the top might come off. So she tried to lift it—and indeed it shifted up, but only about an inch, enough to disengage the top row of hexagons from the ones below. In that position she found she could turn the lower rows. Apparently, it was like a cylinder padlock. Each row of hexagons was a tumbler that needed to be turned and aligned correctly for the box to open. She did not have the combination, but knowing the way Magister Pregaldin's Vind mind worked, she felt sure that there would be some hint, some way to figure it out.

Once more she studied the honeycomb inlay. There were

six rows. The top one was most regular—six blond hexagons followed by six red hexagons, repeating around the circumference of the box. The patterns became more colorful in the lower rows, but always included the repeating line of six blond hexagons. For a while she experimented with spinning the rows to see if she could hit on something randomly, but soon gave up. Instead, she fetched her slate from her backpack and photographed the box, shifting it on the table to get the back. When she was done, she found that the top would no longer lock down in its original position. The instant Magister Pregaldin saw it, he would know that she had raised it. It was evidently meant as a tamper detector, and she had set it off. Now she needed to solve the puzzle, or explain to him why she had been prowling his apartment looking for evidence.

She walked home preoccupied. The puzzle was clearly about sixes—six sides, six rows, six hexagons in a row. She needed to think of formulas that involved sixes. When she reached home she went to her room and started transferring the box's pattern from the photos to a diagram so she could see it better. All that afternote she worked on it, trying to find algorithms that would produce the patterns she saw. Nothing seemed to work. The thought that she would fail, and have to confess to Magister Pregaldin, made her feeling of urgency grow. The anticipation of his disappointment and lost trust kept her up long after she should have pulled the curtains against the perpetual sun and gone to bed.

At about six hours forenote a strange dream came to her. She was standing before a tree whose trunk was a hexagonal pillar, and around it was twined a snake with Magister Pregaldin's eyes. It looked at her mockingly, then took its tail in its mouth.

She woke with the dream vivid in her mind. Lying there thinking, she remembered a story he had told her, about some Capellan magister named Kekule, who had deduced the ringlike structure of benzene after dreaming of a snake. She smiled with the thought that she had just had Kekule's dream.

Then she bounded out of bed and out her door, pounding

down the spiral steps to the kitchen. Hunter and Maya were eating breakfast together when she erupted into the room.

"Hunter! Do you have any books on chemistry?" she said.

He regarded her as if she were demented. "Why?"

"I need to know about benzene!"

The two adults looked at each other, mystified. "I have an encyclopedia," he said.

"Can I go borrow it?"

"No. I'll find it for you. Now try to curb your enthusiasm for aromatic hydrocarbons till I've had my coffee."

He sat there tormenting her for ten minutes till he was ready to go up to his office and find the book for her. She took the disk saying, "Thanks, you're the best!" and flew upstairs with it. As soon as she found the entry on benzene her hunch was confirmed: it was a hexagonal ring of carbon atoms with hydrogens attached at the corners. By replacing hydrogens with different molecules you could create a bewildering variety of compounds.

So perhaps the formula she should have been looking for was not a mathematical one, but a chemical one. When she saw the diagrams for toluene, xylene, and mesitylene she began to see how it might work. Each compound was constructed from a benzene ring with methyl groups attached in different positions. Perhaps, then, each ring on the box represented a different compound and the objective was to somehow align the corners as they were shown in the diagrams. But which compounds?

Then the code of the inlaid woods came clear to her. The blond-colored hexagons were carbons, the red ones were hydrogens. The other colors probably stood for elements like nitrogen or oxygen. The chemical formulae were written right on the box for all to see.

After an hour of scribbling and looking up formulae, she was racing down the steps again with her solutions in her backpack. She grabbed a pastry from the kitchen and ate it on her way, praying that Magister Pregaldin would not have returned.

He had not. The apartment still seemed to be dozing in its emptiness. She went straight to the box. As she dialed each row to line up the corners properly, her excitement grew. When the last ring slid into place, a vertical crack appeared along one edge. The sides swung open on hinges to reveal compartments inside.

There were no gold or rubies, just papers. She took one from its slot and unfolded it. It was an intricate diagram composed of spidery lines connecting geometric shapes with numbers inside, as if to show relationships or pathways. There was no key, nor even a word written on it. The next one she looked at was all words, closely written to the very edges of the paper in a tiny, obsessive hand. In some places they seemed to be telling a surreal story about angels, magic papayas, and polar magnetism; in others they disintegrated into garbled nonsense. The next document was a map of sorts, with coastlines and roads inked in, and landmarks given allegorical names like Perfidy, Imbroglio, and Redemption Denied. The next was a complex chart of concentric circles divided into sections and labeled in an alphabet she had never seen before.

Either Magister Pregaldin was a madman or he was trying to keep track of something so secret that it had to be hidden under multiple layers of code. Thorn spread out each paper on the floor and took a picture of it, then returned it to its pigeonhole so she could puzzle over them at leisure. When she was done she closed the box and spun the rings to randomize them again. Now she could push the top back down and lock it in place.

She walked home a little disappointed, but feeling as if she had learned something about her tutor. There was an obsessive and paranoid quality about the papers that ill fitted the controlled and rational magister. Clearly, there were more layers to him than she had guessed.

When she got home, she trudged up the stairs to return the encyclopedia to Hunter. As she was raising her hand to knock on his office door, she heard a profane exclamation from within. Then Hunter came rocketing out. Without a glance at Thorn he shot down the stairs to the kitchen.

Thorn followed. He was brewing coffee and pacing. She sat on the steps and said, "What's the matter?"

He glanced up, shook his head, then it boiled out: "One of the suspects I have been following was murdered last night."

"Really?" So he *did* know of Gmintas in hiding. Or had known. Thinking it over, she said, "I guess it was a good time for a murder, in the middle of the mourning."

"It didn't happen here," he said irritably. "It was in Flaming Sword of Righteousness. Damn! We were days away from moving in on him. We had all the evidence to put him on trial before the Court of a Thousand Peoples. Now all that work has gone to waste."

She watched him pour coffee, then said, "What would have happened if the Court found him guilty?"

"He would have been executed," Hunter said. "There is not the slightest doubt. He was one of the worst. We've wanted him for decades. Now we'll never have justice; all we've got is revenge."

Thorn sat quiet then, thinking about justice and revenge, and why one was so right and the other so wrong, when they brought about the same result. "Who did it?" she asked at last.

"If I knew I'd track him down," Hunter said darkly.

He started back up the stairs with his coffee, and she had to move aside for him. "Hunter, why do you care so much about such an old crime?" she asked. "There are so many bad things going on today that need fixing."

He looked at her with a tight, unyielding expression. "To forget is to condone," he said. "Evil must know it will pay. No matter how long it takes."

"He's such a phony," she said to Magister Pregaldin the next day.

She had returned to his apartment that morning to find everything as usual, except for a half-unpacked crate of new artworks in the middle of the living room. They had sat down to resume lessons as if nothing had changed, but neither of them could concentrate on differential equations. So Thorn told him about her conversation with Hunter.

"What really made him mad was that someone beat him," Thorn said. "It's not really about justice, it's about competition. He wants the glory of having bagged a notorious

Gminta. That's why it has to be public. I guess that's the difference between justice and revenge: when it's justice somebody gets the credit."

Magister Pregaldin had been listening thoughtfully; now he said, "You are far too cynical for someone your age."

"Well, people are disappointing!" Thorn said.

"Yes, but they are also complicated. I would wager there is something about him you do not know. It is the only thing we can ever say about people with absolute certainty: that we don't know the whole story."

It struck Thorn that what he said was truer of him than of Hunter.

He rose from the table and said, "I want to give you a gift, Thorn. We'll call it our lesson for the day."

Intrigued, she followed him into his bedroom. He took the rug off the freezer and checked the temperature, then unplugged it. He then took a small two-wheeled dolly from a corner and tipped the freezer onto it.

"You're giving me the ice owl?" Thorn said in astonishment.

"Yes. It is better for you to have it; you are more likely than I to meet someone else with another one. All you have to do is keep it cold. Can you do that?"

"Yes!" Thorn said eagerly. She had never owned something precious, something unique. She had never even had a pet. She was awed by the fact that Magister Pregaldin would give her something he obviously prized so much. "No one has ever trusted me like this," she said.

"Well, you have trusted me," he murmured without looking. "I need to return some of the burden."

He helped her get it down the steps. Once onto the street, she was able to wheel it by herself. But before leaving, she threw her arms giddily around her tutor and said, "Thank you, Magister! You're the best teacher I've ever had."

Wheeling the freezer through the alley, she attracted the attention of some young Wasters lounging in front of a betel parlor, who called out loudly to ask if she had a private stash of beer in there, and if they could have some. When she scowled and didn't answer they laughed and called her a lush. By the time she got home, her exaltation had been jostled aside by disgust and fury at the place where she lived. She managed to wrestle the freezer up the stoop and over the threshold into the kitchen, but when she faced the narrow spiral stair, she knew this was as far as she could get without help. The kitchen was already crowded, and the only place she could fit the freezer in was under the table. As she was shoving it against the wall, Maya came down the stairs and said, "What are you doing?"

"I have to keep this freezer here," Thorn said.

"You can't put it there. It's not convenient."

"Will you help me carry it up to my room?"

"You're kidding."

"I didn't think so. Then it's got to stay here."

Maya rolled her eyes at the irrational acts of teenagers. Now Thorn was angry at her, too. "It has to stay plugged in," Thorn said strictly. "Do you think you can remember that?"

"What's in it?"

Thorn would have enjoyed telling her if she hadn't been angry. "A science experiment," she said curtly.

"Oh, I see. None of my business, right?"

"Right."

"Okay. It's a secret," Maya said in a playful tone, as if she were talking to a child. She reached out to tousle Thorn's hair, but Thorn knocked her hand away and left, taking the stairs two at a time.

In her room, Thorn gave way to rage at her unsatisfactory life. She didn't want to be a Waster anymore. She wanted to live in a house where she could have things of her own, not squat in a boyfriend's place, always one quarrel away from eviction. She wanted a life she could control. Most of all, she wanted to leave the Waste. She went to the window and looked down at the rusty ghetto below. Cynicism hung miasmatic over it, defiling everything noble and pure. The decadent sophistication left nothing unstained.

During dinner, Maya and Hunter were cross and sarcastic with each other, and Hunter ended up storming off into his office. Thorn went to her room and studied Magister Pregaldin's secret charts till the house was silent below.

Then she crept down to the kitchen to check on the freezer. The temperature gauge was reassuringly low. She sat on the brick floor with her back to it, its gentle hum soothing against her spine, feeling a kinship with the owl inside. She envied it for its isolation from the dirty world. Packed away safe in ice, it was the one thing that would never grow up, never lose its innocence. One day it would come alive and erupt in glorious joy—but only if she could protect it. Even if she couldn't protect herself, there was still something she could keep safe.

As she sat there, The Note came, filling the air full and ringing through her body like a benediction. It seemed to be answering her unfocused yearning, as if the believers were right, and there really were a force looking over her, as she looked over the owl.

When she next came to Magister Pregaldin's apartment, he was busy filling the crate up again with treasures. Thorn helped him wrap artworks in packing material as he told her which planet each one came from. "Where are you sending them?" she asked.

"Offworld," he answered vaguely.

Together they lifted the lid onto the crate, and only then did Thorn see the shipping label that had brought it here. It was stamped with a burning red sword—the customs mark of the city-state Flaming Sword of Righteousness. "Is that where you were?" she said.

"Yes."

She was about to blurt out that Hunter's Gminta had been murdered there when a terrible thought seized her: What if he already knew? What if it were no coincidence?

They sat down to lessons under the head of the copper-horned beast, but Thorn was distracted. She kept looking at her tutor's large hands, so gentle when he handled his art, and wondering if they could be the hands of an assassin.

That night Hunter went out and Maya barricaded herself in her room, leaving Thorn the run of the house. She instantly let herself into Hunter's office to search for a list of Gmintas killed and brought to justice over the years. When she tried to access his files, she found they were heavily protected by password and encryption—and if she knew his personality, he probably had intrusion detectors set. So she turned again to his library of books on the Holocide. The information was scattered and fragmentary, but after a few hours she had pieced together a list of seven mysterious murders on five planets that seemed to be revenge slayings.

Up in her room again, she took out her replica of one of Magister Pregaldin's charts, the one that looked most like a tracking chart. She started by assuming that the geometric shapes meant planets and the symbols represented individual Gmintas he had been following. After an hour she gave it up—not because she couldn't make it match, but because she could never prove it. A chart for tracking Gmintas would look identical to a chart for tracking artworks. It was the perfect cover story.

She was still awake when Hunter returned. As she listened to his footsteps she thought of going downstairs and telling him of her suspicions. But uncertainty kept her in bed, restless and wondering what was the right thing to do.

There were riots in the city the next day. In the streets far above the Waste, angry mobs flowed, a turbulent tide crashing against the Protectorate troops wherever they met. The Wasters kept close to home, looking up watchfully toward the palace, listening to the rumors that ran ratlike between the buildings. Thorn spent much of the day on the roof, a self-appointed lookout. About five hours afternote, she heard a roar from above, as of many voices raised at once. There was something elemental about the sound, as if a force of nature had broken into the domed city—a human eruption, shaking the iron framework on which all their lives depended.

She went down to the front door to see if she could catch any news. Her survival instincts were alert now, and when she spotted a little group down the street, standing on a doorstep exchanging news, she sprinted toward them to hear what they knew.

"The Incorruptibles have taken the Palace," a man told her in a low voice. "The mobs are looting it now."

"Are we safe?" she asked.

He only shrugged. "For now." They all glanced down the street toward the spike-topped gates of the Waste. The barrier had never looked flimsier.

When Thorn returned home, Maya was sitting in the kitchen looking miserable. She didn't react much to the news. Thorn sat down at the table with her, bumping her knees on the freezer underneath.

"Shouldn't we start planning to leave?" Thorn said.

"I don't want to leave," Maya said, tears coming to her already-red eyes.

"I don't either," Thorn said. "But we shouldn't wait till we don't have a choice."

"Hunter will protect us," Maya said. "He knows who to pay."

Frustrated, Thorn said, "But if the Incorruptibles take over, there won't *be* anyone to pay. That's why they call themselves incorruptible."

"It won't come to that," Maya said stubbornly. "We'll be all right. You'll see."

Thorn had heard it all before. Maya always denied that anything was wrong until everything fell apart. She acted as if planning for the worst would make it happen.

The next day the city was tense but quiet. The rumors said that the Incorruptibles were still hunting down Protectorate loyalists and throwing them in jail. The nearby streets were empty except for Wasters, so Thorn judged it safe enough to go to Weezer Alley. When she entered Magister Pregaldin's place, she was stunned at the change. The apartment had been stripped of its artworks. The carpets were rolled up, the empty walls looked dented and peeling. Only Jemma's portrait still remained. Two metal crates stood in the middle of the living room, and as Thorn was taking it all in, a pair of movers arrived to carry them off to the waystation.

"You're leaving," she said to Magister Pregaldin when he came back in from supervising the movers. She was not prepared for the disappointment she felt. All this time she had been trustworthy and kept his secrets—and he had abandoned her anyway.

"I'm sorry, Thorn," he said, reading her face. "It is becoming too dangerous here. You and your mother ought to think of leaving, as well."

"Where are you going?"

He paused. "It would be better if I didn't tell you that."

"I'm not going to tell anyone."

"Forgive me. It's a habit." He studied her for a few moments, then put his hand gently on her shoulder. "Your friendship has meant more to me than you can know," he said. "I had forgotten what it was like, to inspire such pure trust."

He didn't even know she saw through him. "You're lying to me," she said. "You've been lying all along. You're not leaving because of the Incorruptibles. You're leaving because you've finished what you came here to do."

He stood motionless, his hand still on her shoulder. "What do you mean?"

"You came here to settle an old score," she said. "That's what your life is about, isn't it? Revenge for something everyone else has forgotten and you can't let go."

He withdrew his hand. "You have made some strange mistake."

"You and Hunter—I don't understand either of you. Why can't you just stop digging up the past and move on?"

For several moments he stared at her, but his eyes were shifting as if tracking things she couldn't see. When he finally spoke, his voice was very low. "I don't *choose* to remember the past. I am compelled to—it is my punishment. Or perhaps it is a disease, or an addiction. I don't know."

Taken aback at his earnestness, Thorn said, "Punishment? For what?"

"Here, sit down," he said. "I will tell you a story before we part."

They both sat at the table where he had given her so many lessons, but before he started to speak he stood up again and paced away, his hands clenching. She waited silently, and he came back to face her, and started to speak.

* * *

This is a story about a young man who lived long ago. I will call him Till. He wanted badly to live up to his family's distinguished tradition. It was a prominent family, you see; for generations they had been involved in finance, banking, and insurance. The planet where they lived was relatively primitive and poor, but Till's family felt they were helping it by attracting outside investment and extending credit. Of course, they did very well by doing good.

The government of their country had been controlled by the Alloes for years. Even though the Alloes were an ethnic minority, they were a diligent people and had prospered by collaborating with Vind businessmen like Till's family. The Alloes ruled over the majority, the Gmintas, who had less of everything—less education, less money, less power. It was an unjust situation, and when there was a mutiny in the military and the Gmintas took control, the Vinds accepted the change. Especially to younger people like Till, it seemed like a righting of many historical wrongs.

Once the Gminta army officers were in power, they started borrowing heavily to build hospitals, roads, and schools for Gminta communities, and the Vind banks were happy to make the loans. It seemed like a good way to dispell many suspicions and prejudices that throve in the ignorance of the Gminta villages. Till was on the board of his family bank, and he argued for extending credit even after the other bankers became concerned about the government's reckless fiscal policies.

One day, Till was called into the offices of the government banking regulators. Alone in a small room, they accused him of money laundering and corruption. It was completely untrue, but they had forged documents that seemed to prove it. Till realized that he faced a life in prison. He would bring shame to his entire family, unless he could strike a deal. They offered him an alternative: he could come to work for the government, as their representative to the Vind community. He readily accepted the job, and resigned from the bank.

They gave him an office and a small staff. He had an Alloe counterpart responsible for outreach to that community; and though they never spoke about it, he suspected his colleague had been recruited with similar methods. They started out distributing informational leaflets and giving tips on broadcast shows, all quite bland. But it changed when the government decided to institute a new draft policy for military service. Every young person was to give five years' mandatory service starting at eighteen. The Vinds would not be exempt.

Now, as you may know, the Vinds are pacifists and mystics, and have never served in the military of any planet. This demand by the Gminta government was unprecedented, and caused great alarm. The Vinds gathered in the halls of their Ethical Congresses to discuss what to do. Till worked tirelessly, meeting with them and explaining the perspective of the government, reminding them of the Vind principle of obeying the local law wherever they found themselves. At the same time, he managed to get the generals to promise that no Vind would be required to serve in combat, which was utterly in violation of their beliefs. With this assurance, the Vinds reluctantly agreed. And so mothers packed bags for their children and sent them off to training, urging them to call often.

Soon after, a new land policy was announced. Estates that had always belonged to the Alloes were to be redistributed among landless Gmintas. This created quite a lot of resistance; Till and his colleague kept busy giving interviews and explaining how the policy restored fairness to the land system. They became familiar to all as government spokespeople.

Then the decision was made to relocate whole neighborhoods of Alloes and Vinds so Gmintas could have better housing in the cities. Till could no longer argue about justice; now he could only tell people it was necessary to move in order to quiet the fears of the Gmintas and preserve peace.

People started to emigrate off-planet, but then the government closed down the waystations. This nearly caused a panic, and Till had to tell everyone it was merely to prevent people from taking their goods and assets offworld, thus draining the national wealth. He promised that individuals would be allowed to leave again soon, as long as they took no cash or valuables with them.

He no longer believed it himself.

It had been months since the young people had gone off to the army, and their families had heard nothing from them. Till had been telling everyone it was a period of temporary isolation, while the trainees lived in camps on the frontier to build solidarity and camaraderie. Every time he went out, he would be surrounded by anxious parents asking when they could expect to hear from their children.

Fleets of buses showed up to evacuate the Alloe and Vind families from their homes, and take them to relocation camps. Till watched his own neighborhood become a ghost town, and the certainty grew in him that the people were never coming back. One day he entered his supervisor's office unexpectedly and overheard someone saying, ". . . to the mortifactories." They stopped talking when they saw him.

You are probably thinking, "Why didn't he speak out? Why didn't he denounce them?" Try to imagine, in many respects life still seemed quite normal, and what he suspected was so unthinkable it seemed insane. And even if he could overcome that, there was no one to speak out to. He was alone, and he was not a very courageous person. His only chance was to stay useful to the government.

Other Vinds and Alloes who had been working alongside him started to vanish. Still the Gmintas wanted him to go on reassuring people; he did it so well. He had to hide what he suspected, to fool them into thinking that he was fooled himself. Every day he lived in fear of hearing the knock on his door that would mean it was his time.

It was his Alloe colleague who finally broke. They rarely let the man go on air anymore; his nerves were too shattered. But one day he substituted for Till, and in the midst of a broadcast shouted out a warning: "They are killing you! It is mass murder!" That was all he got out before they cut him off.

That night, well-armed and well-organized mobs broke into the remaining Alloe enclaves in the capital city. The government deplored the violence the next day, but suggested that the Alloes had incited it.

At that point they no longer had any need for Till. Once again, they gave him a choice: relocation or deportation. He could join his family and share their fate; or he could leave the planet. Death or life. I think I have mentioned he was not very courageous. He chose to live.

They sent him to Capella Two, a twenty-five-year journey. By the time he arrived, the entire story had traveled ahead of him by pepci, and everything was known. His own role was infamous. He was the vile collaborator who had put a benign face on the crime. He had soothed people's fears and deceived them into walking docilely to their deaths. In hindsight, it was inconceivable that he had not known what he was doing. All across the Twenty Planets, the name of Till Diwali was reviled.

He fell silent at last. Thorn sat staring at the tabletop, because she could not sort out what to think. It was all wheeling about in her mind: right and wrong, horror and sympathy, criminal and victim—all were jumbled together. Finally she said, "Was Jemma your sister?"

"I told you, I was not there," he said in a distant voice. "The man who did those things was not me."

He was sitting at the table across from her again, his hands clasped before him. Now he spoke to her directly. "Thorn, you are unitary and authentic now as you will never be again. As you pass through life, you will accumulate other selves. Always you will be a person looking back on, and separate from, the person you are now. Whenever you walk down a street, or sit on a park bench, your past selves will be sitting beside you, impossible to touch or interrogate. In the end there is a whole crowd of you wherever you go, and you feel like you will perish from the loneliness."

Thorn's whirling feelings were beginning to come to rest in a pattern, and in it horror and blame predominated. She looked up at Jemma's face and said, "She *died*. How could you do that, and walk away? It's inhuman."

He didn't react, either to admit guilt or defend his innocence. She wanted an explanation from him, and he didn't give it. "You're a monster," she said.

Still he said nothing. She got up, blind to everything but the intensity of her thoughts, and went to the door. She glanced back before leaving, and he was looking at her with an expression that was nothing like what he ought to feel— not shame, not rage, not self-loathing. Thorn slammed the door behind her and fled.

She walked around the streets of the Waste for a long time, viciously throwing stones at heaps of trash to make the rats come out. Above the buildings, the sky seemed even redder than usual, and the shadows blacker. She was furious at the magister for not being admirable. She blamed him for hiding it from her and for telling her—since, by giving her the knowledge, he had also given her a responsibility of choosing what to do.

When she got home the kitchen was empty, but she heard voices from the living room above. She was mounting the stairs when the voices rose in anger, and she froze. It was Hunter and Maya, and they were yelling at each other.

"Good God, what were you thinking?" Hunter demanded.

"She needed help. I couldn't say no."

"You knew it would bring the authorities down on us!"

"I had a responsibility—"

"What about your responsibility to me? You just didn't think. You never think; everything is impulse with you. You are the most immature and manipulative person I've ever met."

Maya's voice went wheedling. "Hunter, come on. It'll be okay."

"And what if it's not okay? What are you going to do then? Just pick up and leave the wreckage behind you? That's what you've been doing all your life—dragging that kid of yours from planet to planet, never thinking what it's doing to her. You never think what you're doing to anyone, do you? It's all just yourself. I never should have let you in here."

There were angry footsteps, and then Hunter was mounting the stairs.

"Hunter!" Maya cried after him.

Thorn waited a minute, then crept up into the living room. Maya was sitting there, looking tragic and beautiful.

"What did you do?" Thorn said.

"It doesn't matter," Maya said. "He'll get over it."

"I don't care about Hunter."

Mistaking what she meant, Maya smiled through her tears. "You know what? I don't care either." She came over and hugged Thorn tight. "I'm not really a bad mother, am I, Thorn?"

Cautiously, Thorn said, "No. . . ."

"People just don't understand us. We're a team, right?"

Maya held out her hand for their secret finger-hook. Once it would have made Thorn smile, but she no longer felt the old solidarity against the world. She hooked fingers anyway, because she was afraid Maya would start to cry again if she didn't. Maya said, "They just don't know you. Damaged child, poppycock—you're tough as old boots. It makes me awestruck, what a survivor you are."

"I think we ought to get ready to leave," Thorn said.

Maya's face lost its false cheer. "I can't leave," she whispered.

"Why not?"

"Because I love him."

There was no sensible answer to that. So Thorn turned away to go up to her room. As she passed the closed door of Hunter's office, she paused, wondering if she should knock. Wondering if she should turn in the most notorious Gminta collaborator still alive. All those millions of dead Alloes and Vinds would get their justice, and Hunter would be famous. Then her feet continued on, even before she consciously made the decision. It was not loyalty to Magister Pregaldin, and it was not resentment of Hunter. It was because she might need that information to buy her own safety.

The sound of breaking glass woke her. She lay tense, listening to footsteps and raised voices below in the street. Then another window broke, and she got up to pull back the curtain. The sun was orange, as always, and she squinted in the glare, then raised her window and climbed out on the roof.

Below in the street, a mob of white-clad Incorruptibles was breaking windows as they passed; but their true target obviously lay deeper in the Waste. She watched till they were gone, then waited to see what would happen.

From somewhere beyond the tower fans of the park she could hear shouts and clanging, and once an avalanche-like roar, after which a cloud of dust rose from the direction of Weezer Alley. After that there was silence for a while. At last she heard chanting. Fleeing footsteps passed below. Then the wall of Incorruptibles appeared again. They were driving someone before them with improvised whips made from their belts. Thorn peered over the eaves to see more clearly and recognized their victim—Ginko, the heshe from the Garden of Delights, completely naked, both breasts and genitals exposed, with a rope around hisher neck. The whips had cut into the delicate paisley of Ginko's skin, exposing slashes of red underneath.

At a spot beneath Thorn's perch, Ginko stumbled and fell. A mass of Incorruptibles gathered round. Two of them pulled Ginko's legs apart, and a third made a jerking motion with a knife. A womanlike scream made Thorn grip the edge of her rooftop, wanting to look away. They tossed the rope over a signpost and hoisted Ginko up by the neck, choking and clawing at the noose. The body still quivered as the army marched past. When they were gone, the silence was so complete Thorn could hear the patter of blood into a pool on the pavement under the body.

On hands and knees she backed away from the edge of the roof and climbed into her bedroom. It was already stripped; everything she valued or needed was in her backpack, ready to go. She threw on some clothes and went down the stairs.

Maya, dressed in a robe, stopped her halfway. She looked scattered and panicky. "Thorn, we've got to leave," she said.

"Right now?"

"Yes. He doesn't want us here anymore. He's acting as if we're some sort of danger to him."

"Where are we going?"

"I don't know. Some other planet. Some place without men." She started to cry.

"Go get dressed," Thorn told her. "I'll bring some food." Over her shoulder she added, "Pack some clothes and money."

With her backpack in hand, Thorn raced down to the kitchen.

She was just getting out the dolly for the ice owl's refrigerator when Maya came down.

"You're not taking that, are you?" Maya said.

"Yes, I am." Thorn knelt to shift the refrigerator out from under the table, and only then noticed it wasn't running. Quickly, she checked the temperature gauge. It was in the red zone, far too high. With an anguished exclamation, she punched in the lock code and opened the top. Not a breath of cool air escaped. The ice pack on top was gurgling and liquid. She lifted it to see what was underneath.

The owl was no longer nested snugly in ice. It had shifted, tried to open its wings. There were scratches on the insulation where it had tried to peck and claw its way out. Now it lay limp, its head thrown back. Thorn sank to her knees, grief-struck before the evidence of its terrifying last minutes—revived to life only to find itself trapped in a locked chest. Even in that stifling dark, it had longed for life so much it had fought to free itself. Thorn's breath came hard and her heart labored, as if she were reliving the ice owl's death.

"Hurry up, Thorn," Maya said. "We've got to go."

Then she saw what had happened. The refrigerator cord lay on the floor, no longer attached to the wall outlet. She held it up as if it were a murder weapon. "It's unplugged," she said.

"Oh, that's right," Maya said, distracted. "I had to plug in the curling iron. I must have forgotten."

Rage rose inside Thorn like a huge bubble of compressed air. "You *forgot*?"

"I'm sorry, Thorn. I didn't know it was important."

"I *told* you it was important. This was the last ice owl anywhere. You haven't just killed this one, you've killed the entire species."

"I said I was sorry. What do you want me to do?"

Maya would never change. She would always be like

this, careless and irresponsible, unable to face consequences. Tears of fury came to Thorn's eyes. She dashed
them away with her hand. "You're useless," she said, climbing to her feet and picking up her pack. "You can't be trusted
to take care of anything. I'm done with you. Don't bother
to follow me."

Out in the street, she turned in the direction she never
went, to avoid having to pass what was hanging in the street.
Down a narrow alley she sprinted, past piles of stinking
refuse alive with roaches, till she came to a narrow side street
that doglegged into the park. On the edge of the open space
she paused under a portico to scan for danger; seeing none,
she dashed across, past the old men's chess tables, past the
bench where she had met Magister Pregaldin, to the entrance
of Weezer Alley.

Signs of the Incorruptibles' passage were everywhere.
Broken glass crunched underfoot and the contents of the
shops were trampled under red dirt shoeprints. When Thorn
reached the Garden of Delights, the entire street looked different, for the building had been demolished. Only a monstrous pile of rubble remained, with iron girders and ribs
sticking up like broken bones. A few people climbed over
the ruin, looking for survivors.

The other side of the street was still standing, but Magister
Pregaldin's door had been ripped from its hinges and tossed
aside. Thorn dashed up the familiar stairs. The apartment
looked as if it had been looted—stripped bare, not a thing of
value left. She walked through the empty rooms, dreading
what she might find, and finding nothing. Out on the street
again, she saw a man who had often winked at her when she
passed by to her lessons. "Do you know what happened to
Magister Pregaldin?" she asked. "Did he get away?"

"Who?" the man said.

"Magister Pregaldin. The man who lived here."

"Oh, the old Vind. No, I don't know where he is."

So he had abandoned her as well. In all the world, there
was no one trustworthy. For a moment she had a dark wish
that she had exposed his secret. Then she realized she was
just thinking of revenge.

Hoisting her pack to her shoulder, she set out for the way-station. She was alone now, only herself to trust.

There was a crowd in the street outside the waystation. Everyone seemed to have decided to leave the planet at once, some of them with huge piles of baggage and children. Thorn pushed her way in toward the ticket station to find out what was going on. They were still selling tickets, she saw with relief; the crowd was people waiting for their turn in the translation chamber. Checking to make sure she had her copy of Maya's credit stick, she joined the ticket line. She was back among her own kind, the rootless, migrant elite.

Where was she going? She scanned the list of destinations. She had been born on Capella Two, but had heard it was a harshly competitive place, so she decided against it. Ben was just an ice-ball world, Gammadis was too far away. It was both thrilling and frightening to have control over where she went and what she did. She was still torn by inde-cision when she heard someone calling, "Thorn!"

Clarity was pushing through the crowd toward her. "I'm so glad we found you," she said when she drew close. "Maya was here a little while ago, looking for you."

"Where is she now?" Thorn asked, scanning the crowd.

"She left again."

"Good," Thorn said.

"Thorn, she was frantic. She was afraid you'd get sepa-rated."

"We *are* separated," Thorn said implacably. "She can do what she wants. I'm on my own now. Where are you going, Clarity?"

Bick had come up, carrying their ticket cards. Thorn caught her hand to look at the tickets. "Alananovis," she read aloud, then looked up to find it on the directory. It was only eighteen light-years distant. "Can I come with you?"

"Not without Maya," Clarity said.

"Okay, then I'll go somewhere else."

Clarity put a hand on her arm. "Thorn, you can't just go off without Maya."

"Yes, I can. I'm old enough to be on my own. I'm sick of her, and I'm sick of her boyfriends. I want control of my life." Besides, Maya had killed the ice owl; Maya ought to suffer. It was only justice.

She had reached the head of the line. Her eye caught a name on the list, and she made a snap decision. When the ticket seller said "Where to?" she answered, "Gmintagad." She would go to see where Jemma Diwali had lived—and died.

The translation chamber on Gmintagad was like all the others she had seen over the years: sterile and anonymous. A technician led her into a waiting room till her luggage came through by the low-resolution beam. She sat feeling cross and tired, as she always did after having her molecules reassembled out of new atoms. When at last her backpack was delivered and she went on into the customs and immigration facility, she noticed a change in the air. For the first time in years she was breathing organically manufactured oxygen. She could smell the complex and decay-laden odor of an actual ecosystem. Soon she would see sky without any dome. The thought gave her an agoraphobic thrill.

She put her identity card into the reader, and after a pause it directed her to a glass-fronted booth where an immigration official in a sand-colored uniform sat behind a desk. Unlike the air, the man looked manufactured—a face with no wrinkles, defects, or stand-out features, as if they had chosen him to match a mathematical formula for facial symmetry. His hair was neatly clipped, and so, she noticed, were his nails. When she sat opposite him, she found that her chair creaked at the slightest movement. She tried to hold perfectly still.

He regarded her information on his screen, then said, "Who is your father?"

She had been prepared to say why her mother was not with her, but her father? "I don't know," she said. "Why?"

"Your records do not state his race."

His *race*? It was an antique concept she barely understood. "He was Capellan," she said.

"Capellan is not an origin. No one evolved on Capella."

"I did," Thorn stated.

He studied her without any expression at all. She tried to meet his eyes, but it began to seem confrontational, so she looked down. Her chair creaked.

"There are certain types of people we do not allow on Gmintagad," he said.

She tried to imagine what he meant. Criminals? Disease carriers? Agitators? He could see she wasn't any of those. "Wasters, you mean?" she finally ventured.

"I mean Vinds," he said.

Relieved, she said, "Oh, well that's all right, then. I'm not Vind." Creak.

"Unless you can tell me who your father was, I cannot be sure of that," he said.

She was speechless. How could a father she had never known have any bearing on who she was?

The thought that they might not let her in made her stomach knot. Her chair sent out a barrage of telegraphic signals. "I just spent thirty-two years as a lightbeam to get here," she said. "You've got to let me stay."

"We are a sovereign principality," he said calmly. "We don't *have* to let anyone stay." He paused, his eyes still on her. "You have a Vind look. Are you willing to submit to a genetic test?"

Minutes ago, her mind had seemed like syrup. Now it bubbled with alarm. In fact, she didn't *know* her father wasn't Vind. It had never mattered, so she had never cared. But here, all the things that defined her—her interests, her aptitudes, her internal doubts—none of it counted, only her racial status. She was in a place where identity was assigned, not chosen or created.

"What happens if I fail the test?" she asked.

"You will be sent back."

"And what happens if I don't take it?"

"You will be sent back."

"Then why did you even ask?"

He gave a regulation smile. If she had measured it with a ruler, it would have been perfect. She stood up, and the chair sounded like it was laughing. "All right. Where do I go?"

They took her blood and sent her into a waiting room with

two doors, neither of which had a handle. As she sat there idle, the true rashness of what she had done crept up on her. It wasn't like running away on-planet. Maya didn't know where she had gone. By now, they would be different ages. Maya could be dying, or Thorn could be older than she was, before they ever found each other. It was a permanent separation. And permanent punishment for Maya.

Thorn tried to summon up the righteous anger that had propelled her only an hour and thirty-two years before. But even that slipped from her grasp. It was replaced with a clutching feeling of her own guilt. She had known Maya's shortcomings when she took the ice owl, and never bothered to safeguard against them. She had known all the accidents the world was capable of, and still she had failed to protect a creature that could not protect itself.

Now, remorse made her bleed inside. The owl had been too innocent to meet such a terrible end. Its life should have been a joyous ascent into air, and instead it had been a hellish struggle, alone and forgotten, killed by neglect. Thorn had betrayed everyone by letting the ice owl die. Magister Pregaldin, who had trusted her with his precious, possession. Even, somehow, Jemma and the other victims of Till Diwali's crime—for what had she done but reenact his failure, as if to show that human beings had learned nothing? She felt as if caught in an iron-bound cycle of history, doomed to repeat what had gone before, as long as she was no better than her predecessors had been.

She covered her face with her hands, wanting to cry, but too demoralized even for that. It seemed like a self-indulgence she didn't deserve.

The door clicked and she started up at sight of a stern, rectangular woman in a uniform skirt, whose face held the hint of a sneer. Thorn braced for the news that she would have to waste another thirty-two years on a pointless journey back to Glory to God. But instead, the woman said, "There is someone here to see you."

Behind her was a familiar face that made Thorn exclaim in joy, "Clarity!"

Clarity came into the room, and Thorn embraced her in relief. "I thought you were going to Alananovis."

"We were," Clarity said, "but we decided we couldn't just stand by and let a disaster happen. I followed you, and Bick stayed behind to tell Maya where we were going."

"Oh, thank you, thank you!" Thorn cried. Now the tears that had refused to come before were running down her face. "But you gave up thirty-two years for a stupid reason."

"It wasn't stupid for us," Clarity said. "You were the stupid one."

"I know," Thorn said miserably.

Clarity was looking at her with an expression of understanding. "Thorn, most people your age are allowed some mistakes. But you're performing life without a net. You have to consider Maya. Somehow, you've gotten older than she is even though you've been traveling together. You're the steady one, the rock she leans on. These boyfriends, they're just entertainment for her. They drop her and she bounces back. But if you dropped her, her whole world would dissolve."

Thorn said, "That's not true."

"It *is* true," Clarity said.

Thorn pressed her lips together, feeling impossibly burdened. Why did *she* have to be the reliable one, the one who was never vulnerable or wounded? Why did Maya get to be the dependent one?

On the other hand, it was a comfort that she hadn't abandoned Maya as she had done to the ice owl. Maya was not a perfect mother, but neither was Thorn a perfect daughter. They were both just doing their best.

"I hate this," she said, but without conviction. "Why do I have to be responsible for her?"

"That's what love is all about," Clarity said.

"You're a busybody, Clarity," Thorn said.

Clarity squeezed her hand. "Yes. Aren't you lucky?"

The door clicked open again. Beyond the female guard's square shoulder, Thorn glimpsed a flash of honey-gold hair. "Maya!" she said.

When she saw Thorn, Maya's whole being seemed to

blaze like the sun. Dodging in, she threw her arms around Thorn.

"Oh Thorn, thank heaven I found you! I was worried sick. I thought you were lost."

"It's okay, it's okay," Thorn kept saying as Maya wept and hugged her again. "But Maya, you have to tell me something."

"Anything. What?"

"Did you seduce a *Vind*?"

For a moment Maya didn't understand. Then a secretive smile grew on her face, making her look very pretty and pleased with herself. She touched Thorn's hair. "I've been meaning to tell you about that."

"Later," Bick said. "Right now, we all have tickets for Alananovis."

"That's wonderful," Maya said. "Where's Alananovis?"

"Only seven years away from here."

"Fine. It doesn't matter. Nothing matters as long as we're together."

She held out her finger for the secret finger-lock. Thorn did it with a little inward sigh. For a moment she felt as if her whole world were composed of vulnerable beings frozen in time, as if she were the only one who aged and changed.

"We're a team, right?" Maya said anxiously.

"Yeah," Thorn answered. "We're a team."

Story Copyrights

IAN DOUGLAS's
MONUMENTAL SAGA
OF INTERGALACTIC WAR
THE INHERITANCE TRILOGY

STAR STRIKE: BOOK ONE

978-0-06-123858-1

Planet by planet, galaxy by galaxy, the inhabited universe has fallen to the alien Xul. Now only one obstacle stands between them and total domination: the warriors of a resilient human race the world-devourers nearly annihilated centuries ago.

GALACTIC CORPS: BOOK TWO

978-0-06-123862-8

In the year 2886, intelligence has located the gargantuan hidden homeworld of humankind's dedicated foe, the brutal Xul. The time has come for the courageous men and women of the 1st Marine Interstellar Expeditionary Force to strike the killing blow.

SEMPER HUMAN: BOOK THREE

978-0-06-116090-5

True terror looms at the edges of known reality. Humankind's eternal enemy, the Xul, approach wielding a weapon monstrous beyond imagining. If the Star Marines fail to eliminate their relentless xenophobic foe once and for all, the Great Annihilator will obliterate every last trace of human existence.

LEGENDS OF THE RIFTWAR

HONORED ENEMY

978-0-06-079284-8

by Raymond E. Feist & William R. Forstchen

In the frozen northlands of the embattled realm of Midkemia, Dennis Hartraft's Marauders must band together with their bitter enemy, the Tsurani, to battle *moredhel,* a migrating horde of deadly dark elves.

MURDER IN LAMUT

978-0-06-079291-6

by Raymond E. Feist & Joel Rosenberg

For twenty years the mercenaries Durine, Kethol, and Pirojil have fought other people's battles, defeating numerous deadly enemies. Now the Three Swords find themselves trapped by a winter's storm inside a castle teeming with ambitious, plotting lords and ladies, and it falls on the mercenaries to solve a series of cold-blooded murders.

JIMMY THE HAND

978-0-06-079299-2

by Raymond E. Feist & S.M. Stirling

Forced to flee the only home he's ever known, Jimmy the Hand, boy thief of Krondor finds himself among the rural villagers of Land's End. But Land's End is home to a dark, dangerous presence even the local smugglers don't recognize. And suddenly Jimmy's youthful bravado is leading him into the maw of chaos . . . and, quite possibly, his doom.